T0106615

MYTH MAN

Alex Mueck

iUniverse, Inc.
New York   Bloomington

Myth Man

iUniverse books may be ordered through booksellers or by contacting:

iUniverse
1663 Liberty Drive
Bloomington, IN 47403
www.iuniverse.com
1-800-Authors (1-800-288-4677)

ISBN: 978-1-4502-4725-2 (pbk)
ISBN: 978-1-4502-4724-5 (cloth)
ISBN: 978-1-4502-4723-8 (ebk)

Library of Congress Control Number: 2010932917

Printed in the United States of America

iUniverse rev. date: 9/30/2010

The author would like to thank the following people. My parents, Michael Dadich, Toni Mannino, Brian & Jenn Dunn, Scott Jurow, Rocco Petito, Roseann Parker, Joe Shavel, Steve Demeo, Ewa Graves, Chris McCentee, Roopesh Amin, Lauren Klein, Laura McGrath, Jason Rich, Scott Coya, Phil Fecher, the Brewster/Sullivan gang, Andrew, Tristan and Victoria Mueck, John and Mary Jane Dreyer, William Dreyer, Cleo and John Roberts, Gay Wightman, and my guildies (Voch, Steelshadow (Rogue's fault!), Sotirf, Green Harvest, Solty, Oprhias, Kyogi, Nervous, Beshaba, Xefron, Feefer, Nervous, Littledoor, Markymark, Galfame, Necaise, and the rest of my crazy gang.) Melissa and I would like to thank two great vets, Dr. Roiland and Dr. Cuccaro for all you have done for Paola. I would also like to thank the many religious people who helped me: Priests, Ministers, Rabbis, Clerics, Pandits, et. It was a rewarding experience to gain insights into the various religions. I would also like to thank Parobola Magazine for their excellent work on religion.

This book is dedicated to Melissa Wightman, aka,
Mayor McCheese, and our loving dog Paola

CHAPTER ONE

BULLSEYE ENVISIONED THE KILLER of myths, faiths, and fables. He smiled at the twentysomething, curvy brunette and stared, neither at her inviting smile nor her ample and welcoming chest but rather at the ashen cross on her forehead. Oh, how he would like to place a bullet through her Ash Wednesday smudge, but the fun would have to wait for later.

She made eye contact as the subway closed in on his last stop. Staring at her cross, he unbuttoned the top of his gray overcoat and revealed a Roman collar.

Her eyes twinkled, and the left side of her mouth curved upward. She nudged closer, smiling. "Father?"

"My child," the killer said warmly with a purposeful trace of a mideastern accent. "I see you started your day with God," he said, eyeing her ashen cross again under the brim of his fedora.

Her head dipped demurely, and then she proudly declared, "Mother wouldn't have it any other way."

"God bless her," he said while thinking, *this dirty slut probably performed fellatio last night.* "She must be a great woman, and I see the fruits of her labor have not fallen far from mother tree." His eyes zeroed in on her forehead again.

The brunette smiled. "I must say, I have never seen a priest on a subway before."

He laughed inside, but his lightly darkened, disguised-with-makeup face never wavered. "My dear, God uses many types of chariots to do his good work."

She laughed as the subway jerked and then decelerated.

A mechanical voice plagued by static announced, "Forty-second Street, Grand Central Station."

He spoke over the hiss. "My stop. Remember our sinful nature and recognize God's forgiveness." He folded his hands and bowed slightly.

"Thanks," she said but then thought that he did not exactly seem the celibate type based on the way he had leered at her.

He stepped off the subway and looked across to where the local six-train platformed. He was encumbered with an over-the-shoulder bag, but he decided the weather was scripted for the day and headed for the stairs.

With several steps to climb, he saw a swirling gray sky punctuated by swiftly falling snow. He smiled as the first hard, wet flakes struck his face.

When he emerged on Lexington Avenue, an umbrella flew at him with deadly aim, striking him forcefully in the right thigh. His grin twisted to a grimace. He looked up angrily.

A gaunt, elderly woman sheepishly approached. "I'm so sorry," she pleaded.

The killer smiled and handed her the umbrella. In a halting Indian accent, he told her, "It's okay. Anyway, I have someone else to kill today."

Her eyes widened, and she edged backward.

He smiled.

Tremulous, she asked, "You're, uh, kidding?" Her face twitched like a timid mouse, but her eyes expressed hope, like maybe the cheese was not attached to a trap.

His face was dispassionate, but his tone was serious. "I wish I was." He flashed a smile as if to suggest otherwise and then tipped his hat, revealing a dark bushel of wavy hair. "Be careful in this nasty weather." Despite the gusting winds, his wig held firm.

She thanked him and gripped her umbrella tightly as she departed.

He pivoted and walked toward Fifth Avenue. Making a right, he saw the double spires of St. Patrick's Cathedral rise three hundred feet into the snowy heavens. Across the street was Rockefeller Center, where a sculptured Atlas held the weight of the world on his shoulders.

The killer laughed. The Greek gods once ruled the world only to be replaced by more elaborate fabrications. We're mortals. No god or gods intervened in our mundane lives.

After all, there were no miracles against a well-aimed bullet.

He walked up a short flight of stairs past a few policemen huddled together and stood before two double bronze doors that weighed ten thousand pounds each.

Two weeks prior, a most helpful tour guide provided that factoid and gleefully answered all his questions. Ms. Giovanni appeared dazzled by his alluring smile, Armani suit, and Italian accent.

Despite his contempt for religious places of worship, St. Patrick's was a magnificent church. The stained glass windows, the chapels, and the marble altars—indeed there was much to marvel. Not all religions managed to have such a glorious spectacle as New York City's St. Patrick's Cathedral, so today's deed was an extra thrill.

As he finally strode through the bronze doors, he recalled the legend where St. Patrick banished all snakes from Ireland. The accounts varied, but one thing remained certain—it was as fictitious as the exploits of Atlas. Snakes were not indigenous to the Emerald Isle.

Myths, he raged.

Warm, stuffy air greeted his nostrils, and he gagged in disgust before suppressing his revulsion. There they were—the faithful arriving to bear their crosses. Next to Easter and Christmas, what other Christian holiday drew such attendance?

He especially despised Ash Wednesday.

He gazed at the arriving flock and assigned sins they were here to ask God's forgiveness for: cheating on taxes, adultery, alcoholism, domestic violence, racism, and clearly gluttony, by the size of one woman's girth. Hypocrites. Your worthless devotion.

Faith, he seethed.

He was a lion. The Christian cattle were his prey.

Since the sheep were forming to the right, he headed straight. Just as he stepped forward, a preppie, pencil-pushing plebe brushed into him and moved on without an apology. *Asshole.* He was blabbing with his female companion about getting a picture of the altar of Saint John the Evangelist.

Speaking of assholes. If only this apocalyptic shit-spreader had been killed like his brother James.

Today, if someone uttered St. John's lunatic rants of the apocalypse, we'd squirrel that seed in the nuthouse. Instead, however, his revelations have sprouted and strangled mankind with an atmosphere of gloom. How many times had he scoffed as some windbag preacher forecasted a date for the arrival of this so-called Antichrist? The date always passed. The excuse is always, of course, the human element of miscalculation.

The only plus to the evangelist's ramblings was the wealth of fiction it created, both in cinema and literature. Sure, God usually prevailed, but evil always grabbed a few souls before being vanquished. Today, he'd move the abacus in the devil's direction, although he considered his musings as *funny talk*. Satan was no more real than Hades, Asmodeus, Baal, Iblis, or Loki. They were all just superstitions used to intimidate mankind.

Fables, he stormed.

He was not intimidated. This was a time to spit back at generations of lies with an unholy vengeance. Let them grab their rosaries and other superficial talismans. Their monopoly on our minds is over. It was time to break free of religious institutions. It's a new world order.

Walking forward through the nave, he reached the end of the pews and moved down the center aisle toward the sanctuary.

A few paces farther, he stopped. Slouched and snoring was a disheveled man, who had not seen a shave by the sight of him or a shower by the smell of him in quite some time. A vagrant. Perfect. When life was hell for the homeless, how could such a man believe in God?

He took the shoulder strap off and placed the bag on the floor. Nonchalantly, he sat next to the man, quickly seized his wrist, and with his other hand, injected a needle in his arm. The man stirred. "Peace, my brother," the killer said in a soothing voice. "I'm leaving you a few things. There's some food, but first, rest."

Smells of alcohol and vomit rose off the homeless man's body. The killer winced as he placed two paper bags beside the vagrant. He moved back to the aisle, thrilled to escape the man's aroma. He removed his overcoat and swung it over his right arm. With the same hand, he grabbed the bag and walked with it by his side.

When he reached the sanctuary, he turned right toward the south transept. Along the wall stood the faithful, awaiting their ashes. He turned toward two guards who stood before a rope partition.

With perfect Gaelic precision, he asked, "Dear lads, I'm visiting from Ireland. St. Patrick's Parish of Wicklow." He paused to gesture outside. "I lost my way in the storm. My destination is the rectory."

One guard deferred to the other. The younger, thinner guard appeared to think for a moment and then asked. "What's your name, Father?"

"Martin Balor," he replied, heavy on the brogue. "From Wicklow."

"I'll call it in," the skinny guard said. "Sorry for the inconvenience, Father. He has to check your bag, regardless."

The guard nodded and pulled a device off a belt clip. He turned away and spoke into the thing and waited. After a brief moment, he spoke again, this time much louder.

"No problem. My pleasure," he said without a hint of such. He said the right words but slouched and spoke in a slow, strained fashion. His wavy brown hair was disheveled. His eyes were red and underlined by black creases, like a hungover big leaguer during a sunny afternoon game.

With an apologetic expression, the other guard motioned to the bag.

"I understand, sir. You Americans have been through a lot, especially New Yorkers. Where I'm from, we don't have this concern. Well, unless you're a bloody Brit," he said with a sly smile.

The killer opened his duffel bag. "All I have is a change of clothes and some holy books. I'm attending an interfaith seminar tomorrow."

At first, the man's darkened complexion caught the skinny guy's attention, but the priestly garments and accent disarmed him. Half-heartedly, the guard fished through clothes, linens, books, and one bottle of water. He thought,

The man was an Irish priest. He looked like a decent chap. This didn't fit his profile of a dangerous sort.

The killer gazed over to the pulpit and raged. *How much bullshit had been spewed from that stage over the past hundred and thirty years?*

The guard broke his fury. "You're in luck, Father. There's a way to the rectory without braving the elements again. I'll escort you."

As I suspected, the killer thought as he suppressed a smile. He clasped his hands together. "That's most kind."

A simple phone call a few months prior was all it took to schedule the visit. The real Martin Balor from Wicklow was possibly settling down with a pint of beer and a plate of corned beef and cabbage at this very moment. Tomorrow, Balor would step it up to scotch to forget his newfound infamy. Corned beef and cabbage was cattle food, but the killer enjoyed good Irish spirits. Not just the booze, but also the Celtic legends.

It was also those legends that led to the selection of Father Balor. He'd been scouting a list of Irish priests he'd easily found on the Internet when he spotted the name Balor. He loved the irony. In Celtic lore, Balor was a cyclops creature that represented death. The connection was too good.

A small smile breached the killer's resistance. *Now comes the fun part*, he thought.

They came around a bend to the famous Lady Chapel. The marble walls were accented with narrow pillars that rose into arches and then tapered to long, narrow columns surrounded by stained glass, which depicted more flights of fancy, including the ascension of Jesus to heaven. The killer enjoyed this part of the church. He knew beauty, even if it was in the misguided form of religion.

His brown eyes sparkled. The optometrist, whom he later disposed of, found the request unusual. She raved about his dynamic blue eyes. Why did he want brown contacts? She was sweet, but she was a potential future witness. And, she was a meddling Jew, so she had to die.

His ogling was interrupted. "Just this way, Father," the guard advised.

The excuse for security appeared overtaxed and/or bored. The splendor of the cathedral had worn thin from the monotonous ritual of standing around.

He might have to die.

Behind the sanctuary, in the ambulatory, a staircase descended. It led to the crypt and sacristies. Also, there was an underground tunnel that led to the rectory. This was not part of the tour, but he knew that anyway. The information was public from multiple sources, and his accommodating tour guide was most helpful with his follow-up questions.

His escape plan depended on that information.

"Father Venezia is in the sacristy," the guard informed. "I'll take you to him, and he'll take it from there."

The killer had two plans to ditch the guard. One was to say that he'd been below years ago and knew the way. The other, if he proved a persistent escort, was murder. But the guard's suggestion was even better. He tipped his hat again. "Thanks," he said, keeping it simple. He feared the excitement might kill his Irish accent.

When the cathedral was built, they had to blast out concrete to accommodate the sublevel design. The double green bronze doors to the left led to the crypt. Every deceased archbishop from New York was buried there. He had hoped to provide the ex-archbishops with some added company, but alas, the current reigning fool had tripped, broken his leg, and was currently hospitalized. There were always other holidays on the calendar.

The tour continued farther, and they turned right. The guard pointed to a door. "Enter there. Father Venezia knows your coming." He turned and strolled back to the stairs.

The killer cocked his head in satisfaction. *Does he know? Surprise, you're dead.*

Out of his jacket, he pulled a long bamboo tube. With his other hand, he rapped his knuckles on the door.

Death comes aknocking.

Balor.

From dust you come, and unto dust you will go.

CHAPTER TWO

FATHER VENEZIA PREPARED. DRESSED in white vestments and purple pendants, he was every bit as dedicated as he was thirty years ago when he was first ordained a priest. Preparation was not making the ashes from last year's Palm Sunday fronds (that was the Sexon's task), but rather, Father Venezia prepared through silent prayer.

Ash Wednesday was a time of reflection, a period to recall our propensity to sin. The wonder of God's forgiveness comes at an infinite price. Father Venezia prayed for mankind. The world was at another perilous crossroads. The Devil's minions—oppression, starvation, war, genocide, and indifference—were on the rise. The evidence was overwhelming.

At an early age, Father Venezia felt drawn to God. His father was a fisherman, and every time he sat perched at the stern of his father's boat, he stared across the sea into the misty horizon until he saw nothing. In the nothingness, he felt a deep calling.

As an eleven-year-old, he had asked his father if it was okay if he put a cross on the cabin wall, next to the captain's chair. He was unsure what his father would say. His mother was the one who made him go to church, while his father was strictly a Christmas and Easter guy.

His father had looked him in the eyes and asked, "Do you believe in God, Son?"

Unwavering, he had answered deliberately, "Yes. I do."

His father looked him over and said, "Well then. On the next voyage, God will be my copilot."

Thrilled, he'd run to the church store. On an overcast morning, he watched his father hang the cross on the cabin wall. *Bon Voyage.*

A few days later, he was lying in bed when he heard his mother crying. Softly, he descended the stairs, but a sudden creak gave his presence away.

Even in the dim morning light, he could see his mother's moist, puffy, red eyes. She didn't command him back to his room but instead called to him. He ran to her open, but shaking arms.

An unexpected northern front collided with a strong southern pressure system. The storm was ferocious, and wreaked havoc across the northeastern seaboard. Downed electric lines, an abundance of automobile accidents, broken branches, and uprooted trees clogged the flooded roads. More precious beach land was stolen by the oceans.

At sea, the wind was howling at fifty knots. The coast guard reported thirty-foot swells. Communication had been lost with many vessels, including the SS *Hacklehead*, the ship his father captained.

Mother had already talked to some of the crewmates' wives. Captain Venezia was experienced and seaworthy, but the *Hacklehead* was not meant to brace waves of the storm's magnitude. Everyone was concerned. The worst was feared.

The young boy heard the wind and rain pound the house in tandem. There were other sounds: branches whipping, car alarms beeping, garbage cans rolling, and then something else—subtle, like a small pulse emitted in the chaotic cacophony of the storm's dirge, something deeper.

Sal Venezia spontaneously left his mother's embrace and charged to his bedroom. He leaped into bed. On the wall was a cross. It was identical to the one that hung on his father's boat. He bought two of them. It just seemed right.

He ran his fingers along the cross, closed his eyes, and prayed. He never prayed so hard, even when he had asked God for a brother or sister. Medical complications prevented that dream.

This time, his prayers felt different.

He stayed fixated to the wall until his mother came up to check on him. Desperate, she looked worse than she had an hour ago. He motioned her to sit beside him. With his free hand, he took one of hers and placed it on the cross.

In a modulated tone she'd never heard her son use before, he said, "It's okay, Mom. Have faith. This time my prayers have been answered."

"Yes," she said to her son. She didn't want to scare him, but she doubted the veracity of her words.

He held his mother's hand tighter. "Have faith. Dad will call us tonight."

His mother did not truthfully believe him, but she did look at the phone differently with each ring while they sat for dinner. Pizza and soda were on the table. So was the dire situation. This time, though, the mood was positive. They pictured heroics over the unthinkable. They never used his name in the past tense.

The phone rang again. He stared at the phone, knowing. It was his father.

His mother slid her chair back from the table and trudged toward the counter. She lifted the receiver and dropped her jaw. Her mouth trembled. She looked at her son in wonder. It was a miracle.

When several years later he announced his decision to devote his life to God, his parents accepted the notion without hesitation. As an only child, there was some small pride in continuing the family tree. But they knew their son's calling—priesthood.

Through his years of service, Father Venezia never lost that faith. He was sure of God's hand in the order of things. Following Christ's words, he made it his mission to tend to the poor and less fortunate. Now forty days (not including Sundays) before the glorious celebration of the resurrection, he marked the first day of Lent by renewing his fight for those who required assistance.

He hunched over an open Bible and looked at a familiar verse of the Gospel of Mathew 6:16–18. As he peered through his oblong reading glasses, a knock came from outside.

He thought: *That must be the visiting priest from Ireland they phoned me about.*

Turning in the chair, he called out, "Please come in," and then rose to face the entrance.

The door opened. A man dressed as a priest stepped in and shut the door swiftly behind him. Instantly, Father Venezia knew the visitor was not a member of the clergy. There was evil in his eyes and some rod-shaped device in his mouth.

In shock, he stared wide-eyed as the man's cheeks puffed. His forehead felt an impact. He tried to inspect, but his arms would not obey. He was immobile; his body would not obey his mental commands.

Although he was unable to move, his eyes still saw the intruder. Was this the first few seconds of afterlife, as his soul left his mortal body for the kingdom of heaven?

The intruder clarified. "I know you can see and hear me. You've been shot with a powerful paralytic. You're not dead … yet," he hissed. "Since I have you're undivided attention," he paused to laugh at his evil wit and then finished his thought, "I'd love to deliver you a sermon on your religion's blight on humanity."

Father Venezia wanted to reply, wanted to defend his church, but the drug prevented any response. He watched as the killer reached into his coat and pulled out another weapon. He'd seen enough television to know that the cylinder attached to the gun's barrel acted as a silencer.

The killer seemed to read his mind. "Ironic," he said playfully. "Silent and about to be silenced forever." He chuckled again as he used a tool to extract the poison dart. Then he put the gun against the wound. "Perfect aim. Right in the center."

Father Venezia could not feel the cold steel of the gun barrel pressed against his skin. He saw the man laugh at him with a wicked malice as he pulled his index finger back.

His last living memory.

He lived for God.

He died for God.

CHAPTER THREE

Police Detective Lieutenant Dominick Presto took the loaded 2 cc syringe and raised it vertically to the light to look for air bubbles. Pleased, he positioned it in his fleshy hand, his thumb poised on the plunger.

He lumbered into her bedroom. The room was warmer than the rest of the three-bedroom prewar Tribeca apartment. No fewer than six glass-encased candles cast shifting beams of light across her gaunt body.

Using an alcohol swab, he dabbed her exposed stomach. Her eyes momentarily flickered open, but she squeezed them shut and turned her face into an oversized pillow.

With her frail physique, there was not much meat on her bones. He pinched her belly. It was more loose skin than actual fat. Her limbs were like splayed pickup sticks, crossed and spindly.

Dominick took the needle and pierced her skin at a ninety-degree angle. She bit her lip but held firm. He pushed his thumb, and the .45 cc insulin load entered her body. He withdrew the needle and then placed another alcohol swab over the injection point. Next, he applied a circular bandage.

Presto. He stepped back. "You know I love you, Mom, but I hate doing this even though I know it's necessary."

The candlelight twisted shadows over his expansive width. Comfortably, he was dressed in a triple-extra-large, navy blue hooded sweatshirt and almost matching, baggy sweatpants. His usual leisure attire. His fleshy face bunched up like a beach ball that was slowly deflating. Then he exhaled like he'd performed an arduous task.

Her head came off the pillow. "You're so silly. In a jiffy, I'll be back on my feet, dancing a merry waltz. And don't forget that I've been pricking myself with those damn needles for over fifty years." She jutted her head out like a vain peacock.

Cleo Presto was used to the diabetes, but being bedridden after a terrible fall was another matter. A tumble down subway stairs broke her left kneecap and ankle. She also fractured her right wrist, which made self-injection impossible. It had been two weeks since surgery, and she was getting weary of her confinement.

Dominick smiled. He loved his mother as a mother loves a son. They were a team. It might not be ideal, but they made a good tandem. You have to play the cards life dealt you.

His father had been murdered when he was thirteen. Well, not directly, but he was killed by a criminal cause nonetheless. He'd been a dockworker when an unauthorized and illegal cargo of hazardous waste fell off a forklift.

A chemical company had found a solution to trim overhead costs. To the cheers of shareholders, a cheaper way to dispose of dangerous byproducts was secretly found. On this particular day, the CEO had been on hand for the clandestine cruise a few hundred miles out to sea.

Eight workers were hospitalized. Only two were released, but their lives had been changed forever. Some said the dead fared better.

There was accountability and a large settlement. As a child, he played a role. While mom rushed to the hospital, he grabbed a fishing pole and his new camera.

He'd snuck close enough to get some pictures of men in white hooded suits cleaning the area where his father labored. There was also a man in a suit. Dominick knew that men who wore suits amongst those that do not tended to be important. He made sure he snapped several shots of the well-dressed man.

When he got home, his elation was crushed. The unthinkable had happened. His father was dead. Dominick did not understand. His father was the strongest of his friends' dads. How could he be dead?

But he was.

The next day, he showed his mother the pictures he'd taken at the dock. She phoned her husband's union boss, who sent their attorney to the Presto's residence. The rest was history. The company paid millions in restitution, while the complicit board of directors fired the CEO, but not before it was clear that his immediate future was prison. He had, after all, tripled the stock price in less than two years.

Devastated and broken, mother and son forged an unbreakable bond. When people face adversity and emerge whole, but not unscathed, they harden and form an impermeable alliance.

Twenty-six years later, it was still only the two of them. Living in the same apartment, having the same conversations, playing the same games. Needling each other, but really knitting their cohesiveness.

Dominick looked down at his mother and gave his classic fat, jolly smile. "Ma, the last waltz you did was when we went to Ms. Klein's senior citizen spritzer. And, need I remind you, that was on account of a few too many cocktails. You did three pirouettes, got dizzy, and flopped on the couch. From there you did not venture, other than a meandering bathroom run."

He stepped and swayed in imitation, bouncing into walls. An extra two hundred plus pounds enhanced the visual.

She raised one eye. "Don't fall, Son. Mr. Stagnuts finally hung that expensive chandelier. If he sees it start shaking all over, that bad heart of his might go off kilter, especially if that wife of his starts yapping." She chuckled and smiled at him.

He laughed too. He was no longer sensitive about his weight, to an extent, and his mother's jibes were good-natured, not mean spirited.

He was set for a sharp retort when his cell phone rang from the living room. Dominick looked at his mother gravely.

The call told him a few things. Someone had been killed. This was not just any murder, though. Not if *this* phone beeped. The situation had to be awfully dire for them to call.

After solving the three biggest serial killer sprees to hit New York City in the past decade, he suddenly became anointed as the NYPD guru in such matters.

He needed time off after his last case, plus he wanted to assist his mother during her recovery. He told his boss not to call unless their precinct lottery pool won the mega-millions sweepstakes.

Presto would never be a candidate for the, "most popular cop" award. Prejudice is not always determined by skin pigmentation. Human shallowness also vacillates against the handicapped, vertically challenged, and poorly complexioned. In Presto's case, it was his weight. Presto's successes were attributed to dumb luck, which to a certain extent was true.

Shy in front of groups, Presto chose his words carefully and never palled around with *the guys*. Little solidarity forged, he was a pariah in the precinct. Other than the dialer of the incoming call, he was basically friendless.

So this was a big to-do.

He shook a head full of unkempt hair and waddled out of the bedroom.

CHAPTER FOUR

Presto answered. "Jack? Tell me we won the lottery."

The voice that came back was deep and hoarse from years of cigar smoke. "Not today, pal," he said hoarsely.

Dominick heard his mother's bed creak and knew she was listening in. He would have to speak louder.

"Who asked for me, Jack? Don't tell me I'm popular enough now that I have a psychotic fan club—murderers calling in, challenging the dough-boy detective."

Jack hissed. "Why do you say things like that about yourself?"

"Because everyone else does behind my back. You're upfront. No bullshit. Give me the whole poop. I know this is not a social call."

Fourth Precinct Commander Jack Burton inhaled. He truly empathized with his prized and despised detective. Presto was misunderstood. He meekly voiced opinions contrary to his superiors. When he was right, there was resentment. Accolades and limelight made Presto shuffle to the shadows. He always let others jockey to center stage for their public bows in the winner's circle.

The portly detective was too nice. Too often, our predatory human culture eats people of Presto's personal makeup. They get taken advantage of. Meek, they absorb the abuse like a giant sea sponge, too soft to fight back.

Burton exhaled. "A priest was murdered today in St. Patrick's Cathedral. There are plenty of eyewitnesses and clues galore, but thus far, there are no concrete suspects. The killer dressed as a priest and casually strolled his way through restricted areas. In fact, security led him to the eventual murder scene."

Burton stopped to allow questions. When the detective did not comment, he continued. "I'm not sure if you're a church going man, Dom, but today's Ash Wednesday."

Presto's eyes were closed in concentration, but they suddenly snapped open. This time Presto did interject. "How was he killed, Jack?"

Burton knew his detective was onto something. "He was shot in the head, presumably at close range." The precinct commander paused to muster his next words. "Around the bullet wound, there's a crudely drawn cross in ash and blood."

Presto filled a brief silence. "How was that Muslim cleric murdered? The one uptown, about a month ago?"

Burton gulped. With one question, he showed a possible connection. Burton didn't care what anyone else thought of the detective. He admired the man.

Burton answered. "Gee, Dom, I'm not sure. It wasn't our case. Why do you ask?"

"I recall something about a cleric being killed in grisly fashion," Presto said. "If I am not mistaken, it was also on a religious holiday. Eid al-Adha, I believe."

Presto plopped on the chestnut leather sofa. He pressed a button, and a leg support shot up. Now he was comfortable. When his mind raced, his body relaxed.

Sitting in his office, Burton shook his head. Someone else made the same connection. That was why they wanted Presto. If a serial killer was responsible, he was the guy to at least consult with.

"Listen, buddy, you may be on to something there. I don't know. What I do know is the cardinal contacted the mayor, who called Commissioner Tipton. But our good mayor," he slipped with a touch of sarcasm, "made other calls, starting with the Feds. It's election year. The mayor wants to ensure politically that he's done all he can. New York City does not elect weak mayors."

Mayor Murray Golden was a staunch advocate of the NYPD, and the union enthusiastically endorsed him, but Jack Burton distrusted all politicians. It wasn't that they were all necessarily corrupt or bad people as individuals. Rather, it was the bullshit they seemed to enjoy groveling in. The fake smiles, the hearty handshakes, the cross party mudslinging, the posing for photos with a bundled infant, and the constant panhandling for dollars. It was one giant act produced for their re-election.

"Uh huh," the great detective volunteered. He didn't care for politics either. Not just mayors, senators, and presidents, but even the political gamesmanship that we deal with in our everyday lives. Presto wanted to know something else. "Who's heading the case, and who told you to call me?"

"Let's just say I have good news and bad news," Burton said coyly.

"I have an inkling I know the answers. And they're inversed from my questions," he said and laughed softly. He noticed a leftover platter of sugar cookies and grabbed one. "Lay it on me, Jack," he said and stuffed the find into his mouth.

He had the decency to press mute until after he swallowed and chased it down with a beverage.

Jack also laughed. His friend was right again. "You'll be most unhappy to hear that ..."

"Woo," Presto said mysteriously. "Let me guess. Deputy Chief Inspector Frank Danko is running the investigation."

"Lucky guess," Jack joked.

Ever since Danko volunteered security time to the mayor's campaign, he coincidently received a promotion and landed a preponderance of noteworthy assignments. That meant press coverage.

Ambitious and unrelenting, Inspector Danko did have his positive traits. Honest, he was also known to be a tireless worker. Like a marble block, Danko lived in a gym chiseling his sculpture. His shaved head and dark goatee made him an imposing figure in the interrogation room. His success at extracting information from suspects was legendary.

Both Burton and Presto felt Danko suffered from tunnel vision in his pursuit of a solution.

If the criminal was sloppy, Danko was your man. Matched against a diabolical mind, he was easily manipulated to erroneous conclusions. Several years ago, Presto suspected Danko apprehended the wrong man. Quietly, he kept digging and shortly thereafter caught the real killer in the act. Danko's pride was not assuaged by the fact an innocent man was saved the ordeal of life in prison and a vicious killer was off the streets. That spark flamed resentment and blackened Presto's reputation.

Presto reached for another cookie. *Not bad,* he thought. They hadn't hardened much overnight. "Now, who besides you would embroil me into Danko's case?" Waiting for the answer, Presto pressed mute and munched on the cookie.

"Glad you asked," Burton announced eagerly. "After the mayor briefed Commissioner Tipton, he consulted directly with the deputy assistant director of the FBI who referred him to a man who was involved in criminal religious activities." Burton presumed Presto would comment here, but there was only silence.

Presto decided the cookies only had a few hours of shelf life. Rather then let them perish to waste, he figured it was better to add the calories to his waist. Chewing, he listened.

Burton continued. "Well, the Fed turns out to be an old acquaintance of yours—Malcolm Bailey." Burton stopped for an expected response. Nothing.

Burton continued. "Bailey tells the mayor that the NYPD has one of the finest detectives in the country, and if they were smart, they'd to put him in charge. The mayor responds that he has already done that. To which, Bailey says that he knows Dominick Presto personally, and whatever recommendations he made, the FBI would comply with."

Burton stopped to laugh as he recounted the episode and listened for Presto to chime in, but there was only silence from the other end. He wondered if his delivery were off, because he thought it was funny and figured Presto would get a kick out of it.

Presto actually doubled over with one hand holding his gut, while the other dammed his mouth. Simultaneously laughing and eating was like urinating and running—two functions best left mutually exclusive.

He wiped his moist crumb-laden hand on his sweats. He looked at his thigh and rubbed the stain until it was almost invisible. Satisfied, he sat back and eyed the last two cookies. He reached and listened.

Determined to get a laugh from his friend, Burton pressed on. "So the mayor responds that he's never heard of Dominick Presto, but he has the very accomplished and respected Frank Danko heading the investigation." Burton stopped for a growled chuckle. "From what I'm told, Bailey's response was, 'Who the fuck is Frank Dunce-O? Sir, if you take this matter seriously, Dominick Presto must, at the very least, consult on this case.'"

Burton howled. He knew Presto must have enjoyed that. Still, he heard nothing. "Hey, Dominick. You there?"

Presto scrambled to get his oversized finger over the one-millimeter mute button. "Yeah," he started and began choking on laughter and morsels of food.

Burton pounced. "Here I am wondering why you're not talking, and your stuffing your face with food." Burton paused and sarcastically added, "Gee, Dom, what are you eating for breakfast"

"Egg whites and seven-grain wheat toast," Presto deadpanned.

Burton sniffed like he was besieged by a foul stench. "Bullshit."

CHAPTER FIVE

"Don't do it, Son," Cleo Presto advised. "You can't save the world. You may be a superhero to me, but down in the halls of justice, they treat you like a cartoon castoff."

Presto tried again to feed her the sandwich he'd made for her. Thus far, her only bite was to gnash at him for agreeing to visit St. Patrick's Cathedral. "Mom, are you going to eat or chew me to death?" He moved the food in a small circle in an effort to entice. "I have to get going," he said with a hint of impatience.

"No you don't," she countered. Incapacitated, she still managed to look feisty. "We have plenty of money. You've proved yourself. You've saved lives. You …"

"Not now, Mom," Dominick interrupted. His voice was serious. "Eat this."

"I'm not hungry now," she said coolly.

"Mom, you're acting like a child. You know it's not the money. I like being a detective, plain and simple. And," he said slowly, "my service was requested by Mayor Golden."

Presto saw his mother's determined face falter. She liked the mayor.

A few years back some developers were trying to get their greedy mitts on the small neighborhood park. The nearby residents started a fuss and brought their complaints to City Hall. The park represented a small slice of nature in the concrete jungle. It was sacred land.

Cleo often sat there reading her mystery novels or just people watching. She chatted with friends and occasionally strangers. Sometimes she just sat there and thought about things. The place was special to her. When a petition started, she became energized.

The mayor took a position with the residents over the developers. It may have cost him some fundraising dollars, but it landed him plenty of votes. In fact, the press coverage was significant, and his poll numbers leaped.

Presto watched his mother's face soften. He hid a smile.

"Really? Mayor Golden asked for you?" She grew excited. Her eyes gleamed, dimples widened, and jaw jutted. "I told you the mayor was a smart man."

"Well, that may be," he said coolly, "but he was advised by Malcolm Bailey, an FBI agent I know. From what I understand, the mayor had never heard of me."

"Don't be so skeptical," she reasoned. "He made the right decision."

Presto shrugged at her way of seeing things but decided not to reply.

She suddenly straightened up in bed, like a bedbug bit her in the ass. "Here, give me that sandwich."

Presto watched in shock as his mother wolfed the meal down. He'd never seen his mother eat with such gusto before. That was more his specialty.

She started to speak, but the last piece of food caught, and she gagged.

"What has gotten in to you, Mom?"

She looked up. Her face was red, and her eyes watery. She swallowed a final time. "Now go. Be off. Stop dallying around. The mayor needs you."

CHAPTER SIX

"**M**AYOR GOLDEN MADE THE request to my precinct commander, Jack Burton. I don't want to step on anyone's toes," assured Presto dutifully.

"Me either," snapped Frank Danko. "You might crush my steel tips," he snickered as he pointed to his shiny black shoes.

Most of the assembled crowd in the priest's chapel laughed. The exception was a priest, whose face twisted in disapproval.

Despite the purpose of his visit, Presto felt good when he walked through the grand cathedral. In an odd way, he lived for moments like these.

Danko's glare and snide comment doused his positive spirit. Humbly, he asked, "Frank, may we speak alone for a moment?"

Danko's bushy eyebrows drew together like two furry caterpillars colliding. He appeared prepared to cast another barb but gruffly replied, "Let's step outside."

Presto led the way outside the chapel, which due to its proximity to the sacristy was currently being used for the investigation.

As soon as Danko shut the door, he grumbled, "What?"

Presto thought about what he was going to say, while his cab had crawled uptown. Presto volunteered a half-hearted smile. Danko didn't reciprocate, his expression as grim as the last man on a long line at the welfare office.

"Frank, I'll leave if you want me to," Presto started. "You're running the investigation; it's your call."

"This I know," Danko assured. "Go on."

"The mayor called the Feds. He told them you were in charge, but the guy he spoke to happens to be the only agent I really know. Years ago, we met on a case. Anyway, he mentioned my name to the mayor. Thus, I am only following orders. I'll be happy to follow your orders and go back home. I was on vacation, Frank."

"What purpose would you serve?" Some of the edge dissipated from Danko's tone.

"Merely to consult. I was asked to make an assessment for the Feds. I'm not sure what their role is at this juncture. You can report back to the Feds if you like. If you want me to stay, I'll help in any way I can. We're all on the same team."

He stared at Presto, but the glare was partially gone, except for dim reflection off Danko's shiny scalp.

"Are we? I respect your abilities. Your record speaks for itself, but you already sandbagged me once. You may have been right, but there's protocol. I was running the case. You could have worked your theories through me. You let me take the fall. You grabbed the glory. I was the goat."

Presto understood, although he did not completely agree. Danko leaped at the obvious and was not receptive to other opinions, especially Presto's. But this was not the time to air his feelings.

"I apologize for how things turned out," he supplicated. "My intentions were not as they may be perceived. I think," he said feigning indifference, "that if you give me a second chance, we can work successfully together on at least a professional level. I will humbly accept otherwise if you feel differently."

Danko paused to deliberate. He spent an unusual amount of time nodding, grimacing, and scratching at his hairless head. He didn't really want Presto around. He wanted this case to himself. That could change if the Feds get involved.

"Here's the deal," Danko finally said. "Attend my briefing. Make your report to the Feds. If you have any alternative opinions, theories, or whatever, here's the format I want you to follow. We will work as a team, but you're the player, and I'm the coach. That means you do as I say. If you have any input or criticism, arrange a meeting with me before you disseminate those thoughts elsewhere. And, if I see you acting independently and outside the scope I outlined, I will dismiss you from the case." Danko stopped to pause and posture. "But if you can abide by my guidelines, I would welcome someone of your caliber."

Presto was elated. It had been years since they last spoke, although he had since conjured imaginary conversations. Usually, the outcomes faired worse. Here was a chance to thaw some cold shoulders.

"Thanks for the opportunity, Frank," Presto gushed. I won't let you down, coach," he said with jock-like flair. "Speaking of which, did you see the Mets get bombed last night?"

Danko grounded the levity Presto thought he'd gained. "I'm letting you in for your brain, Dom, not because we're *paisans*. Let's head back inside."

CHAPTER SEVEN

"**W**HILE THE FORENSICS TEAM does their thing, let's review the information we gathered," Danko declared as he stood before a dozen of his brethren, most of who were part of his inner squad. "I want everyone to hold their opinions for now. Let's examine everything before we draw any conclusions. In this case, more than any other I've seen, I think we need to reserve sentiments and judgment."

Presto was impressed. This was a new and improved version. Perhaps humility and time matured the man.

Danko looked tough but casual in his tan slacks, white shirt, and loose, dark blue blazer. Presto noticed that most of his team was dressed identically. Presto felt like an outcast in his corded trousers, argyle sweater, and tweed blazer with suede elbow patches. When he left the apartment, his mother commented that he looked stately. "With my proportions, estate-ly is more like it," had been his self-deprecating retort.

Danko had taken a moment to review notes he had on a table. "We do have a suspect, but he's a dead homeless man. I'll get to him later, and while we are not ruling anything in or out, there is ample evidence that he is not the triggerman."

Yes, this was a different Danko, thought Presto. The old Danko might have taken the easy route and fingered the dead guy. Danko might still be angry with him, but Danko had learned a valuable lesson.

The room was silent. Danko had their attention.

"I'll start with the crime scene and then work backward," he said crisply. "The victim, Father Venezia, was shot in the head at close range, possibly with a silencer. Nobody heard a gunshot, and Chad, our forensic pathologist, suspected such after a preliminary review. And there's one other thing; I'll get to in a moment."

Danko stopped. His lips tightened; his eyes held a steely gaze. "The killer then took the time to draw a cross around the entry wound. Remember to hold off theories on what the killer's motives were," Danko advised. "You'll see what I mean in a minute." Danko picked up a piece of paper from the table and surveyed it.

"What we have here is an overabundance of clues. All the crosses in the

22

room were turned upside down. The sacristy Bible was destroyed. However, in perfect condition was an open Qur'an." Danko paused to grit his teeth and pick up a folder. "In the Qur'an was a highlighted passage."

He looked at his notes and read: "Kill them wherever you encounter them and drive them out from where they drove you out, for persecution is more serious than killing. Do not fight them at the sacred mosque unless they fight you there. If they do fight you, kill them; this is what such disbelievers deserve; but if they stop, then God is most forgiving and merciful."

When he dropped the folder, a loud thump was heard in the tensely silent room. "Once again, I ask you not to pass judgment. There's more."

Presto had questions and almost sat on his hands to prevent raising one like a nervous, gawky high school teen. He'd have to wait until class was over.

"Left in the priest's lap was a young boy's soiled underwear," Danko said with disdain. "There was also a grainy picture of a young lad." Raising the volume, Danko found better footing. "This seems to tie in with the dead bum we found in the pews. Next to him were some paper bags. One contained a needle and what appears to be heroin. The other contained a gun, a .22 Ruger pistol, equipped with a silencer. There's a serial number, but for some reason, I'm not optimistic it's registered in the killer's name. The gun's been sent to ballistics. Also in the bag was an identical picture of the same boy we found on the priest."

Danko stopped and muttered something Presto could not decipher. While Danko collected his thoughts, the rest of the room used the impasse to shift and stretch. Presto found the metal folding chair uncomfortable on his posterior, despite his extra personal cushioning.

Danko cleared his throat and the room quieted. "Besides the dead hobo, we have another suspect. It's still sketchy, and we're still getting statements, but here's another interesting storyline.

"A priest approached two guards. He introduced himself as Martin Balor; claimed he was visiting from a church in Ireland and his destination was the cathedral rectory. They both claimed he sounded right off the boat Irish. Anyway, the guards called security to check the name against a list. It was a match. It's not uncommon for St. Patrick's to receive other priests; it's the largest Catholic church in the United States.

"So, one of the guards escorted this man to the room where the murder occurred. Both the guards and security estimate this was around ten o'clock in the morning. A Father Grich entered the sacristy at 10:20 am, where he found the deceased. He immediately returned to the rectory and called security, who called the police.

"Another priest, Father Lopez, saw a priest matching the guard's description enter the tunnel rectory door. This was about ten fifteen. At about the same time, Father Buchnell said a priest whom he did not know stopped him and asked for the Madison Avenue exit. The priest said the guy seemed friendly enough, and he showed him the way. He did say that the man had an unusual accent, but he was certain it was not Irish. After reflection, he thought it sounded Middle Eastern."

One of Danko's men provided a bottle of water. Danko twisted the cap and took a healthy slug. Like a gavel, he pounded the bottle down on the table.

"We already contacted Ireland. Their authorities visited the real Martin Balor. He is, in fact, a priest from the church on security's list. However, he claims he never contacted St. Patrick's about a visit."

The deputy chief inspector threw his hand to the air. "So what do we have? Right now there are more angles than a protractor." Danko stopped to laugh, and his merry band of followers made it a quorum chorus. Presto was deep in thought and was the lone dissenter.

Danko brought his hands down. "There's the bum. There's this mystery Balor character. There's a possibility of something else entirely. Either way, the killer left us some clues to think about. Hopefully, he left a few others unintentionally," Danko quipped.

"I need to organize and assign duties. Let's break; lunch will be served in the rectory."

The case had whetted Presto's appetite. He wondered what the church spread was.

Danko addressed the room. "You're dismissed. I'll meet you guys in the rectory." He paused, and his eyes narrowed like a poacher. "Presto, stay here. We need to talk. Anyway, you could skip a meal." He smirked.

He stopped to let those in the room laugh derisively. "Just kidding."

Chapter Eight

"You're the brain, Dom. Any thoughts?"

Presto stared, not angry but expressionless.

Danko's thick eyebrows lifted, and his head jolted forward. "You mad?"

Presto was upset, but he not did provide the perverse pleasure Danko was apparently after. His face remained blank. "Not really. I just hope the boys leave some scraps. Must admit, I'm hungry as a forest fire. Ready to consume," he said with relish.

Danko did not appear ready for that response. His face withdrew, the flesh hugging the skull beneath the skin. Then his nostrils slowly flailed, and the old Danko was back.

"You may be a touch flabby, but don't go soft on me, Presto," he admonished playfully. "Bringing you into that room, after all that happened—well, forgive my childish need to save a little face."

"No problem, Frank. Let's catch us a killer," Presto reminded. He didn't approve of Danko's jibes, but he wanted to stay involved. Cases like this did not pop on the radar often, even in the cage of New York City.

"I'm curious," Danko probed. "What do your instincts tell you?"

"A few things," Presto replied casually.

"Such as?" Danko encouraged.

"I'd recommend an autopsy."

"What ... why ..." Danko stammered.

"The victim may have been poisoned, drugged, whatever. I'd check that out to be safe."

"We know how he died—a bullet to and through the brain. Did you doze off during the meeting?"

"No, Frank. I was tuned in to your every word. The priest was shot in the head, dead center. Right?"

"Yes," a puzzled, but furiously thinking Danko answered.

"The aim is too perfect. The killer intended it for the ashen cross."

Danko cut in. "He could have pulled the gun and forced the situation."

"He could have," Presto agreed. "But that is not what my instincts tell me. No one heard the priest call out. There was no major struggle. No sign of desperation on either side."

25

Danko waived his hand. "I did not make any comments about the state of the room one way or another."

"True, but you would have mentioned a disturbance if there was one. The omission assuredly was because there was nothing to report." Presto kept his voice even. He did not want to turn the conversation into a debate.

Danko shrugged. "You're right, of course. There was no obvious sign of a struggle. However, he did have time to leave us some presents. He could have tidied up."

"Once again, true, but that doesn't seem logical to me. Why? I could see if it was a husband doing his wife in or something of that sort, but this is different. This was planned. He left us all these clues for a reason. He's not sloppy. He's prepared."

"I still doubt he was drugged, but I suppose we can never be too thorough," Danko conceded.

"You may be right. He probably wasn't, but it can't hurt checking."

Danko appeared ready to move on. Presto hoped so. He feared there would be little to no food left. All this standing fatigued him.

"You conjure any other ideas, Presto? What do you think we're dealing with?"

Presto resisted answering. Danko had requested holding back any theories. Now he sought his opinion. He did not want to lie or overtly conceal. Danko would think he was out for himself—withholding information to steal the glory just like last time.

"I have a few thoughts rattling around," Presto divulged.

"Stop being cagey," Danko demanded. "The cardinal called the mayor from his goddamned hospital bed. Let's not futz around here. We need to work together," he appealed with a smile. "There's no *me* in the word *team*."

"I" Presto corrected.

"Eye?" Danko said confused.

"Never mind." Presto consented. He had thought maybe Danko was playing cute. "I actually have a question for you."

"Shoot," Danko fired back.

"A Muslim cleric was murdered about a month ago … on a holiday. Do you know any of the details?"

"No," Danko said and smiled. "I happened to be away with my wife at that time. First vacation we took alone in fifteen years. It was great—rekindled the love flame." Grinning, he made a circle with his left hand and crudely jabbed his index finger through. "Know what I mean, big Dom?"

Presto did not really know. He ignored the childish visual. "We need to get that case file. It might be relevant."

His visage grew serious again. "Think there's a connection?"

"Maybe."

"I'll look into it. If there is, this could get dicey."

Presto nodded in agreement. "We may have a serial killer on our hands."

"We don't know that yet," Danko rendered. "Even if there is some connection, it could be a religious hit or some jihad revenge. Who knows, but let's keep all options open, Dom."

Presto grew frustrated. A moment ago he was being asked for opinions. Now he was chided for offering one. He kept silent and looked agreeable. He thought about food again.

"One more thing," Danko added. "I want to see your report before you send it to the Feds. Do a good job on it. Make sure we look competent. I want their help to be …" his eyes a sudden wanderlust, "distant. We can handle this on our own. You may be their liaison, but you work for the NYPD. Don't forget that."

CHAPTER NINE

"Now I got their attention," the killer said aloud as he gazed at a computer photographic slide show. He knew killing a Christian would, especially in St. Patrick's Cathedral.

His latex-covered finger pressed a key, and the slide show started a second time. He did not need his notes to recognize the faces. He'd made a scrapbook of the city's top detectives.

He had mingled amongst the crowd outside St Patrick's Cathedral, who gawked like braking drivers passing an accident. Cell phones were out, and pictures were snapping. Beneath the veneer, we all love when evil touches lives other than our own. Nestled among the camera crowd, he was hardly out of place.

It was easy. After leaving the rectory, he walked one block north to a phone booth. He knew it would be unoccupied. With cells phones, the days of waiting for an available phone were relegated to when you really needed them, like a city crisis. Then the lines were paralyzed, and you had about the same chance of a connection as chatting directly with God. *None*. But just to be sure, he'd cut the phone cord the prior evening.

Only his back was visible within the booth. Opening his bag, he retrieved a water bottle and a washcloth. He wet the rag and then rubbed his face. When the cloth darkened, he turned it over and scrubbed some more. From his pocket he pulled out a compact mirror and flipped it open.

Satisfied, he'd hunched over, removed his fedora, and tugged at the wig on his head. He exchanged them in the bag for a New York Yankees cap and pair of dark, but unremarkable sunglasses.

He leaned back a few degrees and spun his head in both directions. He neither saw nor heard any signs of commotion. Next, he removed his Roman collar and slipped it in the bag; his hand reappeared with a navy blue sweater. Trendy, the style was popular with the city's preppy white male population.

The real risk, and thrill, came in the interlude before the priest's body was discovered when he reentered the cathedral. He had retraced his steps to the now-deceased vagabond and slipped the gun into the man's hands. Then he put the gun in the brown bag he'd previously placed beside the vagrant.

As the photos cascaded the flat-panel monitor, he knew that although this kill had been easy, things would change. He had their attention now.

"Frank Danko," he snidely remarked. "The mayor's butt boy." Danko was pictured standing with a frown. An agitated finger gestured to someone offscreen.

The other pictures were assorted shots of rank-and-file police drones and Danko's gang of gumshoes. Lightweights.

Then came the heavyweight. Check out this load. This guy's got more pounds than a London bank. Despite the joke, the killer was unsettled by the sight of Presto.

He laughed and gestured to a man slumped in a wheelchair. "Funny one, huh?"

Dressed in checkered flannel pj's and a matching robe, the middle-aged man did not reply. Blankly, he stared into space. Unkempt, peppered hair grew down his neck into a forklike pattern. Course hairs briskly poked out of his nose like mini paintbrush tips. There was also a splotchy beard flanked by wispy sideburns. Minimum maintenance was the mission.

The killer looked away from the stone still Medusa victim, but by then, the picture had changed back to the pointing Detective Danko. Amateur.

He thought while he waited for the slide show to commence. *Dominick Presto.* That was unexpected. His contact said he was on a mini-sabbatical. But there the fat man was.

The stakes had been raised. Now the excitement would begin. There would be much press, and he pondered the headlines of the creative New York dailies.

In time, they would try and assign him a nickname. Infamous serial killers are routinely anointed with monikers. Local legend David Berkowitz was the Son of Sam. Richard Ramirez was the Night Stalker. John Wayne Gacy was the Killer Clown. He'd let the police or press come up with something and then correct the record. He always wanted to select his own name and despised his parents for the one they chose for him. Not this time. When the time was right, the world would come to know.

Myth Man.

Chapter Ten

Back at the apartment, Presto went about breaking the law. He was corrupt, his mother joked. Technically, a police officer's job is not to make laws, or question them, but rather the enforcement of them.

A prior mayor passed a NYC law making ownership of any snake illegal. Presto could understand if the snake was poisonous or a powerful constrictor, such as an anaconda. But a harmless milk snake? What damage could the two-foot, skinny as pen, nonpoisonous reptile do? After twenty years on the force in a tough city, he'd never heard of a homicide from a snake, let alone one as harmless as the pretty Aphrodite. And she was a biter. Skittish, she was the only snake he'd ever owned that did so. But her bite was less painful than a green horse fly.

People didn't know better. He'd always fancied pets. There'd been birds, cats, dogs, fish, lizards, newts, rabbits, tarantulas, and turtles. When he was eight, he asked his mom if he could have a snake. She countered with a dog but promised him that when he was old enough to grow a mustache, he could have a snake. At that age, a child's time of reference is off. Elated, he thought that day was just around the corner.

When he turned sixteen, he'd stare at the mirror, looking for some dark stubble over his lip. A few classmates already had signs of growth, but he was not so fortunate. Several months later, although it looked mostly like a dirt smudge, an immature mustache was evident. He ran to his mom. She was shocked he remembered her bargain, but she never broke a promise.

There was something about all of God's creatures that fascinated him. Banning all snakes was ignorant. There was no danger, only fear. Presto knew. Many times he'd watched movies where a snake or spider was used to convey a threat. Often the props they used were not dangerous. He'd seen movies where nonvenomous snakes and spiders were used, and thus, there was zero chance of injury, let alone fatality.

Presto played on that fear in playing a trick on the pledges of his college fraternity. He dropped their pledge pins in the snake tank and told them to retrieve them. Prior to the day, he told them it was a coral snake, which, in fact, was venomous. All but one of them declined. That one pledge comfortably put his hand in. The snake, more scared than the humans, darted into his cave. Presto asked if he was brave or smart. The boy answered, "Smart. I grew up on a farm down south. That snake is not a coral snake or poisonous. Red next to black is a friendly Jack. Red against yellow is a dangerous fellow. That is the rule on snakes."

The pledge was right, but he was one of eighteen. Most people did not know better.

He removed the screen top from a twenty-gallon glass tank. From a Styrofoam cup, he jiggled three fuzzy mice downward. They fell to white sand and rolled, their limbs jostling. The mice were only weeks old, their eyes still closed. They would never see the light of day.

A small spade-shaped head appeared from a rock cave. A forked ebony tongue flicked from a yellow snout that gradually grew black. The rest of the body appeared—long red bands bordered by black, with a yellow stripe in between.

"Good afternoon, Aphrodite," Presto greeted. "Bet you're hungry. I know I am."

The Sinaloan milk snake located the scent and slowly weaved toward the three blind mice. Her head coiled back, and then, almost faster than the eye, she struck. Her shiny, scaled body coiled over her prey, and an unhinged jaw worked over the mouse's maw.

He went to the kitchen to fix a snack. Back at the rectory, the police boys had ransacked the lunch platter. By the time he arrived, there were only two soggy tuna sandwiches and plenty of salad. Danko had passed and pulled a protein bar from his jacket. He had never planned on indulging. "On a strict gym diet," he had said and shrugged his cold shoulders.

Presto procured two burger patties from the fridge and fired up the gas-top stove. While the meat sizzled, he peeled two pieces of American deli cheese, forked two pickle slices, and grabbed the squeeze bottle of ketchup. He grabbed only one bun, but not out of desire to avoid the carbohydrates. He liked his burger beefy.

Presto tramped to his mother's room. Her injury had started an addiction. It was not the painkillers that had hooked many others, but instead the culprit was trashy daytime TV. She was watching a talk show. Today's episode, she gleefully reported, had been, *Geriatric Genital Piercing*. She told him that she contemplated an ornament of her own. "You're gross, Mom," had been his reply.

He saw a commercial with kids rolling in mud, a Labrador retriever running through an open field, a steaming crumb apple pie on a lily white plate, and two senior citizens laughing on a mountain landscaped park bench. Then an insurance company logo appeared at the bottom of the screen, and the voice-over said they have enthusiastically served Americans concerns for over fifty years.

He asked, "Is your smut show over yet?"

"Just about. I've decided that a new hair style is about as radical as I am likely to get at this age."

"Good choice, Mom," Dominick ratified.

She looked up at him and giggled before she said, "Now tell me about the case."

Another breach of protocol; he told his mother everything. More than a soundboard, her advice was practical. He summarized the day's events.

"Danko's using you,' she rendered when he finished speaking.

"I know that," Presto affirmed. "This is for the victims."

Her head lifted from the pillow. "And for the mayor," she reminded.

"Yeah, yeah. Danko's the mayor's boy, but I don't want to argue with you."

The small rebuke made her look away. She fidgeted with the remote, and the volume rose. The distraction made him follow her gaze to the television. An all female audience clapped wildly as a man in a dark pinstriped suit and fashionable cobalt blue shirt came out with hearty wave and smile. He informed his rabid fans that today he'd introduce agencies guaranteed to catch a cheating hubby plus a few women clients who were fortunate to learn they'd been living with a louse.

"Mom," look at me.

She peeked up at him. Her brow was creased like a pair of his slacks, lost to the bottom of his closet. "Yes."

"What's really bothering you?"

She looked away, but he summoned her attention back. "What is it?"

"It's stupid. A motherly thing."

"Go on."

Lying on her back, she gazed up at him like only a mother knows how. "You care about everyone but yourself. I just fear that when I am one day unable, there will be no one to look after you." She drawled to a long pause. "You better find someone who will."

He did not immediately reply. His mother never pestered him about his nonexistent love life or reclusive nature. He smiled at her. "Mom, stop the drama. I'll buy another dog."

His response did not have the desired effect. She seemed to consider something, the way her face plied in different directions like a mobile amoeba.

In the silence, Dominick heard the guy on the television introduce the president of *Cheater Beaters*. He turned to see a husky, shorthaired woman, dressed in a dark-gray pantsuit saunter out from a velvet, maroon curtain. Hearing his mother's voice, he looked back.

"Just think about what I'm saying. You, more than anyone else, should know the world is a cruel place. The ordeal's easier when you have someone. We have each other, but I'm not going to be here forever."

Presto grew concerned. "Is there something you're not telling me, Mom?"

"No," she declared vigorously.

Her voice more convincing then her expression.

He was ready to challenge her, but like déjà vu, his phone rang from yonder. Once again, he knew he had to answer.

Duty called.

CHAPTER ELEVEN

"WHAT'S UP, JACK?" PRESTO queried.

"This is the mayor," a badly disguised voice began. "Are you trying to start trouble? Looking to pad that resume?"

Jack Burton was almost six and a half feet tall and two hundred and forty pounds of solid muscle. He played offensive line in college, and was drafted in the sixth round by the New Orleans Saints, but a severe anterior crucial ligament tear early in training camp derailed that dream.

Mayor Golden, by contrast, was about one hundred and thirty pounds, wet. Diminutive. People were shocked when they met him in person. Commercials did much to augment his stature.

Their tones were diametric opposites—one deep and hoarse; the other high and tinny.

"Jack? What's up? I know you love me, but twice in one day?"

Burton gagged like he swallowed something distasteful. "Got another call. This time the mayor sent his attack dog, Spencer Hoole. Hoole's never heard of foreplay. He doesn't waste time lubing you up. He just undresses and fucks you."

"The name sounds vaguely familiar. What's his problem?"

"You, Dom. I don't get it. The mayor calls asking for your help, and then his top aide calls saying that maybe it's best you finish your vacation. Says the city doesn't need trouble."

"What trouble? What's he talking about?"

Jack wheezed. "Danko made a report to City Hall. He mentioned the murder of the cleric and a possible connection to events at St. Patrick's. Apparently, that made people unhappy. Danko credited you for the theory."

Presto took a deep breath as he processed the information. He'd make his report to Malcolm Bailey and let the buffalo chips fall where they may.

"I only follow orders, Jack," he said impassively. "Level with me."

"My guess is you're history," Burton said with derisive disappointment. "Hoole was clear that his personal sentiments have been adequately expressed to Danko. Apparently everyone was in agreement including our spineless police commissioner. The only reason I cannot say for certain is that Danko said it was only right to talk to you first. Get this; he said he owed you that much." Burton stopped to emit a sarcastic whistle. "But you know what that means. He'll get his rocks off rolling you under the bus. I wanted to tell you first so you were prepared."

"Thanks, I guess," said Presto with a soft laugh.

"Oh, and one other thing," Jack said with a serious tone. "This call never happened."

Presto remained even. Malnourished millions worried over their next meal. This unfortunate revelation was nothing compared to the worries of an empty fridge. Starvation panicked him.

True, he wanted the case. No doubt about it. Right now, though, he was more troubled by his mom's behavior. "When am I supposed to hear from Frank?"

"Tomorrow. Sleep tight, big buddy. You'll always be my ace. It's their loss, frankly." There was an added spice of cheer in his voice, but it was sprinkled too zestfully. Burton's discourse tasted better without the added sauce, even if intended tastefully.

It was a bitter pill, but Presto swallowed it whole and without a grimace. "Hey, Jack. Thanks for the call."

CHAPTER TWELVE

Presto leaned back from his pride and joy, his desk, and reflected on question thirty-six down in today's, *New York Times* crossword puzzle. *What is the largest mountain in Switzerland? Monte* blank. Four spaces. The third was a definite *s*.

Despite the large settlement, or payoff from the company that killed his father, the Prestos lived frugally. These were not cheap people, but they chose not to live excessively. They did not cruise the ubiquitous bar circuits; indulge in costly, unnecessary hobbies; or follow the latest fashion of technological fads. Charitable, they generously donated to the poor, various afflictions like Autism, as well as several animal-related causes.

They preferred to live as if the blood money never existed. Except for his prize.

Most folks, Presto imagined, would have splurged on a yacht, sports car, and vacations. He desired only one exorbitant item—a desk.

He spent more time at his desk than he ever would in a hot car or sailing the seven seas. The apartment study was his haven from the cruel outside world. Here, his mind was clear from distraction. No music. No television. The only sound was a fan that offered white noise.

The walls were decorated in bookbinding's. All together, the four walls contained more than a thousand books, most of which were secondhand pickups from street vendors. He had the essential criminology classics, but most were pleasure reads.

Besides the chair he sat on and the fan that oscillated in the corner, the only other thing in the room was his desk and what rested on it. He purchased it at an antique auction. He felt bad outbidding an elderly woman with a genuine gold-knobbed cane, but he was not about to let the desk slip away.

Made of a rare satinwood, the eighteenth-century, all original Carlton House–styled desk had cost a bundle. Originally a Welsh prince had commissioned the assignment. However, his royal hiney never sat before his request. Beheaded by his son, the desk was later sold to a wealthy (by the very definition, stiff upper lip) English family. It had been stored with a drape cloth in an attic for hundreds of years until it had been found and sold to an auction house.

Here he sat, with his eyes closed, resting. He did not sleep well. Danko's looming sharp axe was not the culprit. Rather, he was lactose intolerant, and a late night ice cream binge, heavy on the hot fudge, left him unsettled.

This time he was ready for his phone to ring.

"Hello?"

"Hey, yeah. It's me. Frank."

Presto raised his inflection and feigned surprise. "Oh," he stammered. "Hi, Frank. Everything okay? Anything I can do?"

Payback time. Presto heard Danko breath deeply. He pictured his giddy smile and sensed the anticipation.

"I'm not sure how to break it to you, Dom," Danko said, like he was delivering last rites. "I'll just spit it out. Man to man. Cop to cop. I trust you will keep this between us."

"Sure thing," Presto replied amiably.

"Let me put it this way. You're not wanted on this case. The recommendation comes from above, way above."

"Alright." Presto leaned forward with a pen and wrote in the open crossword boxes. *Monte Rosa*.

"They put the pressure on me to drop you, but I told them I owed you a talk first."

"Gee. Thanks, Frank. But you don't owe me a thing."

Danko snorted slightly. "You got that right. But on a professional level, I do."

Presto did not know how to reply, so he didn't.

"Anyway, that's why I'm calling."

Presto jumped in. Time to get it over with. "I appreciate the courtesy. I'm okay. I really was enjoying the time off."

"Well, don't get too relaxed," countered Danko.

"What?"

"You heard me. I may be tight with City Hall, but I don't let politicians tell me what to do. I do follow orders, but the commissioner never issued one—only a recommendation, albeit a strong one."

Presto was stunned. There had to be some trick. *I may be a fool, but this isn't April.*

Danko continued. "I may harbor some resentment, but I'm not an idiot. I'd rather deal with you than the Feds. If you're removed, there's a better chance they'll move in. I want you to keep them at bay. This is our case."

"Thanks, I guess," Presto replied evenly.

"Don't take it the wrong way. There's more. I didn't like being told what to do, but it's not exactly like we're buddies. Then I thought I'd use a test to decide your fate. I looked into a few things. First, I spoke to a Detective

Halloway. He *was* handling the case of that murdered Muslim cleric you mentioned. It's now been reassigned to us. There's a definite connection. Sure, we would have later connected the dots, but you gave us a head start. How can I remove you from the case after that?"

Presto was momentarily bereft of voice. He had been waiting for his death sentence and Danko, of all people, provided the pardon and clemency. "Frank, I don't know what to say. Thank you, I suppose, is a good start. It truly means a lot."

"Alright. Don't get all chummy. There's more to tell, and I'm waiting on a few things. They'll be a briefing late this afternoon. Call in later for the details."

"Will do, Frank. Thanks again."

"Get ready, Dom. Whatever this is, I know one thing now. We have a major situation on our hands."

CHAPTER THIRTEEN

"Son of Satan Strikes" screamed the headline of the *Daily News*.

Myth Man was not a happy camper. Actually, he hated camping, and he was eternally, internally angry. This morning he was particularly incensed.

First was the press coverage. Both the *Daily News* and the *New York Post* hailed him as, the Son of Satan. Thus far, they missed the point, but they'd come to learn. They had focused on the upturned crosses. That was for fun.

And the gall of the New York Times. He had not even made the front page. No, he'd been relegated to the Metro Section. Was he not news fit to print? He'd teach them all.

Then his contact had called. Dominick Presto had not been severed from the investigation as promised. Maybe that idiot Frank Danko was smarter than he'd been told.

He knew that the game could not last forever. When the trail got close, he had his escape plan. He hoped to cover as many religions as possible before it was all over. He did not fear Dominick Presto could get him, but he might be forced to end the killing spree prematurely.

Two more weeks: the timetable was the interfaith holiday calendar. Thinking of his next kill brought a small smile to his lips.

He rose from a cracked, faded black Naugahyde couch and walked across the decrepit blue living room carpet to the kitchen. He opened the fridge. Inside, he retrieved a clear, plastic, liquid-filled bag and returned through the living room, down a short hall, and into a bedroom. There was one window, and the blinds were down.

Lying in the bed was the same bedraggled, silent man who had been previously predisposed to the wheelchair. Next to the bed was a metal stand. Myth Man hung the liquid bag from a hook and then injected a needle into the port. He placed the needle on the bedside nightstand and then gently squeezed and rotated the bag, mixing the medicine. Next, he inserted tubing into the bag and affixed a needleless cannula to the end of the secondary tubing. He scanned and then adjusted the drip rate.

No fuss. The man didn't even turn his head away when the needle pierced the infusion point. His patient was most cooperative. The necessary routine of feeding and changing the bedpan was still an ordeal that revolted him. But for now, he had to keep him alive.

For months he scoured the Internet for the disenfranchised. There were Web sites for conspiracy theorists, antigovernment zealots, firearm fanatics, and other citizens not plugged into the program. These were people who tended to have problems with society and strayed from mingling with the mainstream.

Most of the sites had forums where loonies left their crackpot commentary. An alias frees them to express their wisdom to the world. Of course, the government was watching, they claimed, but they posted away. In time, the anonymous enclaves bond together. A real nuclear family.

It took time getting close. He met a few candidates (in disguise, of course) before he found the right one—a malcontent marine whose misgivings were with the military he'd served.

Initially, the guy had no problem with his mission in Iraq. In fact, the marine was eager, but there had not been as much action as he'd hoped for. Later, a fellow soldier convinced him that they were all pawns in global gamesmanship, orchestrated by greedy multi-corporations hell-bent on global hegemony. His only true buddy prodded. *Hadn't Eisenhower warned about the military industrial complex?*

The marine had not turned from hawk to dove. Violence was a necessary means. Freedom was better than dictatorships. We were not the enemy. He believed in saving America, restoring her to the way the Founding Fathers dreamed. Back then, the government kept robber baron industrialists in check, but greed is hard to suppress. Wealth builds power. Power breeds corruption. Good Americans, such as himself, were losing. The masses went about their business, which was in the interest of big business.

Alone, the marine needed an outlet for his anger. The Internet was such a place. At his favorite Web site, http://www.losingoldglory.com, one of the smarter regulars who consistently agreed with him suggested chatting without the prying governmental eyes of Big Bother.

Myth Man smiled in recalling his first encounter with the marine. He'd told the fool he served in Vietnam and had also felt betrayed. The military angle seemed to ensnare the gullible grunt. Naturally, he'd never set foot anywhere near Southeast Asia. He'd read a few biographies and just talked shit. They went from posting messages on Web sites to frequent email exchanges.

After a few months of courtship, the guy broached the idea of getting together. Myth Man played it reluctantly cool, but then slowly and, he thought, cagily warmed to the idea.

Both had stated that they avoid open public as much as possible. They agreed to meet on a Saturday night at eight o'clock. Myth Man cancelled a few prior times. He preferred inclement weather.

The rendezvous point was the intersection of Wall and Water street. The financial district is a literal ghost town on weekends, especially nights. The few police strayed around Wall and Broad streets where the New York Stock Exchange was located.

Myth Man spent hours aging his appearance by some twenty years. His hair grayed, his face paled and sloughed. He walked with a limp and hunched—Vietnam War injuries, he exclaimed. He even hammed it up with an old army jacket, where the stitched name pronounced "Greed." The slacks were that seventies style that reminded him of wallpaper in his old home, hideously large checkered patterns that rattled one's rudimentary senses.

He topped the look off with an old school black bowler hat.

His gopher showed up in denim—pants, jacket, and baseball cap. The boots were army standards. A cigarette hung from his mouth, a habit picked up during the boredom in Iraq, he later explained. He tossed scattered looks, like he expected to see cameras, secret agents, snipers, or maybe UFOs. His build suggested he was once a tough guy, but inactivity made him flabby and soft.

The courtship: a wink and a nod. They drew closer, wary like two tentative combatants. They receded to the nearby shadows, between two streetlights and became acquainted.

He dazzled the denim off the misfit. Void of human contact, the man craved the feigned interest in him. By the time a small drizzle began to fall, they'd covered guns, especially illegal ones, and duplicitous dealings of both the federal and *secret* government.

Like a gift from the god's that did not exist, the rain suddenly intensified. Myth Man began to shiver and cough. The man caught the cue and suggested finding shelter. At this hour, in this desolate location, the only spots open were a few bars. The few residents who lived in the financial district were Wall Street types—greedy sorts who perpetuated big business's stranglehold over the common man. Neither man fancied their company. After a short deliberation, the guy suggested going back to his place. He parked a car a few blocks away. What harm could an old man with a limp cause?

Back in Bay Ridge, the house was as perfect as the subject. It was as isolated as a place could be (in Brooklyn, anyway).

On a corner, the neighbor on the right side, he learned, was an elderly woman who rarely ventured out, except to feed a stray cat that had settled in her yard. On the left, there was a narrow street and then a large barbwire fence that protected the backside of a used car dealership. Directly across the street was a wall that rose buttressing an off-ramp. The final piece of good fortune was a garage with an automatic door opener.

This was his man.

Married once, the marine's wife and kids split to Seattle. His brother had died years ago from Hodgkin's disease. He had no friends to speak of. He was a loser.

The small house in Bay Ridge Brooklyn had been his parents' and was already paid for. He'd been unemployed since returning from the first Gulf War and lived with his folks. When they died, he kept the place and inherited enough money to remain gainfully unemployed.

While they checked the marine's gun collection, which was comprised of both registered and unregistered weaponry, Myth Man stabbed a needle into the man's neck. The guy turned. He was in shock. He trusted this man. Then he collapsed.

He never left home again.

CHAPTER FOURTEEN

"I WANT EVERYONE'S ATTENTION." DANKO strode into the gathered room like an intense football coach set to deliver a fiery halftime speech. Any chattering ceased. Everyone saw the press. They knew this was serious.

"Before I begin, I want to thank you for your hard work. We've compiled quite a bit of information in a short time. If we keep this up, we'll get this guy soon." Danko stopped. His formidable chin angled upward. He looked confident. "We have to. This might be the most sensationalized city murder since John Lennon, and our man is still at large. We're going to come together and work eight days a week until we get this bastard."

From the back of the room, Presto looked for a small smile from Danko. After naming a Beatle, he strung two of their hits in the next sentence. Because Danko's expression never changed, Presto was unsure if it was an unintentional coincidence.

Danko pointed. "Jenkins and Fortunato put together a report of their interviews with all the potential witnesses, a few who came forward after hearing the news. Good job, men."

Presto saw their heads dip and rise.

"It's pretty strange, but let me start with the man we found dead in the church pews. His name is Darrel Mankin. He's been in and out of homeless shelters for close to seven years. Alcohol killed his marriage, his job, and ultimately, life's ambitions. With the city budget crisis, many of these shelters have closed, and guys like Mankin end up on the streets."

The room seemed especially silent. Every cop knew about the budget crisis. The NYPD had been working without a contract for more than a year. The union flatly rejected a four-year deal that proposed no raises for the first two years and then 1 and 2 percent for the next two. Presto knew he was fortunate not to rely on a cop's salary.

Danko forged on. "Mankin may have been a bum, but there's nothing in his record to suggest he's capable of this violence. As for the gun, we can confirm it was the weapon used in the murder." He sighed. "The serial number was a dead end. About ten years ago, a firearms dealer in Brooklyn was robbed. It was an inside job, and the perpetrator was apprehended, but by then, the merchandise had been widely dispersed."

Danko stopped to thank another officer for the report on the gun.

The room darkened, and Danko moved from the lectern. Projected on the wall behind him, an illuminated face appeared. Off to the side, Danko narrated. "Sketch artist Randy Celesnki spent hours with the eyewitnesses. He said their descriptions were generally consistent. The question is how much did our suspect alter his appearance?"

In the dimmed room, the face glowed like a jack-o'-lantern. The visage was unhelpfully nondescript. Void of a prominent characteristic, such as a scar or pronounced nose, he appeared unusually ordinary, but recognizable.

Presto dismissed the rest of the profile, except that he was likely a male.

Danko's voice cut through the darkened room. "The people responsible for the sketches include the two guards, the priests from the rectory, and two people we deem reliable based on our interviews. One was a subway commuter who spoke to a man fitting our description and said he opened his coat and showed a priest's collar. She claims she did not like the way he leered at her. The other was a woman who bumped into him on the street. She told us he boasted about murdering someone."

Danko must have tired of the dark, romantic setting and snapped at someone about the lights. Feet scuffled, and the room brightened.

Danko muttered, "Thanks," and returned to the pulpit. "While all the witnesses were uniform in their descriptions of the suspect, there was one detail that varied—his accent."

Danko leaned forward with his hands on the lectern, his fingers moved slowly, like twin tarantulas. "The two guards swear the man had an Irish accent. Father Buchnell thinks the accent was mideastern, as does the woman on the subway. However, Ms. Edith Hooper, the woman who claims the suspect talked about killing someone that day, is certain the accent was Indian. She was adamant about that, saying she worked in a hospital for years with Indians. The difference was that his wasn't genuine. 'Forced,' was how she phrased it."

Danko threw his hands up. "Who is this guy, a comic impersonator?" He said it without jest, his voice exasperated.

Presto guessed they'd find out more soon enough. This one wanted notoriety.

"There's more," Danko announced. "When I heard about the accents, something occurred to me. At first I didn't make the connection, as I was vacationing at the time and the case was hardly publicized." He paused, craned his neck, and locked eyes with Presto for a few seconds then resumed. "A Muslim cleric was brutally murdered in his Mosque about a month ago. It was also a holiday. I have it written down here; I'm not sure how to say it."

Danko gave it the ol' American try. "I'd al ad hah?"

Laughter and a few snide comments brought a smile to Danko's lips.

Presto smiled, too. There was a connection. Eid al-Adha—the Festival of Sacrifice.

He wasn't mad if Danko tried to portray the lead as his own. Between them, they knew. That was all that mattered.

After Danko absorbed his moment, he waved his hands downward for quiet. "So both a priest and cleric were killed on religious holidays. The priest had the cross on his head for Ash Wednesday. For the cleric, it was much worse."

Danko picked up a piece of paper and read. "Basically, the holiday is about sacrifice. Something about how God wanted the Muslim prophet to kill his son. It was a test, and because Muhammad was willing, he passed, and God slipped in a sheep or ram instead."

Danko brought the paper higher, obliterating his face. "The custom is to kill an animal by slitting the throat and donating one-third to the poor, one-third to friends and relatives, and I guess the rest is all yours." He dropped the paper.

"In this case, the cleric's throat was slit, and he was missing both arms and his legs below the knees. His nose and ears were also sliced off." Danko stopped to grimace. "The arms were mailed to a homeless shelter, while the legs were sent to the cleric's mother-in-law."

"Good to see our culture does not have a monopoly on meddlesome mothers-in-law," Danko joked, but then grew serious. "The nose and ears remain unaccounted for."

He stopped, his face twisted in disgust. "This is a sick fuck that we're dealing with," Danko spat acerbically. "Also found at the scene was a desecrated Qur'an. Next to it was an open Bible with, once again, a highlighted passage."

He let the comment hang momentarily. He read: "And they shall come against you from the north with chariots and wagons and a host of peoples; they shall set themselves against you on every side with a buckler, shield, and helmet, and I will commit judgment to them, and they shall judge you according to their judgments. And I will direct my indignation against you that they may deal with you in fury. They shall cut off your noses and your ears, and your survivors shall fall by the sword. They shall seize your sons and daughters, and your survivors shall be devoured by fire."

In the quiet, everyone pondered the implications. A priest and a cleric killed on religious holidays. Presto felt a nonfood-related surge in the vast chamber of his belly.

Danko used the impasse to slug some water. The liquid seemed to wash away his grave demeanor.

"Another thing," Danko said with a coy smile. "On a hunch, I requested an autopsy on Father Venezia. Cardinal Keaton was kind enough to acquiesce. I was curious how the killer was able to do what he did without any visible signs of struggle. As it turns out, we found something."

Once again, Danko found Presto's eyes. "The toxicology revealed high traces of tetrodotoxin." He stopped to scratch his beard. "This stuff is serious shit. I'm told the book went into more detail, but I did see the movie, *The Serpent and the Rainbow*. This is the same drug. It's ten thousand times more lethal than cyanide. If given in the right doses, it prohibits the nerves from sending messages to the body. Hence, the person can be alive but unable to even blink. That was how, in the movie, they had those zombies. People were literally buried alive."

Danko's bushy eyebrow's raised. "That means the priest and cleric may have been drugged and alive when they were killed. If you think about the circumstances, that's one terrible way to go. It also shows what we're up against."

Presto fought his impulse and remained quiet and seated. It was not because Danko had stolen the credit again. These matters did not concern him. Unresolved murders did. Jack Burton often brought unresolved cases for his perusal. Danko's tidings sparked the memory search engine.

There was a hit; a double homicide in one of those, pay-and-play by the hour motels.

The man was married. She had been divorced for many years. The crime scene suggested she shot him and then turned the gun on herself. However, investigators were suspicious. The two seemed an unlikely pair. Presto was asked to review the case, and he immediately suspected foul play.

He now knew who their killer was.

CHAPTER FIFTEEN

"You pissed at me?" Danko asked after Presto seated himself in front of the chief deputy inspector's desk.

Presto was a trifle testy, but that was due to yet another seat that wasn't constructed for his proportions. Much of his bottom ballooned over the edges, and he was unable to find a comfort zone. Danko, meanwhile, leaned back in a leather recliner.

"Not in the slightest," Presto attested evenly while he surveyed Danko's office. Family man—photos of his wife and kids were in abundance. Beaches, school plays, playgrounds, soccer fields, and baseball diamonds were the settings. Paintings his daughters made were pinned along the wall of his desk. A 'World's Greatest Dad' business card holder greeted all visitors.

"You have a reason to be," Danko said, "but I had my reasons. My motives were not what you think they may be."

Presto was interested but pretended otherwise. "I don't need to know. You might not believe me, but I am not the attention seeker you may perceive me to be. I like detective work and the satisfaction of serving justice to killers. Other than that, I prefer to be home. I avoid the limelight like a bat avoids the sun. I'm here to help, and if I have to pay my dues to remedy our past, that's fine by me."

Danko rolled the seat forward and rested his arms on his desk. "It's natural that you'd think my goal was to usurp you. To the contrary, I was protecting you."

Presto was now intrigued and did not suppress his surprise. "Huh?"

"We may not be the best of friends, but you have worse detractors than me. When I advised that I was leaving you on the case, I took some heat. I explained why. After the toxicology report and lead on the murdered Muslim cleric, you deserved to stay aboard. I'm not saying any names; in fact, this conversation never took place, but I was, more or less, ordered to isolate you, not give you any role."

All Presto could do was nod. First, he's asked to vacate a vacation, and now they want to farm him. He never understood why he was so misunderstood. *Neither do the mentally insane*, he thought and almost smiled.

Danko frowned. "As I told you before, I follow orders. This time it was an order. Before, it had been a suggestion. This made no sense to me, not after I told them about your contribution. They said they want this handled *delicately*," Danko pronounced. "And, for whatever reason, you're perceived as a shit stirrer."

"Clearly, I need to hire a PR firm to disinfect me," Presto quipped.

Danko smiled. "That may be," he agreed. "Last time I told you since I didn't receive a direct order, my decision was that you should work the case. This time, however, it was an order. So, I'll isolate you. That means your name does not appear in reports. I still want you to stay on but understand if you want to quit. Heck, I would. You deserve the credit."

Presto waived his hand in the air. "I'm not quitting, Frank."

"Good," Danko said. "I was hoping to hear that. Not just because I'm reaping the benefits of your insight and hope you can still keep the Feds away but because this case has the potential to explode. I need your help." Danko winked the concession. "I hate to admit that, but it's true."

"I may have something else," Presto stated.

Danko looked shocked. "Already? How? What?"

Presto was not sure if Danko told him the truth. His old nemesis was not one to fib. He appeared sincere in his request for help. Maybe someone else was trying to elbow him off the case. Could he blame Danko for using him? Maybe, but he was hooked by the cast of the lure.

"Jack Burton drops a lot of files off for my review. They're usually unresolved or suspicious in nature. I think one of them is related to this case."

Danko motioned him with a roll of his hand to continue.

"About a year ago, a man and a woman were found slain in a motel. It appeared to be a murder/suicide. But the detective was dubious. Something bothered him."

"What?"

"It was mostly a feeling. The man was one of America's top sushi chefs. She was a divorced optometrist. He was thirty-nine and known as a dedicated husband. She was fifty-seven and had been in a relationship with another woman for the past seven years. Her lover claimed that after her husband humiliated her with his affairs, she'd exorcised men from her diet. They seemed such an unlikely pair in every way."

"Okay," Danko probed slowly. "Go on."

"The man who rented them the room claimed a woman booked the room. The clerk said that was not unusual, neither was the fact that she had a large frumpy hat disguising a drooping head or that she paid in cash with a fake name. That was all very usual for this establishment, where people pay by the hour and hope the thrill lasts that long. What was unusual was that she paid for two days and asked not to be disturbed. In his ten years, nobody had paid for more than a night's stay.

"His boss told him to look out for criminal sorts who might try and misuse the privacy their business afforded. A chubby, middle-aged woman was not the sort to vandalize the place, sneak in others for a party, make illicit drug deals, or commit murder. The motel attendant ventured she was catching up on lost time."

A lost Danko stepped in. "I have to stop you, Dom. Not to be rude, but cut to the chase. If you say it's fishy, I believe you. You don't have to convince me. What I want to know is how does it relate to this case?"

Dom put his hands up in apology. "Sorry, I get carried away. The chef's name was Akito Ito. You might not know him, but," Presto paused to pat his belly, "but us food connoisseurs, know these things."

Revolted, the dedicated fitness buff watched his gigantic guest genuflect. "I suppose so," Danko observed.

"Yes, well, the point being is that Mr. Ito was one of the few Americans with the license to serve the fugu, or puffer fish."

Danko slapped the table in frustrated jest, "Enough with the food. I have an hour before I'm allowed another protein bar."

I'm finally getting there," Presto conceded. "Tetrodotoxin comes from the puffer fish. Hundreds of people in Japan have made fugu their last meal and died. Now it is better regulated. Mr. Ito would have access to the poison that our killer used."

Danko shook his head in wonder. "You think?"

"I do," Presto replied. "I further surmise that the killer used the optometrist, Ms. Schnabel, to aid his disguises. My guess is this man thoroughly scopes out his work beforehand. Different styles of glasses frames can alter one's appearance. Colored contacts are also a possibility."

"If you're right, that means he planned this out a long time ago."

"That's what makes this case special. Most criminals are impulsive. It's the methodic types that pose the greatest challenge."

Danko groaned. "This is going to be tricky. Since it's not outright terrorism, we've been ordered to tread carefully. The last thing City Hall wants is for this thing to explode."

Presto was confused but let Danko continue and hoped he'd clarify. He also wanted the meeting to end soon. He needed to rise, stretch, and find better seating accommodations. He thought about bringing in a seat cushion Mr. Stagnuts provided post hemorrhoid surgery. Still, he wanted to fit in, almost unnoticed, even if it was as difficult as slipping into size forty-four trousers.

"You know politicians," Danko continued. Presto wanted to say, *No, you know politicians personally. I know they're full of bull,* but, again, he refrained from interjecting. "They all have to pander to every ethnic and religious group. Also, he'll never say it, but because he's Jewish, I think Mayor Golden wants to remain above the fray in this possible Christian/Muslim holy war."

"Holy war?" Presto blurted in surprise. "Terrorism?"

"Yeah. You were right about the Muslim connection."

"I know," Presto replied, "but I'm not sure I agree with the prevailing wisdom in City Hall."

Danko's eyes bulged in astonishment, not like a birthday boy entering a surprise party, but more like he caught a sucker punch to the gut. "What? I thought that's why you mentioned this Muslim thing, like we had some jihad going on. That's why you made everyone downtown nervous."

Presto breathed deeply and then exhaled through his nostrils long and hard enough to blow out a candle. He needed the respite to keep the edge from his voice. "I never said anything about a jihad, terrorism, or holy war, Frank."

Thump. Danko's large fist gaveled his desk. "What exactly are you saying?"

"I don't think I need to reiterate my words," Presto answered calmly.

Danko leaned back in his chair and gazed at the ceiling. His left upper lip hung in the corner like he'd been hooked.

Presto knew he was upset, but this wasn't his fault. He waited for Danko to respond.

Still back in his chair, Danko's head rolled and straightened. His eyes found Presto's. "Maybe I jumped the gun. I reported the connection, and we all assumed it was either terrorism or some religious war. You seem to have all the answers. What's your theory?" There was a slight edge to his tone, but Danko seemed more leery than angry.

"Frank, I never said those theories are wrong. I'm saying that I never suggested them. But now that you ask, I doubt this has anything to do with terrorism. It may be some holy war, as you stated. But, where's the precedent? In Jerusalem, where many faiths have roots and there is the constant specter of terrorism, religious leaders are not usually targeted. And if they are, it's not in the ritualistic fashion we have here. Our case, I believe, is the working of an individual. I think we have to be as careful and as delicate as advised."

Danko rubbed his smooth head. "Okay, Dom. What about those underlined religious passages? City Halls has a right to think this is, like some modern crusades."

"Yes, but maybe that's what the killer wants us to think. He intentionally left us many clues. There's some that are diversion, and others, possibly, that may be his motivation. We need to be open to all possibilities. If we don't get this guy soon, Frank, we'll know his game soon enough. That I fear."

Danko appeared relieved. "That all makes sense. You've been hot so far. I'm not in position to disagree. I've given everyone assignments. I want you to freelance. Do what you do best. If you come up with anything, call me."

"Sounds like a plan, Frank," an eager-to-rise Presto said agreeably.

"I'll assign some manpower to that case you mentioned. Maybe we'll find some names, a lead. I plan to visit that mosque where the cleric was slain. I'll get you the file beforehand. I'd want you to accompany me."

"Thanks," gushed Presto. "That's a most welcome idea."

CHAPTER SIXTEEN

"Shit!" Dominick Presto literally cursed. Aphrodite had a penchant for defecating in her water dish. It's common amongst reptiles. Although it made for easier cleaning, it meant entering her domain. Despite his stealth attempt at lifting the top, she became alerted to his presence.

Aphrodite was coiled with her head slightly raised and drawn back like a crossbow—not a good sign. He smacked the glass, and she darted to her rock cave. He kept his hand next to the glass, ready. With the other, he quickly reached for the water dish. Her head reappeared but not before his hand was clear from the tank.

After dumping the contents in the toilet, he cleaned and filled the dish and returned for round two with Aphrodite. He employed the same routine successfully, and when his hand was free, he fastened the screen top back on.

Aphrodite detected a presence. Prey? Her tongue darted in and out, and she slid out from her cave. She came out and inspected, her tongue darting in search of the disturbance. Despite her edginess, Presto still cherished her. He loved pets, but most required constant care and attention. He appreciated the minimal requirements of a snake and was fascinated with its simplicity. No arms. No legs. The swallowing of its prey whole, bones and all. It was a touch of nature in the un-Eden life of city living.

Was man any better? A snake kills to live or protect. When a man hunts to feed his family or kills an interloper, he's lauded. Man is different from his fellow earth mates in his ability to wantonly destroy other species of life, as well as each other, for reasons other than food and safety. Presto found man's nature far more heinous than Mother Nature.

Presto believed in order, ecosystems, balance, and equilibrium.

Taking advantage of his mother retiring early, he rumbled to his office, but not before removing a tub of vanilla fudge swirl ice cream from the freezer and then nuking it in the microwave for twenty seconds.

Spooning large chunks of ice cream into his mouth, he thought, *What's the purpose behind these murders?* A holy war of some fashion had been the immediate assumption. Logical. The thought had also occurred to Presto, but then he dismissed it. The theory was a product of the immediate evidence. There was a Bible. There was a Qur'an. Therefore, we have a holy war.

He was certain religion played a role but not the instant obvious interpretation offered by Danko. Religious extremism would not postulate in this fashion: the accents, disguises, and overt clues. These were not simple assassinations. They were the work of the same person or persons. If it was not some retaliatory religious war and was the work of an outsider, what would be the motivation?

Presto presumed the immediate assumption was partially right. He was not sure of the ultimate end game, but he knew the killer's intention. Flaming religious passion could stoke the fervor of the faithful. That was their suspect's goal, Presto deduced. Incite a holy war.

He picked up the phone and dialed Jack Burton.

"Dominick," Burton answered cheerily, "thought I'd hear from you."

"Whom else would I go to?"

"Your mother. And since she's prettier and smarter than me, I guess you're not seeking advice, but answers. That, or your having a lovers quarrel," he snorted.

"I'll ignore that but concede that my mother's been acting odd lately. Maybe she's just getting stir-crazy sitting in that bed."

Burton grunted. "Then you should spare her your humor."

"I'm ignoring your jibes tonight," Presto said amused. "I want to talk to you about the case."

"I've heard smatterings already."

"I bet you did."

"Smatterings were an understatement. It was more like *splatter*ings."

"Who was it this time? That guy you told me about, Spencer Hoole?"

"No," Burton said abruptly, but with a trace of humor. "Actually, it was my boss."

Presto gulped. "Commissioner Tipton? I know. He got to Danko as well."

"Right, as usual. Ironically, it seems, you would have been dismissed had it not been for your buddy Danko. That was the most shocking thing I've heard since my wife asked if I'd buy her a vibrator."

Presto smiled at his friend's saucy commentary. Through the phone, he heard a screeching voice in the background. "Jack! That is not funny. Tell Dominick that's not true! He should know what an immature buffoon you are."

I heard her," Presto said with a laugh. "You tell that wonderful wife of yours that I know you better and that I eagerly await my next visit; not to see you, Jack, but for her scrumdelicious cooking."

Jack relayed the message to his wife, and they all laughed. Although Presto had yet to find his life mate, being in the company of a truly loving couple as the Burtons proved the merits of marriage. He recalled his mother's earlier comments about finding someone. He frowned and then pushed the thought away.

"You're a lucky man, Jack. Count your blessings."

"I know, Dom. You're right. Abby's lucky to have me. She should count her blessings."

After a small lighthearted commotion, Presto said, "You're horrible, Jack. Still teasing and courting like an immature teenager."

"Keeps us young," boasted Burton, "but enough about us. Talk to me."

Presto told Burton how Danko stole the credit but then claimed it was to protect him from detractors. "I wasn't mad that he presented my ideas as his own. However, once again, Frank jumped to conclusions." Presto then recounted the holy war theory and added his twist on it.

Jack said, "You think someone's trying to start a conflict? Why?"

"I've been mulling that over, but the details must be kept from the press. Thus far, we've been surprisingly successful, which leads me elsewhere."

"Huh?"

"Considering the details of the cleric's murder, I'm shocked that this was not front-page news. Someone made sure this was kept quiet. I understand the reasoning, but am surprised at the success. I'd like you to dig up those contacts you have and see what you unearth."

"You want me to shovel the shit without causing a stench," Burton equivocated with a coarse laugh.

"Exactly. Not to be paranoid, but I don't trust anyone. I'm used to being ostracized, but this is different. I need to be invisible."

Burton chuckled deeply. "You're too big to hide. Unless," he said slowly, "you're a magician, Presto."

"Hardly."

"I once saw some guy on TV make an elephant disappear."

Through the phone, he heard his wife scold, "Jack Burton. You need to learn some manners and stop being a clown."

Presto smiled. Jack was one of the few genuine people he knew. Burton did not ignore his weight or poke fun for malice. In the superficial world of image and fraud, Jack was a throwback. Presto could see him on the frontier—gritty and gruff but a gentleman.

"Tell Abby thanks. Next time, we'll punish you by cutting you out on that key lime pie she makes for dessert."

CHAPTER SEVENTEEN

"Your move," Myth Man hissed across a chessboard to his silent partner. Recently, he thought about ceasing dialogue with his comatose housemate, as it reminded him of Norman Bates conversing with his dead mother.

Myth Man was no psycho. He was quite sane, he assured himself. His murders were not dictated from the dead but designed to release religion's lock on humanity. History was with him, he told himself.

Finally, unlike Mr. Bates, Myth Man conversed with a living entity. Was this no different than talking to a dog? He supposed it was. A dog would respond in some fashion. Maybe a cat? They were glorified stuffed animals, he thought. Whatever. He decided that he enjoyed it. No backtalk, and it broke the monotony.

While rummaging through the house, he found a computerized chessboard. Had to have been the old man's, he figured. He doubted the freeloading paranoid had the wherewithal to understand the simple complexities of chess. This dummy was not astute enough for the board game Stratego. Tic-tac-toe was more likely his speed.

A master planner, such as himself, of course, appreciated and excelled on the checkered battlefield. But even he knew his limits. The game showed his vulnerabilities.

He pressed a button and awaited his fate. The screen flashed, and a buzzer rang in taunting fashion. He bowed his head in defeat. After conquering the other settings, he'd yet to win on the master level. He was good, but he could be beaten. That is why Dominick Presto concerned him.

He took the loss well. Recent tidings had pleased him. He was advised that Presto had been marginalized. There was also the chance Presto might quit being handcuffed by his own police department. *A man of his intelligence, like me*, he assumed, *must have pride in his work. Bright minds think alike.*

At least the morning's headlines delighted him. He smiled as he traveled the disinformation highway. All the regional papers led with the same story. He almost died and went to heaven (metaphorically speaking, of course, as there was no holy Shangri-la) when he found the story on CNN's home page.

Holy War screamed two of New York's more sensational dailies. A few were more subdued, which annoyed him, but the details were well chronicled, nonetheless—all by a very high-level source.

Both the cleric's and priest's deaths were provided in their goriest detail. It was reported that the police successfully suppressed the details of the cleric's death and wanted to squelch the connection to the recent slaying in St. Patrick's. The source claimed that police feared it was some new form of terrorism or a modern-day crusade. It was reported that the top theories were that a fervent Christian assassinated the cleric and then a Muslim retaliated by killing the priest or that a Shiite Muslim killed the Sunni cleric and framed the Catholics.

The source said he felt it was his duty to tell the truth, even if it meant potentially angering a few religious zealots.

Myth Man selected a Web site from his favorites list. The monitor screen changed. Centered was a giant white cross. Oak trees were scattered in the foreground. Poking out from the trunks was sometimes an arm, leg, or head but always a pointed rifle.

Welcome to the New York chapter of the Christ's Crusaders.

The New York branch was one of the nation's smallest. Most members were located upstate in small hick towns where a double-sized trailer was considered luxury. Also sprinkled in the mix were doctors, teachers, law enforcement officials, and those with other everyday occupations. One guy claimed he was the mayor of a town. All of them remained anonymous but claimed they were ready to report to duty when the time called.

Membership was not monetary but messianic. You had to pass a test on the New Testament. Myth Man knew the lies and passed their sophomore Sunday school Internet test.

He had listed NYPD detective as his occupation.

He chose the message board link and a sign-on box appeared. He keyed in his password. He bypassed topics like Preparing for Armageddon, How to Arm Yourself with NY's Draconian Gun Laws, and Personal Dealings with Christ and instead opted for the Lord's Live Forum. At that moment, seventeen members were signed on, a record number. Normally, the count was single digits.

He smiled. Messages scrolled up the screen like an outgoing wave. Everyone was fired up about the recent news. Some said it was a war; some said it was a sign; all declared themselves ready no matter the calling.

Most of Christ's Crusaders were fundamentalists who tended to dislike Catholics, something Myth Man thought about exploiting later. Yet, when it came to a possible conflict between Islam and Christianity, they apparently forgot their differences with the Vatican.

Myth Man typed.

Disciple of the Dawn: As you know, I'm a detective, and I have the goods on the St. Patrick's case.

Angel of No Mercy: There you are. Tell us. We need to know.

Sister Christian: Disciple, I fear the worst, although the end will be glorious. I just prayed over my sleeping children. Help us clarify.

Lord's Trumpet: Hush everyone. Let him talk.

Lord's Trumpet: I meant write, not talk. Sorry. ☺

Idiots. One thing Myth Man gleaned preparing for his mission was how stupid the rank and file were. They made him feel superior. It was tough being so clandestinely clever in this clueless culture of ours, but not for long. They would learn his wisdom.

Disciple of the Dawn: The politically correct are trying to bury the truth. They're afraid that if the public knows, there may be acts of violence committed against honest, law-abiding Muslims, if there is such a thing.

Trumpet of God: You got that right, brother! Let's all wait until he's finished before we ask questions. Please continue.

In this orchestra of outcasts, Trumpet was brass and out of tune. The man had turrets on the keyboard frets. Myth Man considered tracking down the asshole when it was all over.

Disciple of the Dawn: The suspect only used a phony Irish accent when he spoke to the guards and gained access to the sacristy. The other witnesses who positively identified the suspect swear the accent was mideastern. Then there's the quote from a Qur'an that was left behind. This we know. The question is who killed the cleric? I say who cares, but it certainly wasn't a Catholic who overdosed on Hail Marys. The evidence does not suggest this was the work of a Christian. Here's what the police and the complicit media are not telling you: The man who killed that Muslim also had a mideastern accent. I can tell you all of this because I know a detective on the case. He's considered the best. You may have seen his name in the papers, Dom Presto? Anyway, trust me, he knows the deal, but they are trying to keep him quiet. He's very angry and confided in me.

Myth man stopped to send the message. These nitwits needed small bites to digest. He also required a sip of water

Trumpet of God: Hello? Disciple? What happened?

Trumpet of God: Don't leave us hanging. Where are you?

It was maybe a ten second timeout, but Trumpet had to blow his horn. Yes. When the murder spree ended, Trumpet's epitaph would be Taps.

Disciple of the Dawn: Patience, brother. My daughter had a math question.

Trumpet of God: Accept my apologies. A child is a gift from God. Continue.

Total tool.

Disciple of the Dawn: I'm quite blessed. So, my source, Presto, tells me there are two theories. These Muslims have different sects like we do in Christianity, and like us, have had wars. The cleric was considered moderate, by their standards, and perhaps some fundamentalist nut job whacked him. Then, either the same guy extended his reach to the Catholics, or some follower of the dead cleric sought revenge on a Christian knowing a Bible had been left behind. That is the more popular theory. The other possibility is this is a trick by the Jews. You know those Jews. They're sneaky. They want us Christians involved in their conflict when, in the end, they shall both perish before He returns. Those mideasterners are all the same sort. The Sephardic Jews can pass as Arab, so maybe this was a Mossad thing or something. Who knows? But this contact, Dominick Presto, said it is one or the other. Obviously, there's forensics and much more evidence that tie it together, but the police and politicians are afraid. You know, they can only bash us Christians. Presto said that the lead detective, Frank Danko, and the mayor are trying to squelch this. It is an outrage. Please leave my friend's name out of it, but you need to get the word out about this. I apologize, but I must go as I have to read my lil' angel's report. I will be back soon. God bless!!!

This was a blast. Myth Man was happy. Who said work couldn't be fun? He loved getting the religious digs in. Christ's Crusaders—ha, what a bunch of misfits.

Trumpet of God: Thx for the scoop, buddy. I will be sitting here waiting for your update. I do appreciate …

He exited that Web site and then clicked the favorites menu again. The Muslims and Jews had their fundamentalist fanatics as well. Next up was the Men of Mahdi. He'd get to the Jews later. There was more mischief to spread.

Chapter Eighteen

Ahmed Shaziq picked up his pace and tried to gauge how many of them were in pursuit. His ears tried to pick up the sound of their feet. Three was his guess, but when he walked past a loitering group of taunting teenagers, there had been at least six. In a panic, he also thought he heard car doors shut and the sound of a car kick over.

He was confident he could out run the three on foot. Ahmed never smoked, and at age thirty-seven, he was still in excellent shape. He had only jogged two of his planned twelve miles, so he knew he had a lot left in the tank. But even an experienced marathon runner was not going to evade the speed of an automobile, especially in the open expanse he now traveled.

Headlights. Tires screeched. "There he is. Get him!"

A beat up Pontiac four-door cut in from the right. Ahmed broke left toward the East River when his foot caught a crack in the pavement. His arms flailed in front of him as he smashed down on the cement. He heard jubilant voices as he fought off the pain and tried to rise but fell when an object slammed into his back.

"Strike," a voice heralded. "Nice fastball, Vinny."

"Jerk," a deep voice grumbled acerbically. "Don't use names. Now I may have to kill you along with this sand-nigger."

"Oops. Sorry, Vin."

Ahmed was scared. He had feared backlash when the priest was murdered in St. Patrick's and a Qur'an had been left behind. He'd suffered through the stigma that stained Muslims after September 11, 2001. He considered moving his wife and three children to Canada where a relative of his relocated, but America had been good to him. He performed selective surgery at New York Community Hospital and was able to afford a nice home in Mills Basin. He enjoyed his routine, his life. His children excelled in school. There was much to be proud of. As the group approached, he prayed to Allah that he would see his family again.

Six boys approached, spaced apart like on oncoming net. Ahmed clasped his hands and pleaded. "Please, I beg you."

They laughed. "Hey, Bin Laden," spat the one named Vinny, as he wielded a large metal object. A thick gold chain hung from his meaty neck and rested in a heavy patch of fur exposed above a white tank top. "See this," he said holding a large metallic tool. "This is my sand-nigger-be-good wrench." More laughter cascaded down on Ahmed.

He implored, "I'm a good American. I'm a doctor and worked around the clock after the towers fell. I love this country. You must believe me."

"Yeah," a voice mocked from the side. "Well, this country doesn't love you. Killing priests now? We've had enough."

His friends grunted, "Yeah."

Ahmed did not think he could talk his way out of it, but he tried. "I save lives, not take them. I understand your anger, but it's misplaced. I'm a good person with a beautiful family."

"That's all we need," cursed Vinny, "more of you camels humping and breeding over here. Go back to your deserts."

Ahmed's gaze swept over his attackers. He saw it in their eyes—the anger. There was no getting around it. He hoped his prayers were answered.

"Let's get it over with," he heard. Then the blows reigned down.

*****

"Can't you do something?" the man whined from the back seat. "I don't have all day."

"We're stuck, sir." Abdus Ghaffar commented, pointing out the obvious.

"On purpose, I bet," scorned the man. "Probably trying to jack up the meter."

Abdus shook his head. There was no point arguing. As is customary, he asked the guy which route he preferred, the FDR or avenues to get downtown. The man dismissively grunted, "Whatever."

They started down Second Avenue, and he complained about all the traffic lights. Ahmed then turned left and headed for the FDR, which should have been clear at this late hour. As soon as they ascended the ramp, a wall of cars greeted them. Flashing lights reflected off the buildings, guard railings and cars. An obvious police action.

Ahmed had been driving the streets of New York City for nearly seven years. The job may have been monotonous, but it also taught him something. When you are faced with a situation that is beyond your control, don't make matters worse expelling unnecessary energy. No sense getting hot and bothered.

Tonight was different. He was not able to harness that patience. Earlier he'd heard things from a friend that fueled a restless anger. His friend had a source in the highest rankings of the NYPD. He knew the lead detective,

Dominick Presto. Apparently, the episode at St. Patrick's was a Jewish plot. Both the cleric's and the priest's murders had been staged to breed conflict between the two religions. Even though the police knew this, the Jews control everything. There is no way a Jewish mayor would allow that story to get out.

The Imam at his mosque consistently advocated restraint and peace when Muslims were attacked. His friend's feelings, however, were starting to resonate. *For how long must we be stereotyped due to the sins of a few? It was time to be proud of whom we are instead of traveling in small circles, ostracized. Allah is God, and Mohammad is his prophet. We must not let these Jews try and shame us.*

When Abdus saw the man on the street with his arm in the air, he almost passed when he saw the yarmulke on his head. But the night had been slow, and he needed the money. The guy had a nice suit and probably was a wealthy man. Maybe there would be a friendly tip at the end.

Now gridlocked, foot fully suppressing the break, he knew the tip was fictional history.

"Uh hum," the passenger said with sarcastic disdain. "Hey, pal, I appreciate the waterfront scenic route, but I can see it well enough from my high-rise apartment. I need to be there in fifteen minutes. Make it happen," he badgered.

"Looks like an accident ahead," observed Abdus. "I'll try and get off, sir, but as you can see, that's everyone's plan."

"Fifteen minutes," was the man's rebuttal.

Abdus gripped the steering wheel and strained to maintain his composure. He tried to forget he had a passenger and waited to get off the parkway. He was just getting to the exit when the man informed him that fifteen minutes had passed.

"Sorry, sir."

"Yeah. Well, with the meter rising like my temperature, you can forget any tip. If I had known it was going to take this long, I would have chartered a helicopter. It's going to wind up costing about the same anyway," he derided.

Abdus focused on self-control, but the traffic and comments eroded his will. His friend's comments replayed in his mind. *Fuck this rich Jew*, he thought. *Meddling, trying to frame Islam.*

The light ahead turned red, and Abdus slammed on the break. *Whack!* Abdus looked up to the rearview as the man retracted his hand from the plastic partition. His face bulged in fury.

The passenger yelled. "Are you fucking kidding me? You could have made that light," he snapped. "I'm taking your name and number and filing a complaint. You messed with the wrong guy," the passenger warned.

An internal switch fired. Abdus padded his jacket and felt the knife. Too many cabbies had been mugged and killed. They could take his money but not his life. New York would not permit him to carry a gun, and most knives were illegal. So he decided to keep a bag in the car with Tupperware and a butter knife, fork, and spoon. The frequently sharpened steak knife stayed on him, just in case.

With the passenger still fuming, he turned onto York Avenue, but instead of going straight or right to a faster avenue, he turned left towards the FDR, but this street did not access the parkway. It was a desolate dead end.

"Huh," the man gasped. The hostility ebbed by worry.

Abdus hit the breaks and up-shifted to park. He spun out of the car and ripped open the passenger door. The man scrambled back as the assailant dove forward with the knife and plunged it in his stomach. He screamed, but Abdus quickly withdrew the blade and found the throat.

The passenger was silenced.

*****

The phone rang off the modern décor, which partially consisted of sloped plastic chairs centered by a lime green leather couch, a bronze sculpture that looked like two morphing humanoids, and splashy prints found in a trendy Soho gallery. Dressed in costly, brand-new faded and torn blue jeans and a plain black T-shirt, Adam Goldfarb's white tube sock–covered feet froze to the floor. Ready for another glass of cabernet sauvignon, he had uncorked another bottle to stymie the nervous anticipation.

Adam deposited the glass on a hallway credenza and went to the couch where his phone lay. He hoped the news was good. Then he'd skip the wine and instead celebrate with champagne. He had all the good stuff, naturally.

The cause was just. After all, how much could his people take? The Jewish people have endured enough persecution. Enough. It must never happen again.

Rage boiled beneath his small, bookish exterior. His contact was right. Israel was no longer the only front. The war had been escalated to American soil. Although he loved his country, Jews were still a minority. If things turned, it could get ugly. But that was not about to happen.

Reprisal, his contact demanded. Two could play that game. His source reinforced his thinking. If the Muslims wanted to continue the fight here, the Jews had to be ready to fight back. The Christians may turn on them as well. The source claimed there were Christian fundamentalists afoot with a campaign to bring about the rapture. It included cleansing America of those who do not follow the cross. Whatever the challenge, he was ready.

His source appeared credible. He met him on a message board where a bunch of anti-Semites were bashing Israel. This guy posted the strongest responses, both defensively and offensively. They exchanged emails and although he never met the man, he communicated with him more during the past year than his frequently vacationing wife.

When he asked to meet over some coffee, the guy declined, claiming he worked within the government and could not reveal himself. He said he took a risk using the Internet but was confident his system was secure. However, because of his position and access, he was unable to take action, except tell the truth.

Intercepts and informants had reported that an offshore entity received a slew of cash that had been raised for supposedly charitable purposes. Instead, the purpose was to fund terrorist cells with plans to attack Jewish American interests, which included bombing synagogues, as well as targeted killings.

The informant said that they knew the primary moneyman, but for suspicious reasons, the investigation stalled and seized, and was never operable again. He mentioned a detective who knew the truth. His name was Dom Presto. Presto was equally frustrated by his superiors' conspired silence. It was the government's stonewalls that led his source to an alternative strategy. Find someone who had the means and the balls to disrupt the Muslims' sinister scheme.

The bagman in New York was the perfect choice. Professor Abu Jafri had gained considerable notoriety for his message of peace and harmony. The charismatic professor called for a reformation in Islam. He espoused women's rights, democracy, and tolerance. The government even used him to prop up their image. His harsh criticism of radicalized Islam resulted in purported death threats. Undeterred, Jafri continued to preach his liberal theology.

Adam saw him on a circuit of news shows and actually liked the guy. He seemed legit, but it was too good to be true. The image was a front, and a perfect one at that. The source was sure of it. No wonder those death threats were never acted on.

If Jafri died, the money pipeline would be disrupted. It was only a breech, but it would be a strategic blow. Everyone would assume that the fatwa for his death was finally realized, especially if the plan was executed accordingly.

Being a New York City criminal defense attorney had put Goldfarb in touch with some unsavory sorts. The worst of them was a man named Galvin Dent. Although his stated occupation was an elementary school gym teacher, he had the cash to pay Goldfarb's hefty legal rate.

Dent was on trial for the murder of two prominent men who worked the diamond trade. Dent told Goldfarb the truth. It was an assignment. Dent boasted credit for seventeen other murders. He freelanced: organized crime, personal vendettas, spouse removal, and whoever passed his screening test, which started with upfront greenbacks. If the authorities learned of his prior deeds, it was possible he could be the first person to face the death penalty in New York since 1963.

Goldfarb advocated that Dent had acted in self-defense. He was caught leaving the scene, yet the cops found no money or diamonds on him. The unregistered gun was left at the scene, but the prints were wiped. Dent said he had accidentally stepped on one of the victim's feet in a restaurant parking lot. Words were exchanged, and one pulled out a gun. The athletic gym teacher wrestled the gun away and was forced to use it when he saw the other reach for his gun. The other gun was found, and one of the victim's prints was present.

The case went well. The jury took to Mr. Dent. The defense brought legions of character witnesses who attested to Mr. Dent's virtues. The icing on Dent's unjust desserts was a witness who suddenly came forward.

A woman who was in her midfifties and was a bank executive claimed she witnessed the altercation and took off when she saw guns. She said the deceased initiated the altercation. The jury came back in an hour with a not guilty verdict.

In the courtroom, as Dent hugged him, he whispered, "Counselor, if you ever need to dispose of your wife or some ass wipe at your country club, call me. I hope you liked my star witness. Money talks." Then he smiled at the jury and bowed with clasped, appreciative hands.

Goldfarb answered the phone. "Hello?"

"It's me," Dent announced. "It's done. We're even. If you need me again, it'll cost you," he said with a light chuckle.

"Jafri's dead? You're sure?"

"Jafri is my twentieth hit. That's almost as many hits as The Beatles had."

"Probably," said Goldfarb who was now anxious to terminate the call.

"As long as I'm ahead of Michael Jackson," Dent joked.

*****

Ahmad Nasif decided it was time to ratchet things up. He'd come to America to inflict damage upon the infidel whore. Three long years in hell he waited. His cell's supposed mantra was that September 11 should be an Islamic holiday, but the leader of the cell kept planning and preaching. They could not act until orders had come from the head of the cell syndicate.

Nasif had enough. He wanted action. Muslims were being targeted, and still they sat on the sidelines. They had an anonymous contact, an apparent Muslim police officer. The man claimed there was an honest cop named Dom Presto who'd been silenced. Presto claimed there was an alliance between fundamentalist Christians and conservative Jews that orchestrated the recent killings. They wanted a holy war. The enemy was Islam.

Nasif went to his closet with a hammer in his hand. After clearing some hung clothes, he went to the left side. The closet was lined with wood panels, one of which had nails that protruded slightly.

After working the board free, he pulled out a crude vest that was often referred to as a suicide belt. This one was packed with C-4 explosives and steel ball bearings.

A half hour later, Nasif was on the streets dressed in an oversized trench coat that covered the deadly fifteen-pound vest. His destination was the Fifth Avenue Synagogue. This orthodox synagogue was where Goldfarb worshiped. Nasif had no love for Abu Jafri, the man Goldfarb had contracted to kill. He knew Goldfarb was in custody. He saw it on TV, and Goldfarb's attorney used Pretso's name. Nasif knew better. But if Goldfarb was part of the murderous alliance, then others at the synagogue must be also. Plus, they were all Jews anyway.

As he got near, he thought of his brother, killed by an American bomb that supposedly went off-target and struck their home on the outskirts of Baghdad. Then he thought of heaven. He was a martyr.

He was ready to kill. He was ready to die.

Allah Akbar.

*****

Assi Rick followed a trench coat–wearing man approaching the synagogue. His hand went to his mouth, and he softly spoke into it. Years on the Gaza border taught him well. His instincts sabotaged several suicide bombers' attempts to slip into Israel.

Today, and now every day since the recent spike in religious hate crimes, four men rotated as undercover security for the synagogue. Previously there had been two, but with the recent outbreak of hostilities, the synagogue decided on extra staffing.

Rick watched his partner step out from a parked cab. Rick quickened his pace and was now only twenty yards behind the walking man.

The man tried to brush by his partner. Then, suddenly, the man swung an elbow back to the security man's head, and his partner crashed to the sidewalk.

Rick watched the man in the trench coat run straight for the synagogue. He pulled his gun, aimed, and fired. He hit the man, as planned, in the legs, and the man went down screaming.

The suspect cursed in Arabic. Then he stopped, cursed again, and quickly tried to roll closer to the synagogue. His hand went inside his coat.

Rick fired. He had to.

The man's skull ripped open, and he rolled no more.

CHAPTER NINETEEN

"DOMINICK, COME QUICKLY," PRESSED Cleo.

He heard his mother groan. Worried, he launched himself from his desk chair. His feet pounded the wood floors like a pedal thumping a double bass drum. In a huff, he entered her room. In bed, she was propped up on pillows, her expression taut.

Alarmed, he asked, "What's wrong?"

She looked past him. He followed her gaze to the television. A man and a woman were talking. Captioned on the bottom of the screen, in bold, stark letters it read, "RELIGIOUS VIOLENCE."

Dominick wasn't surprised. He expected a backlash. His request to hold a press conference and explain that the same man likely murdered the cleric and priest had been rebuffed by upper channels.

"Your name was just cited by some lawyer. His client was responsible for the murder of that Muslim professor they have on TV all the time."

Now shocked, he questioned, "Jafri?" Incredulous, "Me?"

"Yes," she said softly. "This is not good." Her eyes closed, and her face twitched like she had a toothache.

"Mom," he summoned, "what's not good? What did he say?"

She bit her bottom lip. Pain and resolve. "Dominick, the lawyer said his client is a hero. They're claiming Jafri's fight with the fundamentalists was all show. In reality, he was a mastermind of some terrorist cell. The attorney's client paid a hit man to take Jafri out before he unleashed a fanatical rampage."

"Jafri a terrorist? I don't buy it."

"Funny you should say that," she said uneasily. "They're naming you as the source."

He smacked his forehead in disbelief. "What?" he demanded.

"Yes," she said grimly. "The lawyer said you were prevented from pursuing Jafri for unexplainable reasons."

"No," he said, knowing she was delivering the news verbatim.

"It gets worse," she informed gravely.

"Worse?" Dominick grimaced. How could this be? "Tell me." He leaned back and braced himself against the wall.

Her words came soft and fast in the manner that urgent, but disheartening news is often delivered. "The man asserted you had evidence implicating Jafri but that a high-ranking detective, Frank Danko, blocked you."

"Oh no," Dominick said involuntarily. His head snapped back as if he took a hard jab.

"Uh huh," she nodded in unison. "Apparently, Danko told you it wasn't his fault, but the orders came from high above. The lawyer cited Commissioner Tipton and Mayor Golden and strongly hinted the conspiracy could go deeper."

Reeling from the combo of blows, he knew he'd been cornered. Then he thought he heard a bell chime signifying a reprieve, but it was only his phone.

His mother had not seen the sun in months, and her pigment was pale and without luster. He never recalled such a hollow feeling in the pit of his belly. He left the room and went to the phone as if trudging through a heavy fog.

"Hello," he answered distantly.

"Is this how you pay me back, asshole?" Danko's voice boomed. "After I pitched and went to bat for you?"

"I, uh ..." Presto stammered.

"I can't fucking believe you. Again? You've betrayed me twice. The only reason I'm not on my way over is that there are more important men than me waiting in line to get to you. I'm going to sit back and watch them feast on your fat carcass."

His phone beeped. He looked. "Private," read the screen. All of his associates on the force were unregistered. He ignored the call. He couldn't cut out on Danko.

"Frank, I didn't betray you or anyone." Presto tried to sound convincing but knew his tone was weedy.

"Bull-fucking-shit, you gigantic Judas."

"You have no reason to believe me, but for some reason, someone is screwing me. I believe the truth always eventually reveals itself. I hope so, because I would not and did not say these things. My mother just saw it on TV. She told me."

"Really?" Danko spat sarcastically.

"Frank, why would I do this? I never spoke about Professor Jafri to anyone. We're working on a separate matter, which may now be related, but you cannot find a person on the planet that will testify that I ever even discussed anything about Jafri. This is bullshit, Frank. Think about it. Why would I recklessly ruin my career on the force? Someone wants me off this case."

"Well someone succeeded, Dom," Danko hissed. "I've been honest with you all along. This time, the decision is mine."

"How couldn't you? I understand. But if it takes me until the day I die, I will clear my name with you, Frank."

"That may be so. It doesn't really matter what I think," a less acerbic Danko replied. "It will be your most important case, because if not, your career's likely over. If I may say, it would be a shame—waste of a good detective."

"Thanks, Frank. Do me one favor? Nail the bastard, or bastards, behind the murder of the priest and cleric. This thing's become a full-blown crisis. Save the city, and it's possible you may save me."

"I don't know what to think. I was angry, still am. But ..." he trailed off. "Let me go," he said slowly.

"Okay. Thanks and good luck, Frank."

"Yeah." Click.

Presto looked at his receiver. There was a message, which he retrieved. It was Jack Burton.

"*Holeeey sheeeet*," Burton's charred voice began. "Dom, Dom, Dom, what is going on? Get back to me, buddy. This is NG. Not good. Tipton called. I'm to inform you that you've been suspended. You'll be reviewed in two weeks to determine your fate. There must be some explanation for this. I hope. Oh yeah, the order to keep the cleric's murder quiet came directly from Commissioner Tipton, but my guess is it was really that spineless mayor's decision. Call me immediately."

It was official. The fight was over. TKO.

CHAPTER TWENTY

IN THE DAYS THAT followed, Presto moped around like a dethroned prizefighter. Dispirited, even his mother's sunny disposition did not penetrate the dark gloom. She had Mr. Stagnuts deliver a few comedy movies, but none brought that carefree, booming laughter that she knew so well.

Presto felt helpless. He had no idea how he could clear himself unless he was allowed access to his accusers. Even then, he knew that his reputation was forever tarnished. Not that it was ever sterling to begin with.

Life's normal pleasures were no longer fun. Feeding Aphrodite was a chore. His cherished Trident maple bonsai almost died from lack of watering. In spirit, the tree represented his current state—small, pruned, and neglected.

His meals tasted bland. He thought nerves suppressed the appetite, but his calorie intake was consistent. He just didn't gorge with his usual zest. Food was fun. Now it was a necessity.

Even his books, which provided so much escape through the years, could not puncture the melancholy. The characters seemed as bland as his food within their cardboard settings. Fiction could not change reality.

After feeding his mother, he retired to his office. For once, his mother did not suggest another fun homespun remedy to break his gloom. He loved her for trying. They'd watched movies and sports and ordered the best take out in town, but none of that was going to recapture what he lost—his reputation, his pride, his calling.

Presto believed that each of us is born with gifts. Some of us unwrap them; others never realize their concealed, but inherent potential. It could be athletics, engineering, medicine, law, teaching, politics, mechanics, technology, singing, or any of the other professions in the grand game of life.

It was this belief that nagged at him. He was born to be a detective. He may have hated the politics of being a cop, but he loved the work. Now it had been stolen away. He hated self-pity, but boy was he six feet deep in it. He knew others had it much worse. He had a great place to live, an over abundance of food, and plenty of money. Other than his admitted case of self-indulgence (obesity), he did not suffer any medical ailments. All in all, life was good.

None of this made it any easier, though. He wanted his job back.

At the moment, he sat in his darkened study. The fan whirled softly. A crisp breeze blew over his dormant body. Eyes closed, he dreamed of a different life, outside the big city—upstate, out of state, maybe even Canada. Get away from it all. A change of scenery might be best.

Anonymity.

Then the dream faded like the contents of his fridge. He could never be anonymous. He stuck out like a bloated thumb. He wasn't a farmer or an outdoorsman. He was a New Yorker. He was a detective.

He looked over his library for the hundredth time and then repeated the same ritual on the Internet, aimlessly checking his favorite sites.

He heard the doorbell ring. *Damn*, he thought. *Mom probably has Mr. Stagnuts bringing more movies or pastries.* He heard his mother call out. Like an angry bear prematurely woken from hibernation, he growled and lumbered from his lair.

"I wonder who that is?" his mother called from her room unconvincingly.

"Yeah, I wonder why I look so big in the mirror," he muttered.

He opened the door. "Yeah, come in."

"Surprise!"

Startled, his mouth opened. "What?"

Grinning like two expectant kids on Halloween night, Jack and Abby Burton stood outside his door. The festive difference, from what Presto scented, was they had brought the treats, and it was he who had been tricked.

Abby wore black slacks and a showy floral blouse. Her bronze curls shined. Presto guessed she was at her salon this very afternoon. She looked radiant. Jack Burton was his comfortable, casual self. He had a blue lattice cotton sweater and worn, but unblemished blue jeans that met brown loafers. Even though he looked a bit preppy, he still reeked of masculinity, along with cigar smoke, by his sheer size alone.

Burton gestured to his wife. "Last time we talked, we discussed having you over. Abby, my dear," he said patting his wife slightly on the rear, "had one lucky day at the track. I called to tell you, but you didn't answer."

"Yeah, well. Sorry ..."

"Don't start now, Dom," he said with a smile. "As I was saying, with the unexpected money, we decided to remodel the living and dining rooms. The kids decided to stay with their friends for the night, and Abby cooked for all of us. Too much food and no comfortable place to eat, so we figured we'd stop by knowing how much you appreciate her cooking."

Pretso looked at Abby. "He's lying. My mom put you up to this."

Burton jumped in, his hand up in protest. "Dom, that's terrible."

71

Abby was too honest and sweet to lie, so she said nothing, but her lips tightened. Presto knew better but was thrilled to see his friends, even if this was his mother's doing. "Come in. Come in. Here, Abby, let me take that bag from you."

"Thought you'd never ask, D-e-t-e-c-t-i-v-e Presto," she said with a sarcastic laugh.

Presto led them to the living room and then deposited the bag on the kitchen counter.

"Let me get my mother ready."

He ran to the room and lowered his voice. "I can't believe you."

Defiant, she replied, "I have no idea what you're talking about."

"Yeah you do, but it's okay, Mom. I appreciate what you're doing. Oh, and by the way, I love how you had me find and dress you in that stylish outfit by claiming you wanted to feel normal again. You're hilarious."

"But ..."

"No buts. Let's get your butt in the wheelchair."

He pushed his mother to the living room. Burton handed him a drink at the finish line.

Pretso sniffed the glass. "Smells strong."

"It's Johnny Walker Blue. Good stuff. Eighteen years old, and I just popped her cherry."

"My God, Jack," Abby said, wagging a finger at her husband. She looked at mother and son. "You two don't know. He still acts like an eighteen-year-old."

Cleo watched her son laugh. The best part was that her son probably didn't realize it was his first chuckle in days.

The night was a blast. They ate. They drank. They laughed.

Everyone saw Presto was having a good time, but no one bothered to point it out. In his own nondegrading way, Burton ribbed Presto all night.

Later, they played board games. At three o'clock in the morning, Presto was screaming about bad letters and a rematch after a rare Scrabble thrashing.

The plan worked. She had tricked her detective son.

A mother knows best.

CHAPTER TWENTY-ONE

It was a glorious beginning. Two murders down, one close to fruition. Religious hate crimes were at an all time high. Extremism was on the rise. In order to sell his message, Myth Man needed to expose mankind's collective stupidity. Take them to the peaks and valleys, and a level plane will be found.

The media was in a cooperative frenzy. He didn't have to plan for that; it was a given. From the headlines, editorials, political cartoons, and reader feedback section, the theme was religious tension.

It was almost worth detouring from his plan and sticking with the denominations he'd already provoked. Could he skip the Hindus and move the Jews up to Purim? Perhaps he should have planned better. After consideration, he stuck with his original script. The cops would know soon enough, and maybe he could escalate things yet.

He thought of better things, the best being the fall of Dominick Presto. It took awhile to get rid of his weighty presence, but the end result was well worth the wait in mental calories lost. His contact said the disgraced detective had not contacted an attorney or union official in his defense.

Presto, it's magic. Myth Man made the fat detective disappear.

Confident, Myth Man walked past a washer and dryer and opened a door that led to the garage. He was wearing the homeowner's clothes. This time it was a thick and badly stained flannel shirt, which he did not tuck into denim carpenter pants that looked antiquated enough that the crackpot carpenter Jesus might have worn them. A biker leather jacket finalized the "I'm tough" look.

How did his patsy have so much trouble with the ladies?

He had the perfect wheels, too—a 1977 Chevy van. The interior had a displeasing pungent odor that persisted through two air fresheners. Littered garbage, including soda and beer cans, graced the passenger floor space. The van was in poor shape. A stale coat of paint would have helped immeasurably over the body that was half Bondo. Better that it was not too flashy. Why draw attention? Besides, the most important part was the engine, and the 350 still looked pristine and had plenty of juice.

Inside, he tossed a duffel bag on a passenger seat and started the van.

He hit a remote button, and the garage door opened. After he pulled out, he pressed again, and the door shut. Before entering the street, he rolled the window down. He needed some air. The car smelled like a medley of perspiration, farts, and whatever stale scent the topless girl air fresheners consisted of.

He set out early to avoid typical New York traffic. The destination was a Kali temple in Jamaica, Queens.

Originating around 4000 BC, Hinduism is one of the world's oldest religions, based on oral texts known as Vedas, which are considered the eternal truth. They were only written down when we reached the degeneration age. These and other texts add and reinforce the Vedas of a polytheistic religion that believes a human soul is reborn thousands of times, in many forms, unless one reaches moksha, or a release. Myth Man likened it to the Greek gods. He preferred polytheism to monotheism. At least the bullshit was more fun to swallow.

Today was the holiday Maha Shivaratri. The day honors the time Lord Shiva, one of the three gods who make the Hindu trinity, created and married Parvati. One of their zoomorphic children, known as Ganesh, has an elephant head, because his father did not recognize him and beheaded the boy while he'd been protecting his mother. Shiva replaced it with the first creature he saw, which happened to be an elephant.

Despite his anger for people hooked on religion, Myth Man loved this shit. Better than the doom and gloom of the major monotheists. Kama sutra, baby!

Like most religions, the Hindus had different sects. While homage was typically paid to all the primary gods, some Hindu temples favored certain deities. After a short deliberation, he selected a temple that catered to Kali, a frightening manifestation of the mother goddess.

Kali is depicted with four arms. Two hands are empty, but in her third is a sword while the fourth holds a severed head. Naked except for a skirt of severed arms, Kali has a third eye centered in her forehead, a cobra around her neck, a necklace of skulls, and a long dangling tongue that drips with the blood of her victims. Kali was one of his favorites except, disappointingly, she is a destroyer of evil and creator of life.

A few minutes off the Van Wyck Expressway, and he was in a different world. The predominant West Indian culture was evident with the ethnic restaurants, window fashions, and places of worship. He turned left onto a residential street and slowed as he passed the Kali temple, which was a converted house. Modest.

He parked a few blocks from the temple and killed the engine. He looked around, saw no one, and slipped into the back of the van. He sat on a bench, opened a black bag, and pulled out his makeup kit.

As a child, he learned to hide, not for fun with games like hide-and-go-seek but to escape. His father was a stern, religious man. Discipline and punishment were necessary in molding a child.

As a youth, Myth Man continually wet his bed. His father decided he found the solution to the problem. He made his son urinate in empty apple juice bottles over the course of a few weeks, and then capped and collected the samples. Each morning, he inspected his son's bed.

It happened one early Sunday morning. Myth Man woke and immediately felt dampness and then humiliation. He ran from the bed and grabbed an undershirt and new underwear from his dresser. He tried to dry up the wet bed sheet, but it did not help much. He took off his soggy underpants, slid them under his bed along with the shirt, and put on the new briefs. He grabbed his bedside iced tea and dumped it over the saturation spot.

There were two quick knocks on the door and it opened. His father strode in. "What in God's name is going on?" His father sniffed the bed and then smelled him. "You trying to cover something up, boy?"

"No, I, I spilled my drink."

"Don't lie to me."

"I swear," he pleaded, scared.

His father continued the inspection. When he looked under the bed, Myth Man gulped.

"Uh huh," his father announced, pulling out the wet garments. "I'd make you put them back on, but I got something better." He smacked his son in the back of the head and yanked him from the bedroom to the bathroom. He left the boy and told him to strip.

Inside the shut bathroom, Myth Man heard his father return and leave several times. After several minutes, the door opened. In each hand, he had the urine filled bottles. He dumped them in the tub and then repeated the ritual with the rest of the stock. The frothy pool was a few inches deep. For good measure, his father unzipped, and added some volume and warmth.

"Get in," he ordered.

Naked, he wanted to beg for forgiveness, but he knew he could not overcome his blatant lie. He thought about calling out for his mother, but she was meek and as scared of the man as he was. It was then, as he stood over a tub of urine, that he first entertained the idea of killing another human. Sure, he'd experimented with animals like frogs, birds, and squirrels. Then he was in control, and death was methodically realized. As the aroma of urine invaded his nostrils, he felt something different—a rage.

If he had the power, he would have done his old man right then and there, but instead, one foot went in the tub, then the other.

"Down," his father commanded. "You sleep in it; you bathe in it."

On the toilet seat was a Bible with a bookmark. His father handed it to him. "Read, sinner." He opened the bathroom door and sat on a chair he'd dragged from the kitchen. He whistled, read the paper, and monitored his son for an hour.

Events like that made Myth Man dream of the power of invisibility. But he knew that was impossible. But then another thought occurred to him. He'd seen enough TV, mostly at friend's homes, to grasp the magic of makeup. Age, gender, weight, height, and eye, hair, and skin color could be manipulated. You could even be a creature, like a zombie in those horror movies he enjoyed.

He researched. There were books by professionals in the craft. With his paper route money, he began to purchase items like wigs, beards, mustaches, foundations, powders, and grease paints and began to create his own prosthetic devices.

He stretched and exercised to grow limber and allow body contortion. He learned different styles of walk, especially important when passing as a female with the usual slight hip sway. He purchased audio lessons by a renowned vocal instructor. He practiced and excelled.

When he was thirteen, his father came home unexpectedly and caught him dressed up as a woman. He caught a beating and a lecture on what the Bible said about homosexuals. He swore his father had it wrong and explained his fascination was the art of disguise. His father didn't believe him, and for weeks his father peppered him regarding his interest in women.

His story was a half-truth. There was a sexual side to his attempts to pass as girl. He wanted to visit places restricted to a man like women's bathrooms and locker rooms, especially the one at the town pool. He dreamed of seeing his neighbor, Heather Honeycutt, naked. He was not sure how his father would have taken the truth, so he decided to leave that tidbit out.

Seated in the van, he reached deep into his bag of tricks and memories. This time, he was to play an Englishman who just spent seven years in Calcutta, which literally translates as "Kali's steps."

He used an Indian accent when he called the temple pandit. He said he knew an Englishman who said the he spent years studying with a shaman in Calcutta that dabbled in the occult. He fled India and claimed the goddess Kali now possessed him. Now in New York, he was looking for someone who could release the spirit from him. The Englishman was very wealthy, he explained, and would make a substantial donation. The pandit agreed to meet, alone, at his hour of choosing.

Myth Man strapped on a fake belly that had a spongy realistic give if poked. On his back, he stuck a sword. He pushed his legs through baggy, thick-corded trousers and then pulled on a loose white cotton turtleneck sweater. He wore shoes that were a size and half too big but were stuffed at the heel for comfort and realistic footprints. After each kill, he donated the shoes to the homeless. He was a swell guy.

The wig was full and mostly gray. He applied matching fake eyebrows and then went about aging his face.

The mirror told him when he was finished. He put on an overcoat and grabbed a case holding a loaded syringe. He looked out the back of the one-way mirror and cheerfully stepped out form the van.

The man he was meeting was considered a Sadhu, or holy man, who owned nothing but a water bowl. Talk about having nothing but a pot to piss in. Myth Man smiled. Naturally, the Hindu was willing to take his promised donation of ten thousand dollars. The pandit explained the money would help fund a more glorious temple.

He walked under a canvas-covered arch that led to a red door. As he strode forward, on either side of the walkway stood white marble statues dressed in cloth. The stoned sentries watched the killer walk by.

He reached the door, and the sense of anticipation grew. Stupid Hindus. People are starving, and you don't eat bovines?

Holy cow, here I come.

CHAPTER TWENTY-TWO

KAMAL VALKAR HAD BEEN in America for thirteen years. After today, his long held dream might finally be fulfilled. Most of the Hindu temples were converted from homes, warehouses, and grocery stores. They deserved something better, not for sheer grandeur but to give purpose and unite the local community as well as Hindus across this country. They had a foothold, and this money could provide the traction to run a temple worthy of the deities.

The ascetic pandit had no use for money. He had long distanced himself from material goods, but money was a necessary evil in today's world. The temple needed electricity and blessings of fruits and incense for the gods. The community was generous, and they managed, barely, to get by.

He was dubious when he received the request to help a man possessed with Kali. Even the caller suspected the Englishman, Roger Yardley, was not all there, but he vouched for his character and wealth.

Valkar trusted the deities would reveal the truth. In the meantime, he pushed away thoughts of the Englishman's arrival and performed the morning's aarti. He dipped his hands into a metal aachamanakam cup composed of sacred water from the Ganges, Yamuna, and Kaveri's rivers.

Today was a holiday honoring Lord Shiva, so Valkar began at his station. He sprinkled three spoonfuls of the same water over a large conch shell and then blew it three times. Then he lit an odd number of incense sticks. This time it was nine.

Deep in thought, he rang a bell while he gyrated a small flame in his other hand. The hand circled seven times.

Next came blessings to the gods. He offered praise by bestowing gifts of bananas, strawberries, and flowers.

The pandit went from station to station and honored the temple's gods. He always ended with Kali.

As a boy, he feared that he was cursed. His mother died delivering him to the world. There were also complications. His left foot was noticeably clubbed, and his forehead bulged. Weak and sick all the time, no one thought he would survive.

His father, brother, and sisters looked at him differently, not because he had deformities but because his creation brought their mother's fatality. He was convinced that this life on earth was doomed.

As a boy, he enjoyed going to temple. He prayed his next life would be better than the one he was now living. In the meantime, bad luck stalked him like a starving tiger.

When he was ten, he went fishing with his brother and a friend. He lost his uneven footing and fell into a swirling river. Unable to swim, his brother jumped in, pushed him to shore, but then got swept downstream. His head hit a rock, and by the time they got to him, it was too late. Seeing his older brother and hero's face, eyes rolled open, slack mouth, and lifeless expression brought him to an uncharted depth. Years later, he wondered if they could have saved him if they'd known CPR.

Life at home grew more difficult. With much time alone, he devoted it primarily to prayer and education and was well regarded at both school and temple.

Solidifying his belief that he was cursed were the events surrounding his thirteenth birthday, which also marked the anniversary of his mother's passing.

His father and oldest sister had set out early that morning to the village market. They never made it back.

Their car lost control and rolled down a ravine. It took days before they were found, their bodies over a hundred yards from the wreck. They had survived and tried to crawl back to the road, but his sister perished first, and her father chose to give up.

The death of his parents, brother and sister, as well as his abnormalities pointed him to the field of medicine. He was gifted and quickly earned a reputation in the Indian medical establishment.

While his career flourished, his personal life continued to wither. For the first time, at age twenty-seven, he became close with a woman, a fellow doctor. They dated, became serious, and planned to marry. A week before their wedding, she suffered a brain aneurysm while attending to a patient afflicted with dysentery.

The day of his fiancé's death and hours before Valkar received the devastating news, he saved the life of the son of a man who owned the second largest diamond polishing company in India. The fourteen-year-old was thrown from and then trampled by his polo horse during a heated match. The parents insisted that Valkar treat their son.

Valkar took pleasure in helping others, and the day, he thought, seemed especially gratifying when the surgery was a success, and the boy's condition stabilized. Then he received the news of his fiancé's death.

That night, in a state of despair, he heard an inner voice like a beacon of light fighting through swirling, dark clouds. In the shifting murkiness, a face appeared, one he recognized—Kali.

She spoke: "Kamala, from death comes birth. This is natural. You must accept this. Oh, Kamala. Each life's soul is tested, none more so than yours. There is a reason. It is time to end your endless cycle of soul transmigration and achieve moshka. Your luck is about to change, but that is another test. What do you do when your luck turns for the better? What if you came into a sudden fortune? Do you live in luxury or without? Kamala, you have faced much evil. Now I shall devour it. Oh, Kamala, what will you do?"

Kali can look frightening. Yet, Kamala had never witnessed such beauty. As her face dimmed, scattered, and disappeared, he felt a short remorse. Then hope.

He tried to interpret the message when he was prodded and yelled at. Thinking he was being visited again, he tried to concentrate but then became conscious that it was his sister, and only surviving sibling, that summoned him. She had come to stay with him during his mourning.

"Kamala, wake up. I'm sorry to intrude. A man is here. He says you saved his son's life."

Annoyed that he could not meditate the message, he rose from his bed.

In his living room was a man dressed in a tan suit with a crisp, white button down shirt. He looked about fifty with white at the temples slightly wrinkled skin. His fingers and neck glittered with diamonds, as did his beaming smile.

"Doctor Valkar," he addressed with a light bow. "My name is Atal Bhutu. My wife and I cannot thank you enough. We are in your eternal debt. You were better than the accolades praised upon you."

Kamala blushed. "I always try my very best. Your son is strong and brave. Without his will, my work would not have mattered."

"You are most kind," Bhutu replied. "We're devastated to hear about your loss. My condolences, doctor."

A bolt of grief pained Valkar, but he thanked the gesture.

Bhutu let the moment of silence pass. "We made a significant donation to the hospital but wanted to thank you personally with something as well." He smiled generously.

"You have already thanked me with your kind words. That is all the blessing I could ask for."

"That may be, my good doctor. I have more money than even my biggest rival. When you have more money than the gods, you should reward the good like they do."

"My staff works hard and are less compensated. They deserve your generosity more than I."

"I somewhat agree," Bhutu countered with a smile. "That is why I dispatched my staff to go find them. They will be rewarded as well," he said like a man who was used to doing business. He smiled triumphantly. "But I came here personally. Your staff deserves my thanks but not more than you, doctor. Oh, Kamala," he said raising his voice, "I do not take no for an answer."

It appeared he was stunned speechless, but Valkar had a flashback to his vision. *Oh, Kamala. Your luck is about to change.*

Valkar snapped back to the present and smiled. "I'm not sure what to say. Obviously, I have been through a lot. My mind is out of focus."

"I will fatigue you no more, my good fellow," Bhutu replied warmly. He clapped his hands, and a servant appeared with a black suitcase. He gave it to Bhutu and left. Bhutu then handed it to Valkar. "Once again, my condolences. Thank you for saving my boy." He then reached out, shook Valkar's hand, and left.

Valkar stood there for minutes without moving, when his sister came from behind. "Open it," she advised. "Nobody deserves this more than you."

He opened it like he worked for the bomb squad, carefully and with trepidation. When the lip snapped back, he flinched. Stuffed inside were rupees. It was the most money he'd ever seen. A black velvet box sat atop with a note beneath.

He read the note first: *I know something about polished gems, particularly diamonds, but also people. Everyone we met assured us that you were the very best. Not that many people can be wrong. Now, you saved our son. Inside is something small, but special.*

Valkar opened the lid, which sprung back. Sparkle. Inside was a diamond. The hue was pinkish.

"Oohhh," his sister marveled. "That is a beauty. I bet it's worth more than the money."

She would know, but so did he. As always, he did his homework before buying his fiancé's engagement ring. This was much bigger and far grander.

During the following weeks, he visited a Kali temple several times and spoke with the pandit. He went into trances, meditated, and listened. Then he made a decision

His sister's husband wanted to move to America and open a business. Valkar decided to follow and open a temple. He would dedicate his life to the deities. He gave the diamond to his sister and used the money to buy the house he converted to a temple. He could have purchased something more elaborate, like a large Victorian he'd fancied, but he gave the rest to help his sister and husband prosper in America.

Valkar immediately relinquished all possessions. His only occupation was a temple pandit, which did not earn him a salary. All donations were used to pay the bills and buy the blessings for the deities, and it insufficiently met those needs. His meals were usually gifts from the congregation or visits to his sister's home.

Free from employment, stress, and all the distractions from everyday life, Valkar gave himself wholly to the gods. His life was never better. Well respected in the community, the temple began to draw a large following. People whispered that Valkar was the man to see if you needed a change of fortunes. The sick felt better; the poor found means; the desperate found hope. Valkar was emphatic that he had no power other than to bring them closer to the deities, especially Kali.

As he finished the morning's aarti, he hoped the Englishman was for real. It was time to build something worthy of the gods.

Then he heard a bell ring, signifying his visitor's arrival. He went to the door; his bare feet softly thudded on the industrial carpeting.

Valkar opened the door. There the Englishman stood. His attire was standard semi-casual attire: brown loafers, corded pants, white turtleneck sweater, brown leather gloves, and a gray overcoat. That was normal. His face was something different. Everything was proportioned with no visible defects. Instead, he exhibited signs usually seen from a shaman instilled with Kali's spirit. His eyes were blood red, and his tongue dangled from his mouth.

His tongue retracted, and he spoke. "Kali sent me to you."

The voice did not fit the man. English yes, but it sounded feminine. The man was either insane, an imposter, or for real. Valkar would soon know. "Follow me," he told the portly Englishman. "Oh, and please remove your shoes."

He walked toward Kali's shrine several steps when a sharp pain pierced the back of his neck. Shocked, he crumpled to the floor. From the ground he saw the man walk over him.

Valkar desperately tried to move away and defend himself, but he was unable. His body lay still. Was he frozen in fear? Did he crack his spine when he fell to the ground and suffer paralysis? No. He couldn't even close his eyes. Even paraplegics can do that. This was something different. A dream? He hoped it was, but it felt too real.

His fears were realized. The man laughed insultingly. "Fool," he said, the feminine voice was now very masculine and normal. "One thing you can say about you religious people is you're a gullible lot." He stopped to gesture around. "Look at your gods," he scoffed. "Elephant heads, monkey faces, extra limbs, and other fantastic bullshit. Don't get me wrong; I like your religion better than most, but I still despise you."

Valkar was on his side. He could not see his assailant's face, but he envisioned the glare by the acerbic tone. As he prepared to die, he thought of his vision of Kali. Did he make the right decisions? Could *moshka* be on the horizon? If not, how would his next life be? He hoped it brought him closer to this life's quest. He knew this one was set to expire.

The man reached down and lifted him up fairly easily. He saw the floor as he was carried and then placed in a chair. The visitor held a sword in his hand.

"I wish we had time to chat, but I know it's a holiday. Some asshole will wander in soon enough. My, my, will they get an extra special treat. Today, the gods will get a real blessing."

Mocking, he stopped to laugh. "Yes, a sacrifice to Lord Shiva, with love from Kali. See how considerate I can be? What better honor can you bestow than literally giving yourselves to them? I'll help you do it."

Helpless, Valkar watched the man smile at him. Evil, he was doomed in his next life.

The sword swept through the air, and Valkar's head hung, momentarily, until it fell on the fallen body, where it rolled face down on the carpet.

Myth Man smiled and went about his work.

CHAPTER TWENTY-THREE

Par Malholtra skipped the last few yards to the temple door dressed in her light yellow sari. She rang the bell and waited.

Her friends were still sleeping. She, however, had been awake for hours. Today was Maha Shivaratri. Although the service and celebration was not until the evening, she would spend the whole day at the temple.

At an early age, Par was drawn to religion. While the other neighborhood children played outside, she preferred to spend time at her bedroom shrine. And there was no place she'd rather be than, of course, the Kali temple with the pandit, Kamala Valkar.

She had asked her parents if she could talk to the pandit. She wanted to help. Surely there was something she could do. She knew he recognized her dedication.

Par was thrilled the pandit agreed to her proposal. Today was her first chance to prove he had not erred in entrusting a fourteen-year-old girl.

Par rang the bell again and listened. A muffled chime came from inside. She stepped a comfortable space back and waited, her foot tapping lightly from nervous anticipation.

After a few minutes passed, she rang the bell again and debated the situation. *We spoke yesterday. Was it possible he forgot? Or did he really not want me after all?* She pushed aside her doubts. *The pandit was a good, honest, smart man. He must be still asleep or inconvenienced.*

Again, she hit the bell, this time with less euphoria. After more time passed, she began to worry. Her concern was no longer for herself; she knew he would not do this to her. Instead, her thoughts were for the pandit. He was old; maybe he was sick or had hurt himself.

Par tried the door. It opened. She took a small step inside, held the open door with her left arm, and announced her presence. She listened. Nothing.

Through the dark, she could make out some of the shrines. A light glowed over Lord Vishnu. "Hello?" her voice quivered.

Still holding the door, she found a light switch and turned it on. The first thing she noticed were red stains in the carpeting. She hoped it was the Red Powder of Holi, which was used as a symbol of sacrifice, but she feared otherwise.

Never had she been this scared. She thought about turning back and getting help. But what if she was wrong? *Silly girl*, they'd say. She might even lose the assignment that she so coveted. And what if the pandit injured himself? He might need her aid.

Her head swiveled like a tank turret looking for danger. Then she saw the first sign that something was wrong. Plaster chunks were on the floor near one of the shrines. She drew a breath and quietly walked over.

"Huh?" *Who would do such a thing?*

Someone had removed Ganesh's head, one of her favorite deities. Her right hand rose to her gaping mouth. This was a violent act, not a feat of surgical precision. Frightened, Par stepped to the door but then stopped. Then from memory, she heard a voice. *Be brave*, her supportive father often advised.

Par turned back and continued into the temple. The red stains were more pronounced, and she quietly kneeled and pressed her pointer finger to a stain. It was moist. She looked at her finger—dark red. Then she sniffed her finger and found the scent coppery—blood. She'd bloodied her elbows and knees playing in the streets and habitually picked at her scabs. She recognized the fragrance.

She tried to summon her father's voice again. Now she was scared. Her legs felt wobbly, like she had a blood transfusion that siphoned her platelets and inserted gelatin. When she looked ahead, her underpinnings collapsed, and she fell to the floor. She cried out, not in pain, but in terror.

She tried to doubt what she saw. It was difficult to look again, but she had to. Par pushed herself from the floor and crawled forward, her sari and hands stained with blood. Although strands of her dark hair blurred her vision, she knew she had it right the first time.

Still on her hands and knees, Par rotated away from the scene at Shiva's shrine. She'd found the pandit and Ganesh's missing head, the latter atop the former.

Like a crab scuttling from a predator, Par frantically crawled toward the door. Out of instinct, she gazed at center shrine, the temple's patron deity, Kali. "No," she moaned from the sensory overload. She began to hyperventilate as the tears gushed from her eyes while warm liquid pooled around her crotch.

Par stared again at the replica of Kali. Above Kali's head, in her upper-left hand, was an authentic bloody sword. In the arm below hung the severed head of the pandit.

Par fainted.

Chapter Twenty-Four

"Do you know what a crisis this has become?" Spencer Hoole looked around the yellow and green décor of a meeting room in Gracie's Mansion. The fireplace glowed softly compared to the heat simmering among the gathered.

Hoole's eyes shifted around until they focused on the mayor. "It's starting to affect your numbers. Your approval rate is at an all-time low. Then he faced the couch across the room where Police Commissioner Tipton and Deputy Chief Inspector Danko sat.

Hoole requested a casual Sunday morning get-together to get a handle on things.

The Mayor had tan slacks and a trendy blue button-down that was less crisp than usual. Both cops wore blue jeans, although Danko's were further worn. Tipton had an outdoorsman flannel, while Danko sported his NYPD fleece pullover.

Hoole, who stridently emphasized *casual*, had a charcoal pinstriped suit with a sensible, muted yellow silk tie. All business, Hoole believed clothes psychologically sorted and ranked man. Today, he wanted to dominate and overcome the size advantage he gave to the chiseled Danko.

"I must say, Commissioner Tipton, that your inability to remedy this crisis is a concern for the mayor. Need I remind you all of the ethnic diversities in the city? Hate crimes are at an all-time high, and it could get worse if we don't figure something out. After that buffoon Presto leaked all this conspiracy shit, the public thinks we're hiding something. Had we not advised sacking that crackpot?" Hoole asked rhetorically and did not pause for an answer. "We have the city economy humming, a balanced budget, and low unemployment; everything is simply peachy," he said evenly and paused to give the two officers a hard look. "But, this," Hoole cajoled as he gestured his hands in the air with a wave of futility, "is a public relations disaster."

Tipton went to speak, but Hoole addressed Mayor Golden. "I can only do so much, sir. You're either perceived as being biased by your religion or just the opposite—paralyzed, afraid to take action that may show favoritism. You can't win, sir. Unless these men," Hoole gestured to Tipton and Danko with disdain, "can do their job, you're career, let alone re-election, is in jeopardy."

Mayor Golden nodded in thought. Tipton looked crestfallen. Danko picked at his nails. His hands had to do something rather than yearn for Hoole's neck.

Mayor Golden looked like a cartoon mouse sniffing nervously about with his small head and oversized ears. "It's not my fault," he whined helplessly. Lost was the stern, steady made-for-TV smile.

"Of course it isn't," Hoole consoled. "But," he said deliberately, "my polling shows that they want decisive leadership. Action! In a crisis, the fickle will either blame you or rally behind you. Someone must be accountable."

Hoole stared at the two cops. Tipton offered a stony smile. Agitated, Danko's right fist momentarily flexed. He wanted to speak but thought it was the commissioner's place to respond.

With his eyes still on the two cops, Hoole finished his thoughts. "If you own a ball club and they underperform, the fans get restless. They start pointing fingers. If the failures persist, the fans will turn against the product."

Mayor Golden winced at the word *product*, but his cocky strategist continued.

"The right thing for ownership is to shake things up. Clearing the decks is better than staying the course on a sinking ship," Hoole smugly finished. The only audible sound was short snaps from the burning fire and Danko's knuckles cracking.

Danko looked at Tipton for solidarity, but his visage was distant, almost dismissive. There was no comfort in his gaze.

"Uh huh," Tipton said with his finger in the air like an apprehensive elementary student. "We're doing all we can. Most of these hate crimes have resulted in arrests," he said with meek pride.

"That is true," the mayor said hopefully.

Hoole shook his head. "All true, but unfortunately that's not the point. My poll numbers show a public that is uneasy and wants accountability."

Danko could not stay silent. "Fuck your poll numbers," he seethed. "We're working our butts off. We're ..."

"Frankly, I thought you cared for the mayor," Hoole interrupted. "You see," he taunted haughtily, "I actually do. It also happens to be my job to ensure the mayor keeps his. I don't intend to fail him as, thus far, you have."

Danko was not used to men mocking him. He swallowed his venom and grimaced. He could not, unfortunately, act out his wish of slapping Hoole around. He thought Tipton should step up to the plate, but he remained on deck, not swinging his powerful bat.

Collecting his cool, Danko said, "Let's not make this personal. I do care. You know as much as anyone how much free time I gave to the campaign."

Hoole stayed derisive. "You've been rewarded like any other contributor to the mayor's campaign," he countered. "Don't kid yourself that you've attained your rank purely on merit."

Danko seethed. This was like being continually zapped by a solo mosquito with your hands tied behind your back. It was sure hard not to swat the pest.

Coming to life, Tipton cleared his throat. "We're all here because of the mayor, and we all want to our best. Let's lay our cards on the table and clear the air."

This was not the endorsement Danko had hoped for.

"Indeed," Mayor Golden announced. "Let's do that, but," he said to Hoole, "I think we need to have some press conferences and better explain all we're doing. We have not made the case."

"Huh," sighed a crestfallen Hoole.

"Yes," Mayor Golden asserted. "There are precedents, Spencer. We have a serial killer on the loose. This was his third victim, by no means a record," he scoffed with the confidence that made him NYC's choice. "How long did it take us to finally unearth Saddam Hussein, let alone Bin Laden?"

"True," exhaled a deflating Hoole. "But I'm reporting to you how the public perceives things."

"We agree then, Spencer. We must change the perception. That's your job. And their job," the mayor said with a flick of his hand toward the cops on the couch, "is to catch this beast. You, them, and me; we all must do our jobs better."

"You're the boss," Hoole offered lamely.

"You got that right," commanded Mayor Golden with vigor.

Danko's emotions swung like a soap opera. He could almost embrace the mayor. Hoole, on the other hand, looked like a scorned, jealous lover. Beaten for today but dreaming and scheming about a rematch. Tipton sat there like a useless gift from a foreign dignitary, still and silent.

Mayor Golden suddenly smiled. He recounted the recent hot story where he was photographed with his hand on the naked ass of a guy in leather chaps. He marched in the annual gay parade with a homosexual councilman who had delivered the vote for him. Suddenly a man ahead of him stopped and, according to the mayor, backed up and then bent over as the mayor's striding hand found the prankster's rear. Naturally, it was front-page news and was even used as material in the late night TV monologues.

"Saturday Night Live called and wanted me to do a Heineken skit. You can guess the punch line. With difficulty, I turned them down."

Everyone laughed, even Hoole. As planned, the mayor's tale, and self-deprecating humor changed the atmosphere. The temperature cooled.

"Hey, at least we'll get rid of that fat fuck Presto," croaked Hoole as he tried to joke his way back into the circle.

"My guess is he'll be thrown off the force," weighed in Commissioner Tipton.

"I should hope so," Hoole asserted. "The man is an embarrassment. His actions hurt our approval ratings."

"He certainly did," agreed Tipton.

Hoole looked to Danko. "Frank, I don't mean this in a bad way, but you should have ditched him when previously advised. The guy's trouble."

"Then don't take this the wrong way, Spencer," Danko said coolly. "Everyone knows that Dom and I are hardly pals. The Feds recommended him to the mayor, but I stand by the decision to keep him. Presto's responsible for solving some of the most high-profile cases the city has ever seen. He was right about the use of poison and the source of it, which connected an unresolved case. There were other things too. He deserved the chance."

Danko was not sure if he was defending himself, Presto, or maybe the both of them.

Hoole smiled like a parent reasoning with their child. "That may be so, but with the benefit of hindsight, we can see that, unfortunately, turned out to be a mistake."

"You may be right. We'll see. Even I believe someone is innocent until proven guilty."

"Please?" chided Hoole.

"Come again," an incredulous Commissioner Tipton said.

Danko leaned back, casually. "Like I said, we'll see. He may not be a friend, but I respect the man. He's too smart. This seems too out of character for him. Honestly, I'm dubious."

Sensing a turn in the conversation, Mayor Golden clapped his hands together. "We all know what we must do. Let's do it."

Chapter Twenty-Five

"Inspector Presto, are you ready to begin?" asked Conrad Lyon, who chaired the three-member ruling panel. His nickname was Lion, not just because of the surname but because of his bushy, blonde mane and calm, aged face. He'd growled and clawed his way to where he now sat.

"I am."

The day had finally arrived. Presto no longer viewed the date like a man on death row. His nerves were fine, and he managed to enjoy a hearty breakfast of Belgian waffles topped with vanilla ice cream and sides of home fries and bacon. He wanted closure, one way or another.

Presto saw the nervous glances the three men cast amongst themselves. Jack Burton had already tipped him off that there was talk Presto had something up his sleeve. Word circulated that he'd refused union representation. Some thought it was because he was pigheaded and too cocky to seek counsel, but most of them thought otherwise.

All three members of the panel were uneasy. Presto appeared without any notes or witnesses. There was pressure from above to be hard on Presto, but his reputation and strange, carefree manner were beguiling.

Lyon rubbed his sturdy jaw, stared at Presto, and said, "We understand you waived the right of representation?"

"Yes," Presto replied casually as he sat with his hands folded on his lap.

"You understand the charges, and possible consequences?"

"I do."

Lyon stared deeper as if trying to break Presto's goodwill. His prey smiled back and appeared to be humming a song. He had to admit, the fat chap did not act like a man who carried a burden of guilt. Wary, he was cautious. "Do you have anything to say before we go over the charges?"

"Please," Presto requested politely.

Lyon had figured as much. "Go ahead," he said pleasantly. He was curious if the man had anything.

"Thanks," Presto said. "I want to save you fellows time. How can I refute charges based on statements from attorneys representing individuals who allegedly committed criminal acts? Those men have not stood trial yet, so their story has yet to be examined let alone cross-examined. I don't know these people; everyone knows that. How I'm the source is beyond me. The truth is, of course, I cannot fully defend the charges. Furthermore, I will not bring forth any of the character witnesses that requested permission to speak or offer the letters they sent on my behalf. I see no need rehashing an unblemished career or the accolades and reviews received throughout."

Presto shot a conciliatory grin. He wanted to get it over with. The room had no windows and seemed as stuffy as his suit, which was much tighter than when he'd worn it a year ago. "I serve because I love it. Because I know in my heart that this is a farce, my conscious is clear. To me, there is nothing more that I can say. Render your judgment."

All three men lightened up. That was it? It could not be this easy. Lyon licked his maw. "That's nice, Detective, but we need some answers to make a proper determination. That's due process."

"Fine. I thought we'd avoid the courtship and get right down to fucking me, because we'll all know how preposterous this is." Presto's voice remained lighthearted, not intimidated, but not defiant.

"Yes, Detective. I see you have no faith in the process then?"

"Faith is too strong a word. Hope may be more apropos, like throwing down a few chips at a roulette wheel. You cannot influence the outcome, and the odds are against you."

The three men leaned together and whispered. Lyon looked hungry, ready to strike. His shoulders squared. He gritted is teeth and sniffed. "You're a detective, an accomplished one at that. Then you must have theories to who is behind this," he looked to the air with a sly smile, "character assassination."

Presto knew this was a good question. He did have two theories, and both would lead to trouble, but he answered honestly. "Whoever it is obviously has an agenda to remove me from the case and simultaneously fuel religious tensions." Presto intentionally stopped for the moment.

After it was clear Presto was not offering more, Lyon circled in. "I see. Can you get more specific on who would do such a thing?" His voice was serious in tone but skeptical in delivery.

Presto inhaled deeply. He was done. "Whoever it is, they have inside knowledge on the case I was assisting on." He stopped again.

Lyon's eyebrows rose to elicit Presto further, but they narrowed when he did not. "It would seem to me then, that only a select few people could do such a thing."

"Yes, that would appear to be the case." Pretso said slowly.

"Hmm," Lyon ventured in feigned thought. "Am I taking a leap to surmise that the person or persons you suspect are perhaps the same people that you defamed in the evidence?"

"It's possible, but ..."

Lyon pounced. "The ol' conspiracy theory, eh? You know how this looks, especially since you present no defense?"

"I do," Presto said. "But there is another possibility."

Lyon flinched. Was Presto baiting him? "Go ahead," Lyon commanded.

"There is another person who might want me off the case."

"Who?" Lyon said uneasily.

"The killer."

"The killer?" Lyon said slowly. His grin returned.

Presto wanted to get it over with. Lunch break was not scheduled for another two hours. "Someone tried and succeeded in bringing friction amongst the different religious factions. That was the culprit's agenda, to foster hatred and violence. Why would I do that?"

On the prowl, Lyon huddled with the panelists again before he addressed Presto. "To summarize your defense, either the killer set you up because he feared your investigative prowess, or a fellow officer and/or someone in the government framed you?" Lyon snorted dismissively.

"Something like that," was all Presto came up with.

The panel huddled again. Presto heard the axe sharpening.

Lyon flashed a triumphant smile. He was set to speak, when some commotion was heard outside the door, which suddenly opened. The cop who was stationed outside stepped in. "There's a FBI agent outside. He insists he be admitted."

Before Lyon could respond, a tall figured brushed past the officer. Presto smiled as he watched the surprised looks on everyone's face. Atop the agent's head was an ivory Stetson fedora. An open black cashmere full-length coat revealed a pinstriped three-piece suit. The man had a regal air about him. He was at least six three but not wiry. At fifty, he looked athletic and well fit. His barely lined face was a politician's dream, strong but not stern. Dark round-framed glasses added to his dated, debonair style.

As he approached the front, the man stopped to survey each individual closely. When his eyes found Presto, his face softened. "Dom, good to see you. Steak dinner tonight? It's on me."

"You bet."

Lyon coughed to get attention, but the man ignored it. He winked at Presto. "Let's just say, I don't owe you one any longer."

"Excuse me," Lyon roared. "What is the meaning of this," he said waving his arms. "And who, sir, are you?"

The man kept smiling at Presto. Then, he slowly turned to Lyon. The left side of his face dipped slightly, and he removed his hat revealing a full compliment of graphite hued hair. He looked something like a sturdier Woodrow Wilson.

"Malcolm Bailey, FBI," he said with a clean midwestern accent. "I'm here to save your asses from embarrassment, lawsuits, and, more importantly, from committing a terrible injustice." He removed his jacket and folded it onto an empty chair and then placed his fedora atop.

Lyon shook his head and huddled with his comrades. They were essentially honest people who tried to weed out the unethical. Despite the pressure, they were suspicious that Presto was indeed capable of the charges. They separated, and Lyon nodded. "If you have something to say, tell us."

Bailey looked down at the panel. "I head a division in the FBI that concerns itself with religion, especially extremism. We monitor various groups using different means, one being Internet surveillance. It came to my surprise when Dominick Presto's name appeared."

Bailey stopped speaking and walked over to the panelist's table. He grabbed an empty plastic cup and poured himself some water. He took a gulp. "Thirsty," he said and walked back with the cup and placed it on the table were Presto sat.

"As I was saying, we found this pattern with Dom's name. It was always the same message. They know Dom Presto and therefore the truth." Bailey stopped to chuckle. "Ridiculous," he said and laughed harder. "My guess was, as usual, Dom," he said, and pointed at his friend who tried his best to suppress a smile, "was on to something."

Bailey sniffed the air and cast a sharp look at the panel. They shifted about. They were now in the hot seat. This was becoming more than they'd bargained for.

Bailey shrugged. "So you can imagine that it came as a great surprise when I learned that someone was stupid enough to actually believe that Dom Presto incited hatred and slandered the very department that he's dedicated his life to. Preposterous," scoffed Bailey, who suddenly pulled a black plastic device from his jacket. He stared at it and smiled.

The room was quiet. The panel was confused. Bailey grabbed his jacket and hat and put them on. "Let's go," he said to Presto.

"What?" a shocked Presto, and exasperated Lyon gasped simultaneously.

Bailey looked at Presto. "I'll give you a lift home."

Then he faced Lyon. "He's coming with me."

"Wait just a minute," Lyon sputtered.

"I will not," Bailey spat. "It smells in here, and I do not want it lingering on my clothes. I grew up in Montana, Son. I like clean air. Don't you boys believe in ventilation?"

Lyon tried to maintain his composure as Presto rose to his feet. "Hold on. I need to report this."

"You do that," Bailey barked, "on your own time. My office has already cleared the release."

"How come I was not informed?" Lyon whined.

"Because it was just confirmed two minutes ago." Bailey pulled his gadget from his jacket. "I got the message that my office cleared this with the mayor and police commissioner. Thank God. I couldn't take much more of this dreadful atmosphere."

Bailey and Presto marched to the door, which opened. The officer that was stationed outside stepped in. "I have a call for Mr. Lyon. It's Commissioner Tipton."

"Nothing like perfect timing," mused Malcolm Bailey.

Grateful, Presto grinned at his old acquaintance.

CHAPTER TWENTY-SIX

Frank Danko sat in his office. The door was shut and a Four Seasons Do not Disturb sign hung from the door. At the time, he thought it would be funny. These days he needed it.

He had been reviewing the case again when Commissioner Tipton called. The murder scene was horrific. He pitied the poor girl who discovered the brutal aftermath. Once again, there were clues left behind. A highlighted passage of the Qur'an sat atop a map of Kashmir. Danko researched and found there was a conflict between the Muslims of Pakistan and Hindus of India over Kashmir, the land along their border.

Danko was not sure about the clues. He was being maneuvered into thinking this was the work of a fanatical Muslim, but was he being steered to a designed dead end? The killings were religious in nature, but why?

They had a pattern. Each murder was on a religious holiday. That should be helpful, but as Danko gazed at an interfaith holiday calendar, he realized how many holidays there were. How many religions would this guy target, and would he go after the same group twice? Plus, within each religion there were various sects like Catholic/Protestant Christians, Shiite/Sunni Muslims, and Orthodox/Reform Jews.

This would not be easy, and although the final outcome at Gracie Mansion faired well, there was substantial pressure to find a breakthrough. Now the dynamics changed again.

Tipton recapped what happened at Presto's hearing. He did not sound pleased. Danko smiled. He was still ticked when Hoole ridiculed him for his decision to keep Presto on the case.

When Tipton finished with Presto, he said, "I have more bad news." Tipton explained that Marcus Bailey, the man who cleared Presto, had information on the case. The mayor, embarrassed by the Presto hearing, capitulated and asked the Feds to lead the case. "Two agents will contact you shortly."

Danko cursed. This was his case.

CHAPTER TWENTY-SEVEN

Back at the safe house, Myth Man administered drugs and nutrients to the homeowner. The rage burned on—a fire that found an appetite and now needs fuel to consume. Souls, not that he believed such a thing existed, were the kindling; Myth Man was the torch. Now the Feds aimed to extinguish his incendiary nature.

His source's tidings had taken a turn for the worse. No more than an hour ago, the FBI had cleared Dominick Presto of any misconduct. Worse yet, they knew *he* was behind the Internet messages. His computer connection was secure, that he was sure of, but he was having so much fun stoking the flames that he wanted to continue the combustion. Well, with the exception of that fool, Trumpet of God. The idea of killing that prick never left the back of his mind.

The NYPD was now alerting all the religious heads that a provocateur was inciting this crisis. Myth Man had wondered why he had been unsuccessful in getting the Hindus to lash out at the Muslims. Maybe those cow-loving freaks were a bunch of Gandhi-like pacifists.

Worse yet, the mayor now brought the FBI in on the case, and Presto had been assigned as their liaison. Not good.

One aspect of his new line of work, which he found difficult, was there was no one to discuss his brilliance with. Myth Man imagined a different scenario where he walked into his true residence, and saw his wife:

"Hey, honey. What do you have cooking there?"

"Oh, just some spaghetti with meatballs, just the way you like them."

Taking off his jacket, he places it and his attaché case on a dining room chair. "Gee, honey, sounds splendid."

"How was work today?" she asks.

"Very productive but problematic. See, it started off well. I was able to, literally execute my plan. I cut off this Hindu guy's head. You know me, I'm artistic, and so I hung his head from the hand of this four-armed goddess. Next I cut off this elephant god's head and put that over the severed neck of the dead Hindu. But on second thought, I like monkeys better than elephants, and they have this monkey god. Was I too imprudent in my haste?"

She smiles. "I am so proud of you honey. I know slicing through the cartilage and a tendon of a neck isn't easy, even with a sharp sword, but I do applaud your decision. Maybe it's a girl thing, but I like elephants better. I find their trunks sexy," she purrs in Myth Man's vision.

No wonder so many serial killers are mentally disturbed. Who to converse with? Myth Man had finally moved past chatting with his drugged victim in the safe house. He thought about it, and after reflection, he did not like what he saw. He was not insane, and he would not act like a psychopathic loony. He was successful in business, maintained a marriage, as well as other hobbies and activities, including his most recent gig as Myth Man.

He felt he juggled his roles well. His wife had no idea, of course. She suspected an affair. He didn't do much to alter her suspicions; it was far better than the truth. Plus, he didn't care for the stupid bitch. It had been a long time, if ever, since she'd uttered anything worthwhile.

He always heard that everyone has a gift but was unsure of what his wife's was. She was neither funny nor smart. A horrendous cook—even steaks and microwave popcorn were an adventure. Lazy—their expensive apartment was a constant wreck. Shallow and uncaring—she hated children, animals, and the misfortunate. She lived forever drunk or on a combo of pills her therapist prescribed, usually a cocktail of both. That was just as well; she was good for nothing more than a weekly screw.

Meanwhile, despite the recent spate of unfortunate news, Myth Man had become one of the most famous men in America. Every celebrity has a shelf life. Myth Man intended to keep his newfound fame for as long as possible before he'd fade off in infamy. True, no one knew he was really the killer, but that was fine. Unlike the idiots who left clues sealing their downfall, he had no intention of getting caught.

It was still a few weeks from his next kill, but the adrenalin was there. He viewed his work as sport. He was player and coach. Winning depended on execution, which required planning. Then came the day. This was how it must feel inside the locker room on Super Bowl Sunday—poised for the kill, then the glory.

He finished administering to his victim and housemate. It was a pain in the ass, but the man had to stay alive until his work was finished.

Satisfied, he headed toward the door, which accessed the garage. Unlike his earlier vision, when he returned home to reality, dinner would be spaghetti, no meatballs, and bland, generic sauce from a jar.

CHAPTER TWENTY-EIGHT

Presto opened the menu, made a selection (filet mignon), and shut it in less than ten seconds. It was a steak house, what could be the fuss, even for a man who considered himself a food connoisseur.

Malcolm Bailey insisted that he order the appetizers and selected an aged sirloin for his main course. He gulped his scotch down before the waiter could escape. "Another."

When the waiter departed, the still-suited Bailey updated him. "After seeing your name, I contacted your precinct and was told you were on vacation, but because I was with the FBI, they directed me to your precinct commander."

Presto smiled. "Jack Burton?"

"Yeah, hell of a guy. He loves you."

Presto knew that, but it felt good to hear it. "You know I love the work, but without Jack, I would have packed it in by now."

The waiter returned promptly with Bailey's drink and placed it on the table.

Bailey grimaced after a hearty sip, not from the booze but instead from bitterness over what this man continually endured. "Well, first thing Jack tells me is that you've been suspended. Being away in Washington, I had not heard the news. When he told me why, I laughed hysterically and then explained what we uncovered. Thrilled, Jack connected us to your police commissioner," he said dismissively. "The man is a useless bootlicker. Says he has to talk to the mayor's office? Who runs the police department, the mayor?" Bailey mocked incredulously.

Pesto smiled. He initially met Bailey on his first serial killer case. Throughout the summer, different string members of the New York Philharmonic were being murdered in their own apartments. Sheet music of pieces they performed was left on their dead poisoned bodies. The profilers made their psych analysis. Forensics offered vague clues. Questions were posed. How did the murderer easily access each location without a struggle? Did the victim know the killer? Why the sheet music?

At first, suspicion fell upon the stern, uncompromising, reclusive conductor, although there was no evidence to suggest his complicity. The murders made headlines and embarrassed the city. After the fourth murder, the Feds provided assistance, led by Malcolm Bailey. But within a week, Presto found the killer.

He had tried to get a meeting with the lead detective, and as with Danko later, he was rebuffed. Presto had attended many of the Philharmonic's shows with his mother, who was a fan of live performances. Without anyone else to discuss the case with, he turned to his mother, something he would do throughout his career.

The musicians killed were not the soloists or more highly regarded orchestra performers. The idea that the murderer was a fan had been discussed, but without a lead, the cops were inconclusive in their approach. His mother was convinced that the dead performers had erred in some way, and the sheet work was the insult to injury. That notion also was not entirely new.

With a keen memory, Presto went back to the shows he attended. He recalled several familiar faces, but two stood out. Alone, they did not appear to be enjoying themselves. One had muttered angrily beside him at a urinal, while the other had been irritable on a concession line and hardly clapped at the concert's conclusion.

He took his memory to a sketch artist. Satisfied, he showed the photos to the remaining orchestra members, who did not recognize either man. Then he took the sketches to the people who worked the box office and several of them pointed to one sketch. He was a regular. He'd always paid cash, and the trail went cold.

Presto canvassed all the stores that sold classical sheet music. At one, a helpful girl also remembered the same sketch as the box office staff. The man had paid cash again, and a search of the sales records was fruitless. Presto left thrilled, however.

Presto went to the lead detective, but he was not granted a forum. He was busy. Presto tried to pass the information along. He was told they'd get back to him. After two days, Presto left another message, but again there was no reply.

His mother prepared a meal and a strategy. Presto had a hunch that the killer was a string musician of sorts. She suggested they split up and show the photo to every conceivable outlet for this skill. They divided music schools and stores by geography.

When he entered a specialty store, the store personnel were in the midst of a shift change. The young man at the counter did not recognize the sketch but explained that he had only started a week ago.

The guy called into the back, and few moments later a man emerged through hanging, string beads. Not only did the owner recognize the caricature, he had a name: Dusty Hunholt. He also had a story.

Hunholt was obsessed with classical music, and as a youth was more than proficient on violin. His teachers saw a master in the making. The gift was stolen when a powerful firecracker took the tips off his left finger. He still played, determined he could overcome his injury, but conceded to Owens he had not, and that without an audience, it could only be considered a hobby.

Hunholt owned an exterminator company, which later explained how he got into the victims' homes.

Presto followed the suspect after he left work. As Hunholt passed a hunched woman in a silk scarf, her cane swung out and tripped him. Before the man could rise, Presto fell on him with a gun to his head. Hunholt cooperated with the handcuffs, but that was more to alleviate the feeling of being crushed than the fear of being shot.

Once handcuffed, the woman disappeared. That was the compromise. He didn't want his mother involved at all, but she would not take no for an answer.

The arrest was a coup for the city but not Presto. It was generally perceived as pure luck, right place at the right time. Bailey, who witnessed Presto being dismissed, sought him out.

The two men were stark opposites. Bailey was debonair, outgoing, confident, and statuesque. Presto wasn't. But they enjoyed each other's company. Bailey, who claimed he could sniff bullshit from a mile away, could not detect a trace from the large, shy detective. Bailey sized him up as having low esteem and high intelligence. Life's experiences introduced Bailey to many men who had those traits reversed.

The waiter brought the appetizers: grilled stuffed mushrooms, escargot, and a goat cheese salad. When the waiter left, they divvied up the food, and Bailey finished his story.

"The mayor's office called back. This dipshit named Spencer Fool."

Presto fought from projecting a half-chewed mushroom.

"Once again, I was not sensing the cooperation I expected and desired. I told this Fool character to get the mayor immediately. I didn't care if he was meeting the president or getting wild with his wife or a mistress."

Bailey paused to stab and savor a portobello. "The mayor turns out to be an agreeable guy," he said sincerely. "I summarized the situation and told him my office would courier information that will prove that the charges against Dominick Presto are unfounded. Then, I had him immediately dispatch the police to the Hindu community. He requested the Feds assist on the case. I agreed. I'm sending two agents to work the case."

"What about you?" Presto hoped to have Bailey around.

"I'll check in here and there, but my immediate focus is another matter.

I'll tell you in a minute but first wanted to inform you that you're on the case again. You'll be working with my two agents."

Presto dropped his fork. "What?"

"That's right," Bailey beamed. He knew his friend was set up for a reason. Reinstating him might shake things up.

"The lead agent is a female, and excuse me if it is politically incorrect to say so in today's culture, but she's extremely sexy." He blew on his hand and fanned it. "The male agent is a bit reckless but sharp. I took him under my wing. My only lament is, like you, he doesn't drink much anymore, which in his case is a good thing. Irish lightweight," he said as he downed the last of his scotch.

"Thanks."

"Don't sweat it, big buddy." Bailey eyed Presto. "Get going on that salad. You look like you don't eat enough greens."

"Does pistachio ice cream count?"

They had occupied the table for two hours before they got around to the dessert menu. Bailey hated to be rushed and hadn't seen his friend in a few years. The big tip at the end always made his restaurant visits worthwhile.

"Dom, I almost forgot to tell you what my main assignment is." Bailey propped his elbows on the table and leaned closer. "I'm sure you've seen that story about that archeological find our soldiers made in Iraq."

The waiter had returned. Bailey selected key lime pie and a glass of Graham Port, while the adventurous Presto ventured for something called the chocolate lover's barge.

"I read something about that in the *New York Times* and then never saw much about it again."

Bailey grinned. "There's a reason, but let me give you the background. Irrigation, dams, and canals altered the Euphrates River. Near the Syrian border, there's a section where the river's water level has dramatically receded. The locals noticed a curious mound that now protruded the river. Some U.S. soldiers heard the clamor and went to inspect the find.

"The mound was a series of large stones. A curious and well-fastened wood staff rose from the pile. The soldiers first removed the curious locals and then set about clearing the stones. When they did so, they found the staff wedged in a wood box, similar to a Christmas tree stand. Underneath were long stone slabs."

Bailey paused when the waiter brought their desserts. Presto's square bowl was filled with chocolate ice cream, fudge, small semimelted chocolate wedges topped with chocolate mousse.

Bailey took a small bite and then took a small sip of the port. "Before the soldiers got a chance to inspect the stone slabs further, an archeological team arrived from London. The team took charge and proceeded in a much more methodical manner. As they cleaned the stone, they found engravings. The writing was Hebrew, a form known as Mishnaic, which was supposedly used prior to Biblical Hebrew."

Bailey stopped to get at his dessert. Presto, the eager listener, had almost swabbed the deck on his chocolate barge.

"When they removed the slabs, they found a stone-fortified hole. Inside was a long, rectangular stone chest, with more Mishnaic Hebrew writing. This caused quite a stir."

Done with his dessert, Presto perched forward, fascinated.

"There were all sorts of theories on what was inside, but before it was opened, the Iraqi government seized control. Israel had requested jurisdiction of the find, but the Iraqis refuted the claim. There would be an uproar in the Arab world, they insisted, and they asserted that since it was found within their borders, it was rightfully theirs. They rejected Jewish historical claims, saying that Muhammad insisted that the Jews and Christians were *people of the book*, and all worshipped the same God.

"That's where the story died in the press. The United States quietly maneuvered to broker a deal. All parties wanted the story to simmer down, but there's an agreement in the works. The Iraqis, for a yet undisclosed, but presumed large sum of money from a conglomerate of sorts, are willing to part with the find from the Euphrates River. But there were two other conditions the Iraqi's insisted on," Bailey said, and took the final bite from his pie.

After Bailey wiped his mouth with a white napkin he lifted from his lap, he continued. "From a PR standpoint, they will not release anything to the Israelis. Instead, they will turn it over to the Americans who will quietly turn it over to a Jewish organization here in the United States. But before hand, the Iraqi's are going to, with our assistance, fake the opening of the Euphrates River find and declare the contents as worthless relics. As you can gather, it's a delicate situation."

Presto understood alright. The recent, exploited, religious tension was testament to the unfortunate divisions that existed. "I know all too well," he knowingly added. "What do you suppose is inside the crate?"

Bailey flashed a toothy smile, his dimples cratered. "This is where it gets interesting. A lot of stuff is being bandied about," he said and twirled his index finger in the air. His left eyebrow rose. "The Ark of the Covenant has been perhaps the most spectacular of suggestions."

"Wow," Presto said. His wide, fleshy face was in awe.

"Yeah, but the prevailing opinion from the scholars who know this stuff is no less spectacular. You've heard of the Dead Sea Scrolls, right?"

"Uh huh."

"Well, the Mishnaic Hebrew that was used on the Euphrates River discovery was also found on one of the scrolls in the caves of Judea. That scroll," he said dramatized slowly, "is known as the Copper Scroll." Bailey stopped and motioned for the waiter. "Hold on a second," he said.

When the waiter arrived, it was not with the same smile he had initially greeted them with a few hours earlier. Bailey asked for one final round, a Jameson and a root beer, both on the rocks.

Bailey looked back at Presto. His eyes no longer sparkled, but instead receded to a watery depth in his sockets as the booze finally took control.

The waiter returned. Along with the drinks, he left the bill.

Bailey seized his drink, stared into the contents, smiled, and sipped. His eyes closed for a few seconds, while the satisfied grin returned. "This Copper Scroll has some lore to it. The scroll is more than two thousand years old and tells of hidden locations where gold, silver, gems, manuscripts, and other desired items were squirreled away. There were sixty-four locations where stuff was dispersed, including some items, apparently, from King Herod's Temple. Attempts have been made to find these locations without much success. The stone crate has fueled much speculation, because of the difficulty it took to transport and hide it within the river. It was hidden for a reason. If it were not for humans messing with that river, this thing would never have been found." Out of breath, Bailey remedied the respite with a slug from his glass.

Presto filled the void. "Wow."

"Amazing, huh?" Bailey slurred. "If all goes well, this thing should arrive in the city in the next several months."

CHAPTER TWENTY-NINE

DETECTIVE DANKO SAT IN his office and waited. He tried forming facial impressions—happy, accommodating, helpful, indifferent, but each attempt withered back to the grim expression he'd carried the past few days.

Danko got up at four o'clock and set out for his morning jog. Some people needed music to motivate their fitness but not him. He found peace through exertion, and with each galloping step and breath, his mind and body felt uncluttered and free. This morning it felt like a chore. Sluggish, he pushed himself thinking he'd find his mind and body's rhythm, but his crescendo never created that harmony.

The shower had not refreshed, and his egg whites and protein shake did not fill. Despite the rejection of his wife's affections at bedtime, she was up to hand him his uniform, fully pressed. His wife had covered for his lethargic scowls, telling the children that Daddy was sick. He loved her for trying and told her so as he left their apartment. Sore, his wounded pride needed time to heal.

Every time there'd been a big case, someone else was there to steal the glory. He knew the stigma, although he never actually heard anyone voice it until Spencer Hoole brazenly attributed his ascent strictly as political patronage. The words had stung, but he knew the best revenge was success, and now that option was all but likely muted as the blue shaded tie he now wore.

This case could have made him. This was big. Now the chance for glory was gone to the greedy hands of the FBI, assisted by Dominick Presto, no less.

What irked him was that he had no doubt the killer would soon be caught. They had a general sense of his pattern, locations, and dates. There were the clues he intentionally left and others he had not, such as carpet threads, hair samples, and other goodies forensics had found consistently through three crime scenes.

A knock from the door froze his face in midmetamorphosis. His cocoon cracked, and instead of something beautiful, his visage gave birth to something bitter.

A large shadow was visible through the frosted glass that outlined his door. Presto, no doubt. "Come in," Danko grunted.

The door opened, and Dominick Presto sidestepped in, shutting the door behind him. Danko watched Presto put his hands in his baggy tan trousers and then look at him, eyes kind and warm.

"Frank," Presto said demurely, "may I?" he said motioning to an empty chair.

Danko obliged with a nod of his head, and Presto slowly guided his rear downward. He adjusted his aged sport jacket, ran his hands across his white button-down shirt, and noted a yellow stain. He liked his eggs with a runny yolk.

Both men looked at each other for several seconds. Danko blinked. "Welcome back, Detective."

Presto noted Danko's frayed look. "Thanks, Frank …"

"I want to apologize for initially presuming your guilt. If it means anything, after reflection, I didn't believe the charges."

Presto waved his beefy hand through the air. "There's no need."

Danko shrugged. "I'm happy your back, just not with the extra luggage. We don't need the FBI, Dom."

"That may be," Presto said agreeably.

"Yeah," Danko huffed.

From outside they heard voices. A series of rhythmic knocks came from the door sounding like a snare drum. Presto glanced at Danko, who gritted his teeth.

"Enter," Danko called out.

A female entered. *This was not just any woman,* both Danko and Presto thought. She was stunning. Brown, lightly curled hair fell above her shoulders and obscured most of her forehead. Her skin was like skim milk, pale and unblemished. Her face featured dimples, high cheekbones, purposeful lips, and eyes that seemed excessively large with her slender features. Her dark conservative suit did little to hide her sensuality. This was someone who spent time at a gym, Danko knew. She stood at five six. Presto guessed she weighed no more than one hundred and ten pounds and was no older than thirty.

Coming behind her, like a quarterback following the cheerleader, was a strapping guy in suspenders. His white shirt clung to his buff physique, which impressed Danko. His face had a tough and beguiling edge that made him alluring to women who liked their men a little dangerous. His hair was dark and a little longer than the standard FBI cut.

Presto thought they were going to introduce themselves as Ken and Barbie, but instead the woman introduced them as, "Agent Carter Donavan," she said as she gestured toward her partner. "I'm Special Agent Lorraine Ridgewood," she added and snapped a business card on Danko's desk.

Danko feigned a welcome smile. "Frank Danko," he said and offered a hand. When Agent Ridgewood took it, he added, "We're happy for your assistance."

Agent Donavan snorted. "You sound thrilled," he said in a strong, sarcastic Boston accent. "Surprised you didn't have a red carpet rolled out to lead us to your office."

Danko's cheek bulged. "You must excuse me. I caught a tough cold from my kids and took some stuff that has me wiped out," Danko lied and hated it.

"Really," Donavan scoffed. "Sorry, when I was at the mayor's office, I got a strong impression from this chap Spencer Hoole that you lobbied to keep us off *your* case. He caged it well. I think one of the telling quotes he attributed to you was, 'I don't want those assholes fucking with my case.'"

Under his breath, Danko cursed Hoole. His face, again, revealed his thoughts. He muttered something and then found his voice. "No good law enforcement official thinks he needs help. I thought we were making sufficient progress."

Agent Ridgewood went to speak, but her partner drowned her out. "Maybe your superiors don't see you as such a *good law enforcement official.*"

"That's enough," snapped agent Ridgewood. She shot her partner a look of disapproval. "It's these interagency squabbles that are partially responsible for not preventing the tragedy on September 11. Like it or not, we're all on the same team. We have a job to do, and we're not going to fail. Let's get down to business." She flashed an apologetic smile for Danko's benefit.

For some reason Agent Ridgewood reminded Presto of a ruby-throated hummingbird he saw as a child. Majestic and small, the bird looked strong and fierce, in control of its airspace.

"Thank you,' Danko replied earnestly. "I'm here to cooperate."

"Super," Agent Donavan saluted. "Where are the donuts and coffee?" He looked from Danko to Presto. "He looks like he could use a donut," he said, and gestured to Presto. "Hey, Danko, before you bring us up to speed, how about rustling up some cop cuisine?"

CHAPTER THIRTY

"**Y**OU LIKE HER," CLEO Presto probed as she prepared the dining room table.

Presto growled, not from the mélange of ziti and garlic bread that wafted from the kitchen but because of her over inquisitive nature. Now that she was back on her feet, there was no escaping his mother's inquiries.

"A mother knows these things." She looked into his eyes but gleaned little. He didn't twitch. He was better at this game than the shaken Danko.

His mother never nitpicked his lack of personal life. Now she was digging with a pickaxe. The last time she asked him about a girl was before his high school junior prom. When he failed to find a date for the senior prom or twenty plus years later, she never broached the subject again.

He decided denial was not the best way to play this. "You're too clever, Miss Love Detective," he said earnestly. "All I said, when asked by you, was that she was the lead agent and composed herself well, especially in light of her partner's obnoxious behavior. Then you asked what she looked like."

Her index finger found him. "It was the way you said it."

Presto spread his hands in submission. "I remarked that she was attractive, in a classy way."

"And you said *she was nice.*"

Presto slapped his right hand to his forehead in mock surprise. "Ah, yes," he exclaimed. "How could I have been so blatant with my secret desires? Like a code-breaker, you found the hidden message within my cloaked assessment."

She wagged her finger again. "Don't mess with a woman that's preparing your food. You're playing with me, right?"

"Mom, of course I'm playing," he said with a dash of smarmy jest. He hoped to end her sudden interest in finding him a mate. "Just for the record, I have a keen eye, especially for the opposite sex. But let's face it,' he said earnestly, "I'm not that sexy." For fun, he pouted his lips.

His mother opened her mouth and waved her arms in protest, but he cut her off. "Mom, it's fine. I'm cool with it but also a realist. Women of her caliber date *GQ* men. Looks do matter; we both know that."

She stifled a small sob. Her head dipped.

"Mom," he beckoned.

She looked back to him.

"You have to stop whatever you're up to. I'm happy with my life. I'm used to it, and always have enough on my plate, excuse the pun," he said and slapped his gut with a laugh, "to nourish and satisfy me."

She returned a soft smile of her own. He could tell she was disappointed, but there was too much spark and illumination to ever dim her for long. "Speaking of food on your plate, here you go, Buster."

Placed on the table were a bowl of roasted potatoes, a plate of ziti, and a foot of toasted garlic bread on a wood cutting board. He dropped the napkin on his lap and salivated.

Cleo banged the floor three times with her cane.

That had been her signal to summon Mr. Stagnuts when she was bedridden. "If you ever need something while your son's disposed, *knock three times on my ceiling if you want me*," Mr. Stagnuts had sung to her. Today they were playing cards, and he told her to use the old signal when she was ready. Ms. Stagnuts had insisted the signal never be performed in the living room. Her eyes notoriously watched every vibration of her prized chandelier.

Presto picked up his fork and began to eat as his mother wrapped up the leftovers. "Feels good to feel useful again," she remarked wistfully. "All these years I took care of you," she said nostalgically. "I was not used to the role reversal."

Presto gorged a large pile of ziti, swallowed, and replied, "Neither was I. Sorry, but I hated doing that needle thing."

"Me too," she agreed unequivocally. "You're squeamish, Son."

"I wasn't that bad," he said defensively.

She grinned back. "You did fine." Her eyes twinkled. "Oh, by the way. The Stagnuts have a niece that will be staying with them for a couple of weeks. She grew up in New Jersey but moved to California about twenty years ago. She's wants to move back here," she said with a gleam. "Arthur and Gina say she's single and a real nice gal."

"Mom," he groaned. "Enough."

Persistent, she continued, "The Stagnuts are old. They don't have the energy to entertain her and specifically asked me if you could spend some time with her."

This was his mother's doing, no doubt. Why was everyone trying to set him up? The killer willed to frame him, and now his mother was trying to canvas and paint him a virtual relationship. Every action had a reason and motive. He wanted to press her when the buzzer rang from the front door.

"Oh, that must be them," his mother exclaimed. She dried her hands and went to the door. "Arthur, Gina. Oh, do come in." she welcomed. "I can use a hand. I baked a crumb apple pie and have vanilla ice cream for a topping," she said and escorted the couple inside.

Based purely on appearance, some couples are perfectly suited for each other. The Stagnuts rolled in like male and female versions of the same DNA samples. The two of them always reminded Presto of a toy he'd received as a child. There was a plastic floatable boat, but the occupants were a family of egg-shaped figurines, known as Weebles. The jingle was, "Weebles wobble, but they don't fall down." Built like barrels, The Stagnuts were the human equivalents of the Weebles.

They were both short and oval, like an inverted body builder. It appeared as if they were both jointless. Neither required a scarf, as their heads morphed into their bodies. Like they were svelte gym rats, they wore tight, eye-popping outfits. Gina was dressed in a hot pink, velour pantsuit, which accented her pearlike physique. Atop her head was a sun hat with a pink bow above the brim.

Arthur waddled in with blue and white striped linen pants that were so loose it was hard to discern he was bipedal. His shirt was silk but a louder shade of blue than his pants. An unlit pipe hung from his lips. Perched on his pudgy nose were thick black-framed glasses with lenses that looked thick enough to have been made from hockey Plexiglas. He also had a black top hat that, along with the dangling pipe, made Arthur Stagnuts look like a pimp snowman. Then Presto looked at Gina in her tight pink velour getup and thought she could have been Arthur's ... *Never mind*.

Gina looked to Presto. "Did your mother tell you that our niece Camille is visiting?" Her voice sounded like a cat in heat, shrill and desperate.

A few choice answers flashed through his head, but Presto instead said, "As a matter of fact, she did. I'd be delighted to spend time with her." He smiled broadly and turned to ensure his mother noticed. She appeared surprised. *Good*. If you can't beat them, then join them ... at least for the moment.

Arthur, also a connoisseur of food, looked at Presto's depleted plate. "Smells good in *here*," he said with a wink.

Arthur was infamous for the clandestine tactics used to dispose of his wife's meals. He used their complicit, and accommodating, dog Skippy on the passable meals. On those not fit for a dog, he used napkins to conceal a large portion and either stuffed it down the garbage pail or flushed it in the toilet. Sometimes those methods were not possible. His wife constantly picked on his clumsiness, not knowing that most of his accidents were staged and usually involved the loss of a home-cooked meal.

Arthur turned toward Cleo. "You told him about Camille's ... ways," he said awkwardly.

Presto eyes widened as he watched his mom, who suddenly looked guilty.

"I did not get the chance. I just mentioned her and then you arrived," she said.

"Conveniently after she gave her three-knock signal," Presto noted.

"Oh, it's nothing," Gina chimed off key. "She's sweet."

Her husband snorted. "Honey, I would hardly classify her as your regular girl."

Gina's right hand went to what would be her hip, and her side jutted out. "Arthur, you stodgy old troll," she said sternly, which elicited a wince from her husband. "She's a free thinker, just a little antiestablishment."

"It's one thing to boycott some company because they're ...," thinking, Arthur waved his hands around trying to conjure his thought, "chopping down eucalyptuses trees for cough drops and thus jeopardizing the existence of our cute friend the koala bear. But," he asserted, "it is quite another to cheer whoever is responsible for these brutal religious slayings."

Gina snorted. "I could smack you. That is not what she said."

Arthur smacked his hands together. "I think that's enough for now, honey. Let's get going." He picked up the food Cleo Presto left on the table and went for the door."

"Just one minute," his wife squealed. "You're not getting the last word," she challenged with an icy stare. Then she looked to Presto. "Don't listen to him. Camille knows this killer is a beast but has no love for organized religion, being a self-proclaimed atheist."

In the background, Presto watched Arthur shake his head. Presto stuck with the script. "I look forward to meeting her, Mrs. Stagnuts. She sounds lovely," he said as sincerely as possible.

CHAPTER THIRTY-ONE

Two cars stopped and double-parked in front of the Kali temple. One sedan was white and blue with roof lights and large letters that said "POLICE" but was often mistranslated as Five-O, pigs, heat, or other popularized slang. The other car was a black Crown Victoria. Although unmarked, the vehicle might as well have had large letters that screamed "UNDERCOVER."

Detectives Danko and Presto stepped out from the police car, while Agents Ridgewood and Donavan vacated the Crown Victoria.

It had been a long day. The two agents insisted they visit each crime scene. They started at the mosque. Danko's previous visit had not gone smoothly, and today's reception had been frosty. Agent Donavan with insults and threats tossed gasoline on that chill and created a firestorm. Within twenty minutes, a small army of Muslim males arrived. They stood silently, shoulder to shoulder. Presto got the message. Donavan did not.

Presto had never witnessed a more horrific interrogation. Donavan did not listen to his partner, even after she reprimanded him for calling the assembled crowd terrorist towel-heads. Three attorneys representing the mosque arrived next, and that ended the first stop on the tour.

On the ride to St. Patrick's, Presto noted that Danko looked amused, but he withheld comment.

Inside the cathedral, it was obvious the two FBI agents had not ridden in tranquil silence. Agent Ridgewood delicately handled all the questioning, while Agent Donavan followed like a sullen, muzzled mastiff.

Although Ridgewood had not uncovered anything new, Presto was impressed by her professionalism, especially following the mishap at the mosque. When they left St. Patrick's, it was readily apparent that Donavan was somewhat less impressed with his partner's work.

"You threw those guys softballs."

Ridgewood stopped. "Excuse me?" She looked equally angry, annoyed, and embarrassed all at the same time.

"You heard me, Ridgewood," he said tersely.

Ridgewood held her ground. Firmly, "Donavan, we'll talk in the car."

Presto thought, as far as partners go, Danko and he were bosom buddies in comparison.

As Ridgewood began to walk to the cars, Donavan said, "You went over old ground. What was the point?" he added dismissively.

"You might not know," she responded derisively, "but covering old ground can reveal inconsistencies, memory recall, and …"

"Nothing at all," he finished abruptly.

"These people are not suspects, and neither were the people at the mosque" she fired back.

Danko and Presto watched the spectacle. Danko's sly grin had increased.

The mellow mastiff transformed back to a rapid Rottweiler. "You don't know that. Those guards, at minimum, were incompetent."

"Newsflash, Donavan, those guards did not also work at the mosque and Hindu temple. And how did you want me to handle the priests? Attack them too?"

"This killer could have accomplices by means of money or complicit persuasions," he countered. "And," he emphasized strongly, "why should a priest be treated differently?"

"Let's go, Donavan," she said firmly.

He would not let go. "Priests have told lies before, Ridgewood," he said sardonically. "You might not have heard, but the church had a little scandal because they covered up for pedophile priests."

"That's enough," she said authoritatively. "Let's go. Now!" She stormed off to their sedan.

Now outside the Kali Temple, Presto watched the two agents approach. While the two did not appear chummy, they both walked over smiling, like the day had gone smoothly.

Donavan's smile became a smirk. "Hey, Frank. You bring any donuts? I'm getting hungry." He licked his lips, clicked his tongue, and let out a laugh. "Just playing. Thought a little humor could brighten the mood."

Ridgewood looked to her partner. "Donavan, if you have a good joke, fine; tell it. But let's try not to rib one another."

"Okay," he said. "I thought of a Hindu joke." He stopped for an awe shucks shrug. "They just come to me," he boasted and tapped his index finger to his temple. "What are Hindus' favorite candies?" Pleased, he smiled broadly.

No one pondered, thus no one answered.

"I stumped you, huh? I'm good."

Ridgewood turned to the cops. "Ready to go in?"

They both nodded.

"Wait," Donavan cried. "Don't you want to hear the punch line?"

Without rancor, she replied. "I could live without it, but I'm sure you'll tell us regardless."

Despite Ridgewood's even tone, Donavan looked miffed. With less enthusiasm, he offered this wisdom, "Dots."

He laughed. His response was three blank looks.

"Dots. You know, the candy?"

"Got you," Ridgewood replied coolly.

Donavan appeared disappointed. "Dots, like dot-heads? You don't find that funny?"

"No," Ridgewood assured. "I don't. We have a girl waiting for us. Let's do our job." She started to walk again.

"Is she hot?" asked Donavan. "I dig the ethnic thing."

Ridgewood rolled her eyes.

"She's fourteen," informed Danko, who held his face in check better than the prior day.

"So," he said incredulously. "Most of them fuck at fourteen. Is she sexy or what?"

Ridgewood was prepared to reply, but Danko said first, "I might remind you, Agent Donavan, that we have a statutory rape law."

"Hey, it's not illegal to think. Shit, if I ever acted out all my fantasies I'd have one hell of a family and a headache."

"That's great to know, Donavan," Ridgewood opined and briskly set forth to the temple door.

CHAPTER THIRTY-TWO

"You cheated," Presto announced. "It's too impossible that those were your opening two words."

Cleo gave a conspiratorial laugh. "When you went to the bathroom, I changed my letters."

"You're too much," he said with a grin.

"I know," she readily agreed.

They sat at the kitchen table with a Scrabble board between them. There were only three words on the table. She opened with *GIRL*. He added R-U-N-T to the *G* for a low-scoring *GRUNT*. With a sly grin, she added the word *FRIEND* to *GIRL*, forming *GIRLFRIEND*.

The Stagnuts had planned to join them for a Saturday night of board games with the Parker Brothers, but Gina developed a headache that required her husband's monitoring. Mother and son decided to play on. After their appointment with the Parker boys, they had plans to visit Mr. Milton Bradley aboard his Battleship.

"Let's start over," she said and began to dump the squared wood letters back in the gray bag.

Presto decided he wanted answers. He was not going to put it off any longer. "Mom," he said. "I want the truth. Why are you fixated on finding me a woman?" She looked away, but he persisted. "There's something you're not telling me."

Her lip quivered. Pained, she closed her eyes. "A mother does not want to see her son alone."

He did not respond. Her answer was why he had not previously pressed the issue. He feared where he had decided to tread.

A tear fell down her right eye and welled by her nostril. "You need to focus on this case."

"Mom," Presto pleaded and grabbed her thin hand. "Fuck the case. I'm talking about you."

She gritted her teeth. "There's nothing to know. I am getting old, Son. Everyone needs someone and so will you ... someday."

His eyebrows rose. "There's nothing to know?" asked a suspicious but hopeful Presto.

She hesitated before answering. Her eyes looked past him. "Not now."

Presto swallowed. "Mom, I love you." He gently stroked the top of her hand with his large thumb. "Please. Talk to me."

Cleo gave a conciliatory grin like the kind politicians use in their concession speeches after a campaign loss. "Promise me that after I tell you, we continue our lives as we always have with laughs and love."

Presto gulped but kept his face even. "Naturally."

"You better," she said with a thin grin, "or I'll never cook for you again."

He cocked his finger. "Don't threaten me, Honey," he said with an Elvis Presley accent.

A more genuine smile split her face. "There's my boy." Her hand squeezed his back. Although her eyes were wet, she looked resolute. "The doctor's found something," she began.

A wave of emotions crashed and flooded the detective's senses. He swallowed again. This time a bile taste left him gutted and hollow.

"It's okay, Son," she said with surprising vigor. "Please, for my sake, don't take the news worse than I did."

Although the revelation had unearthed his deepest realized fears, he was still shocked. Apprehensive of the answer, he asked, "What did they find?"

"Cancer," she replied like he asked for her astrological persuasion. "They found tumors in my lungs."

The dike holding his feelings at bay cracked, and now several tears rolled down his round cheeks.

"Dominick, please don't do this. Now that I told you, I need you to be a pillar of Pyrex, not putty."

He rubbed his sleeve across his eyes and sniffled. "I know. I'm sorry," he replied nasally. "It's just that I love you."

"And I love you," she said now placing her hand on his. "I'm sorry for acting silly trying to find you a woman. It's just my motherly instinct taking over."

*****

Presto lifted his head from the pillow and looked at the digital alarm clock for the umpteenth time since he tried to retire for the evening. 5:00 am. He had not slept well. Each time he dozed off, he woke with a hopeful feeling that it had all been a dream his mother had conjured to fulfill her matchmaking aims. But as the cobwebs cleared, sticky filaments respun his fabrications to threads of reality. Cancer the crab was eating at his mother's life.

He promised to be as brave as she was, but she was always the stronger of the two. Despite his words, the despair made sleep impossible.

This was a killer he could not catch. Perhaps the biggest serial killer in history, Cancer was described in an ancient Egyptian papyri dating back to 3000–1500 BC. Hippocrates, who's anointed as the Father of Medicine, first differentiated tumors as either benign or malignant around 400 BC.

Although the killer was identified, cancer continued to prey. Unlike other predators, cancer was an equal opportunity killer, attacking almost anything in the body, including lungs, brain, skin, breasts, and prostrate. Sure, some of its victims survived, but cancer was still on the loose.

Presto brushed his unkempt mop from his eyes but not the haunting vision from his mind's eye. Death. His legs wobbled as he rose and headed to the bathroom.

In the shower, he leaned against the white tiled wall and willed the water to wash the misery down the drain. Ten minutes later he reached for a giant tropical beach towel, which was just large enough to tie around him.

After he groomed (ran a brush twice through his hair and brushed his teeth) and dressed, he went down the hallway to the living room. He smelled food and heard his mother bustle about in the kitchen. He sat at the dining room table.

Conscious of his promise to his mother, he greeted her heartily. "Morning, Mama."

She came out of the kitchen with a plate of blueberry pancakes and placed them beside a glass of orange juice. "I know you had an early day. Wanted to make sure it started right."

"That's awfully sweet of you, Ma." Like a heavier Ralph Kramden, he bellowed, "Baby, you're the greatest." Presto took a seat at the kitchen table.

She filled a mug of coffee for herself and sat down. "You have to be alert. The killer could strike today."

With the first bite in his mouth, Presto nodded in agreement. Today was Palm Sunday, the next significant religious holiday that followed Maha Shivaratri. Until they developed a solid lead, they planned vigilant surveillance. Police officers had been stationed at every city church, from grand cathedrals to the tiniest of tabernacles. Spencer Hoole had checked in. He said the mayor did not want to hear charges of favoritism if the killer struck in a more obscure location.

Cleo said, "Although you're working Sunday, at least you'll be at church," she said with a wry smile.

After the loss of her husband, Cleo Presto initially found support and compassion from their church. For that, she was grateful. Still, the loss left her bitter. She listened to wisdoms like "God moves in mysterious ways" and "he's off to a better place," but the words sounded like hollow clichés. Bereft of answers, she lost some of her faith.

CHAPTER THIRTY-THREE

MYTH MAN WATCHED THE television with great interest. The FBI had flubbed again, and they were getting grilled before a Congressional oversight committee. This was great theater. Their misdeeds gave him encouragement and a crazy idea.

Thank no god for C-SPAN.

Myth Man enjoyed seeing the FBI director himself squirm in his seat as he tried to explain how FBI agents mistook a toga party in the woods as a white supremacist gathering, a gothic girl in chains as a prisoner for sacrifice, and firecrackers as incoming fire. The result was twelve dead college students.

Next up was some schlep named Agent Hawkins. The guy with the neatly trimmed beard and Brooks Brothers suit looked more like an accountant that miscalculated a tax return than the guy who was in charge of the unit responsible for the massacre.

Maybe the suit was flame-retardant, as Agent Hawkins appeared almost bored as the senators firebombed him with heated rhetoric. The man was unflappable. Myth Man was impressed.

He watched the blowhards go on for hours, and when it was over, he used a TiVo to watch it again and burned it on a DVD. It was more than entertainment. It was educational.

Myth Man peeled himself from the sticky couch and called his source.

"I need some information on the agents working my case."

"Don't bother," the source responded. "I know everything the mayor does, and from what I understand, the Feds have a set date for when they're off the case."

The source breathed deeply, and his voice came over in a quiet hush. "Did you ever hear about that crate they found in Iraq?"

Myth Man shed a wicked grin. "You don't say? Tell me more about that."

When the call was over, Myth man returned to the TV and rewatched the hearing.

He took notes: the clothes, the accents, the mannerisms.

Then he began to practice.

CHAPTER THIRTY-FOUR

WHEN PRESTO ARRIVED AND knocked on the chief deputy inspector's door, a gruff bark told him to enter. As he waddled in, he stole a glance at Danko, who looked more like a suspect than the accredited, and now discredited, detective. Dark wedges underscored his distant eyes. His unkempt goatee was surrounded by a few days' coarse growth. Slumped in his chair, it was the first time Presto ever saw the man not display the posture of a prison guard.

Presto was trying to conjure something to say but had no palpable words up his sleeve that could revitalize the man. "Good morning," he offered.

"Yeah,' Danko grumbled. "What's so goddamn good about it?"

Pretso chose to tread carefully. This was not the same man he met a few months back at St. Patrick's Cathedral. "You're right. It's Sunday and a holiday, and we've been pulled away from our loved ones."

"Speak for yourself," Danko said wearily. "My wife walked out with the kids yesterday. Went to her parents. Apparently, I've been testy and neglectful. Go fucking figure," he said and turned a framed picture of his wife down to his desk.

Maybe to bond, or to shake some gloom from him, Presto nodded in sympathy. "I just found out last night that my mom's got cancer. She'd been acting odd for a while, and she finally told me. So it is somewhat of a black Sunday. I'm sorry to hear that about your wife. I'm sure she'll come to her senses."

"Sorry to hear that Presto, and thanks, but I doubt it," Danko said tersely. "She'll leave me. Her parents never liked me to begin with. She's from money. I'm not. They wanted a doctor, lawyer … a country club asshole for their girl. I can only imagine the influence they're having."

Danko was a wreck. They had a case to work, and the Feds would be here soon. He had to try and snap him out of his funk. "How long have you been married?"

"Thirteen good years," he replied angrily.

Anger was better than despair. "So what does that tell you?" Not letting Danko reply, he said, "You're wife obviously makes her own decisions. She defied her parents because she loved," *oops*, "loves you. You need to be the

118

person she knows. Frankly, Frank, you have not been yourself lately. We'll get through this. I promise you."

A small light flashed in Danko's eyes. "Hey, thanks for listening and your kind thoughts." The light in his eyes brightened further. "Maybe today wouldn't be so bad if we didn't have to work with these two agents. That … that guy," Danko spat incredulously, "Carter Donavan, is an obnoxious clown. How the hell did the FBI ever hire him? He could never get away with that shit in NYPD, I'll tell you that." He still looked haggard, but he no longer sat like a limp noodle.

Presto agreed. He tried contacting Bailey to get some background on the agents, but he must have been busy with that Iraqi crate matter. "He's unorthodox, to say the least."

Danko flicked his wrist dismissively. "No, you're unorthodox, Dom. He's a complete dick."

"I can't disagree."

This was going well, Presto hoped. The anger over his wife was fractured and displaced toward Agent Donavan. Presto was not sure how much that improved things, but at least his mind was not embattled with grief.

"You know what we need," Danko said with a touch of enthusiasm, "some of that Presto magic." He paused to smile gratuitously. "You were off to a hot start, but then you were set up by, presumably, our suspect. Now that you're back, do you have any new ideas?"

Despite the discomfort of sitting in the puny office chair again, he never felt more comfortable in Danko's presence. "Nothing noteworthy. I studied the files you gave me."

"Not much there, huh?" Danko asked.

"Maybe, maybe not," Presto answered with philosophical truthfulness, "but I'm doing a lot of thinking, trying to get inside our killer's head."

Danko's eyes widened. "You're one of those?"

Presto gave a sheepish grin. "No, not really. I just try and see their perspective, the why's and how's. I think I'm also desperate," Presto said with a light chuckle.

"We all are," Danko said and laughed too. "Oh well. At least we have the Feds to guide us," he added sarcastically. "At the very least, Agent Ridgewood is something to look at." His eyes dazzled. "Having her around somewhat compensates for having to deal with that jerk off. I feel bad for her."

"So do I," Presto agreed hastily.

A drumroll pounded across Danko's door followed by muffled words. The anger returned to Danko's gruff visage. Through pressed lips, he bid the agents to enter.

Agent Ridgewood walked in first. She wore a simple, light yellow dress, perfect for Palm Sunday. Her hair was now pulled back in a cloth twist. Agent Donavan followed dressed in faded blue jeans and a dark sport jacket over a white button-down. The top three shirt buttons were unfastened.

"Hello," greeted Agent Ridgewood. She went to say more, but her partner interceded.

"Whoa, Grizzly Adams. What happened to you?"

Danko ground his teeth. "None of your business."

"Donavan," Ridgewood snapped.

Ignoring the warning, Donavan, smiled. "Ah, I get it. Did your wife throw your scruffy ass out?"

Presto's head did a double shake. Danko's sagged.

"Bingo, eh?" He looked to his partner. "Damn, I'm good."

"You're out of line," she replied tactfully.

Ignoring her again, he looked to Danko and jerked his hand back and forth in front of his crotch. "I guess it really is Palm Sunday for you, buddy."

"You're not my buddy," Danko cursed, his chin forward.

Donavan frowned. "Oh, no," Donavan said, dripping with mock disappointment. "This could make the day a tad thorny. You do know that we're partners for the day?"

"What?" Danko spat incredulously. "Partners?" His eyes shifted between the two agents.

"Yes," hesitated Ridgewood. "I thought we might split up, have a cop and agent in two locations?"

"No, no, no," sputtered Danko. "I'm not spending the day with him," he shouted, his finger pointed at his smiling agitator.

"I love you too," Donavan said and blew a kiss. This further riled Danko who slammed a fist down on his desk like an angry judge wishing to silence contempt.

"Let's try this today and see how it works out," she commanded hopefully.

Danko was not assuaged. "We know how it'll work out. Disaster."

Donavan clapped his hands together. "Give me a shot, brother. I'm really a nice guy. We might hit it off."

"In a boxing ring, maybe," Danko challenged, his punctured ego reinflating.

"Yeah, old timer? You better stick to thumb wrestling."

"Boys," shouted Ridgewood. Color filled her pale complexion. She looked to Danko. "I want you to report everything and anything he does wrong. I'm speaking to Bailey tonight." Looking to her partner. "Don't make my report look worse than it already is."

Undaunted, Donavan said, "You got it, chief."

Presto pitied Danko but was thankful the roles were not reversed.

"Hey, Danko," Donavan goaded. "Is there any way you can steer some donuts our way before we set out, or do you have a favorite eatery you hit up? Free of charge, I assume."

CHAPTER THIRTY-FIVE

"I'M DRIVING," AGENT RIDGEWOOD said as they exited the precinct.

Presto followed her to the black sedan he saw the two agents use a few days earlier. At first Presto was surprised to see the dark sedan conveniently nearby, but then he saw the fire hydrant. Presto thought: Would a cop ticket the obviously undercover car? Probably not, but if so, who pays the bill?

"Get in," she gestured as she went around the car.

He did as advised, and the car noticeably lowered on the right side. It did not balance out when Ridgewood's lithe frame got behind the wheel. She turned the key, and the engine came to life. Instead of shifting gears, she stretched back and wiped her hand across her brow. Presto saw no signs of perspiration, but she appeared heated.

She looked over to him, her milky skin translucent in the shadowy vehicle. "Thank goodness I'm free of that lunatic, at least for a day," she said relieved. "Although I sure do feel bad Frank got stuck with him. Donavan promised he'd behave, but I don't believe it. I almost hope he does something stupid, and Bailey finally axes that jerk." Her hand went to her mouth. "I'm sorry. I know Bailey is a friend. I just needed to vent a bit."

"I understand completely," he told her.

Her lips curled up in a supine stretch, and agent minx smiled. "Thanks. Not to just get away from Donavan; I also wanted to talk to you. You can't talk to Donavan. He does all the talking and doesn't listen. He's crazy," she declared.

"He's no introvert, that's for sure," Presto replied.

"No, but he's a pervert. That is for sure," she complained. "And to think he's married. Pig," she uttered in disgust. "He could never get away with this behavior anywhere else, and somehow he does so employed by our very own government."

Presto could only stare. She was stunning even in despair. Although Presto was still a virgin, it did not mean he did not appreciate beauty. Beauty never appreciated him.

"I'm sorry," she apologized again. "I'm blabbing away over here. Let's get going."

In typical New York City fashion, she had to shift from drive to reverse several times before the car cleared a tight squeeze. She negotiated the traffic well, and unlike with Danko, they chatted the whole ride. The destination was Grace Church, which was designed by James Renwick Jr., the same architect who later designed St. Patrick's Cathedral. Danko and Presto were back at St. Patrick's in case the killer decided to bring his crusade there again.

A broken-down cab brought the ride to a halt a few blocks from the church. Ridgewood muttered under her breath and pushed away from the steering wheel.

"Don't stress, Lorraine," he said, already using her first name, as per her instructions. "We have time. The cathedral has been under surveillance since yesterday."

She shook herself to a smile. "You're right. I can't complain. I'm with you instead of that louse Donavan. I can only imagine what he'd be saying. He'd probably start with something about women drivers," she said and nosed the vehicle forward.

"I was going to start with something about government drivers being used to red tape gridlock." His tone told her it was a joke.

Her smile showed she approved. "I wanted to tell you something," she smiled awkwardly. "I was the agent who detected the pattern with those Web sites. Your name kept popping up. I made a report to Bailey, who knew you, and the rest is history." She glanced ahead, but they were stuck for the moment. "Bailey raves about you. Says you're the best. Now that I met you, I'm glad I helped with that inquiry."

Presto may have appeared physically gelatinous, but now even his innards felt like Jell-O. He was forever used to everyone rejecting him, especially the opposite sex. She was nice to him. She was also beautiful. He snapped back to reality. "Well, then. I owe you more than my gratitude. You can take anything away from a man, but steal his passion, and he's gutted on the inside, while the exterior becomes petrified. I know that sounds heavy, but that's how I felt. So, truly, thanks for saving more than a career."

She grinned. "Just doing my job, sir!"

They both laughed. "Sir, yes sir," boomed Presto, and they continued to giggle. Her boss, Malcolm, was known for formality and discipline, being a man with a military background and old-fashioned values.

They were close to passing the cab, which had stalled in the center lane. The driver was outside leaning against the hood. His arms flailed about as a bored cop stood with his arms folded, and a bored expression.

Something about Donavan's erratic behavior nagged Presto. Ridgewood blatantly expressed her disregard for Donavan, but there had been some subtle comments about Bailey. He decided to ask her, but she broke the brief silence first.

"I was saying before that I wanted to talk to you alone." Their eyes met. She did not immediately look away, and when she did, it was to check the traffic. Not yet. "After I gave my report and Bailey told me about you, I looked you up. I know you have some experience with serial killers. Don't be mad at me," she said earnestly.

Anger was the last thing on Presto's mind. He waved that notion away.

She continued. "I noted you haven't said much. I figured that has much to do with all the tension, so I wanted to get you alone and talk about the case. Let's nail this bastard then celebrate over some cocktails."

Presto replied eagerly, "Sure."

She smiled and then cheered, "Here we go." They got past the cab, and they had a green light with them for at least one block. But they were free at last.

Presto was pleased. The case had been mismanaged from the get-go. Despite running the case, the fault was not solely Danko's, but his recent behavior had been erratic. Neutered and no longer in charge, he was defused and confused. Donavan was the final Waterloo, surgically removing the horns off the legendary bull.

"You got it, partner," Presto said with a southern twang. His voice returned to normal. "First, I have something I wanted to ask."

"Sure." She turned on Tenth Street, and they saw several police cars ahead at the corner of the church.

Presto spread his hands apart. "I don't know Bailey that well, but I perceive him as a refined, disciplined man who would not tolerate insubordination. Like successful politicians, he commands attention, exudes charm, and demands respect." He watched her face, but she stared ahead expressionless, waiting for the light to change so they could make the final crawl home.

Her silence told him to continue. "What I'm getting at is Donavan seems to be the antithesis of everything Bailey stands for." He finally saw something, a quick smile. "So, it just seems odd to me that Donavan could even be an agent of the FBI let alone working under Malcolm."

Her smile returned, fuller now; partially because she was able to tap the gas peddle. "You either have a keen sense, Detective, or that was as transparent as naughty lingerie." Her head turned quickly, and she flashed an impish grin.

A distracted Presto asked, "Why then? Is he the great grandson of J. Edgar Hoover, or something?"

She chuckled, went to speak, and stopped. Then said, "I really shouldn't say anything."

Presto was disappointed but foresaw this outcome. "I understand," he said slowly.

Her head bobbed, weighing some thought until she found equilibrium. "If you don't say anything and promise to help me on this case, truly help me, like silent partners, I'll explain."

While Presto absorbed her words, Ridgewood steered alongside a parked police car.

"You can trust me. Scout's honor."

She smirked. "You were a scout?"

"No, actually."

"Didn't think so."

They both laughed. Ridgewood rolled down her window and flashed her tin at a cop. Danko had alerted the officers of their arrival. The closest officer appeared surprised by Ridgewood's appearance. He came over to chat, but she rolled the window back up.

"I'll confess to you inside," she exclaimed. "I have my Sunday dress on; let's go and pray to God we catch this son of a witch."

CHAPTER THIRTY-SIX

Y*OU SLEEP IN IT; you bathe in it.*

Myth Man was in the shower, scrubbing with fury. He awoke from a vivid dream where he was a child again and had been camping with his father. Then he reached over in bed and did not detect his wife's presence. Groggy, he figured she'd likely passed out in the living room. An almost empty bottle of booze, a highball half empty, and an overstocked ashtray would assuredly be on the table.

But no, they'd gone to bed together and, for the first time in months, performed sex. No old flame was rekindled. For the both of them, it was purely a need fulfilled.

Then he felt the wetness around his torso and cursed. *Again*! Like a woman's menstrual period, he was good once a month, except there was no approximate cycle to guide him for the discharge, let alone tampons. Plus, it was just not natural. His wife once, and only once, suggested trying adult diapers. One cold look, and she never mentioned them again.

He found a note on the kitchen counter from his wife. She left to visit her sister, disgusted no doubt. His sister-in-law Allison actually held a good job. It was her husband Jimmy, or Jimbo as he liked to be called, who was a louse, jumping from job to job until being eradicated by the boss. Jimbo did excel when it came to loud beer belches and self-professed sports analysis. The two sisters were likely at brunch. Husband-bashing was certainly on the menu as they chewed their spouses into just desserts.

Next, Myth Man cleaned the scene of the crime. The sheets went to the washing machine. He sprinkled a urine scent remover, which his wife purchased from a pet store, around the bed stain, which was not entirely fresh. In eight years of marriage, they were on their sixth mattress. Sadly, it was not from broken bedsprings, he lamented.

He washed off the extra lathering and thought of better things—cleansing the world of religious slime. *Religion Busters*. He saw a circle with all the religious symbols the cross, the Jewish star, etc., and a diagonal slash through them all. He'd love to hang one in his office.

In twenty minutes, he was dressed in a black-and-white striped sweat suit. He made a few slices of wheat toast, margarine, and strawberry jam, which were washed down with a liter of orange juice. Then he slipped his rollerblades in a backpack and put headphones on. The final touch was the mirrored sunglasses.

He suspected his taste in music was unusual. He guessed most murderers liked rap or heavy metal due to the aggression and violence associated in those genres. The sophisticated types were usually portrayed to like classical music, but he hated that as well, especially since he associated much of the music with the church. He wished he could like that death metal music with much of their venom hurled toward religion, but those idiots instead praised Satan, which was equally ludicrous. Plus, they dressed like assholes, with their zombie, vampire look, and the music was without harmony. All the vocalists sounded the same, with their hoarse, Cookie Monster growls.

No, he had more in common with the killer Patrick Bateman in Bret Easton Ellis's book *American Psycho* in that he favored sappy love ballads. Unlike Bateman however, he was quite sane, and not a finicky fuck.

He hit the play button, and Air Supply came on. One of his favorite bands. By the time he got off the subway in downtown Manhattan, he was up to *All out of Love* on the Air Supply play list. He was out of love all right. He hated his wife and despised religion's hold on humanity. This was why he listened to love songs. They made him angry, got him in the right mood.

Ahead was a corner park. Myth Man found a park bench without a snoozing bum and void of fresh pigeon shit. He removed his sunglasses and headphones and popped a squat. He untied his laces and removed his sneakers. Then he pulled his rollerblades out from his backpack and put the shoes in their place.

He rose, took a few strides, spun in a circle, and then accelerated. He smiled, as he enjoyed the speed a simple change in footwear made, when suddenly he saw something on the edges of his periphery. A homeless man, who was apparently awake, came to life and grabbed his backpack. The vagrant was making a break for it.

Would you believe this asshole, Myth Man thought, as he braked and set off after him. In six strides he lowered his shoulder and hit the larger-sized man. Through speed and leverage, the homeless man went airborne and crashed to the cement. Grounded, the sprawled man looked up at him and decided he did not like what he saw. "I'm sorry. Here," he said dropping the booty.

"Leave," Myth Man warned.

The man scrambled away, and Myth Man wondered if he had killed a friend of his in the pews that day at St. Patrick's Cathedral. He leaned down and collected his stuff. "Fuck," he spat. One of the frames on his glasses broke in the fall. Fortunately, the music player's protective case performed its duty well. Minutes later, he was on his way, skating to the passion of REO Speedwagon's *Can't Fight This Feeling*.

The anger in him surged. He didn't fight it.

He took off toward Grace Church. Although it was an early weekend and he was a skilled skater, he treaded carefully past the parked cars. At any moment, a car door might open. When the traffic abated, he strayed a few yards from the parked cars, and if the situation dictated, he used the sidewalks.

His contact told him all about the plan to monitor every religious site on their respective holidays. This was stretching the police force, and he was glad to hear of the inconvenience. Even better was the report he got on the FBI agents. Apparently they assigned some goofy gumshoe who was hampering the case and pissing everybody off in the process, especially Detective Danko. He also learned about Danko's problems with his wife.

Such mischief he'd started. He felt bad, which made him feel good.

He was somewhat surprised to hear that Dominick Presto was supposed to be at Grace Church this Palm Sunday. His contact had no idea if that was a coincidence or based on any deductive reasoning. Not that it mattered. Right church, wrong day. Why kill on Palm Sunday, when he could crucify another Christian without a hope in hell of an afterlife on Easter?

The security did not trouble him. He had a plan, one that he'd cultured for almost a year. The cleric's murder took some guile and planning, but being the first religious kill, it was relatively easy. St. Patrick's posed a challenge, but the police still had no idea of what they were dealing with, and that also went smoothly. His tactics over the Internet hampered the police. It was only after the the death of the Kali pandit that they realized the nature of the game. After Easter, they would also know his name.

Myth Man.

His music-induced reveries were broken by the sight of a few police cars at the end of the block. He brought the right rollerblade back brake down a few touches and decelerated. As he got close, he saw a platoon of cops. He smiled. This was hilarious. What a waste of manpower. Did they think he was going to walk through the cathedral doors with a bazooka and blast the reverend to kingdom come? Ridiculous.

When he reached the corner and turned toward the cathedral, he noticed a woman in a yellow dress. She was on the other side of Broadway, coming toward him. He wondered if she was the female agent his contact told him about.

He slowed to a crawl and watched the diva in the dress approach. He turned his head to watch her destination point. Only a few yards away from him, eating a sandwich while slouched against a sagging car, was Dominick Presto.

Their eyes locked. Myth's eyes fluttered, and his mouth opened in shock. Presto's eyes narrowed. Nervous, Myth Man looked back to the female and willed his legs to move.

It seemed his synapses misfired, but after several attempts, his legs obeyed the message, and he slowly skated away.

As he gained speed, he resisted the urge to look back. He cursed the lure of a woman's body for the distraction and the sneaky bum who inadvertently broke his mirrored glasses.

Chapter Thirty-Seven

Who said lead balloons don't float?

Buoyant, Presto felt like he had futuristic jets boots on as he glided through his apartment door. Seated at the dining room table, with the newspaper open to the crosswords, his mother looked at him incredulously as he hovered over her.

"Was there a break in the case?" she questioned.

"No."

She cocked her head. "Then what's with the glow? You look a little too happy."

Presto shrugged. "I guess it's the thrill of being back on the job."

She shot an inquisitive grin. "That's it?"

"Oh, and Buddha's Bistro is running the all-you-can-eat $5.99 dinner buffet this week, too."

Cleo Presto looked away. She shook her head. "That won't do."

Jolted, he asked, "What won't do?"

"Buddha's Bistro. Good Chinese, no doubt, but the décor is too drab. Hardly romantic."

"Romantic? What are you talking about? I was joking about the buffet special." His feet had now firmly landed. The touchdown felt wobbly.

"Your date," she said.

He flinched. Was his mother clairvoyant? "Date," he said meekly.

She looked at him oddly. "Yeah. Date," she punctuated. "Camille arrived."

Relieved, but confused, he replied, "Camille?"

"Yes, blank brain. The Stagnuts' niece."

"Oh," he said. "Sorry, I've been busy with this case. I forgot about that."

She smiled sympathetically. "I know. Well if you're up to it, she'd love to get together tonight."

"Tonight?" he gasped.

"Yeah, can you blame her with that woman's cooking?" Cleo's index finger went into her throat. She gagged and simulated a vomit attack.

Gina's cooking catastrophes are infamous throughout the Stagnuts' side

130

of the family tree. Arthur often, but always without his spouse present, contrasted his mother's and sister's cooking with that of his spouse.

Presto took a step back. "She'll be here for a while, and I'm not taking her out every night, so she's going to have to brave her cooking at some point. Tonight's no good."

She dropped the pencil in her hand. "Tired?"

"A bit," he said slowly.

The lines in her face furrowed. "Take a nap. When you wake, I'll have a warm meal ready for you."

His immediate reaction was to become trite over his mother's forthcoming inquisitiveness. But despite her wishes, the cancer did change his behavior.

"That won't be necessary."

"What?"

"Cooking. I have plans later."

Her mouth opened in exaggerated shock. "What plan, Buster? Who are you standing poor Camille up for?"

"I'm getting chummy with the guys on the case. They hang at this girlie bar. I suppose it's a thing married guys do," he said with a chuckle, "but they swear by the chicken wings there. Say they're the best in the city."

Unfretted, she retorted. "Have a good time. Get a lap dance."

"What?" His mouth opened. His shock not exaggerated.

"We women know about that stuff. That's what daytime TV is for."

She continually amazed him, even after all these years. He grinned. "And you approve of such conduct?"

"In your case, I'm treating. You need company?" Her visage dared.

He laughed. "I was kidding."

"I'm not."

"Let's reschedule that blockbuster plan. In the meantime, I'm going to my study to unwind."

"Sure. First tell me what you're really doing tonight."

He snapped his fingers. "Thought I sidetracked you there."

"Not for a second, Dominick."

"I could lie, so you don't harangue me. I know how you'll twist things," he jested.

"I would never," she gasped as her right hand found her throat.

"No, not you,' he deadpanned. "Tonight, however, I'm getting a bite to eat with the female agent we're working with. Trust me, Mom, it's strictly business."

She scowled in jest. "Does this agent have a name?"

He countered with a stupid face of his own. "No. Today, with advances in robotics, the government, to save money, has unleashed a new breed of agents.

She's an android." He jerked himself upright and froze like a mannequin except that none existed in his proportions. "I'm agent Ninety-nine, at your service," he said, attempting a feminine voice.

She grinned. "That was good. Now how about her name?"

His stiffness melted back to flabbiness. "Lorraine. Agent Lorraine Ridgewood."

"Is she married?"

"I have no idea. We never got around to personal stuff."

She hissed slowly, like air escaping a depressed tire valve. "Nice try, Detective. Was she wearing a ring?"

"You won't believe me, but I didn't think to take note." Cleo smirked in doubt, but he continued. "Yet, now that you mention it, I don't recall seeing one."

She picked up her pencil and pointed it at her son. "So you're standing Camille up for this hussy, who wants to pick your brain?" Her tone was mock serious.

"Absolutely. It's called mutual cooperation."

She blinked rapidly and asked, "So where are you taking her? If it's just business, why not Buddha's?"

He found his mother's inquisitiveness amusing. "Actually, we're headed to The Blue Tit, that girlie bar I just mentioned. They even have a caricature of the actual bird in their logo, actually two of them, one over each breast of a busty cartoon female.

"Agent Android Ridgewood, not requiring sleep, moonlights as a dancer. The Feds have inserted undercover robot agents within the sleazy, criminal world of erotic voyeurism."

She threw the pencil at him. Despite the ample target, she somehow missed.

Chapter Thirty-Eight

After he jotted some ideas down, Detective Presto kicked back and reviewed his notes. Unlike famous, fictional detectives, he had no magic summary that ended with the solution and killer's or killers' names. He only wished it was that easy. He lacked the panache and oratory brilliance typified by literary sleuths. He was merely persistent and practical.

Instead, he formulated a battle plan. Although he always knew, it was now readily accepted that they were dealing with one man or one organization. They had a pattern. He killed on religious holidays and twisted the holy symbolism with sadistic intent.

Presto doubted they'd catch the guy in the act, and although the extra police presence couldn't hurt, Presto viewed those precautions as politically practical. It was the detective's job to find suspects.

While he was suspended from the case, Danko's team interrogated people of interest. These notes were in the case file Danko provided when he was reinstated. Most of the interviewed were chosen because they were considered extremist or fervent, depending on your take on such matters.

Presto had a different take. The killer was not a religious fanatic. Instead, he was someone who hated religion. Instead of steering right, Presto veered left and did a little research.

Woven within the American tapestry are countless loose threads that are part of our nation's fabric but almost unnoticeable in the grand cultural collage. Most Americans are raised with some religion. Some stay dedicated; others no longer practice. Then there's another category.

Disenchanted with religion, they seek answers elsewhere. America's landscape is littered like strip malls with all types of cults that provide alternative shopping for the spiritual buyer. Some, like Heaven's Gate, had a spiritual closing sale when the group committed mass suicide so they could hop aboard the UFO following the Comet Hale-Bopp.

Religious freedom.

He also profiled another possibility.

There existed another animal, one that was abused in a religious context. They do not merely lose faith; they either hate God for their fate or no longer

133

believe and blame religion for not only their ills but society's ills as well. This man might be harder to find, but Presto unearthed a few points of interest.

When he finished reading, he tapped his pen with a nervous patter against a spiral notebook. He wanted more, but it was all he had. Something wasn't right. He was conditioned to dribble his ideas to the big men, only to be flatly rejected. So why did he feel the pressure dishing it to the lithe FBI agent?

Of course, he knew why, but he did not readily accept it. This was the first time he'd worked with a woman, and … she was beautiful, and, more importantly, she was not repulsed by him. In fact, they were going to dinner. Other than his mother, he'd never been to dinner alone with a female.

Presto was honest with his mother, and himself, that there was absolutely no chance that he could ever interest the likes of Lorraine Ridgewood. Having her in his company, however, was all the satisfaction he could hope for. It was not that he didn't desire the proximity of a woman, but like his childhood dreams of being a thoroughbred jockey, some hopes are forgotten and left to die. Now his desk chair became his saddle and detective work his thrill ride.

He looked at the time on his computer. 6:04 pm. More than two hours had passed. It was time to get moving. He dismounted his chair and left the study. He had heard his mother leave and then come back. He decided to see what she was up to.

He found her on the couch watching TV. It was a sitcom. Some schlep was getting heat from his wife. The man wasn't responding. He sat in a chair looking like he was doomed, but beneath the veneer, rage boiled.

Presto had seen that expression. Frank Danko.

"What time you going?" she asked.

"We're meeting at 7:15."

"Are you going to tell me where you're really going? For real."

He walked over and sat on the couch with her. "Sure. House of Hanabi."

"Good choice."

"She said she was easy going, but when I pressed, she said she'd been on a sushi binge since she arrived in New York."

"She sounds pretentious. Where's she from?"

He had an urge to defend her but held back. "She grew up in a suburb of Kansas City. She said there was great barbecue but not much else. She's been in Virginia the past few years working with the FBI."

"I thought you two didn't get around to personal stuff," she accused airily and winked.

Dominick smirked. "It came up in the context of dinner plans. You know how people are, who did not grow up here?"

"Is she paying?" his mother asked.

His eyes bulged. "Huh?"

"She asked you. She probably has an expense account."

"Even so, the government's not covering Hanabi's."

"I though this wasn't a date," she quizzed.

He bit his lip. "We'll see how it goes," he remarked.

She gave him a soft slap to the leg. "I'm just teasing you." Then she sprang off the couch with energy he had not seen since before her injury.

Presto gazed at the TV. The same father was now sitting on a large, beaten-up couch with a white cockatoo on his shoulder. Transformed, he looked giddy. Around him were his now adoring wife and three over-elated children. He hoped Danko's drama unfolded in a similar fashion.

Cleo Presto reappeared with the same haste she'd left with. In her hand, hung from a hanger, was a new sport jacket. "Look, it's just like your favorite, except there aren't any tears and stains."

He rolled his eyes. "You're crazy."

She laughed. "I'm old. I'm allowed to be."

CHAPTER THIRTY-NINE

Presto CAREFULLY MIXED A swab of wasabi into a small jade-colored ceramic bowl, half filled with soy sauce. The only thing hotter than the green paste in the restaurant was the woman across the table.

Presto sensed peering eyes when he arrived and found her at the crowded bar alone, holding a bottle of Kirin. They greeted, and she gave him a peck on the cheek, much to the delight of the recipient.

Trendy, young adult yuppies packed the bar, and a few guys with booze-fueled bravado were eyeing Agent Ridgewood like an appetizer. With no room at the bar, Presto was thankful when Ridgewood had suggested they check on their reservation.

Seated now, he ogled her as she scoped the menu.

"It all looks so good," she purred without ever looking up.

"Indeed it does," he replied without ever looking down.

Agent Ridgewood was dressed in form-fitting black slacks and a gray cashmere sweater. Presto wondered if it had, inadvertently, shrunk in the wash. Occasionally that happened to him.

Ridgewood finally gazed up, eyes wide. "I have an idea. How about you order for the both of us? Pick out a bunch of things, and we'll share. It'll be fun."

"Yeah, sure," Presto said agreeably.

"You like sake?"

He wavered. "I'm not a big drinker ..."

She put her hands up. "It's okay. I'll just get a glass with dinner."

Presto did not want to sound like a complete dud. "I'm just too busy to get out much. Sake would be great. I order the food; you pick the bottle."

The waiter arrived. "Mr. Presto," he said and bowed, "good to see you again."

Presto replied with a respectful dip of his head and communicated with the waiter in precise Japanese. If his hair were tied back and he was naked except for a thick silk belt, Presto could have passed as a sumo wrestler.

Ridgewood politely asked the waiter a few sake questions and then selected one of his recommendations.

When the waiter departed, Presto explained that this was the restaurant where the murdered chef had worked, presumably for the purpose of acquiring the tetrodotoxin.

After Presto finished, Ridgewood said, "I want to thank you again for joining me."

Presto considered himself the fortunate one but replied with the standard, "My pleasure." He reached into a wooden bowl for some endamame. He broke a shell and deposited the beans into his mouth.

Ridgewood's face did a one-second spasm. "I went out with Cro-Magnon Carter once. Horrible," she spewed. "He harassed the waitress all night, calling her toots and honey. I was embarrassed the whole time. When he tried to stiff the waitress on the tip, I slipped a ten spot on top of his five."

Presto's face grew conciliatory. "Despite what you told me, I'm still surprised Malcolm keeps Donavan on."

"Me too," she said frustrated.

At the church, Ridgewood explained Bailey's apparent bond with Agent Donavan. Donavan had grown up in South Boston prior to the recent gentrification when it was predominantly a low-income, rough neighborhood. His father worked at the fishing docks doing assorted odd jobs, like cleaning and loading. But the father did his best lifting with his pals at Shanny's, a local pub.

As the youngest boy, Donavan watched and learned from his brothers. The oldest died when Donavan was only seven, shot by a liquor store owner he was trying to rob. A few years later, his next older brother was killed drunk driving while trying to drag race across the Broadway Bridge. His last brother also found the bottle and committed suicide after a drunken fight with his girlfriend over her refusal to introduce another female into their sex lives.

Donavan's older sister did not suffer such a tragic fate, but did share the family's lust for booze. Drunk, she was easy prey for hammered horn dogs. By twenty-five, she was a mother of four children. Three had different identified fathers. The fourth child's father was a mystery. She said she passed out at a friend's party, and someone must have taken advantage of her. Her parents pushed for testing, but she refused. The truth was, she was inebriated and a willing centerpiece of an orgy.

Determined not to end up like his siblings, Donavan and his younger sister Allison found other outlets. For Donavan, it was hockey. The speed and aggression were a substitute stimulus for the fake highs of drugs and alcohol. His father succumbed to liver disease before Donavan was admitted to Boston University, but the old man would have been proud that the first Donavan to go to college did so with a scholarship, not to just play hockey but also for good grades.

Donavan played big minutes as a defenseman for the Terriers in his freshman year. He became a fan favorite for his tenacious style, and by the time he graduated, he had broken a Terrier school record for penalty minutes. The previous record holder had been Malcolm Bailey, who was considered one of the best Americans in his era and represented his country in the 1964 Winter Games in Innsbruck, Austria. One of Bailey's teammates was future miracle on ice coach Herb Brooks.

Bailey returned each year for the Beanpot Tournament and got to know Donavan. Right after he graduated, Donavan's younger sister was found naked behind a warehouse wharf. She'd been raped and then strangled, choking her dreams of a career in medicine.

Bailey had contacted Donavan to offer his condolences.

Prior to the NHL draft, Donavan announced that he would not pursue a career in hockey. He felt another calling—law enforcement.

Bailey got Donavan a job with the FBI but in a different division. Donavan worked undercover infiltrating gangs. Although his success was not questioned, his tactics and attitude were. On the verge of being reassigned to a desk in Montana, Bailey took him under his wing.

A thought flashed across Ridgewood's face. "Oh, speaking of Caveman Carter, I heard from him before we met. He claimed that he bonded with Danko today. Said to cheer him up, he forced Danko into a topless bar and got him drunk."

Presto smiled, partially because the comment reminded him of his earlier banter with his mother.

Ridgewood noticed. "What's so funny?"

Presto recapped his mother's jibes, leaving out, of course, the comments she personally ascribed to Ridgewood. As they shared a laugh, their food arrived: A sashimi and sushi deluxe platter. In between the two giant entrées stood a boat of shrimp tails that poked out from a tempura rolls.

The waiter poured a splash of the sake in a glass and offered it to Ridgewood to sample. She brought the glass to her lips and downed it. "Wonderful," she said, and the waiter bowed to her kindness.

"A toast." Ridgewood raised her glass. "To us," she declared. "To making a great team, catching a killer, and," she paused for emphasis, "to be famous. Can you envision the headlines?"

Presto thought: *Yes I can. Beauty and the Beast.*

Instead, he said, "I had enough press for one year. I'd prefer anonymity, which is hard to do with my conspicuous proportions." A frown appeared on her lips, but he continued. "It should be your face that gets exposed. I bet modeling agencies pay better than the government," he joked.

"You're too kind," she said. "Cheers." She jiggled her glass. They both took a sip. "Mmmm, delicious. The waiter picked a good one."

Presto didn't blame the waiter, but delicious was not the adjective that came to mind. Alcohol was not his thing. Poison on the palate.

Presto loved to talk about food as much as he enjoyed eating it. He separated his chopsticks, and then pointed and explained every morsel. The eel, or *unagi*, he described as succulent paradise. The tuna, or *maguro*, was a tasty temptress. Ridgewood looked on, fascinated.

When Presto's table tour was over, at her suggestion, they toasted again.

Ridgewood handled her chopsticks fairly well. Her positioning was correct, but the motion was not yet second nature. Although the sticks looked like dental floss within Presto's chubby fingers, he handled the utensils adeptly as he propelled food into his mouth.

Presto generously mixed the wasabi with the soy sauce. He looked up, and it was here that he made the connection between Ridgewood and the hot wasabi. He cautioned himself. It was okay to fantasize as long as he understood the dream was fantasy. Or, with his physique, science fiction, he mused.

After a few mouthfuls, and compliments on the cuisine, Ridgewood asked. "You want to talk about the case?"

He touched his outside jacket pocket. With trepidation, he pulled out an encased CD-ROM. "Everything I have to say is on this."

Her eyebrows arched, and she did this upper lip movement that wiggled her nose. "Thanks, Dom. I thought we'd just talk about it. I didn't mean to make you work."

"No. It's okay," he assured. "I found it helpful transcribing everything. It's not much, really. Just some ideas, a plan of action." Despite engulfing several portions, Presto felt an empty feeling in the pit of his belly. "I hope it helps," he finished meekly.

Ridgewood took the last gulp of her drink and poured herself another. She looked at Presto's glass and then at him. Presto felt the cue, closed his eyes, pulled his head back, and braved the rest.

Presto grimaced, *sake very sucky*,

"I'm sure it will be helpful," Ridgewood remarked while Presto cleansed his palate with water. She then picked up her napkin and played with it a bit before dropping it back to her lap. "You're different," she added.

"Yeah, well," Presto said unsure of her reaction. He spun his chopsticks nervously.

Ridgewood motioned for the waiter. "Dominick, I mean that in a good way. Most men I seem to deal with think with their dicks."

Presto wheezed. He was not used to this discourse from women. Then again, his exchanges with a female as beautiful as this were usually limited to something like, "let me open that door for you," which was followed by one word (hopefully)—"thanks."

"Maybe it's my lot in life," she continued. "I'm continually battling the male ego—the swagger, the staring, the snide comments." She waited and exhaled. "You just have no idea how it is to deal with."

Presto did not hesitate. "I do, Lorraine. I only wish to do my job and be left alone. I feel the staring. I hear the snide comments. The difference is that it's because I'm fat rather than beautiful." Shocked that he voiced the visual he continued with a big grin. "I wish I had it as bad as you." He scowled in jest.

Ridgewood lips withdrew in an awkward grin. "You're funny, Dominick."

"You can call me Dom. Only my mother calls me Dominick."

"Mother knows best," she asserted. "Then I'm calling you Dominick too."

"Okay."

She clicked her tongue. Then she looked down at her glass and stopped for a drink. "You're a funny guy, but you're too hard on yourself."

"I like to joke around. I'm also a realist." He was slightly uncomfortable but hung on her reply. He decided to test the sake again. It seemed to taste better.

"Oh, I like that you're not conceited. Self-deprecation can be sexy, to a point, but you have to like yourself. If you don't care for yourself, no one else will."

Ridgewood took another slug from her glass. It was empty, and she looked at the bottle, which was also empty, and frowned. She looked for the waiter, who bustled over.

"Sorry. Party of seven needed help with order."

Ridgewood assured him she understood. "I waited tables in college, and it was not as fine as an establishment as this," her eyes rolled around the room. "It was a rib joint, but the greasiest swine were the patrons."

Both men chuckled, imagining what a younger version of Ridgewood must have had to put up with.

Ridgewood continued. "Do me a favor and get me another bottle of that sake. I commend you on the selection."

The waiter smiled, bowed, and departed.

"Don't worry about the bill," she assured. "It's on me."

Presto put his hands up in protest. This was his first night out with a woman. He wanted to pay. "You have a better chance of picking me up than the bill," he joked.

She flexed her right arm. Her bicep bulged slightly under sweater. "I've been working out."

"Unless your father's name is Ichabod, you don't look like a crane to me. And, that's what you'd need to lift this mass."

"Ha, ha. There you go again. But I'd like to pay tonight."

Presto would not be budged. "The answer is still no. I have money. I don't do this job for the stupendous pay, although the pension's not bad."

"Wow," gasped Ridgewood. "Me neither, meaning I don't work for the compensation. I do it for me." She stopped and looked at him with firm conviction. "By the way, is that a new sport jacket?"

"Uh, it's fairly new."

"It's nice."

"Thanks," Presto replied sheepishly.

The waiter conveniently returned with the bottle. With both glasses filled, Ridgewood prompted another toast. "To us. Looks like we have something in common then."

Presto could swear they were drinking from a different bottle. It certainly tasted better this time around. In fact, he felt better. He was no longer apprehensive. Here he was, joking with a living goddess. Now that he thought about it, she never looked as alluring as she did now.

She broke his reveries. "I'll tell you my story in a moment. I promise you it's asphyxiating, but tell me, where did your money come from? Inheritance, you invented some gadget they sell on TV, a jackpot at Vegas?"

Normally he found it difficult to discuss his father's negligent death. Tonight the grief was gone, and the words came easily. "Many years ago, I stuffed the most hot dogs down my throat in an international weenie eating contest held at Coney Island. The prize was big for the day, and Nathan's even signed me for an ad campaign for a few years. You might have seen me in a few magazine advertisements." He looked at her with a boyish grin.

Doubt crept into Ridgewood's face. "Are you back to your old bad jokes?"

Presto took an opportunity to take a swig of the wonderful sake before beaming. "Yeah. I waded into stupidity because my answer is not a joyous tale."

Presto recounted the events of his father's death. The sake and Ridgewood's attentive, compassionate eyes made it easier. When he finished, he stabbed at one of the few remaining portions.

"I'm almost sorry I asked," she said commiserating. "I say almost, because it means a lot that you shared that with me. It tells me a lot about who you are as a person. This is why you're a detective; it seems you were preordained for the job."

Presto nodded. "I treat every victim as if it was my father. Detectives are not supposed to take a case personally and remain detached. I try to feel like every victim, witness, and suspect in the case."

"That's why you're the best," Ridgewood saluted.

Presto's hands went up to ward off her praise. "I'm not." He relaxed. "It's your turn now. What's your story? A black widow that lures men into her web and poisons them while sucking away their assets?"

"Cold," she said with a fake shiver. Defrosted, she added, "I like how you deftly changed subjects. Self-Deprecating and hates praise. Interesting combo," she mused.

Presto squirmed, and she provided wiggle room. "Okay, before I tell you my story, let's finish the rest of this," she said and gestured toward the sushi. "Then we'll see about dessert."

My kind of girl. "Never a bad plan," Presto said. "They have excellent fried ice cream."

She smiled. "Then let's eat."

After they finished, they dropped the chopsticks, refilled their glasses, and drank in unison.

Ridgewood leaned back, but like a real-life optical illusion, her chest thrust forward. Presto quickly examined his hands before looking up at her face.

Ridgewood gritted her teeth, shrugged, and said, "I got married when I was twenty-three. Lance was his name," she said and wrinkled her nose like she scented a bad odor. "We met on a vacation in Cancun. Club Med, no less," she said with a reminiscent chuckle.

"I'd gone down with a few girlfriends. Up until that point, I'd never been anywhere outside a two hundred–mile radius of my hometown," she said with humble wonder. "And I'd just been accepted to the FBI and wanted my one and only hurrah before I joined the real world.

"I didn't have many boyfriends up until that point," she said to Presto's immense surprise. "I grew up on a farm, and there were not many boys my age, and definitely not many that I was interested in. Even if I was, my father made sure the opportunity did not exist. Honestly, I was focused on my studies. My parents did everything to make sure I could go to college, and I wanted to make them proud of their investment and sacrifice.

"So there I was enjoying my one day in the sun. The resort was basically a meat market, and I talked to more men in the first two days than I did in all of college. I met Lance, where else, at the bar. I had done these tequila poppers and was pretty drunk. Lance walked over to chat, but I was tired and told him I was calling it quits. He asked to walk me home, and I declined. Said, 'I'm a waste of your time, I don't put out.'"

Ridgewood giggled, as did Presto, who was thoroughly enjoying himself.

"You know what the bastard said?" Ridgewood asked rhetorically. "Honey, I'd rather leave this country with your number than sleep with anyone and everyone here. I think you're more beautiful than this tropical paradise and mysterious and sacred as the Mayan ruins I visited just this morning." She laughed again, this time harder.

"It went from walking me home to running my life. Lance was smart in his own way. He was five years older and worked in DC with a lobbyist firm. Since I was headed to that region for FBI training and I knew no one else, I figured it was worth giving him my number.

"Three years later, we married, and I thought my life was perfect. We had the posh house, his Porsche, and my Jaguar, and we wined and dined at the best places with some of the most influential people in the country. We both worked hard, and although my salary was a crumb next to his, we were living the American dream.

"Then, Lance started having affairs. Although he was an attorney and could spray shit like the manure machine my father used on the farm, he was a terrible liar."

She stopped to roll her eyes. "The scum blamed my career. Said I didn't need to work, and it was hurting our love life. I didn't want to quit the bureau but did so to save our marriage. I did everything I could to make him happy, but the signals emerged again: late nights at the office, dinners with clients, a sudden interest in hunting with the boys. One week I went back home to see my parents. There was news of a big storm coming, so I changed my flight home to a day earlier. I called home to let him know but got the machine and left a message."

Ridgewood grinned mischievously. "So I walk in, and instantly I hear something from the living room. I look. Hung from our vaulted ceiling is Lance. At first I go to scream, but then I realize he's naked."

She stopped and put her hand over her face, in what Presto figures must be sheer horror, until she erupts in a tipsy, snicker. "In front of him was a woman on a chair giving him a blow job and in back was a she-male sodomizing him from a table we bought antiquing in the Hamptons. There, watching it all, holding the rope that choked my husband suspended a few feet from the ground, was his best friend."

Her impish smile was gone. Presto sensed that despite the bravado, she was pained by the event. Sometimes humor is only discovered in hindsight.

"I left the room, then the house. I knew what was going on in there. Lance was always much more kinky than I, and I tried to please his wants, but I had my limits. One was … I can't believe I'm telling you this," she suddenly said.

"Uh, eh," stammered Presto

"Phew," Ridgewood breathed. "This sake had some punch."

Presto knew it. Her talk and booze had him tongue tied.

"Am I boring you or being too forward? I'm sorry."

Presto, who often dined alone, assured her. "Not at all, Lorraine."

Ridgewood gave an embarrassed look and continued. "Lance wanted me to strap it on, if you know what I mean. I was unnerved by the request and refused. So seeing my husband being fucked was somehow not much of a surprise. The noose around his neck was for erotic asphyxiation, where you deprive yourself of oxygen until climax. This apparently makes the effect more mind blowing; Lance tried to explain to me," she said and shivered. "The irony is I almost choked him when he told me about it."

Presto was stunned. This sounded like a tale from one of the television shows his mother watched while bedridden. "I'm sorry," he told her. "That must have been a terrible shock."

She was nonplussed. "Thanks. I'm behind that now. Lance didn't contest the divorce, and rather than air dirty laundry, I was offered a substantial settlement. Hush money. It's nice to have, but there's more than money.

"Like you, I wanted to work and rejoined the agency. So I did not come back for the money, but I will admit, I lost most of that hush money it in the stock market. Stupid Lance recommended Bernie Madoff to manage my money, and I lost everything," she said sadly.

She grabbed the sake and topped of their glasses. She put the empty bottle down. "What about you, Dom? You ever married?"

Presto tensed. "No."

"Smart—nothing wrong with being single. You're probably like me. Nice people get screwed in relationships. Look at poor Donavan's wife."

"Yeah."

"I guess living in a big city like this makes it easy being single. There are people everywhere. You must have no problem getting dates."

The only dates Presto enjoyed were palm dates, the fruit and his hand. "You have no idea," he said.

Ridgewood asked. "How about that fried ice cream you told me about?"

Presto was always more comfortable talking about food than himself. "You're going to love it."

And they did.

CHAPTER FORTY

Mʏᴛʜ Mᴀɴ ᴡᴀs ʙᴀᴄᴋ at the safe house. He'd already attended to his housemate, who now looked nothing like the former marine. Withered and gaunt, he reminded Myth Man of a wooden nutcracker soldier, with his blank stare, gaping mouth, and hanging, unkempt, hair.

The man started to develop bedsores. Myth Man had long tired of nursing him, but time was winding down. The game could not go on forever, and seeing Dominick Presto this morning was enough to sprint to the finish line. His goal of making it to Christmas appeared dim. Soon, very soon, he'd execute his grand finale.

After leaving his patsy, Myth Man decided to use the Internet. For fun, he picked a new screen name, The Deacon, and checked up on some of his old friends.

The Deacon: The end days are approaching, brothers and sisters.

Trumpet of God: Welcome to God's village, neighbor. New members are always welcome.

I'll dismember this member one day, Myth Man promised.

The Deacon: Thanks, brother. My mission here is from God. Since a child, I've been blessed with visions from our Savior. He told me Armageddon approaches. We've seen the storms, famine, wars, and the cultural debauchery. This Easter Sunday, a man of God will be crucified. It's the final sign. The Horses of the Apocalypse are ready to leave Hell's gate. Grab your Bibles. The time is near.

Trumpet of God: I'm ready, Deacon. I built me a bunker. It's fortified with food, guns, a gas generator, books …

The Deacon: *Signed Off*

How could someone he'd never met annoy him so much? Suddenly he felt tired. He got up and fell onto the Naugahyde couch. He knew he should head home, but he preferred to face his wife drunk or, better yet, asleep.

Then he fell asleep.

He dreamed.

The boy, who just celebrated his ninth birthday, watched his father and another man across the campfire. His father bowed his head and offered a prayer thanking God, asking for his forgiveness. The boy heard the other man snicker as he looked down at his meal, which included rainbow trout from the day's catch. Both men drank whiskey. It was the first time he'd seen his father drink.

They ate in relative silence. The boy was confused. He knew the other man, who was built like a farm tractor and whose face was permanently etched with a sly, leering stare, was no friend of his father.

He'd seen the guy show up at their home a few times, always at night, and each time his father was apprehensive. It was the only times he'd ever seen his father intimidated. His father always ushered the man away from the house where they talked in private.

One time, the boy climbed out his window and crawled through bushes to get close enough to listen. He did not hear the reason, but he knew the situation. His father owed some money—a lot. This man was sent to collect, and his father did not have enough to make the man happy. Rather, the man threatened his father. Said that if he wasn't paid in full the next time he came, other arrangements would be made.

The boy tried to find his father's eyes, but his old man stared at his food. The other man, however, stared through the cackling fire. At first, the boy was scared, but then the man smiled warmly and blew a kiss. His mother did the same thing when he left for school each morning. Maybe the stranger was a good man.

After dinner, the man said he knew a small cave a few minutes away that was loaded with Indian arrowheads. He suggested they take a few lanterns and investigate before tent time. The boy was eager, but his father declined, despite his son's urging.

When they arrived at the cave, the man led the way. The boy was disappointed when he realized that the cave was small, no bigger than his living room. He was hoping to find stalagmites and stalactites.

He began to wonder where the arrowheads might be, when the man stopped and steered him to the back corner. The boy figured that must be the spot. A sleeping bag was rolled up in the corner.

The man puts a hand on the boys shoulder and says, "Sometimes it's up to a boy to help pay a man's debts."

The sinister tone put a chill in the boy's bones. He hears a zipper pull down and feels something hard poke his upper back.

Myth Man woke up and looked at his watch. He'd slept for two hours, but felt hardly refreshed. Something was nagging at him. A memory popped up and winked at him. Despite his concentration, it flees, leaving a painful void.

As he moved to get up, he realized his midsection was saturated. *You sleep in it. You bathe in it.*

The rage was back. "God, if you do exist. I fucking despise you."

CHAPTER FORTY-ONE

Apartment door 9B opened. The sleeping giant seated against the hallway side of the door lost his back support, and his head slammed down against the panel wood floor within. *Bang*.

"Ouch," Presto moaned.

"What are you doing out here?" Cleo Presto asked her son as she stood over him. "I recognized your snoring."

At first Presto was too groggy, but then he remembered. Between an unsteady hand and a bad case of the *dropsies*, he was unable to get the key in the lock. He decided the doorstep was not such a bad place to take a nap. He needed sleep.

"Uh. I, um." For some reason, Presto felt like a drunken teenager, being questioned by his mother. Maybe she wouldn't notice. "I felt dehydrated and faint. I needed to sit down and must have fallen asleep."

She laughed then suddenly left him. He heard her steps bound away. As he tried to get up, he heard her return.

She pushed him back down. "This is hilarious," she chortled. She began snapping pictures of her son.

Presto realized what was going on and threw his arms in the path of the lens. This only made her laugh louder. "I'm sorry, Dominick, but this is priceless."

She snapped images of his ascent: hands that tried, and failed, to push off the floor, a reach for an imaginary support to gain leverage, a rollover and aborted push up. All the while, Presto groaned like a weightlifter exerting himself. Finally, he got to his feet.

He bounced back and forth against the brick hallway like a bowling ball without the gutters to correct his awkward aim before he crashed through an open frame and onto his bed.

When Presto opened his eyes at the sound of his alarm clock, he moaned and immediately massaged his temples. His mouth felt like he'd sucked on a bathroom hand dryer.

Parched, he tried to get up. His head howled in pain, as if his ascent brought altitude pressure. His bowels roared, and his face grimaced. His iron belly, forged to withstand the hottest of spices and an expansive culinary range, was severely wounded. Unconscionable.

For the first time in his career, he considered calling in sick but dismissed the thought as soon as it came into his head. For a myriad of reasons, he couldn't do that. When he got out of bed, he realized he'd slept in the prior night's clothes, including his new sport jacket.

When he emerged from the bathroom in a deep-blue cotton robe, he immediately smelled food. Like a bloodhound, he followed the trail to the source.

"Morning, sunshine," his mother said and peered at him. "How do you feel?"

Presto grunted something inaudible but was easily translated as, *like a giant pile of dung*. He fell into the kitchen chair and rested his head on his folded arms. He groaned again.

His mom brought over a plate of scrambled eggs, breakfast sausages, home fries, and toast. Presto eyed the plate. It looked as good as it smelled. He brought his head up, slowly. Almost a minute passed, and he still had not picked up the fork. This was unusual. In fact, it was a personal record.

His mother noticed. "That bad, huh? How much did you drink?"

"We drank two bottles of sake." The mere mention of sake had his stomach cartwheeling.

She sat at the table. "You'll be okay, a big guy like you."

Presto smiled weakly. "I suppose you can say I'm a heavyweight who's a lightweight."

"You were never a drinker, thank God." She paused to cross herself. "I can even out drink you."

He smiled, stronger. "We could market that as a televised event: battle of the sexes, ages, and weight classes. Might take off. I could see it being a cultural phenomenon." He grabbed the fork and twiddled it like it was a device he was not sure how to use.

She ignored the commentary and instead said, "I told you this woman was bad news. How much did she run the bill up to?"

"I paid, but that's not the point. She has her own money. We're alike; she works because she wants to make a difference." He recapped the story of Ridgewood finding her husband's kinky escapades, and their subsequent divorce settlement.

"Gold digger."

Presto sighed. "You're as terrible as I feel right now."

She looked at his plate. "Why don't you eat, and I'll tell you about Camille. I met her last night."

"My appetite is shaky enough." Presto groaned. He played with the eggs and then took a bite. No violent eruptions, yet. His mother, however, looked radiant, with an eager grin and excited eyes.

"She's exactly what you need. A challenge. She's pretty, smart, and witty. And you two are match. She's water; you're earth."

Pretso snorted, almost coughing out some eggs. "You don't believe in astrology, Mom."

"No, but she does to a certain degree."

Presto rolled his eyes. "She sounds well grounded."

"No, that's you," she retorted. "You're a Capricorn, which is earth, meaning you're well grounded. You're practical and disciplined."

"Does that mean she's not?" Presto began to forklift the food down his gullet. Food proved the panacea once again. His headache dissipated, and each mouthful salved the breech in his belly. Then he sipped some orange juice. *Much better.*

This time, Cleo Presto rolled her eyes. "No, goofball. Those are just your sign's characteristics. She's intuitive, artistic, and imaginative."

"Does that mean she's a know-it-all, moody, conceited space cadet?"

She ignored him. "Find out this Lorraine's birthday. I bet she's a fire sign. That means you would find her attractive, but it wouldn't work. Earth tries to smother fire and gets burned trying to ground their ardent nature."

Presto stopped eating. He couldn't believe he was listening to this. He pressed the back of his hand to her forehead.

"What are you doing?" she asked.

Presto gave a grave look. "I'm checking for a fever. Clearly, you must be ill."

She smacked his hand away. "You silly goose."

"You're the silly goose," he said with a chuckle.

"Then you're a silly swan."

Despite her age, there was a lot girl left in her. "You're too much."

"By the way, my sign is Cancer. How apropos is that?" She spoke without a trace of sorrow.

Presto's stomach suddenly seized. He tried to keep the moment lighthearted. That's what she wanted. "Fitting. I'm Capricorn. Does that mean as I ram I like to lock horns with hard heads like you?"

"Now stop being naughty," she reprimanded in jest. "All I'm saying is listen to Camille. She's very convincing."

"Really," Presto deadpanned. "So were Hitler, Manson, and that refrigerator mechanic con artist who tried to rape us."

She sniffed away his comments. "You can't help it; you're Capricorn. That's the skeptic in you, but you need a water person to lubricate your crusty, parched earth persona."

Presto almost coughed out a mouthful, as he garbled something. He took a drink to unclog the pipes. "Don't see Camille again. Next time she'll serve cyanide-spiked Kool-Aid."

"In your condition, it seems the poison girl was the black widow from last night, who spun you with her charms."

Presto gave up. "You win. I'll take out Camille tomorrow night. I'm exhausted. The only thing I'm doing after work is stopping at the pet store to get a mouse for Aphrodite."

His mother now looked like the one who just ate a king-sized breakfast, fat with satisfaction. "Trust me. You'll like her."

"Whatever you say."

"And find out this Lorraine's birthday. If she's a fire sign, I get to pick the next five movies we rent."

Presto tilted his head and waved. "With your taste in flicks, if you were right, I'd be forced to lie."

CHAPTER FORTY-TWO

Danko pressed a button and terminated the unscheduled conference call with city hall. "Ha," he shouted with a diabolical grin.

Agent Donavan gnashed his teeth, barked twice, and howled. "*Rrrrr*. We ate em' alive." He jumped up and high-fived Danko.

Presto and Ridgewood looked at this newfound camaraderie in shock.

Presto recalled the cartoon *Tom & Jerry*, where after years of battling, the cat and mouse became friends. Pretso never liked the show thereafter; it became pointless.

"That might have hurt my career, but I don't care." Danko spoke as much to himself as he did to the room.

Presto had been the last to arrive at Danko's office. Ridgewood cast him a knowing look. They were to brief Commissioner Tipton and Spencer Hoole, representing the mayor's office. Immediately, he noticed that Danko was neither nervous nor tense. In fact, he seemed to relish the encounter. Presto soon learned why.

When the phone rang, and before Danko picked up, Donavan said, "Remember. If they give you a hard time, I'll take care of it."

Frank Danko played the straight man, Carter Donavan the clown. On the other end of the line, Tipton was assertive but diplomatic. Hoole was the hard ass.

Danko and Ridgewood briefed them. Ridgewood credited Presto when she outlined their strategies. Presto was surprised both because he was rarely credited and more so that she had found the time, after their binge, to have thoroughly read his notes.

As soon as Hoole went on the attack, Donavan shrieked so loud and long that everyone but the screamer muffed their ears. He then stomped his foot and yelled, "Got you, sucker." He then apologized and claimed credit for the disposal of a cockroach.

When a ruffled Hoole tried to readdress himself, Donavan interrupted. "It's a bad connection. You're coming through all *mumbly*. Can you speak up?"

Ridgewood looked aghast but not Danko. Now he was amused by Donavan's antics, but then again, he had no love for Hoole.

When Hoole reassumed, Donavan prodded him, "Louder." Hoole raised his voice, but Donavan coaxed him again to speak up. Hoole was practically shouting when Donavan interrupted. "Let me play with this thing a second." He actually walked over to phone and jiggled the cord. "Try again." Hoole went to speak and Donavan shouted. "Hold on." Again, he toyed with the cord. "Sorry, but you'll have to be real loud. We got bad acoustics over here." Donavan poorly stifled a snicker.

Hoole began to shout. He tied the mayor's re-election to the case. Donavan interrupted yet again. "With all due respect, Mr. Tool, I …"

"The name's Hoole," the phone roared.

"What did he say?" Donavan rhetorically asked the room. Into the phone he said, "Hard to hear you. Did you say, Stool?"

Hoole lost his cool and cursed. "Hoole," he screamed.

Donavan enjoyed playing the badger against this attack dog. All snarl. No bite. "Fool, Drool, Cesspool, whatever your name is. The point I wanted to make is everyone knows the Feds are in charge of this case. If anyone thinks the mayor's campaign will falter on this issue, then either your boss is a lame duck or all the quacking I'm hearing is from a guy whose doing a fowl, think homonym, job."

Danko put his hand over his mouth to suppress laughter. Not Donavan. He laughed hard into the phone.

Hoole tried to speak, but Donavan stopped him. "If you ask me, your mayor seems stiff. He needs a makeover, some trendier clothes. He needs to mingle. Get some PR with him on the subway; jogging in central park, and knocking a beer back somewhere. I'm not talking Tavern on the Green. No, some dive bar with a pool table, and a young, but still voter-eligible crowd. He's missing the metrosexual look altogether. Instead he looks asexual. Get some photos of him dancing with a hot chick. The young people will love it. The older men will be envious, and the older women will think it's cute. Being dangerous always excites women. Then trot out his adoring wife. His poll numbers will soar." He briefly paused. "Hope you were taking notes."

From the phone's speakers a muffled commotion was heard, followed by Tipton's voice. The commissioner tried to clear the obstacle discourse. After a few words, he let a more subdued Hoole back in the dialogue.

Donavan peered closely at the phone and then pulled out his cell. He dialed a number, and the auxiliary line on Danko's phone rang. "Hold on a moment," Donavan warned. "Phone's ringing, and this call might *actually* be important." He then pressed a button and put Hoole and Tipton on mute.

Donavan put his cell phone on Danko's desk and preened himself. "The art of war. Fluster thy enemy. They don't want an update, but a chance for that winy, political hack to fire a few salvos at hard working, decent law enforcement officials. Let them stew a bit."

Ridgewood finally said something. "Donavan, I think you made your point. Enough."

He smiled at her. "You got it, partner." He closed his cell and pressed the mute button again. "We're back," he sang. "Would you believe it? That was the killer on the other line. He wanted to tell us he was most thankful that a bunch of nitwits in city hall fell for his gambit in incriminating Dominick Presto. He claimed he wanted to send a thank you card. We provided Spencer Mule's name and address."

"Fuck you," hissed Hoole. "Let me speak to Danko."

Donavan grinned. Now he had Hoole unhinged. "Holy James Watson, Mr. Graham Bell. He can hear you."

"I want you to stop talking," Hoole screeched.

Donavan pushed aside a reproachful glare from Ridgewood, put one finger in the air, and then responded to Hoole. "Is it permissible if I hum, yodel, or whistle?"

The banter continued for another five minutes before a completely exasperated Hoole screamed like he'd been electrocuted, and then there was only a dial tone.

After Danko and Donavan commemorated their newfound chumminess with their high handclasp, the team prepared for a day of fieldwork. Once again, they decided to split up. The synergies worked.

No more meetings. It was time for good old-fashioned detective work—investigate and interrogate.

CHAPTER FORTY-THREE

MYTH MAN ANGRILY TERMINATED the call with his contact. *Damn, Dominick Presto.*

Fear he had not felt since a child swelled along with his bladder. He ran to the toilet. Relieved, only in the gastronomical sense, he returned from the restroom and tried to plan for the information his contact had relayed.

Presto put together a list of names that he deemed people of interest. "Your name's on the list," the contact stuttered.

This meant the jig was up, after only three religious murders. There were so many more he wanted to get to. *Shame*, Myth Man thought. That meant his contact's time was almost over too. He'd been useful but, like the dummy he'd drugged back in the safe house, instrumentally expendable.

Myth Man, however, was not as saddened as expected that the spree was coming to a close. Inside news involving some mysterious Iraqi crate coming to New York under the auspices of the Lubavitchers piqued his interest.

He was pleased with his new plan. If he could pull it off, he'd be a legend. Son of Sam would be his junior forever.

CHAPTER FORTY-FOUR

"THIS IS SOME PIZZA," Ridgewood mumbled as she swallowed a bite and dabbed her lips with a napkin. She cleared her throat and added. "The only pizza I knew as a youth was the frozen kind. I should add that the nearest supermarket was an hour drive. The sushi, the steakhouses, the pizza, the variety is so good in New York."

Presto had already gorged a slice of meatball and patted his girth like the prior evening. "As you can see, I wholeheartedly agree."

She laughed this time. "If we don't catch this guy soon, and I stay in New York much longer, I'll need a new wardrobe." Then she added. "What do you make of the people we met thus far? Not much?"

Presto agreed. "No, but each suspect crossed off narrows the list. I figure the city has a population of about 8 million. Let's just say half of those are men, and another half are between the ages of thirty to sixty; that's 2 million people. We just whacked three off that number."

"I like your optimism," Ridgewood said and took another bite.

Their first stop had been at an affluent Tudor home in Jamaica Estates. The home was owned by Jacob Barnaby, a multimillionaire in his late thirties who never worked a day in his life. His parents both came from wealth, and his father invested and increased the family fortune through bribes to politicians, zoning board representatives, and various contractors, which made him one of the top real estate barons in New York City. Later, he expanded his reach to the Hamptons.

His parents met an untimely death on the night of the Fourth of July when their yacht blew up in the Long Island Sound. Initially, it was assumed that the Barnabys' boat must have caught fire due to fireworks that they assuredly had aboard.

The yacht was raised. Investigators determined a large explosive, not sparklers and bottle rockets, had sunk the boat. While Denton Barnaby had his enemies, the one who most prospered was his son, Jacob, who inherited in total assets and life insurance $80 million dollars. Jacob had an alibi, and nothing to incriminate him surfaced.

Jacob Barnaby had the same ruthless traits of his father but a different philosophy. The son saw his father as driven by greed, a delusional empire maker. Jacob thought differently and rebelled not against the spirit of capitalism but rather the excesses. A corporate hegemony controlled the world, and the masses were distracted with meaningless issues, entertainment, and religion. While the masses bowed to a likely fictional god, money and power was the religion of the elite.

Jacob aired his views in cable advertisements and a small manifesto he self-published. His vision resonated like a new religion. His followers, called Jacobites, bussed and flew to gatherings of world leaders and formed choreographed protests that made them sound reasonable and appealing rather than the typical brand of anticorporate rabble-rousers.

While Presto was doubtful that Jacob Barnaby was the serial killer (his face was too well known), it was possible he was giving the orders or had an overzealous member taking matters into their own hands. The group fit his profile.

They rang his door's buzzer at 10:00 am. Jacob answered the door naked except for tight, black briefs and a bottle of Dom Perignon. His full, dark, shoulder-length hair and bushy mustache reminded Presto of The Beatles, circa *Sergeant Pepper's*. Presto's fine nose also detected stale traces of marijuana and fresher sex. Neither scent was based from his personal experience.

Ridgewood and Presto flashed their respective badges and asked for a moment of his time. He seemed too pleased to see them. Barnaby turned and whistled. "Get decent. The Law's here," he warned. "Follow me."

The next thing Presto noticed about Barnaby was the tattoo that canvassed his pale back. Depicted, with some liberty, was the White House. A large for sale sign was planted in front of what should have been the rose garden but instead was a vacant strip mall. The trees were replaced with smokestacks and oil rigs. The White House was, in fact, no longer white. Instead, the portico, columns, and walls were splashed with identifiable corporate advertising logos.

They arrived in a long rectangular room that was once probably a living room but now looked like a hippie lecture hall. A group of recliners, couches, and beanbag chairs faced a lectern. The other side of the room had a stocked bar, and a light rig hung from the ceiling over a checkered dance floor. Two young women, both blonde and nearly identical, were sprawled on the couch.

Presto and Ridgewood were introduced to Amber and Desire, whose definition of decent was the cover of red velvet sheets. Ridgewood asked for privacy, but Barnaby refused. If they wanted his cooperation without an attorney (excluding himself) present, the girls would stay.

After a few minutes, it was apparent that what Barnaby really wanted was an audience. He might as well have stood at the lectern. No, he knew nothing about the murders. No member of his tribe would do such a thing; the Jacobites' doctrine preaches nonviolence. Then he went on a tear.

He praised Ridgewood and Presto for the commitment to justice and honest work. They were misguided in task, he explained. While finding a ruthless killer is noble and necessary, the real killers and crooks are left to pilfer, exploit, and kill with all their tactical means: advertising, slave labor, tax write-offs, bribes, lobbyist, offshore havens, and price gouging.

When he briefly turned his back, Ridgewood stepped on Presto's foot as a cue to leave, but escape was not easy. He never paused or offered an opportunity to interject. At one point, he walked directly in front of the seated Ridgewood. She consciously kept her eyes on his face, even when he slowly gyrated his hips and ran his hand, slowly, around his package.

Barnaby's antic's excited his two companions who went from snuggling to saliva swapping. Both of their tongues were pierced, which elicited an odd clinking sound. Ridgewood's foot found Presto's toes, this time with more inertia. He felt the import of her innuendo and Italian leather flats.

Presto pulled Ridgewood to her feet and announced they were through. Barnaby protested, but they escaped.

Next on the loony list was a Flushing townhouse owned by Keith Highland; at least that was his stated name on his birth certificate. Now he only answered to the name Andromeda. His story was that he'd not been abducted but rather chosen by an advanced race of extraterrestrials to deliver a critical message.

Half human, half insects warned him that the world would face an apocalyptic fate by 2015 unless man changed. We're under an intergalactic microscope, he warned. If the human race does not get its act together, there would be a cleansing, and a DNA modified breed of humans would start over, back in the Stone Age.

One cure Andromeda prescribed was abolishing all religious faiths, which were all fostered to confuse and separate us in the vein of the Tower of Babel. He advocated that because he had the answers, the world could unify behind his revelations.

Presto was sure he'd heard Andromeda's reasoning somewhere before.

Presto almost believed Andromeda's extraterrestrial claims when the front door opened. Standing there was a short, frail man, who after closer inspection did not posses any hair. His head was bald, and his eyebrows and eyelashes were gone. He also wore a snug, metallic-colored body suit.

As soon as Andromeda saw Ridgewood, he glowed like a firefly. "A fellow chosen one," he announced as he ushered them inside his residence.

"You must be mistaken," Ridgewood assured.

"Hardly," he reassured. "That divot in your upper cheek is a scoop mark."

As far as the religious murders, Andromeda had nothing to hide. He'd voluntarily take a lie detector test and go under hypnosis if Agent Ridgewood would do the same for her abduction experiences.

When they left, Ridgewood remarked, "Men are from Mars; women from Venus. Andromeda's so far out there, he's not in our solar system."

The last stop on their misguided tour was the Redemption Tabernacle of Corona. They were there to see Reverend Maximilian Trotter. Reverend Trotter was a controversial figure in New York.

First, while the tabernacle may have been a house of worship and Trotter a self-proclaimed reverend, he was best known for his dire fundamentalist preaching. Trotter also had a record. He served time for interstate gun trafficking.

His basic tenet was that America was at a crossroads, facing a battle for the soul of the nation. America could embrace the Lord and return her heart to Christ as our nation was intended, or we could side with the devil. The ancient trickster was winning and grinning. The scales tipped in his favor and were close to the breaking point. Mankind has ignored God's warnings, thus famine, war, disease, and *un*natural disasters abounded.

Trotter's utopian vision of America was similar to a coast-to-coast version of the Quakers. There would be no mindless forms of lewd and violent entertainment. Bars, brothels, and our thirst for materialism would be no more. Any sect of Christianity not subscribing to this mission was complicit and committed treason against the almighty. First, America needed to defeat her enemies within and then abroad.

Time with Trotter was short. Defensive and abrasive, he did not take questions well, especially when Ridgewood asked how much income he garnered from his newsletters, books, and DVDs that he hawked on his Web site and local cable stations. He was an agent of God. How dare they? His mission required money, and God wanted him to complete his task.

The reverend called her a wicked Jezebel, and they were shown the door.

Presto was aghast as he watched Ridgewood absorb liquid off her pizza with a napkin. She'd wasted all the tasty juices.

"You know," she said, "all this grease makes me think of the oily characters we met today. I wonder if Donavan and Danko had any luck."

They had divided the list by city county, and Danko and Donavan were in the Bronx. The best guess was the killer lived in the city, although with the time gap between murders, Presto conceded he could hail from Hong Kong.

Something occurred to Ridgewood. "Oh, I have to remember to call Malcolm. He left a message on my personal cell phone, not the government-issued one, while we were at dinner last night. I had it off, as I think it's rude to take calls while eating out." She sipped at her Diet Pepsi.

"Malcolm called just to check in, see if he could help in any way. He's been preoccupied with some top-secret project. It's fascinating. Did he mention what he's been up to?"

Presto figured it had to do with the find in Iraq. Bailey had a lot to drink that night and probably said things he shouldn't of. Presto chose to play ignorant. Bailey had come to his rescue. "He mentioned his work focused on religion, but that was about it."

Her eyes turned downcast. "Sorry, then I shouldn't really say anything. I want to report back to him when we're through for the day."

Pretso nodded.

"Speaking of which," grinned Ridgewood, "which whacko is next?"

Presto gulped his fountain soda, which he preferred from the conventional can or bottle. "The next guy comes without a congregation: Terrence McNally. If you scan his name in Lexus/Nexis, you'll find quite a few links. He's originally from the Boston area. McNally's name came up in the murder of a priest when investigators found a letter from McNally that accused the priest of molesting him thirty years prior amongst the deceased priest's possessions.

"There was nothing to make the charges stick. However, I cued on him for a few reasons. The priest had been killed with Ricin, another powerful toxin like we have with our case." Presto paused to lift his dangling sport jacket cuff from a grease pool.

"After a divorce, McNally moved to Queens. He's employed as an actor, does off, off-Broadway. I watched him," Presto reflected. "He's adept with disguise. One minute he's a crotchety elderly, and the next he's a very passable middle-aged female."

As Presto spoke, he was conscious that Ridgewood truly listened to him. She never looked away. He spoke freely, without trepidation. He wanted to catch the killer today, but he'd lament the loss of her partnership.

Presto continued, "McNally made the news a few years back when he wrote and directed an off-Broadway play. The story had a bunch of religious leaders—priests, rabbis, clerics, etc.—in a variety of different skits. In one, they embraced religious unity while they simulated a locker room orgy. In another, they decided to let God decide which religion was supreme. They played a game of Russian roulette to determine the winner. There was none. Each night it came down to two contestants. When the guy shots himself, the bullet went through his brain and killed the finalist beside him."

159

Ridgewood grimaced. "I am not the most religious person in the world, but that's evil."

"The play got bashed from all the religious groups, but as is the norm, the bad press made the play a hit. And as the dollars rolled in, McNally was interviewed quite a bit. If you read those interviews, you see a man who is not just poking fun at religion or even sees his work as art but rather someone who harbors hatred toward these very institutions."

Presto sighed. "I thought he was worth checking out."

CHAPTER FORTY-FIVE

Reunited in Danko's office, Ridgewood summarized their day. "We then met Terrence McNally. His background looked promising on paper, but he had an airtight alibi. He was in Europe for six weeks internationalizing his play when the Ash Wednesday and Maha Shivaratri murders occurred."

"Oh well," Donavan sang. "Tell us again about the underwear guy with the two kissing babes. Hell, we didn't get anything titillating like that in the Bronx. Should have known better being a Red Sox fan."

Presto slumped. He felt guilty that his list had been such a failure. "Sorry this didn't work out. The last thing I want to do is waste our time."

"Nonsense," declared Ridgewood. "You put a lot of thought into that list."

"Yeah, buddy," agreed Donavan. "How were you to know that Toby Conklin was seven feet tall from his rambling piece you found in the Letters to the Editors section?" He gave Presto a toothy grin.

Danko agreed. "No need to apologize, Dom. It felt good to get off my ass, and get out on the streets again. In theory, everyone we met made sense, and we've yet to exhaust the list. My detectives have been combing the streets for months and have nothing to show for it." He stopped to shrug. "We need this guy to make a big mistake."

CHAPTER FORTY-SIX

"WHAT TIME IS CAMILLE coming down?" Presto inquired. He lay on the couch with his dirty sock–covered feet hung over the armrest.

His mother, who had sat quietly at the kitchen table at work on a newspaper puzzle, stomped her foot enough to get her son's head to resist gravity. "No sir, Buster. That's not the way a date works."

Amused, and in agreement, he answered, "Mom, you're old-fashioned. That's not the way it works anymore. Feminism's changed since the Annie Oakley and Susan B. Anthony era."

"I should give you a good slap on the behind. I'm not that old, and I know better. When I was injured, I watched all those daytime smut shows. I'm aware things are different, but it does not make them better or proper. Call her and invite her out. Then pick her up."

Horizontal, Presto snorted "Mom, you're so melodramatic. *Pick her up*," he imitated. "The days of hot rods and drive by burger joints are long gone. The Stagnuts live downstairs."

"Oh, the good ole days," she swooned. "Camille is lovely. She's fun; you're going to have a great time."

"Look at me. I'm pumped." He closed his eyes and snored.

CHAPTER FORTY-SEVEN

Presto's first impressions of Camille were favorable. First, she spared him the visit and suggested they meet in the building lobby. When he arrived on time, she was already there. *A punctual woman?*

She carried an easy look. She wore a simple cream cotton knitted sweater, aged blue jeans, and tan, worn loafers. Her dark, wavy hair was cut above her shoulders in a casual bob. She was a few inches shy of six feet, and her frame was curvy, but in a jock sort of way. Her jaw was strong, purposeful. She looked healthy.

Camille reminded him somewhat of Sigourney Weaver, when she had played Dian Fossey in *Gorillas in the Mist.*

"So where are we going?" Camille asked.

"Albano's. The food is wonderful."

She winked. "How can it beat my aunt's home-cooked Italian meals?" Camille said and laughed.

When they arrived, the owner personally led them to a table next to a small indoor water garden. With passionate detail, the owner described the night's specials.

"I like your mom," Camille said. "She's funny."

A concerto misted the room with soft tones that blended with the warm, homespun décor.

Presto sighed with a twinkle in his eyes. "Please don't tell her that," he begged.

The appetizers had arrived, prosciutto melon and carpaccio. Presto was pleased Camille had not suggested an alcoholic beverage.

"So, what's it like being a detective? You must get a great deal of satisfaction solving a case."

"I do," he said modestly. "Usually it's routine and boring, but then you have your glamour cases. I like to figure things out. Maybe that's from my mom. She's a puzzle freak."

"I heard about this case you're working on when I was in California."

Presto breathed. "Yeah, this one's a stickler, mainly due to the notoriety of it. The reality of it is, there have been only three murders thus far."

Camille dunked bread in olive oil, not all that concerned when some drops hit the tablecloth. For once, Presto thought, the other side of the table was as messy as his.

"Yeah, but when you mess with people's religions, you're playing with brimstone and fire."

Presto agreed. "We've already seen that acted out in the streets. Hate crimes spiked, but fortunately, that's subsided."

The waiter arrived and cleared the appetizer plates and presented their main courses.

"What brings you to New York?" Presto wondered.

"Ultimately, a job prospect, but the impetus is change. I've never lived a stagnant life. I guess you can say I'm impulsive. I get an idea, an interest that I become passionate about, and I yearn to learn, live, and master it."

"Tell me; I'd love to hear." After Presto said that, it occurred to him that he truly was interested in Camille's life. She was different in many ways than Ridgewood, but like the FBI agent, she did not look away from him. How could this be possible that after a life without women, he was on successive dates?

"You sure?" Camille asked.

"Yes," Presto assured. "How'd you end up in California? I heard you were originally from New York."

Camille swallowed a bite of her risotto. Her face lit up the dim setting. "I went to college at the University of San Diego. I was a good student, but I spent much of my time playing beach volleyball. A tour promoter scouted me, but I wanted to make my parents proud by using my college degree for something. So I was torn"

She bit her lip and gulped. "That's when tragedy struck. My parents were killed. It was an electrical fire. They'd been asleep, which, I suppose, was a small blessing."

"I'm sorry," offered Presto empathetically. He thought of his own father and why his mother had not mentioned this.

She thanked him. "When I was slapped with how finite life is, it changed me. I decided to pursue every dream and whim possible. It started with professional beach volleyball. I made good money and appeared on ESPN2 a few times. I only wish my folks were around to see that," she said with tainted pride.

After a pause, she cast a girlish smile. "While in Hawaii for a tournament, I met Bugz, the bassist from that band Rebellious Ruffians. He was vacationing there but looking to buy property."

Camille read Presto's blank look. "Rebellious? You never heard of them?"

Presto was not used to topics he had no knowledge of. He shrugged. "Sorry."

"They were a punk band from LA. They were real big in the late nineties."

"Oh."

"Well, we hit it off, and I moved to Los Angeles and eventually in with him."

Presto smirked, and with a dopey accent, remarked, "Sounds like a bug out."

Her hands were spaced in front of her as she replied, "More than you know," and then curled her right hand up implicitly. "It was fun for a while— the touring, the wild parties, the drinking, and yes, sorry, Mr. Policeman, the sex and the drugs."

Presto threw his hand to his head in mock shock. "You really do learn something new every day. So what happened with Bugsy?"

She laughed. "He was fun, but after awhile, it was too much. I went from the pinnacle of health to post-teenage wasteland. Also, I was no longer living my dreams but Bugsy's," she said and flashed a pouty smile.

"I always wanted to write, so I broke up with Bugz and moved to San Francisco. Prior to that, when I was with Bugz, I met a lot of various people in the entertainment industry. Directors, actors, agents, screenwriters, and others. The contacts helped, and I was able to get published."

Presto loved to read, and the notion of writing a book had occurred to him. Surprisingly, he did not want to try his hand with mysteries or anything to do with police work. Besides a cook book, he fancied the idea of doing an Arthurian book that focused more on the once and future king's early mystical life.

An appreciative Presto asked, "You've written a book?"

"Yes. Eight, actually."

Presto gazed down at his plate. Food was still there. He hated to admit it, but not even Ridgewood had slowed his consumption rate to this point. Camille was combustible energy in the dark, seductive setting.

"What sort of books do you write?"

"I've changed, but I started with fiction."

Inquisitive, "Wow, tell me what you wrote about."

She giggled. "In the beginning, sex mostly."

Presto's mouth dropped. "My, my, my," he gasped.

"Hey, it sells," she attested. "At first, I wrote about what I know, the L.A. music scene. It was written through the eyes of a starstruck groupie. Through my contacts, it got some press, and it did reasonably well."

"What was it called *Memoirs of a Groupie*?"

She grinned. "No, but not a bad hindsight title. *Angel in Hell*—looking back it's sophomoric, but I'm still proud of it.

"I'll be online tomorrow looking for a first edition. I want it signed," he demanded playfully. "I gather you write nonfiction now." He raised his eyebrows tacitly.

"While in San Francisco, I really changed. I ate healthy, jogged, hiked, swam, and even played volleyball again. With my body and my mind finally clean, I began to look at things existentially. I began to notice that the environment around me was ill. I wanted to nurse Mother Nature and became involved in environmental causes. Not just rally's and rhetoric, mind you," she cautioned.

Camille's head bopped, and her chemical-free hair bounced. "I toured the arctic, dived oceans and lakes, climbed mountains, and stayed out at sea for weeks on end. I learned there is no place that's sacred. Man's fingerprints are everywhere.

"Motivated, I went back to school, earned two more degrees, and through a friend, got a job at the San Diego Zoo as herpetologist."

Presto beamed. Camille was different. His comparison to Dian Fossey had not been that far off.

"A herpetologist? Like you're a doctor for herpes?" Presto played dumb. He knew a bit about herpetology himself.

Through a twisted grin, she said, "No. It's …"

Presto cut her off. "I know. I was kidding. I own a snake."

This seemed to excite Camille. She leaned closer, and Presto was able to smell nothing but pure human, not a hint of artificial fragrance.

"What kind?" she asked. "I own a few myself."

"She's a Sinaloan milk snake. She's beautiful. I named her Aphrodite."

"Aw," Camille moaned maternally. "That's so cute, a big man like you with an inchworm for a snake."

Presto pretended to look offended. "Hey."

Still close, she grabbed his hand. "I'm teasing. I love *Lampropeltis triangulum sinaloae*. I have an albino Nelson's milk snake, which is similar. In addition, I have a blood python, a sand boa, and a Gaboon viper."

"Wow," Presto said. "I believe the Gaboon packs the longest fangs of any poisonous snake. Its venom is also extremely toxic."

Camille let a light whistle escape through her teeth. "Very dangerous but generally docile. Mine has a nice, crusted horn formation above the nostrils." She put her two pointer fingers on either side of her nose and narrowed her eyes. She hissed and snapped her head forward.

Startled, Presto jerked backward. They both laughed.

They finished their meal while Camille completed the chain of events that brought her to New York. The Bronx Zoo herpetologist had just passed away. The venom that killed him was not from one of the many poisonous creatures he cared for but rather a bee sting.

With Camille's credentials from the San Diego Zoo and the praise she garnished from her recent books, the position was hers if she wanted it.

Presto insisted they order pastries for desert. Albano's had some of the best tiramisu in the city.

The conversation turned back to the case.

"Are you religious, Dom?"

Presto had considered that question recently. The world did sometimes seem godless. There was so much pain and hate. Religion offered answers but not solutions; however, Presto still held faith. There had to be a purpose, a higher calling. "I am not a regular, but I choose to believe. What about you?"

For the first time, Camille was not instantaneous in reply. Her pause ignited an answer. "I believe in everything and nothing. I believe that there is a higher power but do not believe in any one religion. I believe in the soul but not its fate in heaven or hell. I believe in astrology but feel that men and women decide their own fates. I believe in science but do not uniformly equate it with progress and believe it can equate with an intelligent design. I believe the government is corrupt and lies and yet believe there are honest civil servants with noble aims. I can believe in paranormal stuff like aliens and ghosts but think that most of the reported sightings and experiences are the works of imagination and greed. I believe in some conspiracy theories but think most conspiracy theorists are nuts. And I believe in love but also believe it will always elude my discovery."

She finished with a calm energy and added, "Then again, I may be crazy. Look," she exclaimed and reached into her breast pocket. Her hand withdrew and opened with three dark, polished rocks. "Healing stones," she announced with a sheepish shrug.

Pesto exhaled. "Crazy is right, woman. You sure you didn't pull them rocks from your head?"

Camille threw her napkin at him. "You scoundrel."

He handed the napkin back. "Okay, Camille the Clairvoyant. What about Elvis? Dead or alive."

A snippet of air escaped her lips as her eyes fluttered. "He's clinically dead, of course, but his work makes him immortal," she moaned in her fake trance.

"Very good, genie. J.F.K., lone gunman or something more sinister?"

Camille snapped out from her ruse. "Now that you mention it, what about that? You're supposed to be the detective. Try and explain this to me. How could ..."

CHAPTER FORTY-EIGHT

"Thats some storm," Cleo Presto told her son as she gazed out a window that pattered a fast beat from the pounding rain. "I pulled out your rain gear, boots, and poncho."

"Thanks, Mom."

She was pleased when he recapped his night with Camille. She became ecstatic when he said they made another plan. Presto honestly looked forward to it. Camille planned a behind-the-scenes tour of the Bronx Zoo.

It was not until Presto left the building that the ferocity was realized. It was impossible to manage an umbrella in the whipping wind. The streets were flooded. An empty Styrofoam coffee cup floated by, hugging the curb. It reminded Presto of a ship traveling the coast looking for beachhead. It also reminded him of Camille. He picked it up and dropped it in the corner garbage can.

Maybe God smiled on his good deed. He spotted an empty cab. Once inside, Presto hoped the visibility was better from the front seat. He was barely able to see past the hood.

He arrived at the precinct in one piece and lumbered as fast as he could to the entrance.

Danko waived him into his office. Dripping, he took off his poncho and put it on the floor where a small puddle formed.

When he finally looked at Danko, he noted that he looked as bad as the weather. A box of tissues sat beside him.

"Sick," he declared. "Just came on."

After Ridgewood and Donavan arrived, they all cursed the weather boisterously. It didn't take long for them to agree to cancel any notions of fieldwork. The decision was not unanimous, with the one female dissenting. She let them know what she thought of their manhood until she relented when Danko, after several honks, tossed the empty tissue box in the garbage.

The rest of the day they looked over the other investigator's notes and calls from the tip line. They added six more names to their list. Despite the setback, they left feeling something had been accomplished.

The next day was a mirror image of the day prior—terrible weather, but no new names were added, and nerves became frayed.

Ridgewood and Donavan started to spat. He was a man of action not research. Ridgewood reminded him that he *wussed* out due to, a *bit of rain*.

Danko interceded with a hoarse and stuffy apology. Presto remained quiet out of guilt. He felt like he let Ridgewood down. But unlike Donavan, Presto was not a man of action, and he did his best work sitting around.

Their takeout order arrived late (which was okay) and cold (which was not). Glumly, he ate his cheeseburger and soggy fries. He reasoned it was a good thing he was on the right side of the law. The thought of a prison menu diet was enough to keep him clean.

He did make his appetite up at dinner that night with Camille at Buddha's Bistro. She had mentioned that on the West Coast she found the Japanese food to be excellent but not the same with Chinese. With the inclement weather, Buddha's proximity made it a wise choice.

The day spent with Agent Ridgewood and the night with Camille. Presto never had it so good. His upbeat demeanor was noticed. He'd been asked several times why he was smiling. Donavan even questioned him. "Did you get laid last night, bro?"

When he woke up Thursday morning, Presto heard his cell phone beep from a missed call. He checked the message. There were two.

The first was Ridgewood. She was angry and apologetic. Malcolm had called them back to Washington. Malcolm's other assignment was a sudden priority. They'd return on Saturday.

The next call had been Danko, who reiterated Ridgewood's message, although he sounded much happier for the reprieve. He could use a day or two in bed, he nasally explained.

Presto used his time off well. He visited his own precinct and had lunch with Jack Burton. He missed his friend, and they made plans, without Mrs. Burton's consent, to enjoy her home cooking in a few weeks. He wished his boss a happy Easter, which rolled out of his mouth awkwardly. Until this killer was caught, the holidays were tainted.

The respite also allowed more time for Camille. They went to a pool hall where Camille hustled him five straight matches. They shopped, toured museums, visited art galleries, and then went to the Bronx Zoo.

"*Macroclemys temmincki*, or the Alligator Snapping Turtle," explained Camille as they stood in front of a large glass tank within the Reptile House.

The one hundred and twenty pound, prehistoric-looking reptile faced them from within her tank. Her mouth hung fully open and looked capable of engulfing Presto's beefy arm. On the tip of her tongue, a wormlike appendage swayed in the water. Camille explained, although Presto already knew but remained quiet, that the tongue ribbon was used to tempt fish and other prey near its mouth.

"Bertha, she's affectionately called. She's over sixty years old. She was rescued ten years ago from a Texas ranch. There was a betting ring where they pitted different animals against each other—dogs, boar, pythons, bobcats—you get the picture," she said with a sorrowful sigh.

Presto was so happy he could have jumped in the aquarium with Bertha and hugged her. For the first time in a month, his mind was not preoccupied with the case. They had already been at the zoo for six hours, but the last two had been in the Reptile House. Surrounded by cold-blooded reptiles, Presto's heart was simmering.

They arrived at the green anaconda exhibit. There were two snakes resting just outside a water basin. The larger of the two was twenty-five feet and thick as a maple tree; the other was about half the size. Once again, Presto knew, but he played dumb. He liked when she talked. There was a lot of girl left in this woman.

"What's up with these two?" Presto inquired. "Is that the mother and her baby?"

Camille giggled. "Funny you should say that. That's what most people assume. Actually, both snakes are the same age. The larger one is the female, which is usually the case with reptiles."

Presto looked at her sideways. "They're like the opposite of you and me."

She pinched some flab with a prankish grin. "Then maybe we'll visit the chimpanzees and hang with our fellow mammalians. The largest male, Scamper, is a ham, just like you. I heard that a few weeks ago he stole his handler's iPod, climbed a tree, and held the headphones to his ear. Apparently, he didn't like what he heard, because he snorted a loud raspberry and tossed the iPod to the ground, where it broke."

"Maybe it was, *Hey, hey, hey, we're the Monkees*," sang Presto. "Maybe the chimp was insulted."

Camille laughed, which further cheered Presto.

They arrived at a wall-encased terrarium. Presto looked around and then saw a Jackson's chameleon perched on a branch. Its green, splotched skin blended perfectly with the green foliage. Three tan horns, two over the eyelids and one that was longer and protruded from the snout, combined to look like the twigs it was sitting within.

Thankfully, Camille again provided commentary. "I love these guys," she gushed. "I had a panther chameleon at college. I think I was the only girl with a reptile on campus."

Presto supposed she was. She was as rare as the endangered red pandas they'd visited earlier.

When Camille got home that Friday evening, she called with good news. Yes, she took the job, and would he help her find an apartment. He agreed and asked about a celebratory dinner on Saturday. She regrettably declined and explained she was expected to attend a dinner with the Zoo's director and a few patrons. He was disappointed but understood. He was cheered when she mentioned that the two families were spending Easter together.

Ridgewood and Donavan's Saturday flight back was delayed, and they did not arrive at Danko's until two o'clock in the afternoon. The group spent their time on security provisions. It was Easter eve, and every church in the city would be guarded. They departed with hope. Another death would be a disaster.

Chapter Forty-Nine

NICE COSTUME, Myth Man thought sarcastically.

Victor Markov wore a fake beard and mustache. It was a primitive effort, one likely purchased in a Halloween costume store, but it was passable in the dark bar. The knit cap and use of contacts instead of his typical wire frames did give Markov a different look.

Markov's eyes scanned the almost vacant bar. The place was a dump, and at 10:30 pm most of the older patrons had since stumbled out the door. Markov's twitchy eyes and uncomfortable hands embodied his nervous state. He leaned closer across the table and spoke in a hush tone. "I know I want to do this, but I'm still scared."

Across the table, the other man had spent hours with his disguise. A prosthetic chin enhanced his jaw line. A body suit under his clothes made him look beefier. His wig was grayed at the temples and peppered throughout. His skin was bronzed a few shades darker. Although the weather was not chilly, he wore thin, black leather gloves.

"Me too," Myth Man said. "We both have something to lose." He removed one glove, raised his hand, and pointed to his wedding band.

"Are we crazy?" asked Markov.

Myth Man gave him a long smile. "You're the doctor."

"A nurse, but don't you think less of it. You know how important my job is."

Myth Man nodded. "I do. He's an important man."

"He truly is. It's a pleasure working with him, but when I think of us, sometimes I think of him. I feel ashamed."

Myth Man held no empathy but answered, "I know. But no one will know. We'd both be ruined."

Markov exhaled. "I think I'd kill myself."

Myth Man stifled a smile. *I got that department taken care of.*

He watched Markov closely. His voice had a feminine squeak, like he was in the midst of puberty. His accent was classic New Yawk. He liked to touch his face, especially his ears, and he walked in short, quick steps.

"Another beer?" Markov asked after a short impasse. "I'll feel better doing this if I'm buzzed," he said with a nervous laugh.

"I'll feel better when you unzip my pants," Myth Man replied with a wry smile.

"Me too," Markov replied with a mischievous grin of his own and got up to fetch some brewskies.

Myth Man watched him go. Markov was perfect. When he had chosen his target, he'd known the only way to get to him was through his nurse. He had begun to follow Markov.

He was surprised one night to see Markov reappear from his West Village loft. He wore a disguise, but Myth Man was sure it was Markov. This interested him, and he followed Markov into a bar. Myth Man immediately noted all the patrons were male and figured out Markov's game.

A week later, Myth Man followed Markov to a different bar and approached him, timidly. The slow come-on worked with Markov, and an even slower courtship commenced. It started with short phone calls. Then they opened up to each other. Markov confided his identity, while Myth Man continued his lie. Tonight's rendezvous was to cement their union.

Markov returned with the beers. They clinked bottles and drank up.

"You guys must be nervous with this killer on the loose," broached Myth Man.

Markov huffed. "Hardly," he claimed. "If anything, the recent attentions only made security tighter and more of a hassle. The police are everywhere."

No problem. "Yeah, well I hope they catch him soon. The man's a menace."

"You got that right," agreed Markov.

Myth Man took a long chug of his beer. He then took a long look at his watch. "What time do you have to be there tomorrow?"

Markov stretched his face taut. "Five in the morning. He must be cleaned, dressed, fed, and groomed."

"Sounds tough."

Markov shrugged. "I suppose it is, but I wouldn't trade my job with anyone in the world."

Tomorrow you will.

Myth Man gestured to the door and threw a long coquettish smile at Markov. He tried a face he'd once used on his wife It said: *Let's get busy.* "It's getting late then. Want to get out of here?"

Chapter Fifty

The alarm clock, which played church hymns, woke Reverend Noel Perkins. "Lights," he commanded. Then there was light. "Dimmer," he requested. The room softened. "Dimmer," he said again, and the light was perfect for morning eyes.

Easter morning. The resurrection. He quietly sang:

> That Easter day with joy was bright;
> The sun shone out with fairer light,
> When to their longing eyes restored,
> The apostles saw their risen Lord!
> Alleluia!
> O Jesus, king of gentleness,
> With constant love our hearts possess;
> To you our lips will ever raise
> The tribute of our grateful praise.
> Alleluia!
> O Christ, you are the Lord of all
> In this our Easter festival,
> For you will be our strength and shield
> From every weapon death can wield.
> Alleluia!
> All praise, O risen Lord, we give
> To you, once dead but now alive!
> To God the Father equal praise,
> And God the Holy Ghost, we raise!
> Alleluia!

He had a special sermon scheduled for the day. Attendance would be high, an opportunity to embrace the lost ones. Let them recall that today was not about Easter bunnies and candy goodies.

He sometimes cynically feared that his physical condition detracted from his message. *Yeah, leave it to the bitter quadriplegic to moan and groan about the excesses of today's society.*

It had been ten years since God challenged his faith and took everything from him. He never knew what hit them. He'd left a White House dinner in the back of a limo with his wife and two sons. They were on their way back to their Georgetown hotel. Instead, he woke up in a hospital.

Strangely, when he gained consciousness, his body felt no pain. He figured it was the drugs. First the doctors told him the grave news about his family. They'd perished in the crash. Reverend Perkins wished whatever numbed his body could anesthetize his brain. He tried to lash out in anger, but he found he could not move.

The doctor told him that his spinal cord had been damaged above the thoracic vertebrae. All four limbs would forever be incapable of motion. Even his chest muscles were affected. Breathing was no longer an unconscious luxury.

Perkins battled grief and guilt. *Why had God done this to him? Had he erred in some fashion? Was this an obstacle? Should he expect any better fate than the Son of God?*

During his stay at a rehab clinic, he found his voice again. That had always been his gift. It was his oratory skills that made him rector of Grace Church at the age of forty-one. God had not silenced him. He made it his mission to continue to speak out in his glorious name.

His church was now his family, his nurse the caretaker. The man, Viktor Markov, was a living saint. For the better part of ten years, his nurse dedicated his life to him. None of life's needs were possible without him. He took the barbs, the setbacks, the frustrations, and the minimal progress like buttered Teflon; nothing stuck. The man had the patience of Job and the commitment of a disciple.

After nine years, at Reverend Perkins's insistence, Victor Markov moved out from the rectory. The man deserved his own space. Maybe he'd find a woman, Perkins hoped. He felt responsible that the poor guy never had time to find himself a wife.

Perkins looked at the time. Any minute, and his lifeline would be here.

CHAPTER FIFTY-ONE

MYTH MAN DISPOSED OF Markov like yesterday's trash, literally.

After gaining entry to his apartment, he subdued the man with a needle through the back of his scrawny neck. He then utilized a silencer to permanently hush the nervous nurse. He left him upside down in a garbage can with his feet propped against the wall.

There was a time when he would have considered hiding the body. Markov would be a suspect until found. Disposing of the body, however, could be an unnecessary complication. He also knew that Presto would not waste a second of his time on Markov. Plus, Myth Man wanted the instant fame, the name recognition. He'd go down in history with the best serial killers—not because of the total body count (his would be low next to the elite), but because he would never get caught.

His victims were not prostitutes or next-door-neighbor types but something far grander. Sure, a few regular folks, like Markov, the sushi chef, the bum at St. Patrick's, and the bitch from the eyeglass store had to die. Only the homeless man brought an inkling of remorse, but Myth Man easily dismissed it. The vagabond had no real life. Wrong place, wrong time, he rationalized.

There was no need to take one of Markov's suits; he'd already purchased a replica. He did take Markov's workbag, eyeglasses, and wallet. In addition, he left a few things behind, including blood and hair samples from his captive at the safe house.

Myth Man got a cab to drop him off a few blocks from the safe house. When the cab turned the corner and was out of sight, he broke into a fast jog.

Forty minutes later, the garage door opened, and the van emerged. It was 4:20 am. He had a half hour to get there, which should be enough time. He regulated his breath. It was hard to temper the excitement.

Myth Man had always detested Reverend Perkins. The blowhard had already been too influential, but after his, dare say, tragedy, the man became an icon. The guy was a fool. How could he reconcile the loss of his family and the use of his limbs? Perkins was so inebriated with Jesus Juice that the man's faith was now incredulously stronger. *Hello?*

The Reverend thought he was spared to deliver God's message. Divine fate.

Hogwash. By pure luck, he survived the limo wreck. This Easter morning there would be no divine intervention. No resurrection. No different than the pigeons that shit all over the church. You're born, and you die, just like all earth's creatures. There was no God that favored our lot.

Myth Man was fortunate to find a parking space a few blocks from the cathedral. He felt no urge to look at the mirror one last time. He knew it was perfect. He was Markov.

Two uniformed cops stood outside the rectory door. They were in heated discussion over a three-game slide by the Yankees. The season was two weeks old, but one adamantly called for the dismissal of the manager.

Myth Man approached. "Good morning," he said in a manner that suggested the unfortunate hour they were all up. "If you ask me, I say fire his ass."

This got cheers from one officer and a frown from the other, who then said, "You guys have no patience."

Myth Man waited for them to open the door, but they hesitated.

"I don't want to be late. He'll get snippy with me." He gave them a knowing look.

"Sorry to trouble you, but you know the situation, with this being Easter especially," the formerly crestfallen cop informed. "We know who you are, but we have to see ID and the bag."

Myth Man pulled out a wallet and handed it over to one cop. He opened the bag for the other.

"What's that?" asked the cop who inspected the bag.

Myth Man looked innocently down. "What, the power tool?"

The cop looked at him. "Yeah."

Myth Man smiled sympathetically. "The Reverend's wheel chair. It's been acting up. I'm going to play with it. Hopefully I can fix it." He held a harmless expression and rubbed at his ears. That story was farfetched, but he counted on their ignorance. It would be a shame if they were smart. Then they'd needlessly die.

"Hmm," the cop said.

The cop with the wallet announced, "It's okay. It's him."

The other cop seemed mollified. "I know. I just want to make sure. Can you imagine the shit we'd get if the Rev gets whacked?" He looked to Myth Man. "This killer likes to dress up and impersonate people. Sneaky fuck," he muttered. He grabbed a receiver off his belt. "Nurse is here."

The door opened.

Myth Man hopped in, like an Easter bunny.

CHAPTER FIFTY-TWO

THE INTERCOM TOLD PERKINS that Victor Markov had arrived. He called for the lights to increase their illumination. "Let there be light."

When his attendant came into view, he thought the light change affected his eyesight. He squinted at Markov, but something was not right. Gone was Markov's customary cheerful whistle. When he entered the room, Markov turned his back and did not immediately greet him, let alone check the computer that monitored Perkins's vitals. Odd.

"Is something wrong, Victor?" Reverend Perkins remembered the nurse had said something about a plan the prior evening. He hoped it was a date, but by the looks of it, perhaps it went poorly.

"No problems here, cripple," answered a voice that sounded like Markov but wasn't. The accent was right but not the tone. The words echoed with haughty disdain. The man turned toward the bed.

Perkins peered closer. The clothes, the bag, the hair, the glasses, were all vintage Markov, but this was not his nurse. This was the killer he'd been warned about. As the connection registered, the man stepped forward with a needle. Unable to resist, he tried to call out, but the man's free hand covered his mouth. After a minute, the man stepped back. An impish grin split his face. "Normally, my victims are all freaked out when they try to move and can't. But not the paralyzed preacher; you're used to the feeling," he said sardonically and winked. "Can't talk though, huh? The Lord's Larynx has been forever silenced," he mocked.

The man sat on the edge of his bed. "Easter," he spat sarcastically. Besides this whole Father, Son, Holy Ghost nonsense, the whole holiday is a farce. The very name Easter is derived from the pagan goddess Oestre. Then you stupid Christians couldn't settle on a day to honor your Christ. To fool the pagan masses, the majority picked a day to align with the pagan spring festival."

He paused to cast a hard look. "I'm the exterminator. My mission is to rid this planet of the disease known as religion." He stopped to sing the opening lines from, John Lennon's *Imagine*:

> Imagine there's no heaven,
> It's easy if you try,

No hell below us,
Above us only sky,
Imagine all the people
living for today.

Imagine there's no countries,
It isn't hard to do,
Nothing to kill or die for,
No religion too.

The killer shrugged. "Sorry, not much of a singer. As you can guess, I never made the church choir."

The killer came closer and patted Perkins's body. "Your death shall not be in vain. Think of this as your glorious moment. Your epiphany." He smirked. "May your crucifixion help end a religion that started with such a gory spectacle."

Reverend Perkins tried to ignore the blasphemy. With a body 90 percent immune from sense, only words could inflict pain. He thought of his wife and children. Despite what this devil's minion believed, he was certain he'd meet his family in a better place. He wondered what happened to Victor.

"Oh, by the way," the killer said, interrupting and almost interpreting Perkins's reverie. "Your nurse was gay. Funny I know that, and I met the man only a handful of times. You've spent a decade with him and never knew it. Why? Because your holier than thou bullshit has condemned and ostracized this man as a sinner. Unable to exercise his own free will, he was forced to manifest a separate, duplicitous life." The killer snorted. "He's dead. Now so shall you be."

The killer got off the bed. He opened Markov's bag and took out a nail gun, camera, and radio. He pressed play, and Wagner's mythical opera *The Ring* filled the room. "Ah, there's nothing like music to soothe a man at work."

Helpless, Perkins sat there as the killer surveyed the room. "That'll do," he said. Then he sauntered over. "Surely you know that the wounds typically depicted on Christ's hands are another embellishment." He grabbed one of Perkins's arms. He pointed. "The hands would not support the body's weight. Have to use the wrists," he said as his thumb caressed the planned penetration point.

He let Perkins's arm fall. "Sorry, we don't have a giant wooden cross for you, but that wall over there should do. Ready to meet your Faker?"

When he finished his work, Myth Man exited the rectory. One of the cops on patrol inquired, "Is there a problem?"

Myth Man cast a look of reassurance. "Not at all, buddy. I have to run back to my place for a moment. The Reverend wants to hang something that will always be remembered."

Myth Man stopped to open his bag. He took out the recently used camera. "Oh, before I forget. Is it all right if I take a picture? The Reverend thanks you for volunteering your time to protect his church. We hatched an idea that we think will give you ample recognition."

"Gee," said one of the cops, who lifted his cap and brushed his hair back. "That's mighty kind of him."

The two officers stood erect on either side of the door. They squared their shoulders and puffed their chests.

Myth Man digitally captured their pose. "Thanks, gentlemen. You'll see in a day or two; every top police official will know what fine work you two do."

The two cops grinned.

Myth Man put the camera back in the bag and put the strap around his shoulder. "Be back soon."

Of course, there would be no return. It was Easter. He had plans at his wife's sister's house.

CHAPTER FIFTY-THREE

PRESTO'S PRIVATE PHONE RANG, jolting him from a dream of an unlimited shopping spree at the new gourmet supermarket that opened a few blocks away. A look at the clock told him he'd not overslept. Presto's innards tightened. It was the killer. He'd struck again.

Presto rolled out and stumbled from his king-sized mattress. Phone in hand, he fell into a rocking chair by a window that overlooked a dull brick wall.

It was Danko. He sounded as tired as Presto felt. "Bad news."

"Who, what, where, when, how?"

Presto heard Danko suck in his breath. "Your spot, Grace Church."

"Oh, no," Presto cried. "Please don't tell me Reverend …"

"Perkins, yeah," finished Danko. "I'm here now. Do me a favor; get those two agents to meet here." His words trailed off like the end of a sad song.

As Presto walked to the gothic cathedral, he noted the rising sun, which hung over the towering spire like a late fired warning flare. The fact that he considered Grace Cathedral a high probability target did not assuage his grief; there were no moral victories here. If anything, it made him feel worse.

As he neared the main cathedral doors, he saw throngs of police who looked like they were ready for action but had little to do. The streets were blockaded. There would be no Easter Mass this year.

A detective that worked under Danko spotted and beckoned him. He led Presto back to an exit recessed on the east side of the cathedral. The door led to the Parish Room, which connected the rectory to the courtyard garden.

He found Danko. "Forensics inside," Danko explained and then motioned to the victim's door with his head. Despite the dark circles under his eyes, Danko's voice had strengthened since the call. "I can't believe what I saw in there. It's evil," he asserted angrily. The bulged vein in his temple was back.

They both heard Ridgewood's and Donavan's voices. For once, the conversation appeared civil. "Let's grab them, and I'll brief you outside. I can use the air," Danko said wearily.

They intercepted the two agents, reversed back through the Parish House, and went outside to the garden. They walked several yards along a tiled path near an antique, black light post. The trees' spring flowers began to bud. New life. New death.

Presto turned and gazed back at the church. From his angle now, it looked as if the sun sat impaled on the spire

Presto never had this view of the church. He took in the arched windows, the pointed buttresses, and the immenseness of the stone cathedral. He could not fathom the work of something this grand. He once tried his hand with military-type models but never advanced beyond the novice level. His last effort, a Panzer tank, went from a fifty-piece model to almost a hundred after he smashed his foot down on the aborted jalopy.

"This is good," said Danko. "I needed some space, and we have to wait until forensics is finished. I was only allowed in a secured square of the room that they'd cleared. I saw enough."

Danko recapped what he did see. Tacked to the wall was a crude, cloth cross. In an effigy of Christ's crucifixion, Reverend Perkins was nailed through his wrists and feet to the wall. A fake crown of thorns was placed on his head. On Perkins white nightshirt two words had been written in blood: Myth Man.

Donavan, who had been jogging at the time of the call and was dressed in a running suit, coughed. "Any chance the killer was just looking for a handicapped parking sticker?"

No one laughed. Not even his new friend Danko, who looked away embarrassed.

The good vibes between the two agents ended on that comment. "You're an asshole, Donavan. Have you no shame? No, don't answer. Stay quiet for a while."

Donavan recoiled like a snake in retreat.

Ridgewood then turned to Danko, the edge still in her voice. "What about security? I thought there were police posted at every church entrance in the city? How did he gain access: force or trickery?"

Danko's face twitched defensively. "Well," he said tentatively, "we have to check something out, but it looks like chicanery, again." His shoulders drooped. Frustration oozed perspiration from his pores despite the cool April day. Adrenaline and coffee were the chemicals that kept him awake. "I'll tell you what I know."

Danko explained that the only man purportedly to have entered Perkins's room was his nurse, Victor Markov. Markov left about a half hour later. Said he had to get something and never returned. Officers were dispatched to his apartment. We should hear something soon," he said with tempered optimism.

"The way I see it," Danko continued, "is there are four possibilities, and I think you can discount two and shortly the third. Either someone entered and left whom we don't know about, or the killer may have been disguised as cop or clergy. That leaves either Markov being the killer, or the killer disguised as Markov. We need to find this nurse to rule out the first three."

Presto found Danko's reasoning sound. Those were the likely scenarios, and he also shared the view that the killer was disguised as Markov. If that were true, that meant Markov was dead.

Ridgewood pressed politely. "What else did the cops say about the nurse?"

Donavan had another thought. "What I want to know is why Perkins didn't have a female nurse, in one of those sexy after-hours outfits that my wife won't wear, tending to his needs? After all, he's single now."

Ridgewood, like a cobra, spun quickly, and her head rocked slightly from side to side. Her gaze was venomous. With no tune to charm, Donavan decided to pipe no further.

The minitension was broken when Danko's phone rang. Everyone focused on the call, reading Danko's face for clues. When he hung up, they knew. "The nurse is dead."

Ridgewood stomped her foot. "I can't believe this. Who is this guy, a Hollywood makeup artist?"

"He must be," said Danko in hopes of crediting the killer's guile over ineptitude. "They had photos of all the staff. They said the guy was a dead ringer for the ID." His demeanor, like a storm to come, darkened. "There's one other thing."

Ridgewood asked the obvious. "What?"

"It seems this psycho likes to take pictures," he said with some shame. "He asked the two officers to pose for a picture outside the door. Why do I have a bad feeling about this?"

"Oh, no," Ridgewood said. She knew the implications, none good.

It was then, for the first time, that Presto realized he'd been in Ridgewood's company for several minutes, and he'd hardly cared. Was it the hiatus they'd spent apart? Perhaps it was the drama of the moment. Or maybe, just maybe, it had something to do with Camille? He pushed away that thought.

Now that he noticed, he knew it had nothing to do with her appearance. Despite her understandable anxiety, she was as comely as ever.

Ridgewood turned and saw Presto looking at her. She gave him a hopeful smile. "Dom, what are you thinking," she said slyly, and then added, "about the case."

Presto had a few thoughts, but her *gotcha* flustered him. "Uh, I think we learned a few things."

"Like what?" Donavan challenged. "Crucifixions are on the comeback?"

Ridgewood fixed her partner with a steely stare and went back to Presto. "Go on."

"It may seem meaningless, but we know the name he wants to be known by. It tells me he's got an ego. He craves an identity; he wants the notoriety. If he's taking pictures, then it means he's reaching out, and like a mouse that ventures farther from his hideaway looking for a bigger piece of cheese, there's more exposure and risk." His voice became certain. "Let's use that to our advantage."

"How?" Danko asked.

"A few ways," Presto answered. "He wants a forum. That's a mistake. Let's use the press to our advantage. Let's insult him. I sort of like Son of Satan, but I'm sure the headline writers have others. He wants respect. Let's not give it to him."

"We might just piss him off more," Ridgewood said.

"Come on," Donavan said, ignoring his silent moratorium. "How much more testy can you get than dismemberment, a bullet to the forehead, a decapitation, and now a crucifixion?"

CHAPTER FIFTY-FOUR

DESPITE IT NOT BEING a Catholic church, Presto sat in a pew, lowered his head, and prayed. He first thought of his mother. Nothing malignant should ever touch a soul as benign and pure as his mom. He knew from Camille that she'd been to the doctor several times while he'd been at work, and yet his mother never mentioned it to him. Why?

Presto then thought of the murdered victims. Despite Myth Man's crusade against religion, these were decent men, not shady quacks. Had Perkins not suffered enough from the limo wreck? And what of this poor chap Victor Markov?

Then Presto turned his prayers to Frank Danko. His former foe left an hour ago after being denied sleep for more than thirty hours. With downcast eyes, drooped head, and dragging feet, he bid his forced farewell and returned to an empty home. Holidays can be a bad time to be alone, especially after his estrangement, and he took the murders as his personal failure. Presto wished him a therapeutic rest and a miracle panacea for his family issues.

Then he turned directly to God. *Hey, big guy, or girl. I'm no sexist, but either way, no matter which religion is right, or even if we're all wrong, there has to be a reason why a species as advanced as us, across almost all ethnic groups, believes in something divine. So I know you're out there, and I hope you're listening.*

Help us eradicate this evil. While my badge may be a shield rather than a religious talisman, my charge is an extension of your commandments. You made the rules, and some don't live by them. They're an affront to the tenets of peace and love. Please give us the guidance and strength to find this pawn of perdition.

Oh, and finally, if you may see fit, can you ensure that Mrs. Stagnuts's concoctions are not the only leftovers from today's missed Easter meal?

Presto had already phoned home to tell his mother he would not make the feast. He called Camille too. Both already heard the news of Perkin's murder. Good news travels fast; bad news travels faster.

Pretso heard the patter of short, quick steps echo in the quiet cathedral. It was Ridgewood. "Forensics may have found something."

"Really?" Presto was surprised but reserved. It could be nothing. Thus far, they found plenty of evidence, most to all of it planted, but nothing that led them to a suspect.

"They found blood on Markov's shirt that is not his own blood type. They also found a hair sample match at both Markov's apartment and in Perkins's bedroom." Ridgewood sat in the pew beside Presto. "Hopefully, this evidence is the killer's. Doesn't help us find him, but if we do, we'll have a DNA match."

He looked at Ridgewood; her skin was paler than usual. "That's good news." Presto was still dubious but didn't want to sour Ridgewood's spice. "Where's your pal Donavan?"

"On the phone with his wife. We already reported everything to Malcolm. He's coming to New York, something to do with this big assignment he's been working on, but while he's here, he's going to assist on the case."

Ridgewood and Presto looked at each other. She let her head fall against his side. "I'm scared of what's to come, Dom. I fear this Easter was a prelude to a nor'easter."

Presto arrived home at nearly ten o'clock in the evening. He found two notes on the kitchen table. One was from his mother. She'd had a few glasses of wine and went to sleep. She left a plate for him in the microwave. There was more in the fridge. She was kind enough to mark anything cooked by Mrs. Stagnuts with an *X*. Presto thought a skull above the *X* would have been more apropos, but he was thankful for the warning nonetheless.

The other note was attached to a pink, green, and white Easter basket. Fake green grass was strewn about like Presto's morning mane. A brick-sized chocolate Easter bunny sat upright in the grassy bramble, guarding foil-wrapped eggs.

It was a difficult choice—milk chocolate or Camille's words. He took the note.

Dear Dom,

I resisted drawing a happy bunny rabbit with big goofy ears. Let me simply say that like the rabbit I wanted to draw, I'm all ears. Any time you want, give me a call, and I'll hop on up. ......Camille

CHAPTER FIFTY-FIVE

COLD CALCULATOR—MATH MAN ADDS *Two More* screamed the headline of the *Daily News*.

Math Man?

A finger tap brought up the *New York Post*: *Son of Satan Psycho Strikes Again*. Huh? He looked at the caption below. *Reverend Perkins and Nurse Murdered: Killer Invokes Moth Man Legend*.

What?!

There must be some mistake. Myth Man rubbed his eyes hoping to cleanse his sight, like a sip of mineral water does for the palate. He looked again, but nothing changed.

Myth Man woke on a dry bed, like a boy on Christmas, eager and energized, despite it being a Monday workday. He expected voluminous coverage of his heroics with headlines that would bring him the infamy he so richly deserved. Today was the day he was supposed to be crowned a cultural icon. This was unacceptable.

Testy, he read on. The sexy FBI agent he saw outside Grace Cathedral a week prior briefed reporters, and she was surprisingly forthright. She candidly explained that the killer had murdered Markov and impersonated the nurse to gain entry and ultimately kill Reverend Perkins.

She even told how Perkins had been nailed to the wall, calling the deed heinous and evil. She went on to say that the killer left a message. Investigators were unsure if it was a reference to Perkins or the killer himself. She said the message was written in blood, which ran, but it appeared to be either Math or Moth Man. "We're not sure what this means," she added.

Myth Man stopped there. *Impossible*. It had been clear as day. How could a *y* be mistaken for either supplicated vowel? He pulled out his digital camera and connected it to the computer. He found the picture of Perkins in his Jesus Christ pose.

Myth Man didn't have to magnify the picture to read it clearly. The *y* was perfectly legible. "Myth Man," he howled, banging the mouse like it was an interloping rodent.

Why would they do this? They knew he had a camera. They had to consider he'd photograph his graphic art. Clearly, they meant to frazzle him.

They were wrong. How dare they steal his moment of glory? Wait until the press sees the truth. *I'll show them,* he stormed.

CHAPTER FIFTY-SIX

REVEREND PERKINS'S MURDER SHOOK Mayor Golden personally. Every occupant of Gracie Mansion over the past twenty years had been well ingratiated with Reverend Perkins, and the mayor was no exception. Neither was the president of the Unites States, who called to say he'd be in the city to attend the funeral. The president's normal, velvety voice was as coarse as burlap. It pained Mayor Golden to hear his president, a four-star general, choked up. He felt responsible.

He'd shut his door and asked not to be disturbed. He was to meet the press in a few hours and personally wanted to pen his remarks. He also needed peace.

The killer, as his detectives predicted, strove to correct the record. He emailed numerous news outlets, which chose to still cooperate with the investigation and refused to print or yet comment on his first public statement. A short while later, the photos had been uploaded on numerous Web sites.

The killer had his moment of infamy. He summarized his manifest of religion's blight on society. But, most of all, his chosen name was public: Myth Man.

The mayor looked at the pictures. It pained him to see Perkins crucified in his own bedroom. *At least, for once, no one will blame the Jews,* he thought with a sad laugh. Then he thought, *Since a rabbi had yet to be killed, perhaps the killer was Jewish?* He hoped not.

The mayor empathized with the two cops that guarded the rectory door. Their faces were visible, and the killer conveniently provided their last names, presumably read from their shields.

*How many lives had this Myth Man destroyed? And now he asked for the public to rally to his messag*e? The mayor understood the premise of his ill-conceived rant. Yes, religion used for miscreant purposes was bad, and things such as genocide and extremism were unfortunate byproducts of the history of religion. His people knew all too well, but it was not the whole story on religion. Absent were the hope, care, shelter, and nourishment that had enriched billions worldwide.

The mayor had witnessed firsthand the intercooperation and deepening of understanding between the main religions. That was what America was about and why his parents had immigrated to this land of freedom, where citizens can worship without fear of persecution.

One nation under God.

How could Myth Man's message resonate? Not every victim had been a religious leader. There was the optometrist, sushi chef, and homeless man at St. Patrick's and now Reverend Perkins's nurse. What about them? Were these unfortunate, but necessary deaths to fertilize the revolution with Machiavellian manure?

Maybe his political career would be the next thing destroyed by this menace. He was tired of Hoole, who blamed the police. Every distraction was time wasted. If Danko's team was not doing the job, then it was Commissioner Tipton's job to make that evaluation. Thus far, his self-appointed commissioner had been ineffectual

They had the FBI's assistance. This morning, the female agent, Ridgewood, he believed, said that her boss was due in town.

Mayor Golden decided to remain defiant in the face of evil. He'd stand by the police department, not offer excuses. They got beat this time, but it was not due to lack of effort or preparation. His talking points had a list of religions institutions they'd guarded, down to man-hours and overtime costs.

Golden liked the idea of needling Math Man. The mayor agreed with the Yoda principle: anger led to loss of focus and error. Hopefully more tangible clues would develop.

The mayor planned to offer not one of Hoole's valid factoids in his speech. He had a different mindset, and that's why he wanted to be alone to pen his own words. Some said that was political suicide. Maybe the pundits were right, but he had to go with his gut. New York elected him for being his own man. It was time to differ with the handlers. If he lost an election over a serial killer, then the job wasn't worth it anyway.

Mayor Golden would first honor the memory of the victims. As for his stance on the investigation, he stood by the police and had a message for the killer with an appeal to the public.

America was founded on religious freedom and tolerance, not a utopian, totalitarian vision that disavows spirituality and faith.

He would issue a challenge. President Ronald Reagan once mused at the United Nations, what would happen if the world were suddenly attacked by an alien race? His message was that a lot of our differences would suddenly evaporate. Golden saw this menace in the same light.

The killer's original aim had been to create strife and intolerance, and initially, he succeeded. But what if now the opposite occurred? We, the people who do believe in God, might learn a valuable lesson and not one the killer intended.

The mayor phoned prominent religious leaders of various faiths and told them his vision. They agreed to appear as a powerful backdrop to his speech about religious freedom and tolerance.

Myth Man may slay a few more souls, but he was not going to gain the hearts and minds of the people.

CHAPTER FIFTY-SEVEN

Presto and Ridgewood entered a new Madison Avenue high-rise with floor-to-ceiling windows and a lobby fortified with a Starbucks, a newsstand, a swank saloon, and a swankier salon.

The twenty-fifth floor was occupied by Iron Fortress Systems, a fairly recent startup company that specialized in safeguarding computers from viruses, Trojan horses, and other computer threats. The founder of the company, Dean Fallow, was next on their Manhattan list.

They used their respective badges to bypass building security. "I hope we hit the jackpot soon," Ridgewood remarked. "Like we knock on the door, and he opens and confesses with his hands ready for cuffs." She brought her wrists together and submissively raised them.

Presto sighed. "I bet this one won't go so easy. Fallow, to me, was one of the more intriguing suspects."

Dean Fallow once served as the computer technician for an upstate university. He was popular with students and loved by the faculty for revamping the outdated technology and tirelessly assisting the computer illiterate, which at the time was close to 100 percent.

At a faculty party, he got into a heated argument about religion with a theology professor, Jerry Timmons. He was a computer, math, science, guy, Fallow told Timmons. God was an outdated concept, contrived in the age of ignorance. Religion was the con of the millennia. "Where is God today? I don't see him," Fallow asked with rhetoric spite. When Timmons tried to reply, Fallow turned his back and left in a pompous breeze.

The next day there was a buzz on campus, not just amongst the faculty who knew of the nighttime altercation but also within the student body. Several fraternal organizations allegedly found packages on their doorsteps. Inside was a CD-ROM of the very married Jerry Timmons. Insert the CD-ROM in a computer, and Timmons's face popped up along with a menu of choices: Frequent Correspondence, Photos, Videos, and Frequented Web sites.

The Correspondence file brought up Timmons's email exchanges between single women, married women, hookers, underage females, and underage males, basically anything bipedal. The photos and videos all starred Timmons.

Timmons had always been viewed as anal. The photos only tweaked that perception. In most, it was obvious the other participant, or participants, had no idea they were being filmed. The exception was a transvestite hooker. The Frequented Web sites menu, while less damaging, further evidenced Timmons's secret salacious life.

Rightful suspicion fell on Dean Fallow, which he vigorously protested. He blamed fraternal pranksters, but his denials were dismissed, and he was fired. Fallow sued, successfully, claiming no proof was ever submitted. The settlement was not exorbitant, but it was enough for him to pursue another dream. Ten years ago he moved to New York City and dabbled in a few things; some worked better than others, but he eventually started the company he presides over now. Computer security became a necessary business.

The elevator ascended and abruptly opened. Ridgewood and Presto walked out onto a speckled tan and blue carpet and walked toward the receptionist. A young, bored female smiled when she saw them. "May I help you?"

Ridgewood explained that she could. Without showing their badges, they asked if they could see Dean Fallow. The receptionist obliged and phoned, presumably, Fallow's office. A short moment later, a waxen female appeared; she looked like she'd never seen the sun for fear, unlike the foolish Icarus, that she'd melt.

The candle woman led them through double doors that opened to a standard office, a large room portioned by drab cubicles with offices along the exterior. They headed to a corner office that was by far the largest in view. They were led inside.

A plain-faced man with short-cropped brown hair rose from behind his desk, hand extended. His figure was lithe, yet athletic in a swimmer's build type of way. "Good afternoon. What can I do for you?"

Ridgewood and Presto showed their badges. Fallow's face faltered. He went to the door and shut it. He motioned to the two chairs before his desk.

Presto surveyed the office. The floor-to-ceiling windows could be disconcerting if you were prone to vertigo. Potted plants were situated on either end of the window, with Fallow's desk in the center.

Presto watched Fallow. A few things occurred to him. The man's appearance was within their profile, but there was something else that nagged at him. When he researched this lead, he found one grainy shot taken during his tenure at the university. The company's Web site did not have Fallow's photo, and yet, he looked familiar in a recent way.

Something about this first impression nagged him. When their eyes met, Fallows grew as if they registered recognition. Fallow's eyes quickly shifted to

Ridgewood, where they now rarely wavered. Presto could not blame the man, but he sensed this was not based strictly on sex appeal.

"Yes?" Fallow asked. His hands were clasped, but his fingers still wiggled. A forced sense of composure.

Ridgewood began, yet again, with general questions about his whereabouts at certain dates and times. His answer for Easter morning was in bed with his wife and later at a family get-together.

Presto took notes, but his eyes rarely glanced down at the paper. He watched Fallow who seemed overly preoccupied with Ridgewood. Where could he have ever seen this man?

At this point, most of their interviews fizzled due to the obvious. Fallow had survived to round two, and Ridgewood continued.

"Mr. Fallow, we're investigating the murders of the city's religious leaders," she ruminated and stared, hard.

Fallow's reaction appeared to be one of relief. "Oh, that," he trivialized. "I thought you were here on some trumped up charge from one of our competitors. They think my wisdom and foresight is a byproduct of illegal hacking." He dismissed this notion with a smirk. "But this business, I'm curious; talk to me." He now leaned forward, interested. He shot a quick glance at Presto but went back to Ridgewood.

"Your background fits our profile," Ridgewood said.

Fallow cast an awkward smile. "I take it this meeting is not for my proficiency in computers, chess, and pistachios then."

From Presto's angle, he could see the side of Fallow's grin. He asked a question, but not for the verbal response. "Ah, I love those pistachios too, Dean. I'm a salted guy myself. What about you?"

Fallow faced him and answered, uneasily. "I prefer them without the salt. Doctor says I should avoid sodium," he divulged with a too-quick, tepid smile.

Fallow looked away again, but Presto was sure he'd seen this man recently. Like being unable to summon the right word, Presto could not place it.

Ridgewood evenly said, "Mr. Fallow. It's about your past."

He unclasped his hands, and he tugged on one of his cuffs. "Hmm. I have an inkling I know what this is about, and I'll answer candidly, but why the charade. Be specific," he offered.

Without a beat, Ridgewood said. "Yes, the Jerry Timmons matter. The killer seems to share your disdain for religion. And, yes, our killer also has some expertise with computers." She stopped to let that resonate. "You can understand the connection we drew."

Fallow shrugged. "No, I understand. While it is true, I think religion is a farce and have not always behaved in a pristine ethical manner, I'm not a killer. My unloving wife," he stated with a reedy expression, "will hopefully attest that I was by her side on at least a few of these murders, unless she plots to rid me," he said with a trying laugh. "You may reach her at any time."

He stopped and shot Ridgewood and Presto a conspiratorial look. "I may have information for you."

Fallow eased closer in confidentially. "As these murders got a foothold in the press, I was reminded of someone whom I'd interviewed a few months back. He looked like a nice enough chap, served his country in the Gulf War, but he returned home bitter and without work.

"If the guy kept his mouth shut, he would have had a job. The guy professed to know of me by some means that I cannot recall," Fallow said. "The guy tried to forge a quick camaraderie on similar philosophical grounds. I confess; at first, I liked the guy."

With his eyes still squarely focused on no one, Fallow continued. "Maybe it was his training, but the guy began to talk in a militaristic fashion—mobilize platoons, body bag the believers. It was all so crazy."

Fallow looked to Ridgewood for understanding. He got nothing.

Fallow smiled. "I saw the debate with Timmons as a matter of education," Fallow ventured. "As humans progress, we'll cast away the gods created in ancient and superstitious times. It will eventually happen, but I don't foresee it in my lifetime. The guy I interviewed advocated speeding up that development in a nasty way."

Fallow drummed his fingers on the desk. "Naturally I did not employ this man, but I have to say that for the first time in a while, I thought of him when I read the paper. It seems an uncanny coincidence that you are before me now. Maybe there is a god, and you are one of his angels," Fallow stopped to smile at Ridgewood. "You certainly look like one, and perhaps you're here to receive this message." He nodded to Ridgewood and grinned. "Or I'm wrong, and the connection is a mere coincidence. Either way, ask anything that will clear me and speed up your case. I have no need for an attorney."

Ridgewood thanked him and asked, "I guess a name of this man you described, for starters, would help."

Fallow frowned. "That I do not know, but I could describe him perfectly. However, as a data collector, it's possible I have his name in storage." He gestured somewhere outside his office. "We recently upgraded our systems; have to in our world. But I keep every hard drive that I've owned personally and professionally since that Timmons's incident. Access to someone's hard drive is more revealing than a diary." He chuckled to himself. "If you give me some time, I'll get to those drives and see if I can find this guy's name."

"Gee thanks," Presto amicably responded. He lifted his rear and procured his wallet. He handed the two business cards to Fallow. "Keep one. We'd appreciate if you give us a call whether you glean something or not. On the other, please, if you may, list all your contact numbers in case we need to reach you."

Fallow took the cards and hesitated before he set out and completed the request. When Presto received the card, he overtly only touched the edges, and dropped it in the inside pocket of his sport jacket. Inside was an open evidence bag. Presto's fingers found the thread and sealed it.

Ridgewood looked to Presto, searching his face for his thoughts. He winked.

Ridgewood finally returned a smile to Fallow. "I appreciate your unsolicited assistance," she said easily. "First, I'd like to ask you a few more questions."

CHAPTER FIFTY-EIGHT

Presto rubbed their two knives together, as if he were sharpening their edges. He returned Ridgewood's knife and cut into his porterhouse steak with exaggerated relish. Ridgewood laughed at his theatrics, while Presto wondered how he lived all these years without the company of a female friend.

Presto realized that being in the presence of hotness was not difficult, as he once feared. He recycled jokes between his two dates successfully and learned to ask the right questions that allowed the women to carry the conversation. It was like detective work. He was having a blast. Plus, the best part was, dates seemed to revolve around food—familiar ground.

Ridgewood suggested dinner to cover the day's events, specifically Dean Fallow. Ridgewood was harder to turn down than a free meal, and Presto wanted to flesh out his thoughts with her.

After feasting on the main course, a porterhouse for three, they sank into the meat of the matter. A slightly suddenly troubled Ridgewood asked, "So you think you've seen Fallow before? There are only so many places that could be."

Presto sucked in some air like he was ready for a task of great exertion. "I think I may know where but am hesitant to make the conclusion, because if so, Fallow is our man, and I do not want uncertainty to lead us in the wrong direction."

Ridgewood jolted alert. "Where? Tell me. From the moment I laid eyes on the guy, I feel like I've seen him before. Recently. He looks too damn familiar, but I just can't place it."

This intrigued Presto. "If memory serves me right, last week, Palm Sunday, at Grace Cathedral." But then he spaced his hands in a *who knows* gesture.

Despite his caution, Ridgewood gyrated her body in a little seated samba celebration. "Oh, Dom, we could use a break," she squealed. "That must be where I remember him from too." The connection seemed to relieve her, but she noticed he was not quite as bubbly. "What's wrong?"

He sighed. "We could be wrong; a mind trick projecting a wish." He saw her face scrunch in doubt. "The man I saw looked different but similar. But, we know the killer's penchant for disguise. I can't be sure, and even if it is

Fallow, we have no proof. I have a hunch that whether it's Fallow or not, this will not end as routinely as we like."

Ridgewood chose to stay upbeat. "You may be right on all counts. Fallow could be an innocent man, but if not, Dom, this is a break, and evidence may surface if we get a warrant. Remember we've found hair and other evidence before. Then there was the foreign blood on Markov."

Presto could not dispute her optimism. "We'll see. Unfortunately, I think our man is too cunning for this to be transparent and dissolve like tissue paper."

"What do you make of this story Fallow told us about the guy he interviewed? Imagine if this lead turns out to be the Myth Man."

Despite a table void of food, Presto sniffed, but it was a whiff of disbelief. "He may turn out to be, but not the actual killer."

Ridgewood knew what he was getting at. "Ah, that means you truly suspect Fallow."

"I suspect I'm still hungry," Presto said with a laugh. "Now how about dessert?"

Ridgewood huffed. "I shouldn't, but why not. You're a bad influence," she reprimanded, "in a good way," she grinned.

"The Calorie Kid strikes again."

"So will my dentist."

After they ordered dessert, she asked if they should call Danko and apprise him of their feelings on Fallow.

"I figured I'd wait until tomorrow. I want to be better sure of myself."

Their chocolate soufflé arrived, and the smell and taste killed the conversation for several minutes, minus mimed eye gesticulations and moans of pleasure.

Presto finished his dessert uncomfortably before Ridgewood. With salivating difficulty, he watched her finish the last several mouthfuls.

As soon as she took the napkin from her lip, he asked, "I need a favor."

She reached for her mineral water. "Sure, what?"

"I want a list run of every name possibly associated with Fallow's life: every person in the town he grew up with, classmates and teachers throughout his scholastic career, co-workers, relatives, you get the idea."

"I do. What are you looking for?"

Presto chose to lie. It was not because he wanted to keep secrets from Ridgewood or because, as he was often accused, he was trying to go it alone and gain the glory. This was different; it was personal. Myth Man had inside information. Someone set him up. He wanted to know who that was. The connection would also affirm Fallow's guilt. Despite his hesitations with Ridgewood, he sensed Fallow was their man. "I want to cross-check his name with a multitude of things like security at the cathedrals, police, a whole bunch of things."

Ridgewood smiled mischievously. "Sounds like a whole bunch of bull, but you're the famous detective. I'll get you what you need."

"Thanks," gushed Presto.

She smiled and then said. "Oh yeah, I liked your *old* trick in getting Fallow's prints. Too bad you couldn't get some hair and blood samples to compare them with the recent clues we got."

"That was more to rattle him. We have no prints. Let's keep in mind that thus far, most of the clues have been planted."

"My, my, you are the ever cautious one. Maybe I'm too hopeful."

"It's okay, Lorraine. I prayed today for the first time in ages. We could all use a little hope right now."

CHAPTER FIFTY-NINE

Myth Man opened the safe house garage door and entered the now dilapidated kitchen. He'd check on the homeowner in a minute. First he had to make an important call.

He pulled out a stolen, secure cell phone and dialed. After a few rings, his contact answered. Myth Man got to the meat of the matter. "I had a visit today from Detective Presto and Agent Ridgewood."

"She's a real ball buster but better than her partner, Agent Donavan."

Myth Man smirked. "You don't know, man," he said literally. "She badgered my balls until they were sandblasted blue. That's not nice, since she was so pleasant the last time I saw her. Meanwhile, Presto barely said a word. It didn't matter. He knew. I could tell."

"Sure you're not paranoid?"

"No," Myth Man declared emphatically. "Presto knows. It had to end sometime," he lamented. "That's obvious. One more, and I'm done."

Myth Man heard the man breathe deeply. Then, "Bail now, buddy. You're famous. You've made your mark. Set the plan. Be a phoenix, die, and live again."

Myth Man knew the advice was sound. Why risk it? He wanted one last thrill and was not sure yet if he could execute his plan involving the Iraqi crate. Either way, it was almost time to shift the blame and disappear. Pretso would have his doubts, but the Dankos of the world would want the case wrapped up. With no murders forthcoming, over time, the man in the safe house would go down in history as Myth Man. On his deathbed, Myth Man would reveal his genius.

"I'm going tonight. It's a Sikh holiday. I'll be careful. If I can't do it, I won't."

The man sniffed. "You're my friend, but I'm also saying this from a financial standpoint. I think you should quit."

"You'll get your money," Myth Man said evenly. "Tonight."

"Where?" the man stammered.

Myth Man laughed. "What's the matter? You don't trust me?"

"No, I do," the man said with the conviction of a prostate surgeon responding to the question, *Will this hurt?* "But I am the one person who knows your identity. Do you trust me?"

"I do," Myth Man said with utter conviction. "Naming me only incriminates you. Anyway, let's meet at a public place. A bar. We'll toast to our success and to the day when we may meet again. The money will be in the briefcase. You give me the papers and the keys to the car."

His contact did not respond immediately, but when he did, there was noticeable relief. "That sounds like a swell idea. I'm buying."

"With all that money, you better. Oh, by the way, what's my new name?"

The guy laughed. "Chip Dexter."

"What? Couldn't you find something more anonymous?"

"Listen, all that matters is that it's clean. No kin came forward. His death has never been reported. You got a decent bank account. The guy was a professional gambler. He had no friends to speak of, so Chip Dexter it is."

The name annoyed him, but he knew his contact was right. "Thanks. Meet me at Mash Mill at 3:00 am."

"Be careful."

Myth Man grinned. Betrayal is a beautiful thing. Judas was a personal hero.

After he hung up, Myth Man prepared. He carried two bags to the bedroom and placed objects in the comatose man's hands. Then, around the safe house, he scattered evidence that would incriminate the ex-marine. Makeup kits and various disguises were placed in the bathroom cabinet.

In the parents' old room, he deposited paraphernalia from all of the crime scenes on a dresser. Lastly, he took off his latex gloves and removed his wedding ring. He returned to the soon to be dead man's room. After registering the man's prints on his ring, he returned to the parent's room and placed the wedding ring next to one that had belonged to the sushi chef he'd disposed of.

Myth Man returned to the garage, opened the van doors, and removed another duffel bag. He removed two wire-connected IEDs from the bag. He placed one on the bed; the other he rigged to the front door.

Myth Man had to credit his victim for the final idea of his plan. When the man showed him the two improvised explosive devices a friend in the service had smuggled out of Iraq, the idea came immediately.

He carried the now-emaciated man he'd spent the worst part of five months with and sat him by the front door next to the explosive. He left and then returned with a few of the man's guns. He propped a Chinese made AK-47 assault rifle in his hands.

"Sorry, pal. It's been real and all. We've had fun, haven't we? No hard feelings."

Myth Man looked around one final time before he grabbed his laptop and marched through the kitchen door to the garage. The garage door opened, and he walked out into a starless evening. Heck, they were in Queens.

As he reached the sidewalk, he looked back to the safe house for a final time.

It was nearly one o'clock in the morning when Myth Man arrived at the Gurdwara in Richmond Hills, Queens. He wore a blue turban, darkened his skin, and sported a fake trimmed beard. The clothes were retro and out of style. Myth Man came to the conclusion that the average middle-aged Sikh male drew his fashion tastes from aged sitcoms on the rerun circuit.

As he hoped, Myth Man did not detect any police presence. Normally, his kills were several weeks apart. There was no way they expected this. Not even Presto.

The Gurdwara he approached was similar to the Kali temple in that it was merely another house on the block. To Myth Man's amusement, the previous Sikh center had burned to the ground, and the Sikh's were forced to set up smaller centers in the meantime.

A relatively new religion, it was started by the first of ten Gurus, Guru Nanak, who was born in 1469. Unlike most other religions, Sikhism was not based on mythological lore, which made it an unlikely target for Myth Man.

If he had his druthers, Myth Man would have rather taken his anger out on the Mormons, Jews, or maybe even a celebrity cultlike group such as Scientology for the last hoorah, but alas, the show could not go on forever.

Baisakhi was New Year's to both the Sikhs and Hindus, but for the Sikhs it was held in special regard. The day honors the creation of the Khalsa, or Sikh brotherhood.

The tenth guru, Gobind Singh Sahib, called a meeting in 1699 where more than fifty thousand attended. He brandished a sword and asked who was willing to die for their faith. His call was met with silence. He asked again and again. A man named Daya Ram took the challenge. He was led back into a tent. After several moments, the guru emerged with a now bloody sword. He repeated his call until another man accepted giving his life for his faith. Once again, he was led back into a tent, and only the Guru emerged, his sword fresh with blood.

The Guru repeated his message until five men were taken back to the tents. Then, the five men emerged in new robes and were baptized as Khalsa, or pure ones, who were to be part saint, scholar, and soldier.

Now, Myth Man would also venerate the memory with a modern day Khalsa of his own: an army of the dead.

Outside the Gurdwara door, Myth Man took out his phone and dialed. He was ready.

Sikh and destroy.

CHAPTER SIXTY

Pritam Lochab, at last, fell into his favorite, albeit beat up, recliner when the telephone rang. He expected the call; only he had hoped the man would be late. He was as tired and ragged as the frayed chair that supported him.

The day's festivities had been had been splendid. As Granthi, or reader of the Guru Granth, the Sikh's scripture book, he was also owner of the house that acted as a Gurdwara.

The day started early and ended late. Breakfast, lunch, and dinner were all served in the makeshift dining hall which was a converted basement. He cherished every day, especially one that drew attention to the tenets of his faith. Yet, since he passed the big six-o, he found himself easily exhausted. Thankfully, sleep was not far away. He had one more matter to deal with.

About six weeks earlier, a man he'd never seen before attended a service. Afterward, he lingered around and then introduced himself as Amar Deepinder. He said he was on business in New York and wanted to scout the area for a possible relocation from Chicago. The visitor was likeable and well-versed in his faith.

A few weeks later, Deepinder called again and explained that indeed he was moving to New York City. First he'd come alone and find a place to live. Then he'd bring his family. He did say he lamented the loss of their Cultural Center and pledged to provide a *significant* contribution to make the new center one of the finest in the United States.

Lochab expected to see Deepinder for the Baisakhi festivities, but he called and explained there were flight delays due to a storm in Chicago, and thus, he would not arrive until late that evening. An hour ago, he called again, in a huff. A hotel clerk had called him a terrorist, and there had been a heated exchange. Deepinder explained he could not dishonor his faith and spend the night in such an establishment. He asked if he could spend the evening at the Gurdwara.

Naturally, Lochab accepted. He empathized with Deepinder's experience. Mistaken for Muslims, many Sikh's had been subjected to racial attacks along those lines. He would never turn away a brother in need, and a proper Gurdwara stayed open twenty-four hours a day.

Lochab answered the phone. "Amar?"

"Yes," he answered. "I'm outside now."

"I'm coming now." Lochab went to the door. At the hallway entrance, he faced a painted image of Guru Granth Sahib and bowed before he continued on.

Lochab opened the door and invited his guest in. In proper tradition, Myth Man had removed his shoes and also bowed to the Guru; his head touched the ground. He then placed a fifty-dollar bill in a bowl beside the picture.

"Thank you for rescuing me, Pritam."

"Think nothing of it," Lochab replied warmly. "Come with me." As he led Myth Man to a guest room, he felt a simultaneous hand on his shoulder and a prick in his neck.

Lochab crumbled to the ground. Confused, he tried to rise but was unable. He looked up to Deepinder, who now leered at him, and spoke in an entirely different accent.

"You know what this is?" the assailant asked. In his grasp was a Kirpan, the sacred sword of Sikhs.

Locab knew but was unable to reply. He wondered if this was Deepinder, the man he'd met earlier or someone pretending to be him. No, he was sure this was the same man. It did not matter. He knew the man that stood over him was the notorious Myth Man.

"Normally, I like to spend some time with my victims and tell them how silly their religion is, but I must apologize. Tonight, time is scarce, and I must be on my way. I know that must be a disappointment. Trust me, the feeling's mutual. Oh well," Myth Man said and crouched with the Kirpan aligned with Lochab's throat.

He smiled triumphantly. "I'm the eleventh guru. Like the original Khalsa, you were willing to die for your faith."

Myth Man looked at his watch, shrugged, and then with fierce determination, split Lochab's throat.

When he was done, he left, but not before taking his fifty dollars back.

CHAPTER SIXTY-ONE

ALTHOUGH HE HAD NOT arrived first, Myth Man entered the Mash Mill and occupied an empty booth in the rear. He saw his contact peeking out from a phone booth across the street. This was confirmed when the contact arrived with the same blue jeans and black loafers that he'd just seen.

The man slid into the booth across the table.

They greeted with a firm handshake and pulled away, wriggling their fingers, something they had done since they'd met at college. They were total campus opposites. Myth Man was shy and stayed to himself, while his counterpart was the ladies' man, fraternity president, and party animal. Friends and faculty were amazed when the student known more for his drunken antics than classroom brilliance graduated at the top of his class. In fact, there was no prior scholastic precedent for his sudden performance. It was not as if anyone witnessed him tackling his books. Booze and broads were his majors.

Ambitious, but not willing to work for it, he heard about a shy student's acumen. In the campus cafeteria, he had approached Myth Man and asked for his help. He offered money, drugs, whatever he desired to help him pass a few classes. At first, he thought his offer was to be declined, but instead, the kid scribbled his off-campus apartment number and told him to call.

A few days later, they met, and what the shy guy proposed was crazy but brilliant. At most, he hoped he could get him to write a paper or two and tutor him enough to get by. Myth Man had a different idea. He asked for two hours alone and told him to return.

When he returned to the apartment and the door opened, his jaw dropped like a hard struck, pocketed billiard ball. It was as if he opened the door to a mirror. Momentarily, he wondered if he had an identical twin that had been separated at birth, but he knew this was the student.

The brain would take the tests for him. He was confident it would work. The brain mimicked his voice and swagger perfectly. It was the kid's price that shocked him.

He figured the scheme would cost him dearly, both in dollars and ass kissing. His father was rich, so he'd charm the money from his mother. Money, however, was not the brain's wish. Instead, he stated three names, all of who were part time girlfriends of the debtor. The brain wanted to bed three of his hottest babes.

Not for a second was he repulsed. A guy needs it, he reasoned, and clearly this kid wasn't getting much. The price was right—free for him, at least. In fact, there was a certain thrill to getting his girls drunk and horny and then leaving the room for some indiscriminate reason, only to have his double appear and finish the job.

The relationship was a boon to both men, and a bond was forged, one that no one knew existed. It had to be that way.

This time his old double was dressed in a turban, and his skin shaded. If he had not known about his planned assault on the Sikh's, he would have never guessed it was his friend. In fact, it had been a long time since he'd seen him in anything but a disguise. "Nice getup." His visage grew more serious. "So, did you? A finger quickly went to his throat and drew back.

Myth Man smiled like he'd hit a game winning home run. "Sure did. It was so beautiful. I feel like a heavyweight champion who retires undefeated but always wonders if he had a few more paydays in him before he's eventually dethroned. I need a break, but in time," he said with a crooked grin, "I may come out of retirement."

The other man exhaled caution. "You'll have a whole new identity. Give it time, but if you wanted to pad the resume and continue the rebellion against the religious hegemony duping mankind, there's no doubt that you could reappear."

"Yeah, but for starters, not having to spend another minute of my life with my wife is worth it all. Bitch," Myth Man snorted. "I'll have to get myself a new honey, a nice church-going girl whom I can corrupt and enlighten."

"Hey, at least your new persona is hip. This Chip Dexter was quite a ladies' man at the casinos. Thankfully, he was more committed to cards than making a woman honest. Dexter, by the way, was a whore. Those high-stakes players always get pussy, even if they pay for it. The guy in the morgue said Dexter suffered from multiple sexually transmitted diseases, but at least you won't have to look like a square the rest of your life. Live it up, in a quiet sort of way."

A waitress who looked as aged as the other colonial relics that made up the dim décor stopped by for their order. When she left, she eyed them with some curiosity. She returned several long minutes later with their drinks. Like old times, they toasted White Russian drinks and enjoyed the silence as they contemplated the end and the future.

Myth Man killed his drink and propped a black and beaten briefcase on the table. Carefully, with the lip opening away from the bar, he flashed the money. He took out a stack and shut the lid. He handed the money across the table. "Buy yourself a new suit and some ties. You looked frumpy last time I saw you on the TV." He pushed the case against the wall next to a print of mounted hunters, who followed a pack of hounds on an apparent foxhunt.

Next, a second, new briefcase rose from the bench to the table. "Everything you need is in here," the contact said. "Take a look if you want." He then pulled car keys from his pocket. "Dexter has some nice wheels."

Myth Man saw the BMW emblem and took the keys. "Thanks."

"Oh, by the way, the car's double-parked across the street with the hazards on. Fear not, there's a large laminated pass on the dash. Any cop who sees that vehicle will likely guard it."

Myth Man looked his long-time associate over for the last time and realized the man had never changed. Despite some prominence, he was still a scoundrel and nothing more than a bureaucratic lackey.

Myth Man reached across the table and patted the man on the shoulder. "I guess this is it."

The man looked both forlorn and excited at the same time. "This sounds cheesy, but it's been real."

"It has. Bye," he said and got up, "for now."

Myth Man walked to the entrance and left. Outside he looked at his watch, specifically the second hand. Then he noticed the blinking BMW and quickly walked over.

Inside the bar, the man grabbed the briefcase and walked to the front. Outside the window, he saw the BMW drive away and out of sight. Giddy, he went to the bar, ordered one last drink, and returned to the same table.

He sipped his drink. It made him think of blue waters, palm trees, and bikinis. He fingered the briefcase. He never knew money could look so beautiful. In fact, he wanted, no, he needed, to see those crisp bills again. His fingers found the snaps and pressed.

Myth Man had slowed and was still only a few blocks away when he heard the explosion. He looked at his watch. He was surprised to discover that more than three minutes had elapsed before his contact, Spencer Hoole, opened the briefcase a second time.

He privately guessed it would take less than a ninety seconds.

CHAPTER SIXTY-TWO

THERE WAS ANOTHER EXPLOSION. This time it was Presto's fist as it slammed down upon his prized desk. The impetus was both anger for knowing who had sold him out and joy for connecting Dean Fallow with Spencer Hoole.

Through the night and into the morning, he poured through the reports he'd requested from Ridgewood. He'd almost fallen asleep as the names merged together. It was like reading a phone book. But then, listed in Fallow's campus directory, he found the name Spencer Hoole.

In reality, Presto could have saved himself time. He primarily suspected Hoole but chose not to be name-specific in his search for a connection to Myth Man. Fallow and Hoole went to college together. Fallow *had* to be Myth Man, and Hoole was his contact.

Although it was nearly four o'clock in the morning, he grabbed his cell with the intent of dialing Ridgewood, when he was startled to hear his phone ring, and see her name appear on the screen. He thought of some paranormal, cosmic connection. Camille would have been amused and have some metaphysical answer for the event.

"Ridgewood?"

"Yeah. You sound awake," she said, sounding edgy.

Presto sighed, but his voice perked up. "I have news for you, but I presume you have something as well, since you called."

"Yeah," she said energized. "Fallow called, frantic. He was cursing us, saying he's trapped in a black van. He said that guy he had mentioned turned up. He accused us of being followed and claims he's been abducted. He guessed they were somewhere in Brooklyn. He gave me the man's name. Gary Sykes. I …"

"Bullshit," Presto interjected. This meant Fallow was on the run and had some patsy lined up from the beginning. Why not? This had been well orchestrated from the get go. His mind raced. "I have to tell you something first."

"What, Dom?"

"Keep this quiet for now. Myth Man had inside info on our case, so I knew someone fed him information. Thanks to the lists you ran for me, it seems Fallow and Spencer Hoole from the mayor's office graduated from college together, top of the class. It's not a coincidence, Lorraine. Fallow *is* our man."

"I believe you. I'll call and get someone to triangulate Fallow's cell phone call. We might as well pursue this name he gave us, Sykes. If it's Fallow, he pointed us there for a reason. Should we go, or should I give Danko a call and have him send someone there?"

"Tell Danko to send someone there, but tell them to proceed with caution. This may be a trap. Like you said, Fallow wants us there for a reason; let's not assume it's a good one. Let's meet at Danko's in an hour."

"I'm tired as can be," groaned Ridgewood, "yet you sound alert. What's the secret? Lots of coffee?"

"Nah, sugar is my caffeine. I had a box of chocolates and rationed them well," he said as he gazed at it. All the different slots that were once filled with chocolate treats were now vacant.

*****

"My God," Presto said as the cab neared Danko's station. There was some commotion ahead, so Presto thanked the cabbie and got out. The first thing he noticed was a throng of news vans. Police officers were everywhere. Something was going on.

Once inside, it was evident something terrible had transpired. On the way to Danko's office, he passed a group of officers, three with grave expressions and another who cried softly.

Danko stood outside his office, talking to a few of his men. When he saw Presto, he gestured him to his office and then followed several long seconds later.

When Danko rounded his desk, he punched the back of his chair back and then got angry when the chair rolled away from him as he tried to sit. Finally seated, he scratched at his thumb. "I lost four of my men tonight at Sykes's place. Another two are in critical condition, not to mention others who were severely wounded. These are not just people who report to me but friends." His voice trailed off, and his eyelids fluttered.

Danko recalled the memories they shared. While Presto vaguely knew only one of the injured, he shared Danko's remorse. Despite any internal differences, the police force was a family that stuck together in dire times.

Danko was in the midst of a story about a camping trip when it occurred to Presto that he'd yet to hear where and how the tragedy occurred. He was about to ask when the two agents arrived. For once, sensing the unrest, Donavan was quiet.

Danko explained he had decided not to act on Hoole yet and instead wait and see what turned up at Sykes's home first. In the meantime, Danko dispatched two of his men to watch Hoole's apartment entrance, just in case he made a sudden, unexpected dash. Danko had planned, with relish, to be at city hall before Hoole's normal 8:00 am arrival time. He despised the man, but for now, it had to wait. The fate of his men was his only concern.

Danko was reluctant to broach what had happened. These were his brothers. His mind drifted to their wives and children. For the first time, he thought about quitting the force. He remembered being elated when he'd been assigned this case. Since then, his family had left him, and now he'd lost friends. He had a hard time remembering the last time he was happy, not counting his drunken spree with Agent Donavan.

Danko tried to fight back a geyser of painful emotions, "Detective Rick Hoglan was on the line when I heard the explosion." He swallowed and continued. "Sykes's place was rigged in at least two locations. The injured and dead were removed, and the bomb squad's been sent in. They'll call when it's safe to investigate further.

Almost on cue, the phone rang. Danko picked up and listened. His face grew still. After a few moments, he hung up. His eyes looked at but through them. "The two men in critical condition … they're dead."

CHAPTER SIXTY-THREE

Presto and the two agents went out for breakfast and gave Danko time to deal with the difficult responsibilities that lay ahead. The mood was like the cafe, bland and gloomy.

In the span of twenty-four hours, they lost Reverend Perkins, Markov, and six police officers. The last time more police officers perished in a single event was the September 11, 2001 tragedy.

Nothing had to be said. Nothing was said. Donavan was thankfully sensible and picked at his food. Presto's appetite was subdued, but he managed to finish his plate of greasy home fries, dry scrambled eggs, and hard, ready to crumble on contact, toast.

When they returned, Danko was even more flushed. He almost wished he'd died in the blast. What did he have to live for? All six of these men were happily married. Yes, it almost would have been easier to die than to call the victims' wives and hear their strained voices, the helpless pleas, the shrieking cries, and the cold, deathly silence.

Danko had a long day ahead of him, but he knew how the night would end. Never a big drinker, he amassed bottles from parties and holiday gifts. Tonight, he would drink until he was numb and hopefully pass out. Despite little sleep, he knew that uninhibited, the night would bring demons that would make rest impossible.

"I have news for you," Danko said in a modulated tone. "Hoole never reported to work. He's also dead. We've been busy with all this," Danko said with a heavy frown, "but in the early morning, a bomb exploded in a small pub. At first, terrorism was considered, but that dive was hardly a worthwhile target. There were no survivors, and Hoole's body was unrecognizable, without getting descriptively graphic. Nothing like a credit card, though, when it comes to durability. His was found, and further tests conclude Hoole died in the blast."

No one mourned or offered any eulogy over Hoole's explosive demise

Presto was reluctant to talk about the case out of respect for the fallen but thought that might be the best way to ease the remorse. "I know this may not be the right moment to discuss work, but it seems to me Fallow covered his tracks and eliminated potential threats." Presto stopped. He did not want to press, despite his feeling of anger and urgency.

Danko raised a hand of reassurance. "Presto, it's okay. You three have a job to do. Go to Sykes's place and see what they found. Please, keep me in the loop. I have to visit city hall. Mayor Golden wants to personally visit the wives of the deceased." There was no contempt in Danko's voice, just sorrow. Despite his deep dislike for Hoole, he genuinely liked the mayor.

Danko's face sagged. "Oh, I almost forgot. Now that you mentioned it, it seems Fallow's wife contacted a switchboard operator looking for information on her husband. She said he'd called and claimed to have been abducted. He said he'd already contacted the cops and told her to, believe this, pray for him."

Despite the carnage at the Sykes house, there was evidence aplenty. In fact, it was all the evidence you could ask for.

They found a costume bag with props, disguises, and makeup. There was a computer hard drive that revealed further incriminating evidence. The refrigerator, which had been partially destroyed due to its proximity to the garage door, still held stable vials of the poison tetrodotoxin.

Lined on a bedroom shelf were incriminating souvenirs. The row of trinkets from left to right were: a wedding ring from the sushi chef and her apparent lover's eyeglasses, the Muslim cleric's turban, the Catholic priest's rosary beads, a finger from the Kali effigy, the grip from Reverend Perkins's wheelchair, Markov's stethoscope, a torn page from Lochab's Guru Granth Sahib, and finally Fallow's wedding ring.

There was further evidence that another man, besides the three officers on what was the other side of the door, perished. Assault rifles were strewn everywhere.

It was every detective's dream—all the evidence you could ask for, case closed. Presto knew it wasn't. Ridgewood and Donavan weren't sold either. They'd alerted headquarters, and pictures of Fallow had been distributed to law enforcement officials countrywide.

Presto was not optimistic.

Chapter Sixty-Four

Commissioner Tipton handled the press and was truthful, by all accounts, but speculation and details were still omitted. Tipton stuck with the facts.

Two religious leaders from the Protestant and Sikh religions were murdered. The police spoke to many people on the case. One was Dean Fallow, president of Iron Fortress Systems. Later, Fallow contacted the police claiming Gary Sykes abducted him. On that tip, the police went to the Sykes' residence in Bay Ridge. The place had been rigged with explosives, and six officers died. When the embers cooled, detectives found Sykes's corpse. They also found guns and evidence that was linked with the Myth Man case, including a drug the killer used and items that were connected to Myth Man's victims. For the moment, Fallow's status was listed as missing.

At Mayor Golden's directive, Tipton also mentioned Hoole's death in the Mash Mill explosion. He went further and stated that, for whatever it's worth, investigators noted that both Fallow and Hoole attended the same university, at the same time. The connection was being investigated.

Danko was preoccupied with the deaths of his men, but Presto heard that his wife decided to be near him during this time of grief. These were her friends too, especially the mourning wives. Presto heard a hint of optimism.

The two agents prepared for Malcolm Bailey's arrival. Ridgewood privately told Presto that Bailey would be in New York until the end of Passover. The main purpose of his visit had to do with another matter, but he also wanted to assist with the case.

While everyone fiddled, Presto burned.

He also missed Camille. He never spoke to her after Easter, and two days later, he found an envelope wedge under his front door. Inside was a note.

If I didn't know what a nice guy you were, I'd think you were blowing me off! Just kidding. I know you've been busy. And let me say that I feel for you. I know you've been through a lot. I'm going back to California to close out my affairs there. It should take a couple of weeks or so. I look forward to seeing you upon my return. Be careful. I did a reading, and your future is dark and murky. Good luck with everything. If you need someone to talk to, I can be reached at (858) 763-4452.

Love, Camille

CHAPTER SIXTY-FIVE

"Another round," slurred Donavan at the female bartender, who wore so little clothing that Presto wondered if she was cold. Maybe the hard work kept the blood motoring, he gathered.

Presto put a hand up in protest, but Donavan ignored it like a runner that blows past a third base coach's stop signal and heads for home. "Yeah, right," Donavan mocked.

What the hell, thought Presto. They needed a wild respite, and Bailey was treating.

Bailey had arrived a few days prior, but he'd been preoccupied. He'd called Presto and explained.

The crate from Iraq was set to arrive to coincide with the Jewish Passover. Negotiations between the U.S. and Iraq governments allowed the Jewish people to claim their artifact, but only if it was delivered to America. The Orthodox religious parties in Israel insisted the find be given and governed under the auspices of a responsible organization. After intense lobbying, the crate was to be delivered on the first day of Passover to the Chabad-Lubavitch, a Hasidic organization.

The story of the crate had made the news, but thus far the press had not reported its destination point. Speculation of the crate's contents was rampant, and a one-hour documentary was even shown on the Discovery Channel.

Presto wiped his brow figuratively when Bailey explained the divisiveness and legal, scientific, and religious wrangling he'd witnessed. He readily admitted his own curiosity over what was in the crate. He hoped, being on the scene, he'd get a sneak preview of the discovery.

Donavan suggested a night out on the town, and Bailey obliged, proud that his old alma mater was "shaking off the skirt."

Danko was in no mood for revelry and still mourning his fallen brothers. Ridgewood and Presto were also reluctant, but after they briefed Bailey, he insisted the team unwind over a few drinks. Donavan claimed to know a decent spot for people their age called Sweet Virginia's.

The few drinks became many. Donavan now lined up shots of alcohol, something Presto had not done since college.

The cute bartender, with low-cut jeans that indiscreetly revealed a black, barbed-patterned tattoo each time she turned her back, served their drinks. The drinks were clear but deadly.

"More vodka?" Presto asked, as Donavan slid the shots along the bar.

"Russian jet fuel," answered Donavan. "How do you think those bastards got that Sputnik thing up there before us? You can't survive the Russian winters without it. Just ask the Germans."

Presto wasn't sold. Neither was Bailey, who declared, "I'm Irish, like you Donavan, not Russian. I only drink Jameson."

Donavan laughed. "Am I letting you down? I drank so much whiskey growing up I practically used it with my cereal. Now, good vodka is the only booze I can remotely handle." Donavan whistled to the bartender and asked for two shots of Jameson and another round of vodka for the rest of the group. "Anyone else object before she leaves?"

Ridgewood squinted like the sun was in her eyes. "Hey, I can knock them back with the best of them, but you're all bigger than me. Let's slow it down a bit."

"I'm twice as big as all of you combined," Presto said gaily, "and I've never been this shitfaced in my life."

They all laughed except Donavan who spouted air like the first steam bursting through a kettle. "Party poopers," he lamented sarcastically. Then he raised his eyebrows and shot glass and downed them both. Ridgewood and Presto did likewise.

Donavan's face split into a grin, while Ridgewood and Presto grimaced like they had chugged Tabasco sauce. The bartender returned with the extra Jameson, and the ritual was repeated.

As drunk as Presto was, he had to admit that Bailey's plan was working. After days of somber looks, everyone was having a good time. Donavan and Bailey chatted like father and son. Ridgewood and Presto grinned at each other and laughed at each other's sudden wit. Of course, the alcohol oasis was a mirage in the mind, but that was the point, if only for one night.

Presto's vision was now blurred, except when it came to Ridgewood. Her visage was crystal clear, and she looked more beautiful than ever. When she left and then returned from the ladies room, his eyes followed her, and he again considered himself fortunate to be in her company.

The party could not go on forever, though. When he saw the bartender pouring the umpteenth shot, he finally succumbed. "Hey, Donavan. Enough. I'm not used to *drunking* this much," he slurred.

"I hear you, big guy. The last thing I want to see is you throwing up. I saw this special where they cut open this huge whale, and ..."

Ridgewood flew off her stool. She stood up to the seated Donavan, and yet there was not much height disparity between them.

"That was out of line, Donavan," she steamed.

Bailey's head swayed, and he wobbled on his stool before he steadied himself. "Carter Donavan" he admonished. "How many times have I warned you about ridiculing others over your own insecurities derived from your unpleasant upbringing? Talent alone will not suffice. Discipline yourself. I can't save you forever."

Bailey was clearly blitzed. A fire burned in his belly. His voice was overly demonstrative.

Presto was a tad surprised to see Donavan acquiesce to his boss and mentor. He nodded slowly, his face taut and relenting. "I'm sorry, Dom. It was stupid of me, and I mean it because, in your case, I like and respect you." He offered his hand.

Presto readily shook. He thought the reaction was overdone. There was no malice in Donavan's voice. He was just being himself. But it was nice to see Ridgewood and Bailey defend him so. Still, he wanted to end the sudden tense moment with a laugh.

"It's okay, Donavan. If I throw up, I promise you won't see any tires or human remains. I'm picky about what I eat."

Presto's inflection worked, and they all giggled. As Ridgewood turned away, Donavan loudly whispered, "Then you should eat Ridgewood. She's a fish." He barked a laugh, like the seals Presto had seen with Camille the day they toured the Bronx Zoo.

Ridgewood spun around. Presto heard her shoe souls screech, like a fast traveling car forced to immediately cut laterally. She braked and smacked Donavan across the face with the force of a high-impact fender bender.

Bailey looked to take control. He rose from his stool like a doddering king leaving his throne for war. "Donavan, you deserved that. This is ridiculous. We were having fun." Bailey gulped his drink and flagged the bartender. "One more round; let's drink and make up."

The call to party did not assuage the two combatants. They stared at each other hard, like two boxers before they're asked to touch the gloves.

Ridgewood spoke first. "You're an asshole." She moved back to her stool in between Bailey and Presto.

As Ridgewood's rear touched the seat, Donavan replied with venom, "You're a cold cunt. No wonder your husband wanted to strangle himself with hookers."

Presto flinched. He felt compelled to respond, despite the consequences. So did Bailey. The words were bad enough, but the sneer in Donavan's voice was triumphant.

A barback with a steroid-enhanced body and shaved, lumpy head grabbed Donavan by the collar.

"That's no way to talk to a lady. I'm *gonna* ask you to leave. If you're a smart boy, you'll exit. If not, I'm *gonna* boot your ass out of here." He let go of the shirt and gestured his head towards the door. "Capiche?"

Bailey again tried to establish his authority. "I'll take control of the situation."

The barback was not assuaged. "No, sir. I've watched this unfold. You're drunk, and you *ain't* doing jack."

Presto, who avoided confrontation like health foods, pleaded, "Hey, let's go outside and get some fresh air and let cooler heads prevail."

Hazy, Bailey was at a loss for words, but Donavan wasn't. "Yeah, let's blow this dump." He looked at the barback, sized him up, sniffed, and said, "Trust me, cue ball, I'd rather not crack that Humpty Dumpty –looking head. Stop with the tough guy act, and go scrub the men's room, or I'll hit you so many times you'll think you're surrounded."

Everyone within earshot stared at both of them.

The barback scowled. Donavan, meanwhile, beamed a sunny smile and casually lifted his jacket from the stool.

Bailey rose, as did Presto. When Donavan stepped toward the door, Presto thought all would end well.

Donavan quickly turned back into Bailey, pressing them against the bar. "I apologize. In my haste to exit this foul establishment, I almost forgot to leave a tip to reward the wonderful hospitality." He rummaged through his pocket. To the bartender, he said, "Thanks, honey. You did a fine job with the shots. Here's a fifty for you."

At first she fidgeted, but the money gained her interest, and she meandered over, with an awkward grin, and took the bill. She winked.

Donavan then flicked a quarter in the air, caught it, and snapped it down on his wrist. He looked. "Tails never fails," he declared. He looked at the coin and then turned to the barback. "It's shiny like your head." He tossed the quarter on the bar, and it rolled toward the barback. "Get a new shave. I think I saw some pubic scruff on the back of your cranium."

The barback snapped like a provoked viper. His fist lashed out, but like a mongoose, Donavan was quicker and sidestepped the wayward punch, which caught Bailey on the shoulder.

Presto, never a fighter and blind drunk as he was, did not flinch. Ridgewood, however, sprung to life, and with a primal scream, she dove into the mix and pulled at the two agents with surprising strength. "Let's go," she screamed.

Like a wave, they all flowed toward the door, all the while, Donavan and the bulging barback traded barbs. An actual fight would have been a competitive affair, but verbally, Donavan slew him like a paper dragon.

Outside, Ridgewood immediately checked on Bailey, who was defiant that he did not feel a thing from the punch. Presto was certain that in Bailey's condition he might not have differentiated if he'd been struck with an iron mace. Donavan declared the night was not yet over and suggested a new bar. Bailey quickly agreed. Ridgewood called them fools and implored them to call it quits.

Donavan looked to Presto, who also declined.

"Awe, I get it." His eyes roamed back and forth from Presto to Ridgewood.

Ridgewood, for the second time, walked over and smacked Donavan in the face. Bailey grabbed Donavan and pulled him away.

They kept walking.

Chapter Sixty-Six

Presto tried to open his eyes, but pain prohibited his brain from sending the appropriate signals. He envisioned his head with an array of needles sticking out of it. Acupuncture amok, which made him look like Pinhead from the *Hellraiser* movies. Gingerly, a hand went to his head, and it felt normal, despite the piercing sensations.

Parched, he tried to summon saliva, but the well was dry. Now, he had to open an eye. He always went to bed with a beverage on his nightstand. Through one slit of an eye, he saw no drink.

His eye closed and then reopened, much wider, albeit for the moment, the other was tethered shut. Something was wrong. Or was he in the midst of some alcohol-prescribed dream? The pain he felt was all too real, so he focused.

There was a nightstand and an alarm clock, but his was different. This was a cheap stock digital model. Presto's was one that was adapted for use with his iPod.

His eyes swept past the nightstand. The walls had Tuscan-colored wallpaper with scattered pedestrian flower prints in black and gold frames. The windows had curtains not blinds, besides the fact that proportions were all wrong. His windows were split. This was one large frame. And there were rugs?

Presto's second eye now opened. This was not his room, and it wasn't familiar. His mind said hotel based on the sparse and generic furnishings. Was he so drunk that he had checked into a hotel?

Then Presto used other senses besides sight. He smelled something fragrant, something feminine. Then he used his sixth sense and detected a presence besides him. He had a hunch but could not believe it. He decided to slowly roll his head over, eyes closed, in sleeplike fashion. After a few minutes, he'd peak.

As Presto built the courage to shift, he suddenly realized that other than his socks, he was naked. He grew more nervous. After a long minute, he slowly turned his head. After a longer minute, he opened one eye enough to catch a hazy view.

Thankfully, she was lying on her side with her back to him, but he could tell by the shape and color of her hair that it was definitely Agent Lorraine Ridgewood.

He clamped his eye shut and delved into his short-term memory. He recalled the incident at the bar and that Bailey and Donavan had continued their binge, so that left him alone with Ridgewood. That's where things went cloudy. Then an image flashed across his mind. He was kissing a woman, passionately. It was Ridgewood. This was her place; she had been living out of the hotel since the assignment.

Still, the details were fuzzy. There was only one thing that mattered. Why was he naked, and what, if anything, happened? Despite the pain in his head, he had a self-deprecating moment in his repose. What if this was his first time, and he would never remember the moment?

He thought about gently putting his hand on her shoulder but decided to wait it out. Ridgewood softly breathed as she laid there still. Twenty minutes later, she stirred and rolled over toward him.

Presto half-opened his eyes when they made contact. Drooping, bloodshot eyes stared back. "Do you feel as lousy as I do?" she groaned.

His eyes glazed over, and he groaned in agreement. "Profoundly." He said no more and hoped she'd talk and fill in the blanks.

It worked.

Ridgewood nestled against him. Under the covers, he felt one of her breasts pressed against him. Their heads rested on their pillows, faces only inches apart. His pulse raced.

"Amazing love potion, alcohol is, huh? We work like two civilized adults for months, and then in one drunken fury, we hop into bed together."

Presto decided to be honest. "I'm sorry, Lorraine. I don't really remember much of anything," he said sheepishly.

In jest, her face became reproachful. "I'm insulted." The coquettish smile reappeared. "Kidding. It's okay. We were both pretty lit. And for the record, we didn't have sex. Close, but no cigar, so to speak."

Presto's eyes narrowed. "What?"

"We made a good go at. Don't worry. I was quite satisfied. You do have some appetite," she said as her eyes twinkled. To Presto's delight, she continued without pause. "But you were a bit too drunk, and well, you know—you couldn't get hard enough." She spoke softly without even the hint of an insult.

Presto feebly mumbled "sorry." His first legitimate chance to break his virginity, and he blows it, with a gorgeous woman, nonetheless. Yet, it was still, by far, his most intimate encounter. Although he thought of Camille, he was thrilled to be naked in bed with Ridgewood. If anything, he would have expected remorse, but she was as sweet as ever.

"Dom, it's okay. Hey, we had fun. Consenting adults, although for our sakes, I suggest we not let Donavan get wind of it. He's simply too immature, and I'd rather not deal with his shtick."

Presto, who would have agreed to anything except fasting, quickly replied, "Deal."

Then Ridgewood leaned on Presto and rolled on top of him. The blanket fell revealing her fully. Presto's eyes bulged.

"Dominick," she said strongly. "We may have been drunk, but I harbor no regrets. I've thought about you before," she said and tussled his bird nest hair. "Let me say this, and then we go back to business as usual. When we're through with the case, if you want to meet again, call me."

Presto was thunderstruck. He figured this to be her biggest mistake since she married her philandering husband. Was it really possible that a guy like him could be with a woman as stunning as Lorraine Ridgewood? It certainly seemed so, as he gazed up at her smiling face. They were now sober, and here she was naked atop him.

"You'll hear from me," Presto managed. Then with more eagerness, "That's a promise."

CHAPTER SIXTY-SEVEN

"I NEVER THOUGHT YOU WERE like every other man, but you're no different," Cleo Presto scolded her couch-prone son from the kitchen. "You got a taste, and now you're philandering around town.

Philandering? Huh?

Cleo was full of patriotic color this morning. She had a bright red blouse. Her slacks were crisp blue that receded to white flats. Her makeup had been vigorously applied. Presto noticed that over the past month, she'd been dressing with more flair. At first, he wondered if she'd met someone. Then something else occurred to him, but he dared not ask.

"It's not like that, Ma," Presto mumbled. His mind, body, and soul called for a therapeutic rest. First, though, he had to wait and listen as his mother cooked him as well as an early afternoon breakfast. "We drank too much, and ..." He left the implication unfinished.

She left the stove and leered. "So did you?" she prodded.

Presto was carefree about his weight, but his virginity was another manner. "Ma," he bristled. "Why are you so nosy?"

Cleo Presto laughed, but then her face grew serious. "Because I'm your mother, and I care. Remember, we're partners."

"Ma, if I were a true gentleman, would I kiss and tell?"

"You should never boast, but to confide in a true friend is different," she said persuasively.

"Is that eggs I smell or bullshit?" Presto jazzed.

"I smell something Belgian," she said sniffing the air with a glint in her eyes. Her nose found Presto. "It's you. You're waffling."

Presto straightened to a sitting position. "Well, for what it's worth mom, we fooled around a bit but were too drunk and fell asleep."

As per the norm, Cleo inquired further. "And what was the reaction in the morning?"

"We laughed a bit and left open the possibility of dating when," he emphasized, "the case is over."

She mulled that over and replied, "So where does that leave you with Camille?"

"To be honest, Ma, I'd be lucky to have either woman. They are both

223

pretty and nice, although each different in her own way. Ridgewood is the professional, aspiring woman. She's sweet but fierce and determined. Camille is a free spirit. She's interesting and brings unique traits to the table for a female. Saying all that, I'd be grateful to have a chance with either woman, but if I had to pick one, I'd say Camille."

Cleo smiled. "Well reasoned. You are a good boy. I never doubted you, even if I sounded indignant. I want what's best for you." She returned to the oven, and the sounds of a spatula, sizzling grease, butter being spread on toast, and clattering of silverware were heard.

Presto was nervous, but he had questions of his own. He asked now, while her face was not visible. "Whatever you ask of me, I tell you. I want you to be honest with me. You lost some weight, and your over concern in my love life has me wondering."

He paused for her to speak. Nothing. "Is there any update of your medical situation you're not telling me?" *There, I said it*, thought Presto.

She strode back to the living room, hands on her hips. "Thanks for the concern. I'm thinner because I've been active again. I see the doctors when they tell me. I have had a few chemotherapy sessions, which accounts some for my appearance. They're testing, making sure nothing's spread. Thus far, things look good, knock on wood," she said and banged the wall a few times.

Presto used every arsenal in the detective playbook as she recapped her prognosis. He watched her eyes, hands, posture, and the way she spoke. On most accounts she scored well. Her initial defiance seemed exaggerated, but from there, her mannerisms suggested she was truthful. He hoped she was right.

"Thanks, Mom. I'm so thrilled that I could do ten pushups right now," boasted Presto as he puffed his chest.

"Ha," she replied. "Don't get mushy. Instead, get off you're *tushy* and eat. Breakfast will be on the table in a minute."

When he was done eating, Presto retired to his room for some rest and recuperation. On the way, he stopped to see Aphrodite. He gasped. The mouse he'd fed to his snake the day prior had been regurgitated on the calcite sand; the vermin's body stretched and slick from the snake's digestive juices.

He looked to Aphrodite, who was curled in the corner where the heating pad warmed the bottom of the tank. At first he thought she was dead, but then he saw the tongue flicker before he was reassured.

Presto caught a rancid whiff as he removed the top. He removed the mouse with one hand and used the other to hold his nose. He flushed it down to the toilet. He wondered if Aphrodite was sick.

He thought of Camille. She would know what to do. That was what made her unique. Then he laughed for a second. His mind heard Camille say: *The snake has long been associated with health and medicine. Most symbols associated with medicine display either one or two snakes entwined in a staff. The single serpent staff is for the Greek god of medicine, Asklepios. The double serpent staff is Hermes, who was later associated with alchemy. Alchemists were often called Hermeticists. So maybe this is a sign. The snake has absorbed the ills and metaphorically and metaphysically cured your mom.*

Presto laughed at his mind's commentary.

That was a good line of new age bullshit, Camille, but I hope you're right.

CHAPTER SIXTY-EIGHT

"I'D LIKE TO SELECT my own team to guard the 770," Bailey told Danko, as his two agents and Presto met inside Danko's office.

Danko looked at Bailey, confused.

"The 770 is the term *Cahbad Lubavitch* use for their headquarters. It's on 770 Eastern Parkway. Crown Heights," informed Bailey.

Danko, who still looked like a ghost of the man he was two months ago, was happy to appease. "Sure. Any reason? It seems the consensus here is that the murders are over, at least for now."

Bailey, who was dressed more like a banker than an FBI agent, explained. "While we may all agree that nothing will happen, the Chabad personally asked for federal assistance

"Fine by me," Danko replied. "Hopefully either Fallow is caught, or the murders stop for long enough that we aren't held hostage on every religious holiday. Seems like there's one every day," he said exasperated.

Danko picked up some notes off his desk, strained his eyes, and read, "In fact, today is," he peered closer, "Mawlid an-Nabi. It's some Islamic holiday, and officers are stationed at every city mosque." He shrugged, as if the futility of it all rested on his shoulders.

Bailey stood next to Donavan, leaving Presto and Ridgewood seated side by side. They looked at each other, and Presto's heart raced. He tried to calm his anxiety.

Bailey had his right arm across his chest with his hand pressed over the upper part of his left arm. Presto wondered if that punch hurt more in the morning.

Bailey said, "After Passover, we'll pull off the case. We'll still assist, but from home. Just maybe that Sykes character was the killer. I doubt it, but who knows. If not, we'll still look for any signs of Fallow, dead or alive."

Ridgewood slapped her hand against her thigh. "It's not right. I feel like we lost; there's no closure, almost like a relationship that ends without a why."

Presto wanted to console her frustration. He felt the same way, and it ate at him too, but he knew better. Empathy might arouse suspicion.

Surprisingly, Donavan seconded her gripe. "I actually agree with

Ridgewood. I don't like this one bit, and I'll tell you, Chief," he said turning to Bailey, "I think it's a mistake to pull Loraine and me off the case just yet. First, we've bonded very closely, and I'd hate to break the camaraderie."

He paused to steal a glance at Ridgewood, who shook her head in dismay. "I agree with, Dom. I think Fallow is the real Myth Man, but I disagree that he's just disappeared forever. He wrote the papers; he had this whole agenda. He may have gotten away, but what did he accomplish?" Donavan looked at everyone and then spat a raspberry.

"He got zip. Religion continues. Hate crimes have dropped. He has no organized following. That pisses a guy like Myth Man off. He may pop up somewhere else, but it could only be a city with the size and diversity of New York. He'll be back, trust me."

Presto agreed to a point. Fallow had the taste of blood. His murders were brutal, symbolic, and well planned. He would be back, but in time. Fallow knew they were on to him. He's too smart to continue in the near term.

Bailey shurugged. "That may be, but how long do we wait? I'm going back to Washington a day after the 770 gig. There are other matters we must attend to. Anyway, I have more than enough confidence in my friend Dominick Presto."

A half hour later, Bailey and Pretso sat at a Greek diner that was Spartan in décor and overdue for remodeling, but the service was good, and the food surprisingly better. Bailey had asked for time alone with Presto, leaving an unhappy Ridgewood with Donavan.

"I wanted you alone," explained Bailey, "partially because what I'm about to tell you, I shouldn't. Since the mayor insists on a police presence for every religious holiday, I want to assemble my own team. I'm not concerned with Myth Man. I'm more worried about a multitude of other possibilities. Can you assemble a small group of officers that you know and trust?"

Presto was not blessed with many close associates on the force. He figured he'd ask Danko. Despite their differences, Presto trusted him. He also knew he could count on Jack Burton. "I'll rustle up a few bodies."

"That's good. We'll have you on the perimeter. I'll be inside." He stopped to cast a suspicious look around the diner that was mostly filled with old men who eyed a video lotto game. Presto guessed that since he heard no screams of joy, no one hit the $10 million advertised prize.

Bailey worked at his spinach omelet and then said, "Here's the plan. With cooperation from Israeli intelligence, the crate has arrived. Under a small escort, an armored truck will deliver the goods to the 770 Eastern Parkway parking facility." He stopped to think. "A small team of rabbinical scholars will inspect the find. Unless something dramatic happens, we should be dismissed thereafter." He stopped again, and then his regal face smiled with adolescent shine.

"At least I get to spend a few days with you before I head back. I just hope I hear what's inside that crate before it's all over. I've become friendly with one of the rabbis, and he said he would need my assistance." His eyes sparkled like a child asked if he wants a new toy.

Presto wondered too. So did others. "I read bids were submitted to the U.S. government."

"Allegedly," deadpanned Bailey, "but true. Serious offers from serious people. Trust me when I say, $100 million was considered lowball."

Presto believed him. When word leaked of the bids and names did not surface, the press began to speculate. Was it Bill Gates, Rupert Murdoch, Madonna, a Saudi royal prince, or any of the many other names they bandied about? Presto did not ask, and Bailey did not delve.

Then Bailey did say something that caught Presto by surprise.

"The rich and famous are one thing, but there are nefarious types out there who think the crate contains something powerful, and it belongs to the U.S. government, or should I say shadow government, rather than the Jewish people. That's what's kept me up at night."

When they finished eating, Bailey said, "That was a rough night at the bar. I can barely remember it. I'm still recovering," he said rubbing his shoulder. "I need some rest. Get a team together. I'll call you in tomorrow."

*****

Presto ran some errands. He rented two movies, Both comedies. He steered clear of heavy drama. Next he stopped at the bookstore. In the *New York Times* Science Section, he read about an interesting book about future technology and, specifically, quantum computers. He was shocked to find the book readily available.

Next was the pet store. He wanted to try and feed Aphrodite again. Hopefully, she regurgitated the last one for good reason, and she was hungry and healthy.

He called home.

"Mom, don't cook anything. I'm off early. I got a few movies, and I'm stopping at Sal's for filet mignon." He shook his head and blinked twice. "No, Mom. I did not invite Lorraine over."

Sal's was a typical long wait. There was always a crowd and always conversation. The staff was overly friendly. Presto preferred life at a slow pace and never minded the wait, while he surveyed all the fine meats, salads, breads, and pastries. He left with a fine piece of meat and insight on why the New York Yankees were *gonna win it all* from Sal's son Rico

He detoured from the butcher to a street food vendor. Gus, the guy behind the grill, was a top-notch cook and marinated his food overnight. But today, Presto longed for a sloppy gyro. With all the walking, he'd worked up his appetite.

Last stop on the spree was a florist. He wanted to buy his mother flowers; just because, he told himself, but of course there were reasons. Sure it was for love, but more so, he willed the woman who dealt with diabetes as if it was a mild case of the sniffles to overcome cancer.

CHAPTER SIXTY-NINE

Presto arrived at Danko's office as buoyant as a 300 plus–pound man could be. His night with his mother was perfect. She swooned over the flowers, devoured the steak, and laughed through two movies. It was like old times, and Presto felt reassured.

Aphrodite ate the mouse, and when he woke in the morning, he saw the lump still in her mid belly.

Maybe things were about to get better, and with that optimism, Presto strode into Danko's office.

Danko had some pulse back. His finger tapped his desk to some unheard rhythm. His head bopped to the same inner beat.

Presto again thought of Camille. She'd have a theory of some sort: a day of positive biorhythms, an astrological anomaly of positive persuasion, or perhaps a theory on sunspot variances.

As Presto went to take a seat, Danko rose and offered a hand. "Morning, Dom," he said like they were regular chums. "Good to see you."

"Same to you, Frank."

Presto noticed something different. The pictures of his wife, which had been momentarily removed, were back.

Danko still grooved to some beat, and his words came out in melody. "I wanted to say what a pleasure it's been working with you. I was wrong about you, and I'm glad my misconceptions changed."

Presto's opinion changed as well. No longer did he see Danko as a cold, stubborn, hasty detective. "Thanks, Frank. Let's just say the respect's mutual." He paused. "Has the status of the case changed?"

"It has," answered Danko. "Commissioner Tipton convinced the Mayor, that the police, at present force size, cannot maintain vigilant surveillance every holiday without serious consequences. There's terrorism, visits from dignitaries around the world, and evidence of a spike in other criminal activity, surely caused by resources being directed to Myth Man. You cannot put all your police yolks in one frying pan.

"Fallow is on the wanted list and still considered missing, but Tipton thinks we've seen the last of him, dead or alive. We'll still keep the case open, but after Passover, we'll all go back to our normal lives. I'm sure Jack Burton misses you."

Presto had yet to find an aperitif to cleanse the bitter taste he felt from the lack of closure. Presto wanted to keep his doubts to himself for the moment. No reason to strum a distorted riff and drown Danko's good vibrations. "I suppose it makes sense. We're detectives. That's our job. We can multitask cases."

Danko smiled warmly. "That's right, until the next big one comes along. If a big case lands on my lap in the hopeful distant future, would it be permissible to seek your assistance?"

"Naturally," Presto said with a deliberate pause, "as long as the offer is mutually inclusive and that I may call you as well."

Danko snorted. "You'll never need my help, but thanks for saying that."

"That's where you're wrong," interjected Presto. "I'm asking for your assistance now."

"This I've got to hear," an amused Danko replied.

Presto leaned his head toward Danko. "You already know where Malcolm has to be for the Jewish Passover. Due to some agreement with the mayor and Commissioner Tipton, he's obligated to have some NYPD evident—in other words, on the perimeter, visible, and out of the way."

Danko laughed as Presto continued. "Bailey asked me to round up a few trustworthy bodies to do that. I'd hate to kill one of your Sundays but hoped we'd all spend one last day together."

Danko bit and pressed his lips in consternation. "I had planned the day with the family. What's the time frame?"

"Then take the day. It's no big deal."

Danko waved the offer away. "How long, Presto?"

"Early. We have to be there around six o'clock in the morning, but we should be free by noon."

Danko smirked. "Should be? What if our pal Myth Man shows up?"

Presto grinned. "What if I showed up a thin, gaunt man? Neither will happen."

"Okay then. Don't go on a crash diet, because if you look thinner tomorrow, I'm going home."

"Deal."

CHAPTER SEVENTY

"I'M FLYING IN SUNDAY, on the red-eye," Camille informed with bubbly zest.

Her tone pleased Presto. "That's great," he managed, as Ridgewood came to mind. He shook away the image of her naked, straddling over him. "Can't wait to see you. If you're not tired, I'd love to take you to dinner Sunday night."

"I would really like that. I have to actually visit the zoo when I arrive, but I'll come home and take a nap, so I wake rested and hungry."

When the call ended, Presto was not surprised to see almost an hour had passed. Time with Camille passed like anesthesia or, as Camille would likely say, like time lost to an alien intrusion.

He left his study and checked in on Aphrodite. Presto felt a lurch in his gut. Lying dead and glazed over from Aphrodite's digestive system was the mouse. She'd regurgitated another. He felt this was a bad omen in more ways than one.

After disposing of the mouse, he went to his mother who was watching TV in the living room. Two politicians were in a heated debate that reminded Presto of two children fighting over a toy. He anticipated a debate from his mother when he'd prewarned her that he was going to dinner with Ridgewood tonight. She knew Ridgewood was headed back to life in Virginia, so she didn't protest much. She gave him a peck on the cheek. "Have a nice night."

Ridgewood called and suggested a last dinner together, sushi, like their first night together. He nervously agreed, as it was the first time they would be alone since their interlude.

They met at the same bar, but thankfully, it was less crowded. She had on a simple black cotton V-neck shirt that contoured her figure like wet paint. Her pants were standard khakis that fell to her open-toed sandals. She gave him a stronger peck on the cheek than his mother, but not in the woodpecker sense.

She immediately told him that there was something she wanted to talk about but wanted to wait until they ordered.

Presto knew the menu enough that there was no need to open it, but he did. He figured she wanted to talk about their night together, and this made him jittery, so Presto raised the menu so he was unable to make eye contact for a brief respite until he relaxed himself.

The same waiter from their last visit came to the table and bowed. "Mr. Presto. So good to see you again." He looked to Ridgewood. "And good to see you, too, beautiful lady, if I may be so forward."

Ridgewood deflected the compliment with a curt laugh.

They both began to work the edamame bowl, and after a few legume pops, Ridgewood spoke. "Besides wanting to spend a last, good night together, I also wanted to talk about the case."

Ridgewood drew as close as the table permitted. Presto had visions of her face *that* morning.

She said, "I also agree that Fallow is at large, and I am not sure if it even has to do with him, but something is peculiar about Sunday." Her eyes narrowed in a conspiratorial fashion. "I probably will over step my boundaries, but our presence at the synagogue has nothing to do with Myth Man. It's something else. I can't go into it." She paused in thought. "Did Malcolm brief you on this at all?"

Presto was not sure if he should divulge Bailey's words, just as he would not betray her trust to Bailey. "Nothing specific. He called it 'perimeter work.' Malcolm told me to assemble a small team of ten officers."

Ridgewood appeared to accept that. "That's more or less where you'll be, along with me. I have outside detail." Her face grew incredulous. "You know the deal with women and religion. We get the bum rap. It all started with Eve and the stupid apple. Probably a myth some guy wrote," she muttered.

Ridgewood refocused her thoughts. "Although I know in detail, our mission and what else is going down, there's something amiss." Her eyes wandered aimlessly, as if a clue could emerge within an abstract vision. "I don't know if it's Donavan or Bailey or the both of them, but I feel something's not right. Ever since Donavan and Malcolm boozed that night away, Donavan has been acting weird. He's not been himself. He's been unusually withdrawn. He's made these strange, negative comments about Bailey, saying he's corrupt. Minutes later, he professes he loves him like a father."

Ridgewood stopped to let her words settle. "I know Malcolm is a friend, he's mine too, but he truly respects you. Maybe Sunday goes without a hitch. Let's hope, but I have a funny feeling, except the vibe is not humorous. Keep your ears open, and if something does happen, be careful, and most of all, don't trust anyone, Dom."

CHAPTER SEVENTY-ONE

J ACK BURTON PUMPED PRESTO'S hand. "Welcome back. Take a seat, Dom."

Presto always preferred Burton's office to Danko's. One reason was a full-sized leather couch along the far wall. The precinct commander was known for long hours, and when duty stole a night from his own bed, he'd catch some sleep on the couch. You always knew when the boss was taking a power nap, because he snored like a growling, prowling bear.

Presto said, "I have a favor to ask." He explained Bailey's request to assemble a team. He asked if he could round out the rest of the squad.

"I need to get eight bodies?" asked Burton.

"No, seven. I asked Frank to help out."

"Really? You guys have grown tight. Are you sure you're not going to ask for a transfer to work with him now," Burton said and added a deep, sarcastic laugh. "I can see you doing dinners at the Dankos', except that I hear they've separated."

"Actually, she moved back in," Presto said with enough zeal to induce another Burton rib.

"That seals it," Bailey certified. "Your fraternizing cost you my wife's home cooking. This must be a racial thing."

"Now you went too far, and I'm not talking about the racism canard," Presto said with mock outrage. "I am not trading in Danko's protein shakes for your wife's edible masterpieces."

"You just like a pretty Nubian serving you. You feel like the *mastah*." Burton could not hold in his ruse any longer and laughed heartily. "How about dinner Sunday night then?"

Despite his disdain for how the Myth Man case concluded, now that he was here in his own precinct, he felt the tourniquet of doubt loosen and inhaled a welcome breath of nostalgia. It was Burton. He was the first to care more about what Presto brought to the table rather than what he ate at it.

Presto was ready to agree to Sunday when he remembered Camille. "I can't Sunday; I have plans. But any day thereafter …"

"Plans? With who? Frank? Next you'll tell me you two are hitting the gym together."

Presto went to object, and his words tumbled like spilled peas. Burton could not contain himself, and he slapped his desk with a hearty laugh. Presto laughed too. It truly was good to be home.

They made plans for Thursday, and Presto was thankful he did not have to explain about Camille, yet.

Presto discussed the Myth Man case at length: the suspects they interviewed and the players involved, Dean Fallow, Gary Sykes, Spencer Hoole, Malcolm Bailey, Carter Donavan, and Loraine Ridgewood. He detailed the friction between the two agents, and to better explain Donavan's fighting spirit, he told of the encounter at Sweet Virginia's.

Burton looked puzzled but excited, like a jigsaw fanatic who just dropped a thousand different wedges on a table. "I'm shocked that you went out to a bar, but Sweet Virginia's, no less." Burton wiped at his lips, which became overly lubricated in his excitement. "Just last night, two people that worked there were murdered, a male and female; both were shot dead in their own apartments." He paused and stroked a few keys on his computer keyboard. "Looks like the male put up a fight. His place was messed up. Blood was found that was not the victim's."

Presto's heart jolted. "Do you have any pictures of the deceased?"

"Hold it there; I'm getting to it." Burton tapped a few keys and opened a dossier file on the deceased. "Here's the female," he said and turned the monitor so Presto could see. "Claire Hutchins."

Presto did not recognize the name, but he knew her. It was the bartender who served them the night they were there.

"You know her?" Burton gazed across at him.

"Let me see the male," Presto stuttered. His mouth went dry. His blood and mind raced but stalled, as if too much gas clogged the carburetor, inhibiting ignition.

Burton punched a key, and the picture changed. Presto had hoped he would not recognize the male. Reason trumped desire. On the monitor screen was the barback who scuffled with Donavan.

Burton snapped his fingers. "Dom, what is it?"

Presto sat there speechless.

"Talk to me," Burton urged.

"I need you to do me a favor. Find the detective on this case and ask him to check a few things for me."

Chapter Seventy-Two

R IDGEWOOD, IN A STENCILED FBI windbreaker, clapped her hands. "Let's do it, boys."

Presto, Burton, Danko, and the rest of the team filed out of the police RV parked on Eastern Parkway, Brooklyn. They spread out to predetermined positions. Ridgewood waited for Presto.

"What's the matter, Dom? You look tired, worried."

Sleep had eluded Presto and so did the answers to the questions that sprung at him in the dark. Something nagged at him that this case was not over. He thought about Fallow, the Iraqi crate, the people who'd been murdered in the bar. Sweet Virginia's. It could not be a coincidence, and with the murders so close to home, the questions continued their stalking pursuit.

He wanted to speak to Ridgewood, or Bailey, but he didn't. Now that he had Ridgewood before him, he wanted to talk about Sweet Virginia's. He said nothing. Not just yet. He hoped that day would prove to be uneventful.

"Just tired," he replied. "Need to catch up on sleep. We all do."

They moved off the sidewalk to allow a few bearded men in black coats and hats pass. "Good morning," one said.

Presto replied in kind, but Ridgewood merely grunted.

He mimicked her displeasure. His right hip shot out and met his hand. In a feminine octave, Presto said, "Girl, are you still mad that you're not allowed to guard inside because of your sex?"

"I am," she said with defeat. "These guys are no worse than any others. Women get the raw shaft from almost every religion. She looked to the parkway when a truck rumbled by. Wrong one. "I think a lot of men just made up a lot of stuff to justify our oppression. I'd like to believe that God made us equals. Two shapes together that make us whole."

Presto thought that was something Camille might have said. Then he padded the bottom of his overcoat. Inside the inner pocket was a cloth sack. Curled up inside the sack was Aphrodite. Not only was Camille coming back to New York today, but she planned to stop and see Presto before going to the zoo. The snake would get a checkup from a professional herpetologist.

Ridgewood took his hand in hers, braking his reverie. "They should have the armored car here in five minutes. Be ready."

*****

"I thought Boston and DC traffic was bad, but this is ridiculous," Donavan cursed the Belt Parkway traffic and pumped the brake for the umpteenth time.

Bailey wheezed. "Tell me about it. I grew up on a farm. Traffic was a narrow horse trail and a ride coming the other way."

The Iraqi crate had arrived at JFK airport in the early morning. It taxied into a secured hanger where the cargo was transported to a level A-9 armored car, capable of withstanding rounds from high-powered rifles. Actually, it was a SWAT truck based on the International Navistar 4700. Two unmarked sedans made up the escort.

"What Jewish holiday is it again?" Donavan asked. "Pea soup?"

Bailey sighed. "Fool. It's Pesach, the Jewish Passover. No more jokes, Donavan. We're all business here on out." Bailey grabbed Donavan's arm tight to let him know he was serious.

They finally reached Eastern Parkway. The police had the street barricaded two hundred yards in both directions from the Lubavitch world headquarters. The three-story stone building looked immaculate, especially considering the squalor they'd passed.

Bailey backed into a sunken driveway until he stopped at a garage, the designated loading area. Stationed there were Agent Ridgewood and Detective Presto.

"Thanks for entrusting me with this," Donavan told Bailey.

CHAPTER SEVENTY-THREE

Rabbi Yeheil Ackerberg sat motionless in his study. Eyes closed. Mouth slack. The only sound in the room was his long, deliberate breathing. By all accounts, it appeared he was catching a well-needed snooze for a sixty-eight-year-old man afflicted with gout and a bum knee.

Sleep had been scarce. Yesterday had been the Fast of the First Born, and then there had been the facilitation of Chametz. The Lubavitchers were growing in numbers. Many of the new members were from other sects that were lenient on allowing possession of any of the five major grains. Assisting each household to comply was time-consuming work but necessary.

Rabbi Ackerberg, however, was far from asleep. His mind raced. Pesach. The day always brought personal joy, but today was different.

His son, Benzion, would ask the Four Questions before Seder. He had high expectations for his seven-year-old, and why shouldn't he? Benzion was bright, compassionate, and dedicated.

He was proud of his son. The rabbi remembered his own youth. His parents ignored G-d and then cursed him for their own begotten ills. They died when he was only eleven. He later learned that they'd been murdered, but the circumstances were murky. He heard talk his father was involved with shady individuals, but nothing was substantiated, and no one was arrested.

Orphaned, he'd been placed in a Brooklyn Lubavitch center for displaced youths. It was there that he first found family and hope. Then he found G-d.

Benzion did not have to find G-d. G-d was with him from his first breath. Every day thereafter proved that the greatest experience could be achieved while you are alive and not limited to the afterlife.

Pesach also brought the arrival of the Iraqi crate. Rabbi Ackerberg was grateful that the crate had come into his possession. It helped to have friends in high places, including the White House, but he would never betray the trust and work it took to bring the crate to America and ultimately under his auspices.

He was keenly aware of the speculation that surrounded the crate's contents. While he doubted it contained the Ark of the Covenant, he did hold hope that artifacts and scrolls could provide more insight to both the ancient Jewish people and the wonders of G-d.

If asked, he was more inclined to indulge in the more practical theory, which connected the crate to the Copper Scroll.

The Copper Scroll was found in Cave #3 in Khirbet Qumran, where the collective find became known as the Dead Sea Scrolls. More than two thousand years old, the Copper Scroll spoke of treasures saved and scattered, like an artifact diaspora, when Nebuchadnezzar razed Herod's Temple in 586 BCE.

Like the crate, the Copper Scroll was written in Mishnaic Hebrew, which contrasted with the rest of the Dead Sea Scroll find, as well as the Torah and most rabbinic literature.

But it was not just what the crate contained that interested Rabbi Ackerberg. It was believed that when the scattered treasure from Herod's Temple was recovered, a righteous king will arise for Israel and gather the tribes of Israel from the four corners of Earth.

The *galut*, exile, was over. Moshiach now!

A buzz was heard breaking his thoughts, and Rabbi Ackerberg opened his eyes in a softly dimmed, book-lined room. He looked at the picture of the Rebbe, Rabbi Menachem Mendel Schneerson, and dipped his head in reverence.

On a desk, a Torah partitioned by a yad rested on white silk. On one side sat the activated beeper.

He expected the day to go easy. An alert was issued that a threat had specifically targeted thc Lubavitchers: the center would be temporarily closed while the police investigated.

No interruptions.

The buzz ended after the designated seven rings. In two other apartments within the center, the beeper had also gone off. Two other rabbis waited there. Both were considered *gedolim*, Torah luminaries. One, Rabbi David Loew, was a scion to Rabbi Yehudah Loew of Prague. The Maharal, legend has it, created a golem in the sixteenth century to act as his protector.

The crate was here. The suspense would soon be over.

CHAPTER SEVENTY-FOUR

Bailey and Donavan vacated the truck. They went to the entrance, a set of double mahogany doors beneath a buttressed window from the floor above.

Bailey rapped the door a few times.

Seconds later, the doors swung open. There stood a short, stout man dressed in black hat fashion with a long, cottony beard and eyes, Donavan thought, that read your life's dossier in a few seconds' glance.

Bailey greeted the rabbi. They'd met and had spoken on the phone so frequently during the past few months that they'd become fast friends. After a few quick words, Bailey introduced Donavan. Rabbi Ackerberg handed the men two white yarmulkes.

Bailey called to Ridgewood. "Watch the truck. We'll be back in a few."

Ridgewood wanted to salute her boss. *Sir, yes sir.* Instead, she chirpily said, "Yes," as if the task was well received.

When the door shut behind him, as planned, Donavan was asked to stay in the foyer. Bailey followed Rabbi Ackerberg back to his study.

*****

Ridgewood tapped her foot furiously, like she kept pace with a high-speed metronome. "It's been like a half hour already. What's going on?"

"I'm not sure, but I'll be angry if those two are getting better grub than glazed donuts, as good as they were," Presto quipped.

For the first time, Ridgewood flashed a hint of anger at Presto. It passed, but traces were still there in her voice. "Bailey had this thing scripted with the rabbi down to the minute."

Serious. "Sorry. I never asked. Now I will. Tell me what was supposed to happen."

She shook in a small fury. "I'm sorry to lash out, but Bailey was supposed to escort three rabbis to the garage. Donavan was to load the crate into the garage and return to the front entrance. Bailey was to assist with the labor. Because of the holiday, they can't open or operate anything. They were going to wait or let a non-Orthodox Jew do the work, but Rabbi Ackerberg and

Bailey bonded. He'll do some grunt work and then leave and stand guard when the find is examined. That was twenty minutes ago."

Presto considered this. "One of us should go to the front door and check with Donavan."

"That's what I'm thinking," she said. "But here's the thing. Because I'm a woman, you should go." She paused for a sly grin. "But that's why I'm going to do it."

Presto was torn between being respectful to religious concerns and feelings for a friend, who also happened to qualify for his sole sexual experience. "No problem."

Briskly, they walked up the driveway, cut under a tall newly budding maple tree, and headed up to the door. She didn't look around, but Presto did, and the few passersby, all Lubavitchers, watched Ridgewood.

Ridgewood knocked. She put her ear to the door, pulled back, and knocked louder.

Presto spoke into the FBI provided relay. "Jack, it's Dom. It might be nothing, but I need you to clear the area."

He heard his friend's voice. "You got it."

In seconds, he saw Burton and three officers approach a small crowd. Presto heard Burton tell the men he needed them to clear the area. Jack Burton was imposing as any man Presto knew, but the men, who did not appear fit for trouble, stood their ground.

Then, they went ballistic.

Presto followed their eyes to the front door and saw Ridgewood's back disappear inside. Presto looked back. Two officers, one of whom was Danko, came to assist with the now screaming men. They managed to move them back twenty yards, but they were hardly subdued. One guy, dressed in more civilian attire, took out a cell phone and dialed.

Danko jogged over. His bushy brows danced. "Dom, what's going on?"

"I don't know. They should have been out by now. Ridgewood went to check it out."

Danko blew out air of despair. "Not good."

"Let's not jump to conclusions yet."

Danko slapped the truck with a watchful eye. "This armored car. Something tells me there's more going on than we've been told." Danko looked to Presto for information.

Presto did not consider anything but the truth. "You're right. I was privy to some info, off the record, and whether right or wrong, I did not betray that trust."

Danko nodded. "My beef's not with you. I hate being assigned to something and not getting the real scoop. It complicates things when shit doesn't go right. Hence ..."

Presto knew Danko was right. Still, he wanted to stall. He hoped Agent Ridgewood would appear with good news, but then he thought about what Danko would do if the roles were reversed. Danko was a cop, and he was honest.

"Frank. Truthfully, there's a reason behind the secrecy."

His words were cut off when Ridgewood called from the entrance. "You two. Come quick." Her voice was casual, but her body language said more. Her eyes registered alarm. Flushed of color, she looked shocked, like she'd seen dead people. Her hand, which beckoned them over, twitched with rapid-fire panic.

Ridgewood's reappearance got the group of Lubavitchers vocal again. A few more were present. Thus far, they were peaceful. Presto hoped there was no reason for that to change. They did not have the manpower to control the situation.

Ridgewood looked worse the closer they got. Her mouth tried to work again, but her lips just quivered. "Myth Man. He left a sign. The rabbis are dead," she stuttered and then faltered forward.

Danko put his arms around both of them, like they were off for a jolly stroll, and pushed them inside. Then he shut the door. Immediately, they saw Donavan sprawled on the floor.

Ridgewood composed herself. Her voice came in low but in quick breaths. "He's alive. The study," she said and pointed.

Danko whispered. "How do you know it's safe? The killer could still be here."

Ridgewood wheezed. Her body grew stiff and straight, like a marine. Her small jaw was angled up in defiance. She looked tough.

"I'm not taking this out on you. My role was lessened today because I'm a woman. When I see my partner down, the last thing I'm going to do is call in the guys to come to my rescue, but now is not the time. It's a disaster," she said, and her voice trailed off. Gone was the flair she exhibited in her defense.

Despite Ridgewood's ease, Danko took out his gun. He looked to Presto. "I have a wife and kids. I play safe." Danko's eyes shifted about. "This is a big place. Take hours to thoroughly check it out."

Ridgewood's voice grew unsteady. "He's not here to kill us. You'll see what I mean in a minute." She stopped to gather herself again. "When I saw Donavan down, I checked on him. There's a pulse. There's a wound to the back of his head."

Presto asked. "Shouldn't we get an ambulance?"

"We're beyond that. I checked each room, scared, but found nothing until I got to the rabbi's study." She shook with anger. "How did we get beat again?"

Danko boiled. "What?"

Ridgewood wiped at her forehead. "I checked. Bailey's on the floor alive but unconscious. Trust me. The three rabbis are dead."

While Presto's mind raced, Danko took charge. "Okay, we need to take action. Clearly we don't have enough men to handle this. I'm calling in backup ASAP."

Ridgewood agreed with a quick nod. "I have to get Bailey, Donavan, and that truck out of here, to an FBI safe house."

"Yeah, worry about the truck. The NYPD will take care of the mess," he said sardonically.

Presto listened to them exchange a few snappy retorts, but words were lost on him. Questions riddled him.

Was this the work of Myth Man, and if so, was it Fallow? If it was Myth Man, how did he do it? Was he inside already, disguised and waiting? Did the crate mean anything? Did the Sweet Virginia murders tie into this in some way? If they did, then there was a whole set of new questions.

Was there ever a Myth Man?

Nothing made sense.

CHAPTER SEVENTY-FIVE

For the first time in a long while, Frank Danko felt like a man in charge. This case was supposed to be his glory. Instead, it had been a curse. Then he remembered something his wife said as they reconciled their differences. *Sometimes things need to get worse before they can get better.*

Danko was pretty sure there was something to that old adage. He hoped so anyway. Right now things were a mess. Hundreds, possibly thousands of black hatters were out in the streets, along with scores of police. News vans appeared like vultures sensing the dead.

Mayor Golden was set to arrive. He planed a news conference with the World Lubavitch headquarters as the backdrop. These murders were personal. Rabbi Ackerberg was a friend, not just a political endorsement. If he was going to lose an election over the Myth Man crisis, he did not plan to go down meekly.

Danko respected the mayor. It was not his fault that Myth Man had eluded capture. The Feds specifically assigned themselves to guard the World Lubavitch Headquarters. He had nothing against Bailey's team, but he was glad this one was on them.

The Feds had since departed. Bailey and Donavan had come too, but were disorientated. At Bailey's request, Presto left with them.

They hightailed it out with the truck. Now he was left with the disaster. All they gave him was a yarmulke.

He never got his answer on what was inside the vehicle, but he wondered if it had anything to do with the murders. Probably not, because there was no attempt to seize the vehicle.

Was this purely another religious hit? It looked like that since only the rabbis had been murdered.

He thought about Fallow. Was Presto wrong about him? He didn't think so. Once again, it had looked like Presto somehow found the right guy. So was this the work of Fallow? Judging Myth Man's previous feats, anything was possible.

For the moment, the case was his again. He thought of Presto—how would he approach the evidence? He knew Presto would not leap at the obvious. Neither would he.

For the first time in a long time, he felt like a detective again.

What to do? Something told him he needed answers now.

The headquarters housed several apartments, rooms, and closets, all of which were searched. He learned that none of the officers stationed behind the center saw anyone leave from the rear.

Normally, they'd rather avoid contaminating a murder scene, but Ridgewood had already been all over the room to check the bodies. It was the right call. No plastic forensic body suits were on hand. She had to see if anyone was alive. Then they had to attend to Bailey.

A blood-smeared nightstick lay next to the fallen FBI Director.

On a desk was an open Torah. Scrawled in blood were two letters: MM.

Danko needed to go back to the rabbi's study. Something he saw bothered him.

He snapped on latex gloves and returned. The first thing he checked was the blood trail. Someone had stepped in blood and done quite a bit of walking. He checked the rabbis' feet. No blood. The footprints were probably the killer's.

He saw the trail lead to a door. Danko opened it. It was a bathroom. He walked into the already lit room. On white tiles were blood prints that had been deliberately smeared. From the shape, it looked like the toes pointed toward the toilet but not straight as if a man were urinating. He also noticed a small red streak on the outside of the toilet bowl.

Danko looked closer. Blood. Was something flushed?

As he backed out, his heart leaped. On the marble saddle that bordered the two rooms was a crystal clear heel print. He photographed the evidence.

He returned to the room. He looked back at the blood trail. There were a lot of prints near where Bailey had lay and also by one of the dead rabbis.

He walked over. Somehow, the rabbi died with a smile on his lips. He'd been shot twice in the head, one at close range from the looks of the scalded tissue. He understood the deceased was Rabbi Ackerberg.

He was set to leave when he saw blood on the man's fingertips. He looked closer. Was it the rabbi's own blood? The blood was not smeared on the pads of the fingers, as if he felt his own wound. No blood was evident on the rest of the hand. The blood had gotten there another way.

Danko squatted and looked closer. Blood was massed under the fingernails of his index and middle fingers. Thankfully, the rabbi did not gnaw his fingernails to receded stubs, like Danko's own hands. Neither finger was cut, but under one nail, and perhaps the other, there was what looked like skin fragments.

This evidence was the connection Danko hoped to find, but he couldn't believe what he was actually thinking. Impossible. If he learned one thing with this case, it was that misdirection could be deadly. Doubt attacked reason. Who to trust?

He dialed his cell phone. After several rings, it connected. He overrode the greeting. "Are you alone?" Danko asked with an emphasis on the conspiratorial.

Picking up the cue, the reply was short. "No."

"Please go somewhere where we can talk and then call me back. It's important." Danko hung up and waited.

Chapter Seventy-Six

Presto hung up the phone and looked at Bailey. His composed, gentlemanly demeanor was no longer evident. Once conscious and alert, Bailey went into a rage. The mission was a personal disaster.

It was an awkward time to ask for space, but he had to. "Give me a minute," Presto said and left before Bailey could ask the caller's identity.

Presto found an empty room. He called Danko back.

"It's me."

"You're alone?" Danko asked.

"Yes."

He heard Danko sigh. "Dom, I'm not sure how to put this, so I'll just start from the top. I think the murders were an inside job." He hesitated. "Real inside."

Presto understood perfectly but asked, "What exactly do you mean?"

"Did you notice a scratch on Malcolm's cheekbone?"

Stunned. "Yes, but ..."

"What about his suit? There are blood spots," he said not so much as a question, but as a statement of fact.

"I think I remember seeing blood. He was wounded."

"On the back of the head," Danko reminded. "Listen, Dom, I found blood and likely skin samples under Rabbi Ackerberg's fingernails. He scratched somebody, and there's evidence the killer went to the bathroom and possibly flushed evidence."

"Frank, are you saying Bailey killed these men?" Presto was incredulous, and yet he had a feeling something was amiss from the inside.

"All I'm saying is something's up. I know this is going to be uncomfortable, but this is a crime scene, and he was in the room. I want that jacket and his shoes. And that goes for Donavan too."

Presto gulped. He'd never questioned an acquaintance, let alone friend and prominent FBI agent. "That is going to be tough."

"I'm counting on you," Danko commanded. "I'm not making an accusation, but they were in the center when the murders took place."

Presto thought for a second. "What about Ridgewood?"

"I thought about that. She wasn't in there long, five minutes tops. No way

247

all that went down while she was in there, and I'm not seeing her dainty prints in blood. Nonetheless, they are a team. Tell them I want all their clothes. Heck, tell them you're giving yours too."

Presto heard a knock at the door and heard his name called. It was Ridgewood. "Frank, speaking of the dainty one, she beckons. I will call you back when I can."

He hung up. "In here," he answered. He went to the door as it opened.

Ridgewood gave an urgent look. "I need to talk to you. In here's perfect."

Presto was still processing Danko's implications. Myth Man had framed people before—Sykes, for instance. Was Fallow back, or had he been wrong about the computer guru? If he was wrong, was today's murder committed by the same person as the previous religious hits?

With these questions cluttering his mind, Ridgewood moaned softly. Her eyes fluttered with nerves.

"Did Bailey say anything more?"

"No. I think he feels shame. He wants to go back to the crime scene."

She gave him a long look. "What were you doing in here?"

"I needed space. Had to make a few calls. Danko checked in." He didn't want to discuss that yet. "Does Donavan remember anything more?"

She looked puzzled, like she wanted to hear what Danko had to say. When she refocused, her face was taut and withdrawn, like she'd swallowed something unpleasant and needed to divulge it.

She bit her lower lip. The words came slow. "Donavan. Well, he's disoriented and keeps retracting what he said or thinks he remembers. Dom," she said earnestly, "I need you here—someone from the outside."

Presto stayed silent. He was not sure what to think yet and gestured for her to continue.

"Who knows," she said and huffed. "They were both knocked on the head. Donavan's brains were already scrambled."

Presto finally spoke. "What did Donavan say?"

She answered. "He says he has this foggy recollection that he was talking to Bailey when he was struck down. He says Bailey was walking slightly behind him, but then he changes. Says he must be loopy, because there is no way that could be. Claims he worships and trusts Bailey like a true father."

Presto massaged his scalp as if he could relax the knot in his brain. It didn't work.

"This is nuts," was Presto's final analysis.

Ridgewood agreed. "You bet. By the way, Donavan has his own opinion. Despite what he thinks he remembers, he definitely thinks this was the work of Myth Man, whoever that may be."

"Does he," Presto said. For some reason, he found that comment interesting.

Ridgewood stood up. She drew close. "What did Danko say?"

"He's further checked the crime scene. Made a few observations."

"Such as ..." pressed Ridgewood.

"No one was seen leaving the building. No one was found inside either."

"What else?"

Presto summarized Danko's findings: the bloody footprints that led to the bathroom, Danko's suspicion that evidence was flushed, the rabbi's bloody fingernails, and the suspicion that he'd scratched someone, perhaps the killer.

The last comment stretched her face. "The last thing I'm looking to do is sink my boss, but he did have a nice scratch on his face." She shrugged. "Then again, he was attacked."

Everything moved too fast. Presto was still trying to sort things. Still, he answered, "Suppose the rabbi scratched Bailey. The tests would conclude whether it was his blood or not. Why would he then proceed to bludgeon his head knowing the evidence he'd left behind? Does he just figure he's an FBI big shot, and he can cover it up, or still yet, blame the plausible theory that he was set up by Myth Man?" He spat the moniker in disgust. "It doesn't make sense."

Ridgewood nodded in assent.

Presto was not through. "Then again, it's possible that when the killer attacked, in a panic, the rabbi lashed out, accidentally striking Malcolm." Presto knew what he said was true, but he was not sure what he believed yet.

She considered that. "Fair points. Listen, if things get sour, I want you to know that I've got your back. I'm not sure what happened to Bailey and Donavan in there, but even if there is a 1 percent chance that they're up to something, I'm with you."

Ridgewood looked into his eyes. Then she hugged him and groaned wearily. "I've had enough of this case." Her words were muffled against his body. After a few seconds, she pulled away. "Sorry. Despite my bravado, I'm still a woman."

"One more thing," Presto said. "Danko plans to treat all of us as evidence to the crime scene."

CHAPTER SEVENTY-SEVEN

"Is HE FUCKING KIDDING me?" roared Bailey. "The only article of clothing he's getting is my boxers."

"No shit," opined Donavan. "Since when are the victims treated like criminals?" He rubbed the back of his wounded head.

Presto felt uncomfortable, and the ante rose when Ridgewood remained silent. He tried. "As you know, it is not uncommon to take the victim's clothes for evidence."

Bailey hissed. "I don't like how this is being presented. This is the biggest disaster in my career, and to grind salt in my wounds like this is too much. You're not presenting this as if Inspector Danko wants our clothes to catch Myth Man. You make it seem like he suspects us."

Ridgewood coughed meekly. "Guys, let's not get crazy here. Like we always say from the law enforcement perspective, if you have nothing to hide, what's the problem?"

Both men stared at her hard, but then Donavan grinned at his superior and gave a wonder-twins activate fist touch.

"He wants my clothes?" Donavan said haughtily. "He can have them. Just tell him that when he's through, I expect them dry-cleaned."

Presto's phone rang. Impeccable timing. It was Danko. Presto's face was a dead give away.

Donavan snorted. "Is that super sleuth Danko on the line? Wonder if he wants a stool sample?"

As Presto pressed the button, he felt as if he had just activated the button that launched a bunker-busting bomb.

"Frank?"

"Listen up, I'm coming to you."

His voice uneven, "Any reason?"

"You're not alone, are you?"

"No," Presto informed.

"Dom, be careful. I have a bad feeling one or more of these agents is up to no good." The line went dead.

The three agents looked to him, or were they watching him? No, this felt natural. They were curious.

"Danko's coming here." He said no more.

"What?" Bailey said acerbically. "Why?"

Presto was not sure what to say. Was his allegiance to a friend who probably saved his career or to his former nemesis but fellow NYPD detective?

"He wants to run the case right. Gather evidence. Talk to us. Be a detective."

The two agents cast him a steely gaze.

Ridgewood inserted herself. "Boys, let Danko do his job. I understand the frustration."

"Do you?" shot Bailey. "I lost a friend and a career. The last thing I need is that moron annoying us as he wastes taxpayer money. But you know what?" he said magnanimously. "I'll give the idiot what he wants. I'll soon be stripped of everything. Might as well start now."

Bailey hung his head. Donavan consoled him. "I'm sorry, but this is not our fault. He began to pace, and his right index finger tapped his left palm.

"Think about it—St. Patrick's, Grace Cathedral. These were high profile hits. He's done it before. I'm sorry, but I've been to Halloween parties where someone dressed as a convincing rabbi. Myth Man's a master of disguise. He must have been inside before we entered and got out one of the many exits or windows."

He stopped pacing. His face was both chummy and resolute. "We got beat this time." He snapped his head like he took a punch, bit the pain, but was back in the fight. "This just means the case is not closed after all. We have work to do."

The "rally the troops" speech did not enlist Bailey. "I must be an idiot to stand by you. How blind could you be? Work to do?" he huffed with lamenting scorn. "We'll be lucky if we're not used as Hogan's Alley props for the new Quantico trainees."

Donavan was determined to see things differently. "Bailey, the reason I refuse to admit defeat is because I can't watch you do so. This guy, Myth Man, is a master, and at least the crate is here, safe and sound."

Bailey was not convinced but chose not to argue further. "I need a few minutes alone. Dom, can you stay behind a minute?"

As soon as the two agents left the room, Bailey drew close. His eyes implored.

"Dom, I need you here. I have a bad feeling that I'm being framed in some way." His eyes grew more importune.

"Why is Frank Danko coming here?"

CHAPTER SEVENTY-EIGHT

Presto had hoped to speak to Danko alone. As fate would have it, he lost the bladder battle, and the deputy chief inspector arrived as Presto dried his hands. When he left the men's room, all three agents were already around Danko, who had a large duffel bag hung around his shoulder. The welcome committee was quick to make the detective feel unwelcome.

"What the fuck are you doing here?" raged Bailey.

"There aren't any donuts here, Danko," quipped Donavan.

Danko bristled then smarmily said, "And I thought we were friends."

They glared at each other.

Ridgewood remained silent and then saw Presto emerge. She went to him. "I'll let the testosterone run its course."

Presto did not reply. He heard the voices rise in volume and vulgarity.

"Gentleman," declared Presto, "lets keep this inside not outside." He pointed to the room Bailey had recuperated in.

As soon as the door shut, Presto was quick to speak. Loudly. He needed to quell this minirebellion now. He was the one person who had an allegiance to both parties.

"Enough. Let's start by acting professionally."

Bailey was not easily quieted. "First, we have to respect each other as professionals," he pontificated.

Presto took advantage of the impasse. "The room," he gesticulated toward an open door.

The party looked around. Other agents at various levels stared at them. The place was a zoo. Reason took hold, and the troops trudged into the room Presto had called Danko from.

Everyone glumly sat down like they were adults who had been assigned detention.

Presto did not relish the words he was about to say, and the first few words tumbled out of his mouth like a feeble roll of dice. "Er, uh, we need to remember that until told otherwise, this is our case. The men and women in this room have a decision to make. Yes, this was a disaster, but even in defeat, we owe our professional best not to succumb."

Presto felt a small air of confidence. No one had interrupted him.

"Malcolm, I respect you more than anyone in this room, but Donavan is right. Your career is too distinguished, and the way I see you—if you're in command of a sinking battleship, you'd be steadfast and resolute to the end."

Bailey tied to speak, but Presto had to get the second part out. "Sorry, Malcolm, but Frank has a job to do. Let's not forget that you were victims in this tragedy too. Frank found evidence on one of the dead rabbis. It's quite possible there are traces on your clothes as well. Let forensics do their thing."

"Dominick's right." Ridgewood agreed.

Thinking of Camille's New Age persona, Presto sent her a futile ESP thank you.

Ridgewood asserted, "Now is not the time for turf battles and egos. Let's hear Frank out."

Both Bailey and Donavan glared briefly at their partner before they turned to Danko.

Danko jumped up, which caused Donavan to tense. "Hey, bud. Let's keep things relaxed."

Undaunted. "I'm relaxed." He winked. "I think on two feet."

Danko smiled broadly. Bailey and Donavan did not.

"First things first." He pulled the duffel bag onto the chair and unzipped it. He pulled out clothes. He smiled again. "It may not be up to your high fashion, but I brought sweat pants, shirts, and flip-flop sandals. I want everyone's clothes and shoes. The men can all change in here. Ridgewood can use the restroom."

At first no one spoke. Then, "This is bullshit," Donavan snorted. "But have it your way, thrift shop boy."

"Cool it, boys," snapped Ridgewood as she left the room.

Presto was tense, not just from the friction in the room, but also because he was uncomfortable undressing in front of others. The last time he undressed in front of anyone was back in the days of dreaded gym class.

Bailey spoke. His tone was calm. Serious. "I'll keep my cool, but I'm going to say my peace."

Danko's voice replied in kind. "Fair enough."

Bailey's shirt was now off, and despite his age, he was in fantastic shape. His lightly haired chest was solidly contoured, while his stomach was cut and fat free.

Presto gulped. All three of them were fine physical specimens. He hoped he could dress under the covers of the conversation.

"Why not lay your cards on the table, Frank? Talk to us. I want to clear the air, because you're not treating us like partners anymore. You're behaving like we're suspects." Bailey finished and removed his pants.

"Yeah, Frank," said Donavan. "What's with the third degree, buddy? You're looking at us harder than you stared at those beautiful tits that day at the topless bar."

Donavan the speed dresser had already changed. He looked at home in the beat-up sweats and T-shirt. Bailey did not. He looked like a guy who slept in a suit.

Danko pulled up his sweats. "I found some evidence. There are so many unanswered questions with this case, but one thing we know is Myth Man's framed people before. He tried to get Dom thrown off the case."

"And, if it wasn't for us, he would have succeeded," reminded Bailey.

"Agreed," Danko conceded.

They looked to Presto. He shrugged. "Thanks," he said sheepishly. His outfit stretched to the limit. He didn't care. He was reclothed.

There was a knock on the door. Ridgewood called. "Okay, boys?"

"Yes," said Donavan. As the doorknob turned, he added, "We're all naked and ready for you, Ridgewood."

She walked in and over to Bailey. "No matter where we may be reshuffled in the deck, when this is over, I'm reporting his behavior." She looked her superior in the eye. "If you were smart, you'd take action first."

Ridgewood saddled up to Presto. "So, Frank," she said. "We're ready for a slumber party. Tell us what you got."

Unfazed by Ridgewood's threat, Donavan smirked. "Looks like we know whose bed you're sleeping in Agent Ridgewood."

Before Ridgewood could reply, Danko spoke. "Let's do that."

"Let's," Bailey said with sarcastic relish.

Danko ignored the jab. This was a rejuvenated man. Finally, the spotlight was his again.

"As I said, we found some evidence. And as I also said, Myth Man has framed people before. There may be evidence that he framed one of you. If he did, I'm bringing the information to you firsthand. And," he said quickly, "even if the odds are less than 1 percent that anyone here could be involved, I'd be negligent not to do this by the book."

"We wouldn't want it any other way, Sherlock," quipped Donavan.

Bailey snapped. "Agent Donavan, do not speak unless you're asked to. When called upon, you will answer without commentary. That is a direct order. Do you understand?"

"Yes. Sorry."

Presto sensed Donavan was hurt or angry. Maybe both.

Bailey nodded to Danko. "Continue."

Sincerely. "Thanks," Danko said. "Other than Ridgewood, I'd like to see everyone's shoes."

Presto sensed Bailey's unease, but he cooperated. The four men put their shoes on a desk at the front of the room.

Bailey grunted. "Frank, you can skip the formalities. Whatever you're checking, we damn well sure know it is not on your shoe. Put them back on."

Danko opened a folder he'd placed on the desk. Out came a photo—the bloody heel print.

"Someone stepped in blood and walked into the bathroom in the rabbi's study. I found one clean print."

Danko grabbed one of his shoes, black leather and squared toe. He turned it over. "As you can see, the prints in the photo are very clean, tightly spaced ridges that angle toward the toe. My Clarks are obviously much different with that wide boomerang-like pattern."

"I see," Bailey grumbled. He grabbed his own and turned it over.

"May I?" asked Danko, who now had latex gloves on.

Bailey handed his shoe over. His eyes looked away but flashed with anger, like a distant but oncoming thunderstorm.

Danko turned the shoe over again. His jaw dropped. No need for analysis. It was a dead ringer. Not only was the symmetry the same, but also the left side of the heel was identically worn. And there was dried blood.

"Holy shit," Donavan said. He then looked to Bailey and shrugged. "Sorry."

Danko did not hesitate. He put the shoe in a plastic evidence bag. "All this means is this shoe left this print."

Bailey snapped. "Of course that's all it means. What do you think? I killed these men?" His voice raged as his face grew red.

Danko looked to Presto. "I make no assumptions. I learned from the best."

Ridgewood put a hand on Bailey's arm. "Take it easy, Malcolm. We know you didn't kill anyone."

Bailey relaxed and managed a weak smile. "Thanks. I don't remember going to any bathroom."

Danko nodded. "That's why we need to piece this together."

They sat down again.

Danko looked to Bailey again. "I have a few more questions for you. Please don't take offense."

"Should I call my attorney?" Bailey half-joked. "Go ahead."

"Your face." Danko pointed at Bailey's wounded cheek. "There's a scratch."

Bailey caressed his cheek, which had been treated. A beleaguered look told Danko to continue.

Presto noticed that despite the tension, Danko did not press. This was diplomatic for the old bull. Still, he feared where his former nemesis appeared to tread.

Danko cast a somewhat sympathetic look, for a bald, bearded, tough, prickly guy. "Do you recall how you got it?"

"Frankly, Frank, I don't recall," he shrugged. "I woke up with it. I assume it was not self-inflicted."

Danko let the answer pass. "Your jacket," he said. He went over to the chair that held Bailey's sport jacket. He came back with it. "I know this may be morbid, but could I ask you to put this back on?"

Bailey put his sport jacket on like it was a straightjacket. He stood erect and posed as if to look fashionable, which was not a funny sight with the bloodstains and the sweat pants.

"Go on, Frank. It can't get much worse."

Danko approached. He pointed at the jacket's lapels. "The blood—there's a good amount of it. It's not smudged, giving the appearance that it was sprayed and scattered."

He stepped back to allow Bailey more personal space. The FBI director filled the vacuum.

"Fuck you."

Ridgewood gasped.

"Easy, Malcolm," cautioned Donavan of all people.

Torn, Presto felt compelled to say something. "Let's relax," he said feebly.

Nobody relaxed, but Danko tried to offer an olive branch. "You can take the jacket off."

"Damn right I'm taking it off," Bailey huffed. "In fact, if you don't get to the point, I'm taking off, period."

All eyes turned to Danko. Silence. His bushy brows bunched up as if conflicting pressures collided. His foot tapped twice. He stretched his jaw.

Finally, words came. "No problem," he said flatly. "I won't apologize for my methods, and you should know that I act without relish."

"Cut the sentiment, Frank," Bailey urged. "I don't believe it's personal. You carry an air of dubious suspicion." He waved a beckoning hand. "Please."

Again, they waited on Danko. This time, they did not wait long.

"Okay, here it is. There was the heel print and a spot of blood on the toilet. That infers someone went to the bathroom. I don't think during or after this carnage that someone stopped to take a leak. Something else was flushed."

Presto watched Bailey boil, but Danko pressed on.

"Then I see your jacket. You had a wound to the back of your head and a nice, but superficial scratch on your face, but the bloodstains are on the front of your jacket."

Danko was on a roll. His mouth picked up speed like a downward soapbox car. Now that he was pressured to divulge his hand, he would do so without interruptions.

"Back to that scratch—as I examined Rabbi Ackerberg, I noticed traces of blood on his fingers. Under closer inspection, there appears to be human skin tissue, along with adequate blood samples, under his nails."

Now his voice was also louder. "All of the aforementioned evidence is on the way to a NYPD lab," he said with a strong emphasis on NYPD. "So this is where I'm at. I say, why the heel print to the bathroom after blood has been spilled? Why the scattered blood stains on your shirt and jacket? Is the scratch on your face from the rabbi's fingernail? And, if so, what does it all mean?"

Bailey tried to say something, but Danko cut him off.

"The evidence says two things to me. Either you were involved, or you were framed. Like I already acknowledged, Myth Man has framed others before, and logic dictates the latter."

The respite finally came for Bailey. "You're fucking damn right it's the latter."

Silence.

Then a voice: Carter Donavan.

"I do remember something before there was nothing."

Everyone looked at him.

"We were inside, and I was told to wait in the foyer. The rabbi and Malcolm left for the study. Then Malcolm came back to talk to me."

Bailey winced. "What?"

"You led me a few feet from the door, and then I felt this blow to my head." Donavan's face contorted in rage. His finger pointed like a dagger. "It was you that struck me down."

CHAPTER SEVENTY-NINE

Chaos ensued.

Malcolm Bailey, deputy assistant director of the FBI, a man as highly respected for his accomplishments as for his unflappable demeanor, lunged at Donavan.

"Liar!"

Donavan was quick and sidestepped Bailey then rallied with a fierce punch that caught Danko in the back as he tried to intervene. Danko groaned like a wounded animal but turned on Donavan with venom in his eyes. "Back off. Now!"

Ridgewood ran to Bailey's side. "No," she implored. "This has to be some mistake. Think about what we're doing." She looked at Bailey. "He was not even in this city when all these religious murders took place."

Ridgewood stopped to stifle a sniffle. She was close to tears. "Why would he murder three rabbis? For what reason? To blemish his career? Because he has some inner hatred for Jews that none of us saw all these years, and that friendship with Rabbi Ackerberg was just a charade? Bullshit," she cried.

Bailey put an arm around her shoulder. "Thank you, Ridgewood. I'd rather have you in my corner than anyone. You, of all of us, are the most practical."

"This is cute and all," commented Donavan angrily. "Let's not also forget the doctor flat out said my head wound was far more severe than yours. You have some explaining to do."

"No, I don't," Bailey said with dripping scorn.

Danko pulled out a BlackBerry, studied it, made an odd face, and then elicited a strange clicking sound. "Actually, you do."

"Fuck you, Frank," Bailey said with even more malice. "I've had enough of your amateur detective show. Use you're fucking brain. Detective 101—look for a motive. Today was the worst day of my life. Why, Sherlock Shit-For-Brains, would I commit this utter atrocity?" Bailey asked with haughty disdain. Then, he critiqued him. "Fucking idiot."

Ridgewood looked desperate to find some equilibrium. "Dominick, you have anything to say?"

Presto didn't. The possibilities were so endless he didn't know where to start. Again, the case marched through his mind like a bloodthirsty crusade. It came down to two things—was this the work of Dean Fallow/Myth Man or not? If not, then this truly was a different ball of wax. It was a boulder of bullshit.

Logic said this had to be the work of Myth Man. But how could he have pulled this off? Did Fallow also have a connection in the FBI? Maybe.

And what if someone in this room was responsible for today? How? Why? One theory came to mind, but he dismissed it as too ridiculous. It had to be Fallow until proven otherwise. He must have beaten them again.

He finally said, "If I am a betting man on whether these murders were committed by Malcolm Bailey or Dean Fallow, I'm doubling up on the later."

"Exactly," seconded Ridgewood.

"Thanks, buddy," Bailey said. "There's a reason you're ten times the detective Frank Danko is."

"Yeah," said Donavan. "Ten times the size."

Ridgewood went at Donavan. This time he chose not to fight back. "I'm sorry. That was stupid, but he's wrong about this. Look at the evidence. How could *his* bloody shoe print be in the bathroom? And I know what happened. He," Donavan said and pointed at Bailey, "smashed my head. You can guarantee that face scratch is from the rabbi's fingernail." His face grew long. "Betrayed, the poor guy probably lashed out."

"Again," challenged Bailey, "what about a motive?"

Donavan suddenly illuminated. "You know, maybe all these murders were your work, too."

Ridgewood came to Bailey's defense again. "Now you're getting ridiculous, Donavan."

Donavan didn't falter. Actually, he seemed overjoyed. "I'll give you not only the motive but the solution to the most famous murder spree in recent memory. Gary Sykes. Dean Fallow. Those boys may have been involved or not. I'm not sure, but there was a mastermind."

Bailey kicked at a chair like it was a bucket under Donavan's feet. "I was wrong about you. I should be demoted. You're either a cunning liar or as dumb as everyone told me you were."

"Nice try, Bailey. You know better. My problem is my attitude, not my intelligence. I don't follow the rules, because they sometimes restrict what is ultimately right. But don't sidetrack me."

"You know what?" Bailey asked. "Tell me your theory. It had such a wonderful start. The mastermind," he scoffed.

Donavan said, "I will. Your sudden fake bravado is admirable." He looked at his sudden jury. "We are forgetting one thing—the crate. Maybe all these murders were a diversion that led to today. The goal was the crate."

Bailey cut him off. "When this is all over, this is not something we will look back on and laugh over. I may get demoted, but I'll have a job. I'll see that you, Donavan, do not."

Donavan tried to reply, but this time Danko interjected. "I agree. It seems a complete stretch that he had anything to do with those other murders."

Bailey gasped. "Gee, thanks, Frank. You've now graduated from Police Academy."

Danko curtly replied. "Don't thank me. Tell me about the crate, Bailey."

Bailey shook his head. Then he looked at the rest of the room, primarily those who he'd briefed. A cold stare reminded them of their oath of silence. "Can't tell you that. The information is restricted, privileged, and confidential. In due time, it may become public knowledge. That's all I can say. Sorry."

Danko seemed to expect that. "Okay. Would I be wrong to speculate that this crate, which was delivered in an armored truck and is classified information, may hold contents that would be considered valuable in a monetary or, say, cultural sense?"

"Frank, I don't know what's inside this crate. No one does. It was to be opened for the first time today. So that would be impossible to answer."

"Bullshit," shot Donavan.

Danko turned to Donavan. "Let me handle this."

He turned his attention back to Bailey. "I know this may shock you, being just a dumb cop, but I think I know about this crate." He looked around the room with a smile. "Hey, I watch TV. I'm a Discovery Channel buff. Could this be that crate that was found in Iraq? If so, from what I recall, millions of dollars were offered for the crate, even though no one supposedly knew what was inside. There was even talk of the Ark of the Covenant."

He stopped, feeling sudden leverage. "Hey, but I'm just a cop. What do I know?"

The short silence was filled with the sound of clapping hands. Donavan.

"No, Danko. You're not dumb at all. You've got the right crate. You've got the motive."

Bailey pointed a hard finger at Donavan. "You realize you confirmed classified information."

Donavan smiled back. "Like I said, I break the rules when it's right. The ends justified the means. You murdered those men."

Presto finally spoke. "If the crate is here, and we found Bailey on the floor of the rabbi's study, how can we surmise the crate was his aim?"

"Fair point," Donavan replied. "Consider this. I think his plan was foiled when Ridgewood dashed in. Notice how at first he wanted to take the truck, supposedly here, solo? And either way, the crate has not been opened. Maybe there is another part to the plan."

Bailey fumed but answered. "I wanted Ridgewood and Presto to work the scene." He glared at Donavan. "Stupid me, I was worried about your head and loss of blood. So, yeah, I wanted you in a hospital. My concern was for your safety and getting that truck to a safe location, which we did," he added smugly. "In the end, we all squeezed in."

Presto waited for a quirky comment. It was tight up front. Ridgewood was forced to sit on his lap. The discomfort, momentarily, ended when Danko asked a question.

"Bailey," said Danko, "I ask you and, in essence, this room this: let's say the evidence shows that the scratch on your face was caused by the rabbi's fingernail. Let's also say that the blood on your shirt and coat was from one or more of the rabbis. We also have your bloody heel print on route to the bathroom with blood on the toilet. Since the print could only come after the murders, the evidence does raise some questions. No?" Before Bailey could reply, he added, "And now, someone that works for you claims it was you who clubbed his head." Over Bailey's growl, he finished. "Where does this leave us?"

Bailey erupted. "I don't care how it looks. And," he said with a dismissive glance toward Donavan, "either his head got scrambled when he was struck by Myth Man, or he's a lying weasel. I hope it's the former, because the later is, by far, more insidious."

Presto was about to speak, but he stopped. He saw a gleam in Danko's eye. He held something back.

"Oh," Danko said. "There is one other thing. I found the murder weapon."

Everyone but Presto commented.

"Why hold out on us?" roared Bailey.

"That's not right, Frank," chastised Ridgewood.

Even Donavan was critical. "Sneaky bastard."

Presto remained quiet.

Danko ignored the disquiet. "He pulled out his BlackBerry again. The information arrived only eight minutes ago. The gun was disassembled and flushed. Lucky for us, the center had a septic tank. Luckier still, the tank was brand new," he said with an awkward grin. "It had been replaced only last week. I don't have all the details yet, and I'm not sure I need them, but a 9mm gun was found, along with a silencer." He stopped to let this sink in.

Silence.

Danko's bushy eyebrows bunched. "We saw no one leave the center. Say

Myth Man did slip away, why flush the gun? The way I see it, either he would leave the gun somewhere obvious, or he'd take it with him. You figure he'd wear gloves. He's been meticulous before. This makes no sense. Neither does the fact that the handle of the nightstick was wiped clean and then left on the floor."

Danko stopped again. He had their attention. He thought for a nanosecond about consulting with Presto but dismissed the notion. He felt like a detective. He felt like a man.

Danko walked right up to a stunned Bailey. "I hope I'm wrong, Assistant Director Bailey, but you're under arrest."

CHAPTER EIGHTY

"I WANT TO TALK TO Presto alone," Bailey said to Danko. "Five minutes, then you can arrest the wrong man."

Danko swept his hairless head. "Like I said, you may have been framed." He turned his attention to Donavan. "Stick around, Buster. We're not done with you either."

Bailey faked astonishment with a smack to his forehead. "That may be the smartest thing you said today."

Danko fixed him a look. "I'm trying to be diplomatic." He looked at Ridgewood and Donavan. "Let's give them a moment."

As soon as they left, Bailey pleaded to Presto. "I didn't do this."

He was ready to explain the thousand reasons why this was preposterous, but Presto stopped him with two words.

"I know," Presto declared as he retrieved his sport jacket out of concern for his snake Aphrodite.

This time Bailey was truly astonished. "Really?"

"Yes. This may still be the work of Myth Man, but I'm going to ask you a favor."

"Anything," implored Bailey. "Anything at all."

Presto never thought he'd see Bailey ruffled, let alone desperate. He was not sure if he could blame him. Yet, in a way, he did.

"You still have the keys to the armored car?"

Bailey looked confused, yet hopeful. "Uh, sure, but they're in my jacket. They're part of the evidence. We can't tamper with that."

"I can. I work with Danko. The keys are not going to the lab. That truck is not staying in this garage forever." Presto winked and retrieved his own set of keys from his jacket. With gloves on, he reached into Bailey's soiled sport jacket and took the truck keys.

"My fingers are not too nimble. Can you take these two keys off this key holder?" Presto asked and handed Bailey his key ring, holding up the two chosen keys. "Switch them with the truck's keys."

When Bailey made both switches, Presto returned one set to the jacket, along with a short note.

Bailey winked back. "We switched three keys earlier, before my arrest, when we first got here."

Presto grinned. "That's right."

Bailey returned a grateful smile. "Want to tell me what's on your mind?"

Presto told him.

*****

The trio returned.

Bailey approached Danko. I'd like to surrender my gun and shield to Ridgewood if that's okay."

Danko nodded. "Sure. I'm doing this as a precaution. We'll run some tests. I hope something clears you."

Bailey softened. "Thanks. You have a job to do." He looked to Presto. "He knows I didn't do this thing. I have faith he'll clear my name."

Danko gulped. Déjà vu. Was he arresting the wrong man, only to have Presto revisit his role by exonerating the innocent and apprehending the guilty? Suddenly, he was not sure he wanted anything to clear Bailey.

"Let's hope so," Danko said meekly.

"Another thing," added Bailey.

Danko swore inside. This was not proceeding as planned. "Yes?"

"Although I may think you're a lousy detective and lack the insight of the gifted ones," Bailey said and gestured to Presto, "I do think you're an honest man. I need a favor."

"Yes?"

"The truck. The keys, I assume, are still in my jacket. I want you to take possession of them. I also want you to get some NYPD here to stand guard and watch that truck until you hear from the FBI director himself."

Danko brightened just a bit. These were requests from a man without a motive. Or were they? He was lost.

"That's ridiculous," opined Donavan. "We have a station full of agents who are adequately qualified to watch a truck if you don't trust me. Or does the conspiracy run deeper?" he mocked. "Maybe I should be more sympathetic. Perhaps an alien anal implant is responsible for your actions. Perhaps Dom or, better yet, Ridgewood can check for you, since they're up your ass anyway."

Danko overcame everyone's anger. "Actually," he yelled, "it's a splendid idea." He then turned his attention to Bailey. "Two of my men are outside. I see no reason to make a scene. If you don't cause a problem, you'll be treated with the utmost respect and held personally in my office until we check up on some things."

"I appreciate the professional courtesy."

Danko led Bailey from the room.

Ridgewood called after them. "Bailey, as soon as we settle things here, I'm coming to see you."

When the door shut, Donavan went ballistic. "We're the Feds. We don't let the police run our show."

Ridgewood waved him off. "It seems excessive, but can you blame him? Oh, you already did," said Ridgewood coldly.

Donavan crossed his arms. "You think this is easy? Bailey's been like a father to me. I could be wrong, but I'm telling you, he knocked me out."

"Well, you didn't give him the benefit of the doubt," Ridgewood scolded. "I'd expect more loyalty from you, even if Bailey was a killer."

Donavan bit his lip in thought. "You have a point," he conceded. "If this was Myth Man, then he's a magician."

Grim faced, Danko returned. "Wasn't easy."

"You did the right thing," championed Donavan.

Danko's face contorted in a wry grin. He looked to Presto. "Why do I feel like I made a mistake?"

"You did the right thing," Presto said.

All heads turned to him. Their faces all registered surprise.

Danko said, "Dom, for once in your life, can you tell us what you think? Did you just let me embarrass myself?"

Ridgewood agreed. "Bailey saved you when you were wrongly accused. If you know something, you should have done the same for him."

Presto looked at Ridgewood. Her pleading expression almost broke him, but he knew he had to do this the right way. "No," he said to her and then looked to Danko. "The evidence points to him. The best I can offer is hope. I still believe Dean Fallow is on the loose and probably responsible for today."

Appeased, Ridgewood said, "Let's hope so."

"Get those keys," reminded Presto.

Danko looked to Presto as if he didn't buy the explanation but said, "Yeah, sure thing." He trudged over to the table.

Danko returned and jingled the keys before them. "Got them."

"Wait," Donavan said and grabbed Danko's arm. "The keys. They don't look right."

Danko looked at the keys with a quizzical expression. "Huh?"

"They're different. I'm telling you." Donavan blinked hard. His head gyrated like two invisible hands smacked his skull to and fro. "The garage. Now! I think we've been played."

CHAPTER EIGHTY-ONE

"THAT MOTHER FUCKER. THESE aren't the right keys," screamed Donavan. The expletive bounced off the parking garage walls like it was a natural cavern.

"Watch your language," reprimanded Ridgewood. "At least the truck is still here."

Donavan cackled, "Well golly-gee, Ridgewood. Isn't that just swell and dandy?" He muttered something inaudible under his breath, but it sounded like 'fuck' echoes with reverb and distortion.

Danko said, "I'll call my men and see what they found on Bailey."

"Super," Donavan said with a sarcastic laugh. "For all we know, the cargo's already gone."

"Take it easy," Danko said. "Bailey's going nowhere. Everything's fine."

As he spoke, the garage elevator opened, and six police officers filed out. A stout man with an oversize head and eyes that squinted in the dimly lit garage addressed Danko.

"I understand there's been an arrest."

Danko ignored the second half of the delivery. "Guard this truck with your life."

They returned to the conference room. Presto found a seat. The others paced.

"I'll call and see what possessions they found on Bailey."

"He probably swallowed them, the feisty old bastard," Donavan quipped.

"Make sure they get some blood samples from him ASAP," Presto said knowingly.

Danko had his phone in hand. "You have something in mind?"

"In a minute. Let's see about those keys first."

Danko moved several feet away and dialed. Donavan continued to fidget in anger. Ridgewood went to Presto.

"Are you here to help or hurt Bailey?"

He wanted to be honest in Bailey's defense, but he believed the only way to flush out the possible guilty one was to pretend otherwise, although he still clung to the notion that Myth Man's identity was Dean Fallow, and Mr. Fallow was still at large.

He said, "Ridgewood, I'm only after the truth."

"I can see," she said snidely. "I thought you were more than that. This is ridiculous no matter what the evidence says."

Donavan meandered over. "Yeah? Explain why the keys were switched, genius. I started to regive him the benefit of the doubt, but this sealed it."

Ridgewood was defiant. "There may be an explanation," she said, but the vigor in the words faltered, as if doubt intruded on each syllable.

Donavan sensed a kill. "Like what?"

Presto spoke. "Perhaps he's innocent and doesn't trust someone here, so he switched the keys and willingly surrendered them to the police. He did ask for them to guard the truck."

Invigorated, Ridgewood said, "Yeah. Exactly."

"Whatever," Donavan said. "Sounds like a crock to me."

Danko loudly snapped his phone shut and walked over. "Dom, I know we need the blood to compare with the evidence found at the crime scene, but you made the request sound like you had something on your mind."

Presto replied, "I think you may find a connection to a seemingly unrelated but, in fact, quite related pair of homicides."

The room was silent. The sound of air ducts in the ventilation system could be heard.

Then Ridgewood griped. "What? You were just defending him. What's going on?"

"Yes, Dom," said Donavan, who towered over the seated Presto. "Explain yourself, secret miser."

Presto did not like the way Donavan hovered over him, but he made sure to watch his face. "Danko was not with us, but the rest of us went out together one night."

He watched, but Donavan did not flinch. No one spoke. They waited.

After several long seconds, Presto continued. "Sweet Virginia's was the place."

Presto could not see Ridgewood with Donavan screening his frontal vision, but he heard her say. "I think we all remember that night."

Presto's heart raced. It was the night they ended shacked up in her hotel room. He found the nerves to proceed.

"The bartender and that guy who had words with you," Presto said as he locked eyes with Donavan. "They've been murdered."

Donavan threw his head back in shock and then sauntered back with the pack. He giggled. "Did you hear that? Presto's ready to make Bailey out to be a ruthless killer because the joint cut him off from his Jameson." He clapped his hands with fervor and rubbed them together. "This keeps getting better."

"What are you saying?" asked Ridgewood.

Presto seated, calmly replied. "I'm saying that blood was found at one of the murder scene's that did not match the victims. There'd been a struggle, and the detective that worked the case believes the other blood was the killer's."

The words hung in the air until Danko, who nudged the process along perfectly, asked, "Are you telling us that you believe this other blood is Bailey's?"

"I am," certified Presto.

"This is crazy," gasped Ridgewood.

Presto shrugged. "I could not agree more, but money does strange things to people—makes them corrupt."

Danko came through again and asked, "But what money could these two barhands have?"

"Actually, none," responded Presto. Then he changed course. "Frank, tell us about the phone call."

He threw his hands up in surrender. "Sorry, forgot. Bailey told the police that he thought he was being set up and switched the keys. He handed them over."

"Just like Dominick said," an astonished Ridgewood reminded.

"Spooky coincidence," said Donavan.

Danko forged on. "I was patched through to Deputy Director Kyle Trinkus. Bailey is to remain in custody. The police will bring back the keys now. I was told to give them to Ridgewood until several hours from now when two new agents will come to commandeer the truck. You'll be happy to know, Agent Donavan, that he thanked the police for doing their duty, but their presence here will no longer be necessary."

Donavan cheered. "Smart man, that Trinkus. He knows we have the killer in custody."

"Actually, we don't," Presto said.

Donavan grunted. "Are you back to Fallow again?"

Presto finally stood. He looked at three of them and then squarely at Donavan.

"No," Presto said. "I'm talking about you."

CHAPTER EIGHTY-TWO

Presto dropped a bomb on the room. Faces registered shock and horror. Mouths moved, yet not a sound was made. The room temperature rose a few degrees. Would there be a counterattack? Presto waited.

Donavan clenched a fist and puffed his chest. The old Boston bully days beckoned. He chewed anger and swallowed. He chose to try and salvage the wreckage.

"All that cholesterol must have clogged your brain. Bailey's blood is all over the place, and you finger me? Don't tell me you think we're in cahoots now."

Presto smiled. "No, not at all. You set him up."

Donavan's face tightened over his skull. He tried to look and sound dismissive. "You've lost it, big boy," he finally said.

Ridgewood looked ashen. "I think I'm the one who lost it. First we're saying it's Bailey, which is preposterous, and now we're saying its Donavan?" She threw Donavan a bitter look. "I prefer the second theory, but are we jumping the gun again? What happened to Fallow?"

Presto looked at her. It was the worst she had ever looked. The bags under her eyes had grown darker, like eyebrows beneath her eyes. Her once proud posture sagged.

Danko stepped in. "Donavan, maybe you should speak to an attorney." He calmly advised.

"I don't need a fucking attorney." His arms spread. "Are you insane?"

Danko grinned, "My wife thinks so." But then he grew serious. "Think about it, Donavan."

"Are you kidding? I want to hear what the mighty Presto has to say."

Presto was nervous. He was not a great detective of fictional lore, and unlike many of his literary heroes, he'd rarely been in a situation where he faced the suspect and had to narrate the case to conclusion. The fact was that he didn't like interrogation. He was as nervous as the suspects. He knew he had to deliver.

"When I heard about the Sweet Virginia's murders, I knew the coincidence was too strong. It didn't make sense. Then it did. Awhile back, Bailey told me something about you," he said to Donavan. "He said you had a troubled past and steered clear from alcohol. The few times you did drink, you were so far out of practice that you got drunk off a few drinks. Bailey was happy for you but lamented that you were an Irish lightweight.

"So I was surprised to see you pound all of those drinks that night. You chose the place. You kept the drinks coming. You were the ringleader, and still, you were the most sober of us all. In fact, Bailey was in terrible shape, but you behaved as you always do—loud and obnoxious."

Donavan chuckled. "The testimony of a drunken man. This is great."

Presto returned a smile. "It gets better."

For the first time, Donavan flinched. Presto saw it. It was the eyes—a flash of registered alarm.

"The one thing I'm not sure of yet is why you killed them."

Donavan laughed hard. "Is this the moment where you expect me to slip with some confession? Surely you can do better than that." His face morphed from Hyde to Jeykll.

"You're right, Donavan. I'll get to the point and explain what happened. As far as proof goes, some is obviously educated," he pronounced, "guess work, but I have the goods to back up some of it."

"Oh, do you?"

"Yeah," Presto assured.

Ridgewood broke her silence. "This I want to hear," she said merrily.

"Fuck you, too," Donavan said.

Presto was no longer nervous. He had hoped it was the work of Dean Fallow, but the murders and then the way Donavan turned against Bailey confirmed his deepest suspicion when he heard about Sweet Virginia's.

"That night, Bailey drank Jameson, and for the most part, we drank vodka, or Ridgewood and I drank vodka. You drank water."

Donavan went to say something and stopped. His mouth churned slowly. "Yeah?"

"Yeah. It was a good story. We were on a tough case and needed a release. The boss is an alky, and you're the saint. So to keep an eye on things, you tell them to pour you water. Better yet, once the boss is wasted, get loud, create a skirmish, and get thrown out. The boss will think it's fun, and you'll get him out of there and home before there's trouble."

Presto stopped. "Sound familiar so far?"

"No," Donavan said. His words were not laced with same Donavan defiance.

"It should. You forgot about the chef, Felipe."

"Cooked by the cook," sang Danko.

"Fuck you, too," Donavan said.

"You're usually wittier than that," Danko observed.

270

"Whatever," Donavan said dismissively.

Presto hoped he caved soon. "After the disturbance you caused, our pal Felipe checked on things. According to the detective on the case, that's the story the bartender told him. Said you gave a hundred bucks for the trouble."

Donavan shook his head. "This is all bullshit, and even if there was a lick of truth to it, why would I pull off this charade and then murder them?"

"Easy," replied Presto. "For Bailey's blood." He stopped and waited. He had to falter soon.

But Donavan just stared back.

Danko said, "Donavan, you might want to call it a day. It's not looking good."

"No. This is good. I need the laugh."

Need the laugh? Now Presto would enjoy this. "In order to frame Bailey, you needed to have his blood in places that it could not be based on the sequence of events, so you got him drunk and took his blood. I had wondered why Bailey clutched his arm the next day. I knew he had been punched. Was it a coincidence the bouncer punched Bailey in the arm where you would later draw blood?"

Danovan grinned. His hand went behind him and returned with a gun. "Easiest target practice I ever had. Time to die, you fat fuck."

CHAPTER EIGHTY-THREE

RIDGEWOOD SCREAMED. "YOU CAN'T do this." She reached for her own gun.

Donavan winked at her. "Yeah? Watch me." He turned his attention back to Presto.

Instinctively, Presto fell in one direction, to his right. He heard the gun discharge. His butt hurt from the fall, but he felt fortunate that he did not land on his left front side and crush his beloved Aphrodite, and also that he was still alive.

He heard a commotion. Danko and Donavan were on the ground, battling like wrestlers—the real kind. Danko must have tackled Donavan split seconds before he fired the gun. Presto went to get up. He had to help the man who just saved his life.

Then came the sound of another gunshot.

Danko groaned in anguish. "Shit," he screamed, followed by rapid breaths. Donavan shoved Danko off him. From the ground, he aimed his gun at Presto again. "This time I won't miss. Like harpooning a whale at Sea World."

There was no escape this time. His last stealth move was saved by Danko's heroics. This time, he was not set squarely on his feet. He made no attempt to move.

Instead, in a final death flash, he thought of his mother and best friend. Now she'd be alone. Next came an image of Camille and how much he enjoyed the way he felt around her. He wondered if they had a future. Then, he went to look at Ridgewood.

Presto heard gunfire for the third time and fell to the floor.

His eyes closed.

Chapter Eighty-Four

HIS EYES OPENED. At first, he wasn't sure where he was. Was this heaven? No. He saw the same floor, the same chairs. Was his spirit surveying his final resting place?

He heard Ridgewood's voice, and then other voices came in frantic unison. The door opened. "Oh my God," came a voice.

Presto looked around. Donavan was motionless on the ground. Blood seeped from his head to the tiled floor. Next to him lay Danko who was also bloody, but alive. His hand pressed against his shoulder in a fruitless attempt to dam the blood flow. A man came into view and eased Danko to his back. Danko's shirt was ripped open, and the man pressed gauze against the wound.

Ridgewood kneeled next to Presto. "You okay?"

His coccyx bone throbbed, but he was hardly in position to complain. Two people were shot. One was dead.

"I'm fine. Thanks. You saved my life."

Ridgewood smiled, but the look was grim. Presto wondered if this was the first person she'd ever killed.

"You'd do the same for me," she said. "Anyway, Danko took a bullet for you. I had the easy job." The grim, tortured grin returned. "I knew Donavan was a bad seed, but not this bad. I still don't get it."

Presto wanted to explain, but first he needed to check on Danko. He gingerly got off the floor.

Danko was on his back. Tape held a thick wad of reddening gauze to his chest. His eyes looked up as he called Presto closer.

Presto went down to one knee and listened.

"I'm okay. It's a bitch, but I think I got lucky."

"Frank, you saved my life."

Danko grinned. "Least I could do. You bailed me out. I was after the wrong man again. Thanks for the note this time. How did I do?"

"You were perfect," Presto said and meant it. Danko was as smooth as his shaved head. "In fact, it was your work at the scene that clinched it."

"You're too nice." Danko's calloused hand reached for Presto's, which had never toiled hardships.

"Call my wife. She needs to know. Tell my matador that her Iron Bull is just fine," he said with a crooked grin. "They're taking me to Beth Israel."

"Sure thing, Frank," Presto sensed that Danko genuinely loved his wife. Beneath the hard exterior was a vibrant heart. "I'll be there, too. First, I need to clean up the details."

The paramedics arrived. Presto waddled away and gave them space. Ridgewood came over.

"How's Frank?"

"He'll live. He's tough, but he's also lucky."

Ridgewood crossed herself. "Thank God." Then she poked Presto. "Are you going to tell me what just happened?"

Presto explained what he knew, but there were still unanswered questions. Presumably, Donavan set the night up at the bar under the pretext of getting Bailey drunk. Presto noticed how Bailey held his arm the next day. Was it a punch or something more? When Donavan turned on Bailey, there had to be a cause. Maybe these murders were not Myth Man's doing.

He suspected the toxicology would show no tetrodotoxin was used on the deceased. He suspected Donavan framed Bailey and left the clues. The bloody shoe print was easy to do, and so was the scratched face from the fingernail. He could have also shot the rabbis with Bailey's sport jacket on or over his unconscious, propped up body. Donavan needed the blood, or why would he risk killing the two Sweet Virginia's workers?

Despite the reason, there was "the why" again. Was the mysterious crate the aim? And, if so, how was he going to steal it, even if the keys were here? Did he plan on being a fugitive? Now those answers may never come.

Ridgewood absorbed Presto's thoughts. "Again, you did a great job." Then her face cringed. "As much as I despised Donavan, I didn't just shoot him; I killed him. It happened so fast," she said and trailed off. Her lip curled in grief, and her voice cracked. "It's hitting home. What about his wife? I know her."

A few suited agents arrived. They wanted information, and they wanted it fast. They talked to Presto and Ridgewood together and then alone.

When they were through, Ridgewood and Presto reunited with Jack Burton, who had finally arrived.

"When Frank called me and told me about the note you left him and to get here as soon as possible, I never expected this," Burton said in awe. "What's next?"

"The truck keys should be here soon," explained Ridgewood. "I'm being directed to bring the truck to another, yet undisclosed location."

Presto told them he was leaving. "I've had my snake cooped up all day, and then I want to check on Frank."

"Bye, buddy," Burton said with a sly wink.

"I'll call you later," Ridgewood said and gave him a hug.

CHAPTER EIGHTY-FIVE

You can never get a cab when you need one.

Presto desperately looked for a taxi with a vacant yellow light on. He didn't see any, but he did see other people with the same plan. "Damn."

He took out his phone and dialed.

"Mom," I need you to listen to me. "It's probably nothing, but I want you to leave the apartment."

"Am I in some danger?"

Presto was not sure. "No, I don't think so, but I can't be too cautious. Please leave now and go to the Stagnuts'. I'll be home soon, if I can get a cab. I'll come for you."

"It's this case, isn't it? I saw the news. Mayor Golden was brilliant, as usual."

"Brilliant, Mom," appeased Presto. He would not lie to his mother. "Yes, it has to do with the case. It's probably nothing. I'll explain later. But a bad man died today, and I don't think he acted alone."

"Why would anyone come here?"

"Because a man died. I didn't kill him, but I accused him. And there's one other thing, but now is not the time. Leave," he commanded.

"I will," she promised. "I love you, Son."

Presto hung up and revisited his need to get home immediately. Still no open cabs, but he did see a police car parked at the end of the block. With cumbersome agility, he managed to slowly navigate around an elderly woman with a prosthetic leg and dashed with the speed of a motivated tortoise.

"Darn." The police car was empty. He scanned the street and surrounding stores. No officer was visible.

Desperate, he did something he'd seen countless TV cops do but never witnessed in all the years on the force: he pulled his police shield out with a fifty-dollar bill. He tapped the window of a beat up, but carefully polished eighties Cadillac.

Presto yelled, "Police emergency. I need you to take me across town."

Two startled youths gaped at him and shook their heads. They kept the window down. Presto surmised they were Dominican from the air-freshener flag that hung from the rearview mirror. Probably afraid they're being hassled

275

by the *man* again. The driver put his hands in the air like he was being arrested.

Presto needed to clear the confusion. He reached for the back door of the Caddy and opened it. It was not the cheetah patterned upholstery that shocked his senses but rather the cumulus cloud of cannabis that wafted through the car like a colliding storm front. If not for the pungent odor, Presto would have guessed the hipsters installed a fog machine for the complete nightclub feel.

The driver turned his head. Like a white zinfandel, his eyes were tinged a watery red. The youth looked scared but offered a crooked smile. "We just borrowed this car like five minutes ago from a friend."

Presto thrust the fifty-dollar bill in his hand. "Take this and buy some more pot. I don't give a shit. I need you to get me somewhere, fast."

The driver's smile mended. "Really? You got it, Big Papi." He slammed the gas.

Presto coughed. "Please roll down the windows before it rains in here."

They made good time as they hurled up Third Avenue. Presto urged the driver, when safety permitted, to blow traffic lights, which the youth successfully performed with an overzealous commitment to duty.

Presto had been worried the youth was too stoned to drive, but thus far he'd done well. He was quite adept at getting cars to move with either a close tailgate, an urgent fist out the window, or a heavy use of the horn. Sometimes all three were employed.

The Cadillac turned a corner and was met by a wall of gridlock. Presto peered ahead. He couldn't make out the exact problem but saw the flashing lights of an ambulance. He looked back. A car moved in behind them. They were stuck.

"Not good, boss," the driver said, reporting the obvious.

Presto dialed Burton. He listened. The news was not good.

"I'm stuck in traffic only a few blocks away. Get someone to my place. Now." He hung up.

The two youths turned to him. The passenger, who sported an askew Yankee hat and large expressive eyes that twinkled with humor, asked, "Is it your wife?"

"My mom," Presto answered.

"You still live with you mom? I thought I was bad," the youth said.

"Long story," Presto replied.

The driver cast him a look of solidarity. "My mamma is way more important to me than any ho. Get out of the car. I'm going to help you out, bro."

The traffic was still at a standstill. They walked around and opened the trunk. Out came a shiny silver, stand-up, gas-powered motor scooter.

"Top of the line, bro," the driver said. "Not meant to hold your weight, but she'll make it for where you got to go."

Presto looked at the scooter with equal parts of appreciation and apprehension. "Thanks, guys."

"Leave it in front of your building. It's a good area. We may get it back."

"I can bring it inside, and you can ring me," Presto assured.

The driver laughed. "Don't trouble yourself, boss." A sly grin emerged. "Let's just say she didn't cost me much."

The driver put out his hand. Presto took it.

"Get going, Big Papi."

They turned the scooter on for him and showed him the basics.

Presto took out his wallet. He handed his detective's card to the driver. "Call me if you ever need me."

CHAPTER EIGHTY-SIX

Presto was conscious of the spectacle he created as he zipped down the sidewalk in the stand-up scooter. Any adult would have looked silly on one of these things. A three hundred plus–pound man was a whole different sideshow. He ignored the turned heads, pointed fingers, and pointier jibes. Fear has a way of whitewashing trivial concerns.

To some, the sight of a police car in front of their residence was a concern. Presto was relieved. Presto eased off the gas and coasted to a stop. The police car was double-parked and vacant. He didn't see any other cars around, so far, so good. He took a deep breath, waved the security pass over the scanner, and entered his building.

Presto was inclined to first stop at the Stagnuts' place to check on his mother, but since the police had already arrived, he went straight to his apartment.

Just as he was ready to work his key into the lock, a thought occurred to him. He reached into his pocket and pulled out the ignition key to the armored truck that held the mysterious crate. He untied the cloth sack in his inner pocket and dropped the key. "Sorry, Aphrodite." He retied the knot.

Then he thought if the police were here, he should ring the buzzer. He would not want to startle them.

He rang the buzzer. A minute passed. No one answered. He rang it again. Nothing. He felt something was wrong but then dismissed it. Everyone was probably downstairs at the Stagnuts' wondering what the big fuss was.

He descended a floor and looped back to a door that was exactly below his apartment. He rang the buzzer and heard Skippy bark. The door opened.

"Oh, hello, Dominick."

"Hi, Mrs. Stagnuts."

"How many times do I tell you that we are all adults, and you can call me Gina?" she scolded.

Presto was not up for banter, but he replied, "All the time. What can I say? I'm old-fashioned."

She smiled. "That's why you're a good man. Our Camille raved about you."

Presto was happy to hear that, but now was not the time. He didn't see or hear anyone. Where were the cops? Why had his mother not appeared at the sound of his voice?

"Mrs. Stagnuts," he said, "is my mother here?"

She looked puzzled. "Your mother?"

"Any police?" Presto stammered.

"Police? What is going on?" She let him inside and called out, "Arthur?" Then she whispered, "He's been on that computer all day. I bet he's looking at porn."

Presto was exasperated, so he said nothing.

Mr. Stagnuts appeared in a large checkered, flannel robe. "Hello, Dom. What's the hubbub?"

Presto tried to speak, but a lack of saliva made his mouth stick. He finally managed. "Have you heard from my mother in the past half hour?"

"No," he said with a sympathetic shake of his head. "Let's go upstairs."

"No," Presto said firmly. "Do me a favor. Call upstairs."

While Mr. Stagnuts retrieved the phone and dialed, Presto took out his own phone. He watched and waited. He could see each unanswered ring etch a line of worry into Mr. Stagnuts's face.

"Hang up," Presto said after too much time had passed. He pressed the send button on his cell.

Mr. Stagnuts reluctantly hung up. "What's going on?"

Presto did not hear the question. Burton was already on the line. He turned to the Stagnuts. "I have to go."

Once outside, Presto updated Burton. When he finished, Burton said. "I hope we're wrong, but if so, wait for backup. I'll have someone there in minutes."

"Do that," Presto said, "But I'm going."

With each step up the stairs, Presto sensed dread. He was not courageous, and he wasn't particularly heroic. The days as a boy, when he stood and photographed the men on the dock who were responsible for his father's death had passed with puberty. He was a man that liked to think, not one to act.

He never imagined he would face actual danger. Yet, here it was, delivered to his doorstep. Anger boiled.

He pulled out the gun he never thought he'd use. With his other hand he turned the key and entered his apartment.

CHAPTER EIGHTY-SEVEN

"HELLO," PRESTO CALLED OUT. Nothing.

He kept a normal pace through the foyer. Where it split (a hallway that led to his bedroom on the left and the brick wall that partitioned to the living room on the right), he crashed to one knee with his gun extended. "I know you're here," Presto said.

"That's good fatso," she said with sudden informality. "I have a gun to your mom's head, so cut the bullshit."

Presto stood sideways with his gun extended, his lower body blocked by the wall partition.

She was right. Ridgewood stood behind his mother, a silenced 9mm gun pressed against her temple.

His mother did not look scared. In fact, her visage exuded tenacity with eyes that prowled and a steel, firm posture. "Son," she called, "listen to me. Do not give in to this hussy. There are two dead cops in the bathroom. And ... ouch!" She screamed as the gun swatted her head.

"Shut up, you old bitch," said Ridgewood. "Dom, give me the key."

Presto considered his options, which were not bad, except for the fact that a gun had just cracked his mother's skull. Yet, his mother had not been subdued.

"Dominick, listen to me. The cancer. I'm dying. Soon. You have a life to live. Do not waste it on me."

Ridgewood's gun struck his mother again, but his mother's dire words brought more pain that the stark visual of Ridgewood's strike. He could not let her words affect his composure.

"It's over, Agent Ridgewood. The police are on their way here. Whatever your end plan is, it's over."

Ridgewood grimaced. "There's where you're wrong. If you think I'm the top of the food chain on this, you're crazy. Burton never got to make that second phone call, according to my source, so unless you had any other bright ideas, I'll take that key."

Presto considered her words. He believed her claim of acting on orders. This he figured. Who it was irked Presto, but for now, he was more concerned with survival. His options seemed as limited as the typical *Restaurant Week* prix fixe menu specials. He was not sure if it was funny that he thought of food in this crisis.

"Only if you let my mother leave," he mustered.

Ridgewood knocked the request down with a shriek of laughter. "You're not in position to make demands. We both know how this is going to work."

Presto did. That's what he was worried about. "I left the key with a nice Dominican fellow who gave me a lift here."

"That's a shame," Ridgewood said. "Then you die." She cocked the gun against Cleo Presto's head.

"No," yelled Presto. "Okay, I have it," he acquiesced. "It's in my jacket pocket."

"Then drop your gun," Ridgewood ordered.

"Damn, my leg hurts," Cleo Presto said. She stretched it for a second and then stamped her foot down on the floor three times.

"You stupid bitch," Ridgewood seethed. She almost laid her hostage out with the gun, but at the last second she slowed the impact of the blow. She needed the shield for a few minutes longer.

Frozen, Presto saw blood trickle from his mother's head.

CHAPTER EIGHTY-EIGHT

"Y ou're not going upstairs, Arthur," demanded his wife. "You saw that boy. He was scared."

Mr. Stagnuts looked at his wife of thirty-eight years. Many people asked how he stayed married to her. He sometimes wondered himself. They were so different. He was funny, free-spirited, and jovial. She was stiff, wary, and maybe even maniacal. He was the *Stag* and she was the *Nuts*. But he knew one thing. His wife loved him with all her heart, and that counted a lot in this world.

His wife was usually right about things, but he heard the distinctive three-knocks. It was a call for help. He couldn't ignore it, and he couldn't look in his wife's eyes and face the disapproving, hurtful look she undoubtedly cast. He knew she was serious when she had not even mentioned that her beloved chandelier still vibrated from Cleo Presto's call.

"I'm going upstairs, honey. If I don't call or return in five minutes, call the cops."

Arthur Stagnuts just hoped the next call would not be for an ambulance.

*****

Ridgewood was in a bind. The bitch stamped her foot for a reason. Why? It could have been some diversion, but she doubted that. If it was, nothing had happened. It had to be something else. Her next thought was that it was a signal of sorts. She assumed it was to the neighbor below them. What did that mean?

The old hag said she was dying. Maybe that meant if she were in trouble, her neighbor would summon an ambulance, or the neighbor was on his way upstairs to help. If it were the latter, he'd probably have the keys to this place, so locking the door was not a likely option.

Both of the scenarios were bad. She had to think fast. If the neighbor was on his way up, she had to act faster, and fat-assed Presto was between her and the door. And if the neighbor arrived, Presto would tell him to leave and call the cops.

Ridgewood panicked. She thought about taking a shot at Presto. Enough of his girth poked out from the wall's partition. She had the silencer. She could blast her way out. That seemed her best option.

She quickly turned the gun and fired.

"Bitch."

✶✶✶✶✶

Cleo Presto hated Agent Ridgewood before she ever laid eyes on her. Now in her presence, she witnessed her outward beauty and her inner evil, yet something deeper irked her. This hussy had used her son.

Her only concern was for her boy. Cancer would soon take her life. She hid her fate from him because she loved him and didn't want their last days spent together in the shadow of gloom. Everyone knew but Dominick. Only her revelation was supposed to come at a later time, under more tender circumstances.

She had to think of something. Then she had stomped her foot three times. She hoped Arthur would come and hear their cries for the police. Right now the hussy had the upper hand. She had to change the dynamics.

It worked, but perhaps not for the better. She heard rapid breaths from behind her. She felt Ridgewood's gun-free hand grow tense and sweaty on her clamped bicep. Next she felt the pressure from the gun release from her temple, and the body from behind shift quickly. She was going to shoot her son.

Cleo Presto propelled herself low and backward, like a cornerback making an awkward tackle. Two shots rang out.

From her back, she could not see her son, and she didn't hear him cry out. A hand came around her neck and pulled her up.

"Bitch."

✶✶✶✶✶

Detective Presto's hand touched the brick wall thankful for stone rather than cheap standard sheetrock, which was as bulletproof as cellophane.

When he tried to roll over, his back screamed with pain. His weight overburdened him, and he could not find the leverage to get on his knees.

Despite the pain, he smiled. Momentarily forgetting his mother's mortality, he briefly savored the clip she threw on Agent Ridgewood's knees.

Then the front door of the apartment opened. There stood Mr. Stagnuts.

Arthur Stagnuts saw Dominick down on his back struggling to get up. He sensed no danger and ran to help.

Dominick's hand went up in halting motion. "Stop," he screamed, "go back and call the police."

He tried to stop his momentum. A bullet over the partition wall did.

Arthur's stout body almost fell on top of him. He couldn't look at his dead friend. Seconds could not be spared. He looked out the open door and saw no one.

"Yes," Presto screamed hopefully. "Mrs. Colby! Go inside, turn every lock on your door, and get the police here. Now!" he shouted and than roared with rage over his dead friend.

He screamed at Ridgewood. "I'm giving you one way out. It works for all of us." He hoped he was loud enough that Ridgewood would think she should have heard an apartment door close.

He listened. He tried to hear his mother. He could hear a struggle of sorts. Good enough, he hoped.

Presto called out. "You're time is short, and you're not getting past me. Here's the deal. I throw over the key. You release my mother. We go down the hallway to my room. You leave."

After several seconds, Ridgewood said, "Okay. You have my word. Throw it over."

Presto felt terrible about using his beloved snake in a dangerous ruse. She'd been lucky to survive his clumsy falls. Surely she was perturbed. He hoped so. He reached inside his jacket and pulled out the cloth sack.

He knew much depended on luck. Aphrodite was a small snake, possibly as light as the metal key and ring. He needed a reason for her to be suspicious of the cloth sack.

"Okay," he replied. "The truck key is in some cloth sack Bailey gave me, along with some other type of ancient ring he was given by Rabbi Ackerberg. He said it had to with what was inside the crate." He paused for credibility. "That's all I know."

"Just throw it over," Ridgewood said.

Presto hoped Aphrodite was testy with all the day's action. He swung his arm around the wall and slung the sack in the living room.

He heard Ridgewood say. "You open it, bitch."

After a few seconds, his mother sarcastically informed, "There. Now do you want me to grab the key too, or do you think there's a mouse trap inside?"

"Shut up. Give it to me."

Then Presto heard music to his ears.

"Ouch! Fuck!"

The hook snared his fish. For a moment, he felt like the kid on the fishing pier again, the thrill of the catch.

The happy tune changed.

Ridgewood screamed. "You asshole. Now your mommy dies too."

"No," yelled Presto even louder. "You listen to me. The snake is poisonous. If you don't do what I say, you will die!"

*****

Ridgewood was in a state of shock. How could everything have gone so wrong? She'd been assured everything had been taken care of. She just had to do her part, but now she saw no way out.

When she reached in the sack, something bit her. She tore her arm out, and there attached to her index finger was ... a snake? She screamed and violently shook her hand. The snake crashed against the floor and slithered away.

Then came Presto's words, "You will die."

She wished she'd never gotten involved with this. It wasn't the money that corrupted her, she told herself. It was her patriotic duty. She was following orders.

Now she was desperate. "Are you fucking kidding me?" she begged Presto. "Poisonous?"

"Yes," his voice rang out. "She's a coral snake, and she's lethal. But if you do what I say, you can live and leave."

Ridgewood's heart drag raced, sudden speed that kept accelerating. Was Presto providing a parachute? Could she trust him? He'd already tricked her.

"Talk to me quickly, or your mom gets a bullet and dies with me."

The hag called out. "Don't listen. Let her die."

Ridgewood struck her again. Again, she defied her pain.

"I love that snake," the fossil actually said.

Ridgewood wanted to pump a bullet in the geezer, but she couldn't just yet. "Dominick?"

Presto called back. "In the fridge, on the shelf below the eggs, are two loaded syringes. Take the pink one, pinch some fat, anywhere, and inject it all. A good amount of time has passed."

"You're bullshitting me," she said.

"You can wait about fifteen minutes and call my bluff."

Ridgewood tensed further. The fat sneak sounded so calm, so certain. She believed him. Why else would he have syringes in his fridge? The big load couldn't handle his booze. She doubted heroin was his thing. She had to give it to him. It was a good trick.

Ridgewood maneuvered the mother up and went to the fridge. She went back to the stove and watched the kitchen entrance. She pointed the gun. "You open the fridge and give me the syringe."

The annoying woman obliged. Ridgewood then ordered her face down on ground. She placed the gun on the countertop and grabbed the syringe. She tried to inject her arm, but she found it difficult to pinch the skin and work the syringe stopper. She rolled her shirt up a bit and found some flesh on her sculptured abdomen.

She injected herself.

*****

Cleo Presto's smile kissed the kitchen tiles. She knew her boy had just bested the hussy. Ridgewood would die.

The two needles in the fridge were insulin and Lithro. Ridgewood injected the latter. While both would be lethal to a nondiabetic, Lithro acted faster, for more dire circumstances. If they could get by for another fifteen minutes, Ridgewood would go into hypoglycemic shock and lapse into a coma. Death was all but certain, especially without immediate care.

None would be forthcoming.

Her son called out. "Talk to me, Ridgewood. What's going on?"

Cleo turned her head and looked up. Ridgewood appeared to be doing a nonclinical self-diagnosis of her well-being. Her fingers flexed. Her eyes blinked rapidly and focused on nothing. Then she ran her fingers through her hair and smiled. She probably felt good about things, seeing that nothing bad happened immediately after the injection. She bought it.

Ridgewood answered. "I just injected myself. I want to give it a minute to make sure you didn't give me rat poison or something."

Presto's voice answered, "I saved your life, Lorraine. After you killed a friend and brutalized my mother. Do as you promised. Release her to me, we'll go to my room, and you can leave."

Cleo saw the sneer on Ridgewood's face and knew it wasn't over yet.

Presto wanted to talk to her, letting the drug surge through her body and alter her blood glucose level to about 600–800 mg/dl. Normal levels were about 110 mg/dl, while people with diabetes, like his mother, had levels around 140 mg/dl. Agent Ridgewood was in some serious trouble.

"Can I ask how you were going to pull the rest of this off?"

Ridgewood answered with a spiteful laugh. "No. No talking. Here's how it works: Head down the hallway. Your mom comes with me to the door. Once it's open, I'm gone, and she's yours. Trust me. I don't want this baggage with me."

Presto didn't like this. "Lorraine, my way works better."

"No, Dominick. When I come around the corner, how do I know you won't shoot me in the back?"

Presto waited a few precious seconds. "Because I just saved your life."

Ridgewood snorted. "That's funny. You're the one that put the snake in the bag in the first place."

"Listen, Lorraine," he said with a slow calm. "Unlike a bullet, the snake bite was reversible. I just want to save my mother."

"You will. Just do as I say, or she dies now. You're a bigger target, and I bet I have better aim, so go to your room now. You can stand where you'll see, but your mom's a screen until we get to the door."

"Please, Lorraine," pleaded Presto.

"Move. Now," Ridgewood yelled at her hostage. Ridgewood struck her again, and Cleo howled in pain.

Presto went down the hallway and into his room. He leaned his head and gun out. "I'm down the hall. Don't do anything stupid."

He heard feet shuffle, and then saw them, but instead of walking toward the exit, Ridgewood came down the hall with his mother in front. She fired.

Debris from the wall crashed around Presto's head. He winced and ducked back.

*****

Ridgewood tried to push the stubborn bitch forward, but granny wouldn't cooperate. She wanted to use the shield further, but she had enough. For a distraction, she fired her gun again at Presto's door. Then she put a bullet in the hag's head.

For a brief flash, she felt joy. She might just get out of this, but the spark she felt extinguished like a strong breeze vaporized her. She suddenly felt weak and dizzy. She willed herself to march forward, but her legs went numb, and instead, she fell. The gun slipped from her grasp. Her pulse raced, and she began to shake. Something was very wrong.

Was the antivenom too late, or was she double-crossed? She gagged.

She saw a gun poke out from the room, then Presto's head. His eyes went to his mother, and his face went white. Ridgewood guessed hers was paler.

Presto went down to one knee and spoke. "Lorraine, if you want to live for real, you are going to talk, and you're going to talk quickly. Tell me who's behind this."

Ridgewood willed to speak, but her mouth was desert dry. She didn't want to live, but she'd talk anyway.

"I was asked to help Donavan set up Bailey and remove him if he became a liability," she sputtered, "but no one had to die if you didn't play the game with the keys. Carter and I were to move the truck, where we would later be carjacked. Bailey would have been exonerated. It was clean. It was all set. I was going to make a bundle for the operation, and," she managed with pride, "be a hero." Her breathing became short.

Presto poked her to continue.

Her mouth began to lose shape as she spoke, like an inebriated ventriloquist. "If it went well, I'd continue in my career for a few years and then retire with millions. If it didn't, we'd still be millionaires."

Ridgewood coughed. It took everything she had to get that out. She tried again. "Imagine if the Ark of the Covenant is really in that crate. Forget the money; think about the power it could possess. People in our government were angered when it was awarded to a Jewish organziation, as loyal citizens as they may be."

Presto pressed her further. "Give me names."

"We got a call from the FBI director himself. He said he was sending an agent to meet us who worked on a special joint mission with the CIA. We were told to follow his orders only. His name was Agent Charlie Hawkins. It was a matter of national security."

Ridgewood gagged.

Chapter-Eighty-Nine

Jack Burton stared at the man seated before him. "Will that be it?" The question was phrased as if he said, *That better be it.*

"Just a few minutes more," the agent replied.

As soon as Burton had hung up with Presto, a man came to visit. He had a neatly trimmed beard, was dressed in a dark suit, and had horn-rimmed glasses, which gave Burton the impression of a banker. He introduced himself as Assistant FBI Director Charlie Hawkins and asked for a few minutes of his time.

Hawkins was led to a small office that looked, from experience, like an interrogation room. Seated across from each other, Agent Hawkins said he was sent from the FBI director to investigate what had happened at The Lubavitch Center. The man asked Burton to summarize the day's events as he understood them.

Initially, everything seemed routine. The agent worked methodically, too methodically for Burton. The guy tediously rehashed everything, even the minutia, in extracting a full summary.

Burton grew weary. "I have to make that phone call. My friend could be in trouble. I told you, Agent Ridgewood is missing. We need to get backup there."

Like the heroic snake, Aphrodite, Agent Hawkins did not blink. "As I told you, we received a call from Malcolm Bailey, who also spoke to Detective Presto. The police and FBI had been dispatched to his apartment moments before I spoke to you. I'm sure everything is fine."

But as more time passed, even the stoic agent seemed antsy. "Yes, that should be it," he finally said. "Let me go check on one thing. I'll be back in five minutes."

Burton waited and fumed. Ten minutes passed. He pulled out his cell phone and was pleased to see a full signal. Previously, he'd tried to follow through on Presto's request to send police officers to his residence when his signal failed. That was when Agent Hawkins had materialized by his side.

CHAPTER NINETY

Tears fell down Presto's face.

He lay on the floor beside his dead mother. Her lifeless head, with entry and exit wounds, lay on his lap. He'd wiped the blood off of her face and now played with her hair.

Presto looked at Ridgewood's gun. He thought about ending his own life. He figured his mother would die before him but not in this way. Killed because of his work and by the first woman he'd shared a bed with. He could deal with the humiliation but not the loss of the only soul he loved.

He clasped her frail hand and thought of her bravery. She had probably saved his life with her tackle. Then he thought of her words. "I'm dying." She'd kept the truth from him. He wanted to be angry and ask her a million questions. Like a blubbering boy, he began to talk to her.

For whom the bells toll, he thought, breaking his reverie, and then realized he was listening to the muffled sound of a ringing cell phone. It was coming from Ridgewood's jacket. He rolled her body over and pulled it off her belt. The number on the screen read "Private."

Presto was not the best impressionist, but he gave it his best college try. "Problems," he said in a huffed feminine octave.

"Agent Ridgewood?" asked a plain but harried voice.

"Problems, Agent Hawkins," Presto tried. He kept the pitch high and the volume low.

"Do you have the truck keys? Is Presto dead?"

"We have to meet," Presto said.

"Agent Ridgewood?" the caller questioned. Then came a short, sinister laugh, and the voice changed to a more modulated, familiar tone. "So you're alive, Detective Presto?"

"You bastard," seethed Presto.

"Now, now," the voice taunted. "It's a shame you're among the living, but I must say my plan still worked to perfection. Sorry, I don't have time to chat. I'm sure we'll meet again one day, Detective Presto." The line went dead.

Presto hit redial, but the call failed. He dropped the phone to the floor. He went back tending to his mother, when a phone rang again. His.

"Burton," he answered frantically.

"Are you okay?" The raspy voice asked.

Presto did not answer, yet. "Were you with some guy Agent Hawkins?"

"Yeah," said a puzzled-sounding Burton. "He interviewed me and left me in this room. Said he'd be back in five; it's now been ten."

"Please, Jack. Find that man and arrest him."

"Leaving now," Burton said. "Can I ask what happened? Did Bailey get the police there?"

Now Presto was confused. "Bailey? No I haven't talked to him."

"This Agent Hawkins grabbed me. Said things were under control, that you had phoned Bailey, and help was on the way."

"No one came, Jack. Two cops are dead. Agent Ridgewood's dead. My neighbor's dead." He paused, and the tears returned. "My mother's dead, too. Ridgewood killed her." With anger, he stifled a sob. "Find Agent Hawkins, aka Myth Man. Now!"

After Presto hung up with Burton, he continued to lie on the floor with his dead mother. He didn't hear the police until they were upon him. His tears and choked sobs deafened their entrance. He told them to look in his mother's bathroom for the two dead officers. One tried to help him to his feet, but Presto declined. He wanted more time with his mother.

Presto did not move until the medics arrived. Seated beside his dead mother, he told the police what happened.

Eventually, he struggled to his feet. If the quick ascent did not disorient him, the next voice ordeal did.

"Arthur," wailed a hyperventilating sob. "No, no, Arthur."

A commotion.

"Let me in," screamed Gina Stagnuts.

Chapter Ninety-One

Presto watched a robin leave the dug up earth and fly away with a wriggling worm snared in its beak. The bird took advantage of the upturned soil that surrounded Cleo Presto's casket. He smiled and thought of his mother and how she would sit in the corner park and enjoy a slice of nature.

He shed tears as he received condolences. But through it all, he smiled. He had to. He owed his mother that much. She saved his life, so he could live it.

Camille stood by him, but her aunt would not come. Presto was advised to stay away from Arthur's funeral.

Mayor Golden was even on hand, and he gave a small eulogy that was truly gracious. Presto was thankful for the eloquent, moving words without the benefit of TV cameras.

Afterward, when everyone left, he asked Camille for a moment with Bailey, Burton, and the recovering Danko. He kept his words brief.

Despite the rabbis' deaths, the police were viewed favorably, while the heat fell squarely on the FBI. The crate was saved and was to be returned to the Chabad center under the auspices of another esteemed group of rabbis. The accolades meant nothing to Presto.

The real Agent Hawkins was found stationed along the U.S./Mexican border. He'd been there for the past few months, without fail. Of course, the FBI director never contacted Agents Ridgewood or Donavan

"I want to thank you for being here," began Presto. "Tonight, I'm going to spend one last night mourning. Tomorrow, I'm coming to work. Agents Ridgewood and Donavan were pawns. We know who did this. I will not rest until I find Myth Man," he declared.

Everyone ratified his creed.

*****

After dinner, Presto and Camille went back to the W Hotel on Lexington Avenue. They went to the bar, rather than their room. After getting two beers, they found an unoccupied couch.

"Thanks," he gushed. He was drunk again, but this time, it felt good. He was sad and happy and thankful when Camille suggested he stay in a hotel for a few days, with herself included. A package deal he could enjoy.

Presto doubted he could ever return to the apartment. He'd take a real estate killing selling the place after the bloodbath inside, and although he did not believe in ghosts, he knew that if he lived there, he'd be forever haunted by personal demons.

They drank more. Camille and the booze loosened him up.

"You know," she said, "it's usually the female that poisons her lover, not vice versa. You're the male black widow," poked Camille.

He laughed. "Don't remind me. The snake saved my life, and I have no way of thanking her."

Camille grinned. "That's where you're wrong. After the police left, I went through your place and put pinkie mice near all the heating ducts. I sat on the couch and read a book with the lights dimmed. She came out a half hour later. I wanted to surprise you, but I saw how sad your face was when you mentioned her, and I couldn't resist."

Joyous, Presto spilled beer on his lap. "Really? Or are you trying to fool me with a duplicate?"

"That sounds like something your last girl would pull." Camille gave a coquettish smile. "How about falling in love with someone you can trust?"

Camille pushed Presto back on the couch. She put her lips to his and kissed him.

Chapter Ninety-Two

T<small>HE RABBIS STOOD AROUND</small> the open Iraqi crate. They shifted through the bowls of pottery, cooking utensils, old clothes, and sandals. After they rummaged through everything, they also found a box with twenty silver shekels. That was a lot of silver in those days, but worth only intrinsic value now.

Rabbi Corson spoke, "This appears to be the belongings of a merchant family that fled Israel. Nothing more."

CHAPTER NINETY-THREE

Y OU SLEEP IN IT, *you bathe in it.*

Dean Fallow watched the news and laughed. The final score had been his best tally yet, and this time, he was not the actual agent of death.

When he thought of playing the two FBI agents, he was dubious it could actually work. But promises of money, an appeal to patriotism, and a human's inability to question a higher authority (see God) were all the ingredients he needed. Turning Ridgewood against Donavan was the only easy part. Sure Detective Presto was still alive, but his original goal of killing the rabbis went splendidly. It was a joyous occasion.

Almost.

He knew Presto would hunt for him. Good luck now that he was in Siberia or, should he say, the New York Adirondacks. Thus far, in one week, he'd seen more deer than people. Maybe he would send the fat detective a condolence card on the loss of his mother.

Today, however, he was traveling to the western part of the state. He left his room with a urine-stained mattress and checked out of the motel. He didn't check in under the name Chip Dexter, mostly because there was no need to record that name at a motel within ten minutes of his destination. The other reason was he just didn't like being Chip Dexter. He liked to be no one and anyone. That was the beauty of disguise.

He hopped into a Honda Civic with stolen plates. He looked again at his disguise in the rearview mirror. Aged, he thought he would look good in twenty years.

He drove through country roads that reminded him of his new hometown. He instinctively looked out for deer. After twenty minutes, he pulled past a dilapidated split-level ranch. Fallow snorted; worst house on the block.

He walked past overgrown junipers, with branches that impeded the pathway to a beaten screen door and knocked.

After a few minutes, a door unlocked, and an elderly lady with her silver hair in a bun and large cross around her neck appeared. "You must be Jonathan," she said.

Fallow gave his best Sunday smile. "Hello. And you must be Ms. Baker. You look wonderful," he charmed.

She led him inside. They crossed a living room that reminded Fallow of when he toured Betsy's Ross's Philadelphia home. Fallow wondered if each owner of this house kept things exactly as their predecessor had. Heck, folks spent a lot of money to live around antiques. Maybe the home was a family hand-me-down.

She pointed to a dark wood-stained door. "He's downstairs in the basement. I'll put some brownies on. My boy loves them."

Fallow descended a few steps and called out. "Luke?"

"Keep coming. I'm right down here."

Fallow continued until he hit pay dirt. Literally. The floor was nothing more than pressed dirt with a few gravel chips here and there. The stone-walled room covered the whole floor of the house. In the recess was a crude bunker with an effigy hung from a pole. Fallow looked closer. The face was black. A crude Jewish star was painted over the heart, and a red turban rested on the head.

On the walls were guns and crosses.

Seated in front of a computer was a paunchy middle-aged man. As Fallow got closer, he saw more hair hanging from the guy's nostrils than sprouting from his scalp.

"Jonathan? The Deacon? Is it really you?" The man went to rise from his chair.

"Don't trouble yourself," said Myth Man. He came up beside him. He pointed to the desktop computer. "So, Trumpet of God. Is this where you do all of God's good work?"

"Yes," the man said and turned his back.

Myth Man took the needle from his pocket and quickly shoved it in the man's neck.

"You're going to die, asshole. P.S., There's no salvation."

The End